HULLBRIDGE

11/16

RAYLEIGH HULLBRIDGE

2014

W/D

EssexWorks.

For a better quality of life

Please return this book on or before the date shown above. To renew go to www.essex.gov.uk/libraries, ring 0845 603 7628 or go to any Essex library.

Essex County Council

GLORIA

KERRY YOUNG

BLOOMSBURY CIRCUS
LONDON · NEW DELHI · NEW YORK · SYDNEY

First published in Great Britain 2013
This paperback edition published 2014

Copyright © 2013 by Kerry Young

Supported using public funding by
ARTS COUNCIL
ENGLAND
LOTTERY FUNDED

With the assistance of a grant from The Society of Authors and the Authors' Foundation.

The moral right of the author has been asserted

Bloomsbury Publishing Plc
50 Bedford Square, London, WC1B 3DP

www.bloomsbury.com

Bloomsbury Publishing, London, New Delhi, New York and Sydney
A CIP catalogue record for this book is available from the British Library

ISBN 978 1 4088 4336 9

10 9 8 7 6 5 4 3 2 1

Typeset by Hewer Text UK Ltd, Edinburgh
Printed and bound in Great Britain by CPI Group (UK) Ltd, Croydon CR0 4YY

A people is not independent once it has shaken off the chains of its masters; it begins to be once it has extirpated from its being the vices of vanquished slavery, and, for homeland and to live anew, rises up and gives form to concepts of life radically opposed to the customs of past servility, to the memories of weakness and adulation that despotic rule uses as elements of domination over the enslaved people.

– José Martí

Gloria

1938

'I hear a sigh across the earth.'

CHAPTER 1

I GRAB A piece a wood and I hit him. And I hit him. And I hit him. And all I can hear is the dull thud like when yu bash open a ripe watermelon and the juice splash all over yu. And then I hear Marcia screaming as she trying to get out from under him. She shoving him off of her but my arm is still moving because all I am thinking about is how he done it to me; and how his hands so rough everywhere he holding me down; and how the coir mattress stick me in the back as I lay there staring up at the rusty old corrugated zinc roof he got on this shack; and how it so hot in here; and how the smell of him, the thick, sour sweat of him, mek my stomach turn and mek me want to heave but I just lay there like a piece of board until it was done.

This is what I am thinking while my arm is swinging and swinging 'til Marcia grab me and we run outta his stinking pit into the air and the rain. We run past the hole in the ground where he burning the wood to mek the coal and into the trees, through the mango and breadfruit and banana and pear. We just tearing our way past everything. We cut through the cane field and run through the bush past branches that catch your arm and roots that catch your foot. Down, down 'til we mek it to the river. And is then I realise I still got the piece a wood in my hand. So I smash it. I find a big rock and I smash it and pull it and tear it 'til there was nothing left but twigs and splinters and dust and I throw the bits into the river. And then I jump in after them because the blood is all over me with the rain meking it run like its own little river of red rolling down my face and all over my hands and soaking into my frock. And that is when it stop raining.

I say to Marcia to get in and wash herself. We take off our frocks and rub them under the water and ring them out and bash them on a rock and rinse them some more. And then I tell her to mek sure she do between her legs as well and she say to me, 'Him didn't do nothing to me yu know. Him just get on top a me when you bust through the door.'

'It nuh matter. Wash away what him intend to do to yu.'

We lay out the frocks to dry on a big rock in the sun and I tell Marcia we must go hide in a bush 'til the clothes dry. I don't want nobody coming down here to find themselves two young girls all naked waiting for them to tempt their nastiness.

When the frocks dry enough we put them on and we start walk back home. I say to Marcia, 'What yu doing up there in the shack with him anyway?'

'I meet him on top road with a whole heap a wood him carrying to go mek the coal. But him rope bust and he got the wood all over the road and ask me to help tek it down the hill. So I do it, and when we get to the shack him say to me if I want come inside for a glass a lemonade so I say yes and that is when him jump me.'

I don't say nothing to her because it too late now for any advice I would be fixing to give. Then she say, 'What we going tell Mama?'

'We not going tell her nothing.'

'We not going tell her?'

'She only going say to yu the same thing she say when him do it to me.'

Right then Marcia just stop walking and turn to me.

'Him do it to you? Him actually do it?'

'Maybe two years back. When I was 'bout the same age as you.'

'And what did Mama say to yu?'

'She say, how many times I tell yu to stay away from that man? Barrington Maxwell not right in the head. Wouldn't nobody have nothing to do wid him if it wasn't for the coal him meking up in them woods.'

'She didn't say nothing 'bout what him do to yu?'

'I just finish tell yu. She didn't say nothing. She just go pick some herb and boil some bush and give it to me to drink. And she say, that going fix anything he might have leave me wid and that was it.'

So we carry on walking and a little later Marcia say, 'Yu think yu kill him?'

'Don't talk like that! We don't know nothing 'bout it yu understand me.'

'But what if him not dead? What if him going come and point us out?'

'Point out what? Point out that him got yu in the shack there trying to ruin yu? Because him never catch sight of me. I come up behind him and I hit him before him know what was what, him so busy holding you down and dropping him pants. Yu just shut up 'bout it now.'

5

All the time we walking my feet stinging from running over the rough ground. When we nearly reach back I find a nice big puddle a water and I throw myself face down in it, and I tell Marcia to do the same. So when we get up the frocks covered all down the front with the sticky red mud yu always get after the rain.

'What the hell happen to you?'

'We fall down Mama.'

'Fall down? Yu know how much scrubbing it going tek to get that mud outta dem frocks? Yu might as well have just tek dem 'round di back and put dem on di fire. You go tek off dem dresses now and put on something decent yu hear me. Then yu go put dem to soak. You two girls got no respect for anything.'

Later, when we sit down to dinner, Mama still vex. She slapping everything on the plate. The yam, the green banana, the salt fish and callaloo. When she pouring out the lemonade she almost miss the glass and have to use her cloth to mop up the spill. She not talking to nobody.

After we finish eat she tell Leroy to go fill the kerosene lamps before it get dark and she start tek 'way the plates. So I go help her and all the time we busy washing the dishes and clearing up she nuh say nothing to me.

Next morning she still vex. She tell Babs to go parcel up the ironed clothes to tek down to Miss Edna and Babs lay out the big square cloth on the table nice and neat and put the clothes in it and wrap and fold the edges good and tight and put the safety pin in the top just like how she see us do it because is usually me or Marcia that do this job. And that is how I know Mama still vex with us because she nuh talking to me and Marcia even if it mean she got her baby Babs doing these chores now.

When she going down the track I shout to her, 'Hey Babs, yu want some company?'

'Don't call me Babs. My name is Barbara I keep telling yu.' And she keep on walking even though she only twelve years old and she can hardly balance the pile a clothes on her head. So I shout Marcia and the two a us run after her 'til we catch up.

'I don't need no escort yu know. I perfectly well able to do this myself.'

Marcia say to her, 'We know you able. But who say we cyan just walk down the road with our baby sister on a beautiful morning just so to enjoy it?'

'I'm not no baby. You only two year older than me Marcia and in time that not going mean nothing.'

When I look back I see Mama standing up at the gate watching us like she fully expect me and Marcia to go help anyway.

We wait on the porch for Miss Edna to come back to us wid the money. She count it out into Babs's hand. All in little copper and thing. And then Babs put the change into the purse Mama keep special for this and we go on our way. Miss Edna didn't even offer us a glass a water. Mama been teking in her washing every week for near on five years and she never even say good morning to us or give us a little thank yu. Nothing. Is all she can do to count out the one shilling and sixpence into yu hand and then sit back on her porch with that sour face a hers, sipping her cold lemonade. And she don't seem to think that we walk all the way down here with that heavy load, and we carry the dirty clothes up the hill in the hot sun, maybe we could do with some water to wet our lips. But Miss Edna nearly white and that in her mind mek her too good for the likes a us.

But when I think we going back home Babs say she got to pick up a few things Mama want from the shop. So I say OK and the three a us walk up the track to the road and start head off to town.

Every truck that come by Marcia trying to wave it down so we can catch a ride even though I keep telling her how dangerous it is, and she say, 'There is three a us. What going happen to three a us?'

But I don't care. I not having us teking no ride from no man. Next thing yu know he got six friends waiting 'round the corner just hanging there for us to get delivered to them nice and fresh off the highway. Ain't nobody stopping for us anyway, so we carry on walking 'til we get there.

When we go in the grocery store Mr Chen say to me, 'What you doing here on yu day off, Gloria? You not get enough of this place all week?'

'Mama need some things urgent.'

We waiting there while Babs picking up this and that like she cyan mek up her mind and that is when the policeman step through the door. He is standing there in his grey shirt and heavy blue pants with the red stripe down the side and the shiny white belt over the red waistband. I think maybe I should run but my feet done stick themselves to the floor so it no matter what I fancy to do. The policeman look at me and then Marcia and Babs and then him say to Mr Chen to pass him the cigarettes him want. Twenty Lucky Strike. Him stand there eyeing us while him open up the pack and tap out the cigarette and stick it in his mouth. And then he reach down him side and I think he going for his gun but is only the lighter coming outta his pocket. Him flick the lid off the little silver Zippo and roll the wheel and mek the flame, and light the cigarette. And all the time he is standing there he is looking straight at me. Then he start to open his mouth and I can feel the cold sweat break out all over my body but I still cyan move. I just stand there wid my feet glued to the dusty wooden floor.

He got the cigarette in his hand and him sticking out his tongue and reaching into his open mouth. Him fetch out a loose piece a tobacco and flick it off the end of him fingers, and then him put the cigarette back in him mouth and drag on it long and slow, staring at me like him really studying me to see which way I going to jump. Him put the lighter back in him pocket and tek the cigarette outta him mouth and blow out the smoke in three little rings and then him say to me, 'My, my, Gloria Campbell. You sure turning into a beautiful woman.'

The next day is Sunday and we have to go to church. Mama always want to get there good and early because if you go too late the place get crowded and she cyan get her favourite seat right up front where she see the pastor good and feel the vibration every time he slap his hand down on the Bible and beg the Lord to forgive us sinners. But the pastor only talk one word at a time, or maybe two, in between slapping the Bible so everything he got to say tek a long time.

'The Bible' slap 'says' slap 'we are all' slap 'sinners' slap. And with every slap we say 'Praise be to God' or 'Yes sir hallelujah'.

'We' slap 'have sinned'. Yes sir. Every one of us. Hallelujah. The pastor say that the Bible tell us that the wages of sin is death. And I start wonder if Barrington Maxwell's death was the wage for his sin or if my death going to be the wage for mine.

He say our sins separate us from God for ever but that Jesus is the way, the truth and the life and that no one comes to God except through Jesus so we have to ask Jesus Christ to forgive our sins. But I cyan see how Jesus going forgive a thing like what gwaan between me and Barrington especially since I not praying to nobody 'bout it. Anyway, the pastor say sin hinders prayer and if yu have wickedness in your heart the Lord will not hear you. So I guess that is that, because what is in my heart is wickedness through and through.

And then we start to sing. *Stand up, stand up for Jesus*. And after that, pastor really strike up the band and the whole congregation is bringing the place down. Everybody inside the church and everybody standing on the veranda and out in the yard is singing and clapping and raising our voices and our arms up to the sky like if we can reach up high enough we can touch God in his heaven.

This little light of mine I'm gonna let it shine. I singing at the top of my voice. Not just from my throat but from deep down in my stomach. I singing because it feel good to just let go even though all I am thinking is what light is there in me to shine.

Next morning when I getting ready for work Mama say she coming wid me and we have to go call by the church. She already explain to Mr Chen how I going be late on account of going to a funeral.

'Who die?'

'Yu father.'

'My father!'

My whole life I been asking my mother who my father is and she nuh tell me. She just say it no matter. 'Him never had nothing good to give yu.' So I just stop ask, and now after all this long time she going tell me him dead.

'When he die?'

'Last Friday.'

'Last Friday? Yu mean the day me and Marcia come back wid mud all down our frocks and yu vex wid us?'

'It not you I vex with. It him.'

'Yu vex with him 'cause he die?'

'I vex with him because he was a wicked man who never did one decent thing in his entire life. He bring shame on everybody that know him and in the end he bring shame on himself. And now he is dead, thank the Lord.'

'So what it matter to you after all this time?' But no sooner than I say it I wish I had bite my tongue because now she going answer me and the truth is I don't want to know no more. I don't want her to go tell me now that my father name Barrington Maxwell after I go beat the living daylight outta him. So when she nuh say nothing I just shut up and go finish dress and follow her to the church.

We sit down in the pew. Mama say Marcia, Barbara and Leroy got a different daddy. That not no news to me. But the peculiar thing 'bout this funeral is that there is nobody there but me and Mama. There not even any dead body. So when I think I was going to go look in the coffin to see who was laying there it nuh work out like that because there is no coffin. There is no pastor, there is no mourners. Is just the two a us sitting there. And when I ask her what 'bout the headstone and all, she say, 'What head- stone? Who yu think going pay for a thing like that?'

The rest a the week I am silently praying to Jesus Christ even though the pastor say he not going hear me, because it seem like I done kill my own father. And then Friday afternoon the police come in the shop and say they just find Barrington Maxwell and he been laying up there in the shack dead all week. That people start wonder 'bout him when he nuh turn up wid the coal and so the police go up there and he is laying there with his head beat in like a watermelon turn to pulp. And he got him pants down 'round him ankle so they have a good idea what going on up there.

I just stand there looking at them while the policeman busy telling Mr Chen all a this news. And then Mr Chen turn to me and say, 'Gloria. You all right?' But I don't say nothing and then him say to me, 'All this bad business. Not the sort of thing a young girl like you should be listening to. You go find yourself something to do out back. Go on.'

I walk and don't look back. I just go out back and weigh out the sugar and parcel it in the sturdy brown paper ready to go on the shelf.

The police waiting for a special officer to come from Montego Bay to tek charge a the investigation. And every day one a them is in the shop telling Mr Chen 'bout how smart this Montego Bay policeman is and how they know is two culprits.

'How yu know that?'

'Is simple. Maxwell got him pants down so him doing something to somebody laying on di mattress there. And then di other one come up behind him and bam! Him head mash up. And I mean mash up good. So that mek two. And knowing Maxwell then one a them is definitely a woman.'

'Yu think yu going catch them?'

'Yah man. These people got no idea what dem a dealing wid. When di man come from Montego Bay him going sort all a dis out double quick. Yu can bet yu life on that.'

But all the time the police busy talking this way everybody know that the evidence is spoiling with all the waiting. Not that they got any evidence anyway. They not got no murder weapon. They not got no eyewitness. They not got anything that going trace back to anybody because the place up there so filthy they cyan decide what to collect up and tek to the police station or what to just put in the garbage. They knee-deep in muck. They can't even get any decent fingerprint, not that they got anything to compare them with anyway. So it seem like maybe they wasting their time even waiting for this man from Mo Bay.

I say to Marcia, 'Maybe you and me should go get the bus to Kingston,' and she agree but Mama not hearing nothing 'bout it.

'What yu mean Kingston? What you two girls going do in Kingston?'

'I get a job Mama. Maybe work in a shop like I do for Mr Chen and I look after me and Marcia.'

'And what about her schooling?'

'She almost fourteen. She nearly done anyway.'

'So yu just going jump pon a bus and leave me here wid Barbara and Leroy to fend for?'

'You tek in your washing and yu do your dressmaking. Rightly yu not have my wages coming in but then you will have two less mouths to feed.'

Mama look at me and then she narrow her eye. 'Yu going go all di way to Kingston just so yu can do di same thing working in some shop and go live with strangers?'

But I don't say nothing. So she say, 'Unless there is some reason you girls in such a hurry to skip outta here.'

And is now like she not so much looking at me as piercing right into me. Like she burning wid her eyes right into my soul. And then after some long time she say, 'Leave di frocks here. I will put dem on di fire when yu gone.'

CHAPTER 2

THE BUS TIP and roll 'round every corner, over every bridge, up and down every hill and valley, through every little town and hamlet between Savanna-la-Mar and Kingston. All along the coast road with the sea splashing up the window all the way to Black River and over the hills through Santa Cruz to Mandeville where we wait under the big tree for the next service to Spanish Town and Kingston. It take us all day and we practically see the whole length a the island hooting and honking and screaming and shouting every time the bus come too fast 'round a corner, or nearly fall down or slide over a precipice, or have to come to a dead stop because it almost run into a cow or goat or man or cart, or because it come face to face with some big truck that carrying bananas or lumber and the driver screech on the brakes and everything that he carrying on top a the bus slide up front and fall off. And we all have to get out and go pick it up, boxes and bags and crates; things that tie up with string and things that just come loose like a roast breadfruit or a few oranges. So yu stooping down in the road collecting all a this together from outta the dirt and under the wheel hoping that these people know what of this belong to them. And then yu get back on the bus and start the whole thing over again with the driver having a few choice words for anybody that want to listen, and the whole bus wid a few choice words for him as well. Me and Marcia don't say nothing. We just do what everybody else do. We sit. We hold on. We brace ourselves. We stannup. We fetch up the stuff. We sidung again. We nuh pay no mind to the woman and her pickney that tussle and fight over every scrap a bulla bread or orange or drop a sugar water that pass between them. We nuh worry ourselves 'bout the chickens that every now and again is running loose on the bus, and the man have to go grab them and truss them up in his little wire cage. We nuh fret on the man 'cross the aisle who want to rub himself up while he look sideways at us like he think we interested in what he got in his pants. We just sit close to one another and stare out the window, and every little while we swap seats so we tek turns in catching the breeze instead a just breathing in that heavy stink a sweat. And when yu have to stand up and go fetch the things outta the road yu feel grateful for the relief from the dress sticking to yu back and yu backside, and catching up between yu legs.

When the bus reach Kingston it stop in West Street and we get off right in the middle a the market with everyone coming this way and that wid the fruit in the basket on top a the head, and the pushcarts wid the crates a beer and soda and every kinda higgler and juicy jockeying for position and arguing and cussing so bad it almost injurious to the ears a two young girls.

'Yu just come from country?'

So we say yes.

'Well yu need to move yuself outta di way. Yu cyan see dis is a busy metropolis?'

We just stand back because we got no idea what he is talking about.

Mama got a friend live 'round Back-O-Wall and she write the address on a piece a paper. When we find the place it is just a room in a dirt yard full a rooms. Inside it got a little bed and table and sink in the corner. Mama say we must call her friend Auntie, so we knocking and peering through the half-open door calling out 'Auntie, Auntie' 'til some feeble old woman turn up bend over rubbing her back like she wear out from so much hard work. It seem like she expecting us so I don't know how Mama get word to her.

Auntie let us in and tell me to rest the grip on the floor in the corner, and she sit down on the one rickety straight-back chair she have. When I look at her I see she not as old as yu would think. She no older than Mama. She just tired that is all. Like life already done finish her off.

'Yu just come from country?'

'Yes, we get off the bus and come straight here.'

'I tell yu mama di place too small for yu to cotch more than a few days. She tell yu that?'

'No, she nuh tell us nothing.'

'Well I telling yu now. Yu understand me?'

'Yes, Auntie.'

Then she start look 'round the place like she wondering where she going put us.

'Gloria, you a sleep wid me in di bed and Marcia I going fix up a cot fi yu under di table.'

'Under the table!' Marcia lift up the little tablecloth and gawk at the space. 'I cyan fit under this table.'

'Yu legs going stick out little bit that is all.'

'Yu really serious 'bout me sleeping down there?'

'Yu got a better idea?' And then she cross her arms and say, 'Yu see anywhere fi yu to stretch out in dis here palace? What did I say to yu 'bout staying here? If it nuh good enough yu can go. There is plenty men out there happy to give yu bed space fi the night.'

'Is all right,' I say to her to calm her down. 'We grateful and we thank yu for sharing wid us what you have.'

Auntie mix some condensed milk and water and get out some saltine biscuits that she must have had in that bag for three weeks they so soft. But we hungry and we eat, and we nuh complain as we crawl into the sacks she sew together for sheets with Marcia's head deep in the shadows and me squash up against the wall feeling Auntie's damp body clinging to me.

The next morning we got to go find some work. Auntie say that finding shop work not going be that easy since Mr Bustamante got everybody on strike and the shops in town all close up.

'Di dockworkers done bring everything to a standstill over di increase in wages dem want and di overtime for Sundays and public holidays. Dem marching up and down King Street meking di shopkeepers close dem shutters even if deh nuh want to. And every week there is some big march or protest and barricade blocking up di road. Even just last week in South Parade dem have to call out di police and army di whole thing get so bad outta hand. And di police dem don't seem no better. Beating every man, woman and chile dem come 'cross. So yu watch yuself when yu go out there. Yu hear me?'

I know what Auntie mean. Where we come from country not so far from Frome so we already hear 'bout all the trouble wid the sugar estates and how Tate and Lyle making all sorta promises 'bout jobs and wages and cottages and schools, and it all turn out to be a pack a lies the newspapers print. So all sorta mayhem break out wid striking and burning the cane fields and police and shooting, and four people get dead and a load more wounded and almost a hundred arrested. So I know.

I say to Auntie, 'Is all right. I not going bother anybody in King Street. I just going go to a Chinaman and tell him how I used to work in Mr Chen shop and see if him want to tek me on.'

'Deh burning down Chiney groceries as well, yu know.'

So what I going to do? I go out there anyway and I find out that Auntie right. There is nothing but trouble and misery out in them streets. Everybody in Kingston been striking. The tram, the bus, the shoe factory, the tobacco and waterfront workers and every kind of labourer. Business come to a complete stop. Plus, there was all sorta crowds just walking the street and causing a ruckus over unemployment and starvation wages, and stoning the police when they asked to move on. And putting Mr Bustamante in jail didn't solve nothing.

'How long yu do shop work for Mr Chen?'

'Two years a going there after school and weekends, and in the last year I working there six days a week.'

'Six days a week! So yu well experienced then?'

'Yes, sah. Well experienced.'

Mr Ho give me the job after I walk the full length a Barry Street squeezing between the long line a horse-drawn buggies to go into every grocery store and bakery and laundry and betting shop there was. He don't want to pay no more than a pittance though. He say he going give me five shillings a week when I know the shop assistants in King Street meking eight or nine. But what I going to do? I tek it. When I get back to Auntie she start cuss 'bout how the Chinaman robbing me and teking me for granted.

'The strikers in Spanish Town do it right when dem go shut up di shop a all dem Chiney and Syrians.'

I just say to her, 'Beggars cyan be choosers.' And she kiss her teeth so I reckon she nuh like me talking to her like that.

So now I got to go find Marcia something to do and Auntie say it best for her to put into schoolgirl service because she only young. Auntie say she know somebody can sort it out and Marcia will get her bed and board in exchange for a little light domestic work. So I agree and Auntie fix it for Marcia to go stay with some family up by Cross Roads. When I tek her up there it seem like a nice place wid a tidy yard out front and a tile veranda. The house modest but it look like they care for it. The live-in maid greet Marcia friendly. She call herself Norma, and she show Marcia where she going sleep, which is a dark little room with a wooden slat of a window that the two a them going share. Next to that they got their own toilet and they can wash themself in the outhouse where they do the laundry.

The lady a the house come outside and look us up and down standing there in the yard. Then she say, 'Norma tells me that your auntie is a friend of hers.'

'Yes Miss.' And Norma say, 'Yes, Miss Vilma.'

Miss Vilma light-skin. She tall and slim. And she holding some American magazine in her hand with a picture of some white woman on the front fetch up like she think she really gorgeous and that everybody who bother herself to read that magazine want nothing more than to be exactly like her, and do everything she do, and have everything she have.

'Your sister has experience of domestic work?'

'We from a big family Miss Vilma. There is always plenty to do.'

She stand there and look at me a little longer, stiff, like she forcing herself to do it.

'I am taking Norma's word for it that she is a good girl.' She jut out her chin at Marcia. 'I don't want any trouble, you understand me?'

'She is a good girl Miss Vilma, I promise yu that. Hard-working and no trouble at all.'

And without saying another word Miss Vilma turn 'round and walk back inside.

I feel bad leaving Marcia there but it better than sleeping under Auntie's table and at least she doing something to earn her keep.

'Yu not going forget about me Gloria is yu?'

'No Marcia. What yu go say a thing like that for? When I can get enough for us to have a place together I will come get yu. I promise. I been looking out for yu all these long years didn't I? Yu think I bring yu all the way to Kingston to just go leave yu here like this?'

She just look at me like her heart breaking at the thought that maybe this is the last time she going see me. I hand her the little grip with her few things in it and I turn 'round and walk outta the yard and shut the gate. And then I turn 'round and see her with Norma arm 'round her shoulder and I hope to God that nothing bad happen to her before I get a chance to come fetch her back to be wid me.

Auntie got the sink in the room but as for some water coming outta the pipe, well maybe it do and maybe it don't. So when I get up from sleeping under the table, which I tek to because I cyan stand the feel of Auntie sweating up next to me, I try catch some water in the pan but there is not a drop a anything coming my way. I look at the standpipe in the middle a the yard and I know I don't want to tek that walk out there, because every time I set foot outside the door there is some little bwoy that got something to say to me. It mek yu wonder how come they learn so young what they got between their legs. Sometimes they even throw little stick at me while the nastiness is coming outta their mouth. Or maybe he just stop what he doing and tek his time. Like he leaning on the standpipe and shut off the water so as to just look at me. And yu think to yourself they not even old enough yet to do anything with what they got down there but they already know exactly what they fixing to do with it. So much so it mek yu feel shamed and want to run and hide but yu too frighten to say nothing back to them. And that is just the children. The grown men, that is something else. That is not shame. That is fear. Like when yu standing in the shower out there in the yard. And the piece a zinc door only covering the middle part a yu. So they can see your head and everything yu got from your knees down. And they resting themself there against some post or they tek up seat on some old crate just so they can watch yu. They smoking a cigarette or maybe some weed. They chilling. And that is when yu realise how naked your feet feel. Even the soap and water that is running over your body and going down the drain seem suggestive because they can see it.

And all the time yu in there yu worried that one a them going step 'cross the yard and come grab up the towel or housecoat yu got hanging there on the two nails sticking out either side a the little cubicle yu standing in. But it nuh happen. Yu just keep think-ing on it, because eventually yu going have to reach out and pick up the towel and haul it over the top a the half-door and dry yourself without bending down too far, and then stick out yu arm for the housecoat that is going to be your only protection to mek it back to Auntie's room. And when it is your time a the month, yu just catch up some water in a pan and wash yuself inside because yu don't want no pink tinge swirling 'round down into that drain like a open invitation to the vultures.

The thing is I cyan decide which is worse. The little bwoys wid dem sticks and foul mouth, or the grown men with them silence and hungry eyes. Sometime they even licking their lips. I cyan stand to see it. But truth is I more troubled when it happening at my back At least if they looking me in the face we both know. We both party to it. The other thing, behind me, is just for them, and sometimes their friends. And all I get is the remains of the whisper and the laugh. The laugh so loud it feel like every man in the place must be joining in.

Not Mr Ho though. He don't take no part in it. Mostly it seem he feel sorry for me. Maybe he would even prefer to get a young Chinaman to help in him shop. But he wouldn't insult a Chinaman with the wages he paying me. So what can he do? He do the same as me. He bear it. But he grin, and sometimes he bow. That is how he protect himself. That is how he keep them coming back to buy the flour and rice and saltfish that is his livelihood. That is the truce between them, even though Mr Ho nowhere near as stupid as they think, and they nowhere near as harmless as he say.

'Is just joke, Gloria. You know men. Tomfoolery that is what they call it. They just passing the time a day wid yu.'

CHAPTER 3

IT WASN'T NO longer than three weeks before Marcia run off from Cross Roads and come back to Auntie's.

'What yu doing here girl? Didn't I tell yu to stay there 'til I come fetch yu?'

'I cyan tek it there Gloria. Miss Vilma, she is evil.'

'What she do to yu?'

'She mean and nasty and she shout at yu if yu nuh do things right, and she turn up her nose and kiss her teeth and tell Norma not to give me no dinner; and she throw things at yu like if she nuh like how a blouse iron or how the food taste, she just throw it, plate and all. And the husband he don't do nothing. He just sit there or stannup and watch her. Never a word him say to her 'bout how she carry on. And the pickney, them no better. They just like her with the temper and the screaming and the stamping if there is something they nuh like. And the way they look at me Gloria, is like they think I just a piece a shit some dog leave behind.'

'What yu talking 'bout shit? Yu nuh worried Auntie going come and hear yu?'

And then she start cry. So I put my arm 'round her shoulder and I stroke her hair and say, 'Marcia it sound bad. I feel sorry for that. I nuh mean for yu to be having this misery put upon yu. But I cyan do nothing. Yu cyan stay here. Yu have to go back to Cross Roads and hope Miss Vilma forgive yu.' But Marcia not happy and in truth neither am I. But what I going to do?

Marcia beg me to let her stay the night and promise she go back in the morning. I try talk her outta it because the longer she down here the less chance Miss Vilma going tek her back. But in the end she cry and plead wid me so much I don't have the heart to mek her go especially after it turn seven and it getting dark. When Auntie come in she vex.

'What di hell dis girl doing here? She nuh in service up di road?'

'The woman giving her a bad time Auntie. She just come down here tonight. She going back in the morning.'

'What morning? Yu think dem going tek her back? By morning dem got some other girl sleeping in her bed, glad to have di chance to do something useful. Glad yu hear me. Not snivelling and feeling sorry fi herself. Glad. Yu know how many people sleeping under a piece a cardboard or zinc sheet right out there in di road? And she so proud that she can afford to run off from hot food and a roof over her head. Because what? Because some woman talk bad to her. If I turn tail every time somebody talk bad to me I would be falling down dizzy from all di spinning 'round I would be doing. The chile have to learn to mek di best a it. Goat feed wheh im tie.'

Next morning Marcia get on the bus and go back to Cross Roads and I keep my fingers crossed that I don't see her again on account a Miss Vilma turning her back. But even though Marcia gone Auntie still vex, and every day she is cussing and clattering the little pot and pan she got boiling the banana and frying the plantain. She say I am crowding up the place and so likky-likky I nyaming up everything in sight. She say the money I give her not enough.

'Yu think it nuh cost nothing to have yu a sleeping and eating day after day like dis? Yu think it nuh matter that every night I get up to sit on di pot yu legs is sticking out from under di table ready to tek a little swing to knock me down and mek a stinking wet mess all over dis floor? Yu think I nuh hear yu breathe and heave and twist and turn all night like yu doing hard labour down there? Yu think it easy for me to have to sit outta di way while yu wash yuself under yu arm and down below because yu too fraid to go out di yard? This little room is only mean for one person. Me. Me and me alone. I nuh tell yu dat di first night yu come here? Dat first day yu just come from country? Yu think it all right to just sidung here like yu take up residence, like yu nuh need to go nowhere? I was doing yu mother a favour. Yu know that? And I never ask no questions 'bout how come you two young girls have to run from country so sudden and so fast. Dat was your business. But now yu come here and mek it my business because day in day out all I have to look pon is your face staring at me like yu think it me forcing yu to live hand to mouth in this pit.'

This is how Auntie gwaan day and night. But the time she really turn hateful was the day she come and find me looking in the bottom drawer a her dresser, and all I was doing was seeing where the smell a the mothballs was coming from. I dunno what madden her so because all that was in there was a few pickney baby clothes all neat and pressed and fold real nice.

'Yu think yu too good for dis place. Yu think yu high and mighty working in di Chiney shop instead a soiling yu hands on other people dirty clothes, or scrubbing dem floor, or cooking dem food, or wiping di pickney nose or better still backside. Yu too good for dat. You and yu sista. So what yu think yu good for? Yu think I don't know? Yu think I don't have eyes in my head to see what gwaan every time yu step foot outta dis room? Yu think I not got no nose to smell di stink a dogs on heat? Yu gwaan like yu think it dem. Like dem coming at yu from every corner fi no good reason. But is not every woman got dem foaming at di mouth. Every other woman living in dis yard can go 'bout her business. She catch water. She go to di toilet. She wash down in di shower. It not no major event. You step out and it like a pack a wolves closing in for di kill. Tracking yu, homing yu. Yu think I nuh see it? What yu think dat is? Yu think it some freak a nature that mek dem turn like dat wid yu? Yu think dem just pick yu out random like it have nothing to do wid you? Well I know dat is what yu want to think, but dat is your little daydream. And if it mek yu feel better so be it. But you is the only one yu fooling. Because just like every man in dis yard got him eye train on you so every woman can see di heads that turn, and di ears that go deaf, and di motion that stop any time you turn out. And every one a dem can feel di stream a cold air dat yu carry wid yu up and down these parts. Yu think yu big woman but you mark my words. Going to yu bed hungry still better than di suffering yu get if yu let some man breed yu. Better sleep hungry than play wid bwoy pickney. Next thing yu know yu a panhandle for dem dirty business. And if yu want money yu know already is only one bank dem want put it into. Di hairy bank. Better di shame a being poor than mixing wid evil. No tek shame and go shake di debbil's hand.'

Auntie seem like she content to say all a this to me. Me no more than a child. It hurtful. Maybe it even hurt more because deep down inside I know she right when she say, 'Breeze nuh blow, tree nuh shake.' So I reckon it time for me to go find some place for a live-in job. Time to leave Auntie to all the nastiness her mind meking and the way her mouth running off even though there nobody listening because I give up wid that weeks back right after she tell me, 'Yu dripping di juice that mek di man dem beg fa jooks.'

But how I going find another job when I working from dawn 'til dusk in Mr Ho shop, Monday to Saturday? I tell Marcia I cyan see her Sunday afternoon no more. Not for a little while anyway. And I start walk the street every Sunday from sunup 'til sundown. Every week I mark out a good neighbourhood and go from house to house knocking on the door or calling through the locked wrought ironwork, 'Hello, anybody home,' until somebody come and shake their head and say, 'No, no help needed.' And then I go to the next house where maybe they sitting on the veranda, or maybe I got to run from the noise of some big Alsatian they got tie up in the front, or maybe I cyan climb over all the baby bicycle and pickney things that messing up the yard, that I know I going spend all my time picking up if they decide to tek me on. So I just pass that one by and hear my shoes scraping over the gravel a the next driveway, and flick the click a the next gate, and smile and say, 'Thank you, Miss,' even though she nuh give me nothing. And all of this wid the sun beating down on me like it cooking me from the inside out except I mopping myself wid a handkerchief because I want to look as fresh as I can for the next person that is going to open the door and then shut it in my face.

'How old you say you are?'

'Twenty years old, Miss.'

'Twenty? You don't look hardly over sixteen to me.'

'They always say I look young for my age, Miss.'

'And you don't have any references?'

'I just come from country, Miss, and the family didn't think to give me no references.'

'But you have done domestic work before? For this family you say in the country?'

'Yes Miss, mother, father and three little children. Wash and iron. Cook and clean. I keep the place nice, Miss, and my food is tasty and nutritious. All I ask is you give me a trial and if after two weeks you not happy I will go look somewhere else. I just begging you for a chance to prove myself.'

'I don't like to employ people off the street like this you know. No references. No recommendation. You could be anybody, some delinquent for all I know.'

'Look at me, Miss, I am no delinquent. I promise you that. I come from a clean, decent, God-fearing family. Church every Sunday; house clean spick and span every Friday; washing on the line every Monday. Routine, Miss, that is the answer. Everything in the right place at the right time. Neat and tidy. Spotless and fresh just like the good Lord mean it to be.' But I can see that I am not meking no sway with her. She standing there with her hand on her hip and a curl on her lip looking down at me from the veranda. She not even ask if I want to take the five steps and go up there outta the sun. That would be outta order because then I would be looking at her eye to eye and that wouldn't do at all.

She not saying nothing to me so I reckon maybe she thinking 'bout it at least. But then she start shake her head and I know it bad news. So I speak up quick, because in all the weeks a walking my Sundays away this is the closest I get to anybody even considering it.

'Miss, I am a good, honest, hard worker. Right now I am working in a grocer's downtown but shop work is not where my heart at. Looking after a family that is what I want to do. And right now all I need is to see the room you have for me to sleep in and settle with you when you want me to start.' And I look up at her with a straight back and a conviction in my eye because I can hear the pleading in my voice and it sound weak and ugly. But she not convinced.

'I am sure you are a good worker and I believe you when you say you are honest, but I just can't hire somebody off the street like this. It would be different if you were just going to work outside like in a gardening position, but not somebody working in the house and helping with the children.'

My heart start to sink. But right then a man step out the house and walk over to where she standing. Him look at me. And then him look me up and down, slow and careful. And then him say to her, 'All month you been telling me how you need some help since the last girl leave so sudden. So give her the job nuh?' And he turn 'round and walk back inside.

The room I got is hot. The window barely big enough to let in daylight never mind any bit a breeze that might dry the sweat off yu skin. It small and it smell like it never catch the slightest bit a fresh air since the day they nail on the last piece a wood and screw on the door. The bed look like it come out the ark. Just big enough for me to lay down sideways with a mattress so thin if yu turn over too quick yu would catch it in the springs. The drawers I think somebody make outta some old orange crate and the hanging rail is nothing more than a piece a old wood. It seem shameful that they would mek somebody live like this while they busy in the house with their big wide open windows that catch the light and drapes that waft on every little gust a wind.

But it no matter. I leave Auntie behind and I was glad and thankful for that because her cantankerousness never stop. Even after I say to her that I was going she was still telling me 'bout how ungrateful I was for the roof she put over my head, and the food she put in my belly, and the kindness she show me and Marcia when we just come to Kingston a pair a country bumpkin who didn't know nothing from nothing. Even as I am walking up the yard to the gate she is shouting out to me, 'A no one time monkey want wife.' But I just keep walking with the tears rolling down my face.

'I didn't tek anything, Miss.'

'The children say they saw you.'

'I don't know how that can be, Miss, because I didn't tek nothing.'

'Are you calling my children liars?'

'No Miss, no. Just maybe they mek a mistake. Maybe they think they see something but it not what they think.'

This is how it is with her every other day. But I cyan think she really believe that I taking food from the shelf, or crockery from the cupboard, or jewellery from her dresser. If she really believe all a this she would have call the police by now. Still, it nuh stop her carrying on wid me. Every time I turn 'round is something else. The pickney, they just cower 'round the doorpost and anytime she ask them, 'You see her?' they say, 'Yes Mommy, yes.' But they know it not true. They know me better than that because when she not here all they want to do is watch me fold the sheets and hang out the towels to dry, and fix the lunch, and tidy 'round the place. And maybe they try their hand at a little bit a ironing like a square handkerchief or pillowcase; or peel some Irish potato for the beef soup; or grate the coconut for the rice and peas. And talk. Bwoy they can talk. They talk about everything under the sun. Yu would never know they have so much to say when yu see these three little girls sitting so prim and quiet at their mama's side. But she don't know nothing 'bout it. She would fire me faster than buckshot if she know what these girls busy doing every day they come back from school, because this sorta activity is no fit thing for these light-skin girls to be doing. No fit way for them to be behaving wid the help. So when she not here, they is this way wid me and when she come they turn tail completely. They distant wid me, and moody and sour, and they eager to say, 'Yes Mommy, yes.' Gloria is a thief.

But it not the pickney that really bothering me. It is him, lean-ing on the doorpost in room after room. I can feel his eyes burning into me every time I reaching up to tek a pot off a high shelf, or getting on my knees to scrub the floor, or even just bending down to pick up a dolly. It mek my body sweat and my hands jerky. So from time to time I drop something and he is there, quick as a flash to catch, to rescue, to pick it up and give it back to me wid a smile like he happy to be of service as he put the pot or can or yam into my hand, resting him fingers on my skin and teking more time to do it than it really need.

The worse time is every morning when I have to make the bed. Rubbing my hands over the sheet to straighten it out. The sheet his body been twisting and turning on all night. Fluffing up the pillow his head been resting on. Shaking out the top sheet that maybe he wrap himself in or maybe he throw off in the night to cool his nakedness, because I never get no pyjamas in the wash for

31

him. Turning down the top, fixing all the corners, putting on the bedspread, running my hand down the pillow line for neatness. And him watching every move with a body so still I can almost hear him breathing. It not so bad when he on the seven 'til two shift because he outta the house in the morning. But when he do the two to ten that is when I really feel it strong in the bedroom.

I don't say nothing to nobody 'bout it. I just carry on and hope that he don't mistake my sweating and clumsiness for excitement. That he don't tek it on himself to start do something more than look.

'Yu sure keeping the place nice, eh, Gloria.' So now I got to turn 'round and look at him.

'Yes sah. Thank you, sah.' He take a couple steps towards me and lean up on the next doorpost.

The kitchen long and narrow, with only one way in and out and he is standing right there in the gap. So I trapped, unless I plan to jump outta the window and maybe break my leg and have to explain to Miss what been going on here. It ten o'clock in the morning. The pickney not getting back from school 'til one o'clock and she gone to office all day 'til six.

'The whole place more settle since yu come here, eh, Gloria?'

'Thank yu, sah.'

'How long yu been with us now?'

'Almost a full six month now, sah.'

'A full six months, Gloria. That is good.' And he tek two more step towards me. Him cotch him hip on the edge a the stove and cross him arms and legs.

'Yu like it here, Gloria? Yu happy working here in the house?'

'Yes sah. It is a good job.'

'And yu like yu room yu sleep in out back?'

32

'Yes sah. It is a fine room. Everything I need.'

'Yu fix it up nice?' That is when my heart stop. Just for a split second because right after that it was pumping like I was running up the mountain to Cinchona.

'I do the best I can, sah.'

'Your best is good enough for me, Gloria.' And then him say, 'Yu know, I haven't seen inside that room for such a long time. Well, almost a full six months.'

So I say to myself, 'How much yu want this job girl? How much yu want a roof over yu head, running water and regular food from the table? How much yu want to spend yu Sunday afternoon, yu only half-day off a week, with Marcia, walking the street or sitting on a bench outside Cross Roads market or catching the bus to Hope Gardens because it free to go see the trees and flowers? How much yu want that?' But then I realise I already done lose the job because either I go willing to him and the wife find out and fire me, or I kick up a stink that nobody going pay no mind to and most likely call the police and have me arrested for a thief, or I just walk outta here right now. Sudden, like the last girl. No last week's wages. No references. And that is even supposing I going mek it past him to go pick up the few things I have in the room out back.

'So what yu say, Gloria?'

Him smiling at me because he know he got me cornered. All I can hear is my own heart beating, and feel the cold sweat a fear on my skin, and the rough, dry hands of Barrington Maxwell on my arms and pushing open my legs and I know I cyan be doing that again. But neither am I going to go grab up a knife or pan. For one thing my arm don't feel strong enough to swing it. And afterwards what I going to do? Go jump on another bus? To where? Spanish

Town? And tek Marcia with me? Or leave her here in Kingston? Or maybe this time they catch me and send me to prison which is where I belong anyway. And what going happen to Marcia then?

'I would just like yu to let me pass so I can be on my way.'

'Wa'ppun, I too old for yu? Too ugly maybe?'

What I going say to him? So I say, 'You are my employer. You are a married man.'

'Since when a thing like that matter to a girl like you?'

I dunno what kinda girl he think I am. Where he get the idea. I always dress prim in the little black and white uniform she give me. I act decent. I talk respectable. And the personal things I have to do I do in my room behind a closed door. So maybe it what Auntie say, I dripping di juice.

'I would just like yu to let me pass so I can be on my way.' And he just uncross his leg and wave his arm and bow like as to say, 'Yes, yu can pass, your ladyship.'

So I put down the bowl a gungo peas I was getting ready to soak for the soup and I dry my hands on a cloth. And I slowly move to walk past him. But just as I get there he stick out his arm.

'So I block yu way now Gloria just to give yu one last chance to change yu mind because yu know yu want it.'

I don't look at him and I don't touch him. I just say, 'I would like you to let me pass so I can be on my way.'

I go to the room out back and change my clothes and leave her uniform on the bed. I put my things in a brown paper bag that the groceries come in, and I walk up the driveway and close the gate behind me. Him sitting on the veranda with him feet rest on the little table reading the newspaper and eating peanuts, flicking the shell over the railing into the yard.

CHAPTER 4

I START WALK down the road to catch the tram downtown even though I got no idea where I going to go. And then suddenly three youths step into my path and decide they want stroll wid me.

'So what yu name beautiful?'

I don't want say nothing to them. I just hold on tight to my bag.

'We not after yu bag yu know. We just want to get to know yu that is all, and give yu some protection as well. It nuh safe for a beautiful young woman like yuself to be walking out here all on her own like dis. Yu nuh know that?' And then they start prancing and circling 'round me. One at the front, one at the back all the time them moving and moving. Trotting 'round me as I carry on walk.

'Yu nuh want say nothing to us? Is not us yu need be fraid of yu know. Is all them other ones out there. All them bad bwoys that just ready to pounce.' And just as he say the word he raise him hands like claws right up in front of me wid a big wide smile pon him face. And the other two laugh.

Next thing I hear is the clip-clop of a horse and the whirl a the wheels turning, slower and slower until it almost come to a standstill right next to me. I keep walking and leave the bwoys standing there patting themself on the back because they think they so smart and funny. But the horse buggy not making like it want to pass me. Then I hear this voice in a loud sorta whisper say, 'Miss, miss.' When I turn 'round it is a Chinaman sitting in the back seat leaning over trying to catch my attention. He broad and square for a Chinaman and even though him sitting down I can see him tall. He well dressed as well in black pants and jacket and a crisp white shirt.

So I say, 'There is something I can help you with?' But him no answer, so I say, 'I hope you are not mistaking me for some other kind of woman. I have you know I am a respectable woman on my way to the store.'

'You have trouble?'

'And that is any of your business? Go 'way man.' And I start hurry but the buggy keeping pace with me.

'Not to be rude, but young lady such as you walking by self with things in Hong Zi grocery store bag catch my eye, and I think you have trouble with youths.'

'What trouble?' And I kiss my teeth. 'You just mind yu own business and leave me to mind mine yu hear me?'

'I can offer ride to wherever you go.'

'What is the matter with yu man? Cyan yu hear me tell yu I don't want nothing? I am walking the street and the last time I check it still a free country so I not committing no crime. Leave me nuh?'

So the buggy tek off and I think thank God. But no sooner than the horse and black canopy disappear 'round the corner the three youths show up again.

'Yu Chiney daddy leave yu in him dust darling?'

'Yu more interested in our company now?'

'Why yu nuh let us escort yu so we can pass di day nice?'

I just keep walking. I know the tram stop only 'round the corner down the road a ways.

'It better yu stick wid yu own kind yu know.'

'The Chiney dem do the same ting. Stick together.'

'Birds of a feather. That is how it is.'

And then they start get closer and closer 'til they brushing up against me. Just here and there, like they touch the hem a my dress, or brush 'cross my back, or catch my arm as they circling round and round.

When I turn the corner I see the Chinaman buggy park up by the kerb. So I quicken my step and when I get up to it I stop. And he is sitting there looking at me. He reach out his hand and I just tek it and raise myself into the buggy and sit down. The driver flick the leather and the horse move off leaving the three bwoys standing on the sidewalk like they cyan understand what just happen.

We go pass Cross Roads and head down Slipe Road towards Chinatown. It feel good to be riding in the shade with the breeze brushing my face.

'You just maybe lose job I think. And you being a domestic that would most likely mean you also lose place to live.' And he look at me like him expecting an answer.

'Yu asking or telling me?'

'Asking.'

'Yes, yu right. Yu happy now?'

'That is nothing for me to be happy about. It seem more like sad.'

I turn my body 'round square on to him. 'And even if it is, what is it to you?'

He just stare at me and after some long while he say, 'I have daughters. One not too different age from you. If man come 'cross my daughter in trouble I hope he stop and offer some assistance.'

When we reach North Street the buggy stop outside Hong Zi Wine & Spirits and we step down and go inside. The store cool and dark with the shelves stack and liquor pile up in boxes and crates all 'round the room, and a big mahogany counter at the far end for people to conduct their business.

'Mr Henry, the truck ready to leave for Spanish Town. Anything else yu want go on it?'

'Show me.' So the bwoy hand the Chinaman a piece a paper and he read down it and say, 'Yes, fine.' And the bwoy tek back the paper and go out back where I hear some big old engine start up and set off down the road. I just stand there and look at him, and realise that this here is Henry Wong, owner of wine merchants and grocery stores where every week for the past six months I have been picking up supplies, and whose brown paper bag I am standing there clutching.

'Is there something yu want from me, why yu bring me here like this?'

'Something I want?'

'Don't play me for no fool. Yu know what I mean. Just because I a domestic don't mek me stupid, especially 'bout the ways a men.'

He tek off his jacket and hang it on the back of a high sorta stool chair that standing behind the counter. Then him roll up him shirt sleeves. Slow and careful. First the left one and then the right. And then he sit down on the stool and fold his arms and look at me.

'I bring you here because this is where I coming. But now you here I not sure what I fixing to do with you.'

'Yu don't have to do nothing with me. I can just walk outta here right now and that is that.'

'That is that? You have job? You have somewhere rest your head?'

'That is no concern a yours. I cyan even believe I am still standing here talking to yu.'

'You want glass water or maybe lemonade?'

'Lemonade! Yu think lemonade going fix my situation?' Him no answer me. Him just sit.

'I know woman in East Kingston, Franklyn Town, run small boarding house. Respectable establishment, prices reasonable. Breakfast and dinner as well.'

'What yu doing all this for?'

Him look at me serious and then him say, 'You want leave? There is door.' And he motion his head.

So I turn 'round and I walk. Just as I stepping outside I say to him, 'How come yu name everything Hong Zi when yu name Henry Wong?'

'Name not Henry Wong. Henry Wong name British immigration officer give. Real name from China, Hong Zilong.'

I walk down to Barry Street and I go find Mr Ho shop. When I get there the place busy-busy. Mr Ho is run off him feet and the little girl helping him don't seem like she have the first idea what she is doing. So I just walk 'round the counter and pick up one of the long white cotton apron hanging on the nail and tie it 'round me and start serve the next customer. Mr Ho see me and smile but him nuh say nothing.

When it time to shut up Mr Ho tell the girl she can go home and he will tidy up and sort everything out. After she gone him say to me, 'You need work, Gloria? Domestic position not work out for you?'

'It turn into a disaster Mr Ho.'

'You want come back shop?'

'Yu serious for real?'

'The girl mean well, Gloria. But she slow and she get confuse. She nuh know what is what, especially since English start fight with Germans and governor make all his regulations over prices. She make mistake. She not so good wid adding, not like you. She nuh know how to please customer, or suggest maybe they try something new, or get little extra, or take advantage of special offer. She just give them what they ask for. That is all. But that not shopkeeping Gloria, eh? We know that.'

I think for a minute and then I say, 'Yu maybe think I pressing my luck but I need a raise Mr Ho. Me not staying with Auntie no more. So when I get somewhere I going have to pay real rent.'

'You not got nowhere to live Gloria?'

'Live-in domestic. Yu lose the job, yu lose the bed.'

Mr Ho knot him brow like he got a earnest fret and then him start look 'round the shop like he thinking what to do.

'So where you sleep tonight?' But I not got no answer for him.

He tek off his apron and start walk into the back room where he got the storage of rice and flour and bottles and cans and such like.

'It not much space and it dangerous with toilet out back but maybe if you manage with pot we lock door and you sleep here. And tomorrow we think what to do.' He pause and then he say, 'I would take you home with me but, you know, too much explaining to wife.'

I cyan face going back to Auntie to ask her for nothing. Anyway, I reckon the room nuh worse than sleeping under the table or up next to her gluing my body to the wall.

Mr Ho say I must go get something hot to eat and he wait for me to come back. But I say no, is OK. I don't need nothing.

'Gloria, you must eat something. If you not want rice then we open can bully beef and pull down some hard dough bread, but you must eat. You have money?' I don't say nothing. 'You take this.' And he reach in him pocket and pull out some change and say, 'Step 'cross street and get rice and pork. Is OK. I wait for you.'

When I get back Mr Ho open the door and hand me a cold soda and say, 'You eat now. I already make space for you in back room and wash out old oil tin for pot. For overnight, you know. You rest now. I going lock you in 'til morning so everything safe and sound.'

When I go in the back room I see he stack up some big bags a flour and throw some old sack over them. And next to that he fold up two more sacks for me to have something to pull over myself in the night if I need to. The oil tin he leave standing on the floor in the middle a the room.

When I finally rest myself down I lay there and think about the life that the good Lord give me and the trials and tribulations He put in my path, and whether He mean for them to mek me strong or if it to break me down. And I wonder when He finally going say, 'All right Gloria Campbell, I pardon yu now and it OK for yu to carry on yu life with the same good fortune and good grace that anybody who been through what yu been through so young should deserve to have.'

The next morning when Mr Ho come to open up the shop he bring a flask a hot coffee and some rice and sausage in a shut pan.

'You have good night, Gloria?'

'Yes Mr Ho. Thank you.'

'Good. You nuh work today. Today you look somewhere live. Then tomorrow plenty time start work. Plus I give you rise. Nine shillings a week. Just like King Street. How that sound to you?'

'Very generous Mr Ho. Thank you.'

'You go wash up out back now and then you eat and then you go see 'bout room.'

I walk up to Henry Wong's wine store. When I come through the door he sitting behind the counter. 'You change mind 'bout something?'

I swallow hard like it is my pride that is going down my throat so thick and lumpy. 'Lodgings in Franklyn Town?'

And he just turn to the bwoy and say, 'Go fetch buggy.'

Miss Sissy run the boarding house. It a old ramshackle place with a lot a rooms and a big wooden table in the kitchen that she must seat a dozen people or more. She say that is where I going eat my breakfast at six-thirty and dinner at seven, and if I not there at dem times I not going get nothing. She tek her hand and brush back her wavy grey hair that she got tie up in a bun but it still loose, and she take a puff on her pipe.

She show me the room with the little bed and drawers and closet and I ask her if she got a room can sleep two.

'Sleep two? What yu planning a doing? Yu cyan be moving no man in here yu know. That is a strict rule a this house. No men, not morning, noon or night. This whole house is for women and women alone yu hear me?'

'I understand Miss Sissy. It just that my sister is in service up Cross Roads and I want if I can to bring her here to be with me and finish her schooling.' Miss Sissy look at me like she suspicious but Henry Wong nod him head like it OK and she say all right.

The room bright and airy and it got two single bed push up against each wall wid a little tile table between and a lamp on it. It pretty and clean, and the rent she is asking going leave just enough each week for tram fare and any little extra me and Marcia need.

When I go get Marcia she cyan believe it. She pack her grip and wave goodbye to Norma so fast I was out the gate again almost before I come in it. When she see the room at Miss Sissy's she happy. She turn and spin and jump and dance in the little gap between the beds and she hug and kiss me. And then she throw herself down on top a the bedspread with her hands behind her head and kick off her shoes.

CHAPTER 5

MR HO SAY the girl not a bad girl, she just need training that is all. So now I got to follow her every step she tek from bagging up the flour and rice, to weighing the saltfish and counting out the cans and stacking the bread on the shelf. I got to watch her out the corner of my eye while she serving the customers young and old, regulars and strangers, as she weigh and count and pack the goods for them, and tek the money and give the change. I even got to see how she pile up the empty boxes and garbage out back. She call Lynette. She small and don't look like she could lift a full bag a rice if her life depended on it, but it turn out she stronger than she look and it seem like she doing all right. Mr Ho happy enough. He glad he nuh fire her because now he got the two a us out front he spending less time serving and that seem to please him. Me, I dunno. Four months later and there is still something not right 'bout that girl. It playing on my mind. I cyan put my finger on it that is all.

The other thing troubling me is Marcia, because even though we settled and she supposed to be going to school Miss Sissy say it not so. Marcia dress every day in the white blouse and little blue pinafore dress like she got on the uniform and on her way but all she do is cross the road and spend the day sitting down in the house over there doing God knows what according to Miss Sissy except she sure it involve smoking cigarettes and drinking liquor, and sometimes when she come back Marcia got to visit the bathroom to wash the make-up off her face. Miss Sissy say it not decent for a child to be spending time, never mind how much time, with women like that. It alarming. That is what she say. And it going lead to bad business.

'Bad business? What yu saying to me? Apart from the child not going to school to get her education?'

'These women, Gloria.' She pick up the tablecloth and walk out back to empty the crumbs. So I follow her. 'They are whores.'

It tek me aback the way she spit out the words at me.

'Yu mean actual real whores or yu just think they loose because they smoking cigarettes and carrying on?'

'Yu nuh see how much men they got marching in and outta that place? All hours a the day and night? What yu think deh up to? Running a boy scout troop?' She shake out the cloth in the yard and then she fold it neat and walk back inside.

I say to Marcia, 'Yu nuh think yu should be trying to get yuself a education instead a spending all yu time across the road?'

'Yu mean wid Sybil and Beryl?'

'It nuh matter what they call. Fetching and carrying after them not going do yu no good if yu want something better than working in a shop.'

'Like teking a more senior position with Miss Vilma? That what yu mean?'

'Since when yu get so fresh? Yu think yu can talk like this to me after the hours I spend trying to keep us outta the poor house?'

'More like outta the penitentiary yu mean.'

'Hush yu mouth.' And I pray to God nobody standing outside this bedroom door to hear her and start put two and two together to mek ten. 'Yu got to want something more than this.' And I look 'round the little room the two a us sharing.

'Yes, that is what I want and going to school to learn 'bout Oliver Cromwell and the kings and queens a England not going do nothing for me unless I am planning to become a schoolteacher passing down all this same claptrap to the next generation who going sit there just like me wondering what all this got to do with meking a living in Jamaica in 1940.'

Sometimes on a Sunday I sit on Miss Sissy veranda and look out over the road where the radio blasting out the calypso and they jigging and jiving with the curlers in their hair and the cigarette in their mouth wearing some long silk robe they must get from Chinatown, all red and yellow and green embroider with flowers and birds and flowing round them with every swish a their hips. When Marcia not sitting with me looking at them, she over there with them looking at me. And in truth she spend more time over the road because that is her preferred activity. She nuh want do nothing else. Not tek the bus to Hope Gardens, or go listen to the military band play their music in Victoria Park, or even go to the beach. All she want to do is run after Sybil and Beryl fetching the next pack a cigarettes and chipping the ice off the block for the next drink. She taking lessons in drawing on the eyebrow pencil and squeezing tissue paper to blot off the excess after yu spread on the lipstick. She painting their fingernails and even their toenails, with the little piece a cotton stick between each toe. And then after she done that she doing her own. Right out there on the veranda in full view a the whole street. Who would think the girl not even finish school yet.

Miss Sissy say I should keep Marcia lock up in the house. That what she need is for me to march her to school every morning and go fetch her back at one-thirty and lock her in the room 'til dinner time.

'I cyan do that Miss Sissy. I got to go to work.'

'The child need a firm hand. That is all I am saying to yu.'

All I hear from Marcia is how Miss Sissy chastising her every day and giving her errands to keep her running to the shop, and fetching this and carrying that like she a delivery bwoy. Miss Sissy even try get Marcia do little bit a housework but Marcia not doing it. Truth is Miss Sissy effort not doing nothing but driving Marcia further into the arms a Sybil and Beryl.

'She call me a whore yu know that?'

'She didn't call yu no whore Marcia. She say yu need to be careful in case yu turn into one.'

'Yu see. The two a yu the same. Yu think that every woman that paint her toenail and pamper herself is a whore. Having a little fun wid yuself don't mek yu nothing. Anyway, how somebody going turn into a thing like that? Like it a accident? Yu cyan do that. Yu have to decide. Yu decide that is what yu want to do. And when yu mek that decision that is your business.'

'A where yu learn to talk like that girl? Yu think yu a big woman now because yu paint on little lipstick and smudge on some rouge? Well let me remind you, you are a schoolgirl and yu would do well to concentrate yu mind on that, not running over the road to go fuss 'round those two with their silk robes and fancy talk 'bout who is deciding what. What you need to decide to do is get a education so yu can earn yuself a living.'

'Yu mean like you every day trailing after that fool-fool girl Lynette and working like a slave for Mr Ho doing everything he want and everything he not even think he want yet? And then coming home so tired yu can hardly get the spoon to pick up the sour mackerel rundown Miss Sissy busy serving up every night. Fretting every week and counting out quattie because yu dunno if the wages going cover the rent and the food and the bus fare. I wouldn't ever want to wake up to one single day a worry like that, never mind thinking that this is the rest a my life. At least Sybil and Beryl having themself a good time while they putting a roof over their head and luscious food on the table.'

The thing that worry me is that I think maybe Miss Sissy half right 'bout Marcia state a mind. Not that Marcia already decide, but that she like the company a Sybil and Beryl too much. And from my point a view it is one thing her being over there with the two a them in daytime doing their beauty treatment but it another thing now she playing waitress at night. That is a completely different kettle a fish.

'Yu busy wid yu mouth running down two women yu never even meet. How would yu like it if somebody do that to you? Just tek one look and decide they know all there is to know. Yu should go talk to them before yu start find fault.'

Maybe Marcia got a point. So when she come tell me that Sybil and Beryl invite us to dinner I think I got no choice but to tek a bath when I come back from work the Saturday and put on a clean frock and go with Marcia 'cross the road, if for no other reason than to be able to say I come face to face wid dem. Miss Sissy huffing and puffing but what I going to do? Marcia not going pay no mind to anything I got to say without me at least taking the time to sit across the table and exchange a few words with these women she calling her friends.

The house got a veranda out front that go narrow 'round the side. It got a room yu step into with some grey and white tiles on the floor but this is not the room we going eat in. Where we going eat is the back room that next to the kitchen with a big, wide door that go straight out into the yard that sufficient and pretty with a almond tree and some yellow hibiscus and white periwinkle, and a purple bougainvillea running all over the back fence. The kitchen is a good size with a little maid room just off it that nobody live in because is only Sybil and Beryl in the house, even though it got another living room with sofas to lounge in and two bedroom each side a the house with a bathroom in between. Four bedroom and two bathroom. Beryl serve up curry goat with rice and salad and afterwards she bring out a pineapple upside-down cake and some gizzadas. She got ice cream as well and what look like a gallon a rum punch. These women know how to entertain, and it taste good. Marcia right 'bout Miss Sissy cooking, but we been eating it so long I almost forget what good food taste like. Beryl's curry goat is rich and thick, hot and heavy. Not thin and watery like everything Miss Sissy put on your plate.

'Yu see much a Kingston since yu come from country?' Sybil cutting her eye at me while she lighting a cigarette.

'No. It well over two years now and all we do is look for work and find it and a few months later look for work again.' Sybil laugh and Beryl follow suit.

'Yu nuh think that maybe the work yu finding yu should be leaving for somebody else to find?'

'Yu have to work. What yu going to do otherwise?' The two a them look at me and then they look at one another and laugh. Marcia start join so I shoot her a stare and she shut up.

Sybil drag on her cigarette, and then she say, 'Yu a good-looking woman, Gloria. Anybody ever tell yu that?'

I look at her through the curl a blue smoke. Sybil is tall for a woman and she sturdy. She heavy set but she filling up her body. She solid. She not carrying no spare pounds. She lighter complexion than Beryl, sorta fudge brown, whereas Beryl is more like chocolate. A square chunk a dark chocolate. She got good teeth as well, Sybil, and a smile that would mek yu forget yu troubles and believe that she was the only person on God's good earth that yu could trust.

'They been telling me that ever since I young enough to tek it vain, and then old enough to know it was trouble.'

'The old women dem say "beautiful woman beautiful trouble" because she attract the man like a moth to a flame. They nuh understand that the beautiful woman not the one that cause the trouble, she the one that get it. That nuh right, Beryl?' And Beryl say 'yah man' and the two a dem exchange a glance.

Beryl say, 'So tell me 'bout life in country. What it like?' I tell them 'bout the sugar cane and banana plantation, and the hills full a orange trees and the river with the water so clear that when yu stand in it up to yu neck yu can still see yu feet clear as day. And then Marcia start talk 'bout Mama and Leroy and Babs and then Beryl just say, 'So how come yu come to Kingston?' And a hush fall on the room.

Marcia start shuffle and Sybil say, 'Marcia tell me some man in a shack would have ruin her if it not for you busting through the door with a big stick in yu hand.' I cyan believe Marcia go tell them 'bout that. I so shocked I cyan even bring myself to look at her. And then Sybil say, 'Yu nuh need to fret yuself. We not going tell nobody.' She turn to Beryl and then back to me. 'Yu secret safe wid us.'

I look at them sitting there so satisfied like they already done figure out the whole a life and know the secret. 'What yu trying to do Sybil?'

'I trying to help yu Gloria that is all. Marcia say yu working in the Chinaman shop all hours a day and night and even though it wearing yu out yu not got tuppence to show for it come the end a the week. And all I am saying to yu is yu could put the gift God give yu to better use. Better use for you. So yu can have something more than the see-through fish soup Miss Sissy feeding yu and the strip-down room yu sharing wid yu sista.'

I reckon Marcia the one putting Sybil up to this.

'What you do Sybil is your business. I got no quarrel with that.'

'What is it yu think we do?'

I cyan believe she go ask me a thing like that. Right out loud. I want to say to her 'I think yu entertaining men for money' but I cyan say it. I don't know it for sure. Not the money part anyway. The men, I seen plenty and I can guess what going on inside, but the money, I don't know. And still, when all is said and done, I cyan believe I nuh figure it right. The only thing that meking me hold back is remembering what Marcia say to me 'bout how everyone think a woman who paint her toenails and dance on her own veranda is a whore. And also, that it would be so downright rude to say it.

So I just sit there and look at her 'til Sybil eventually say, 'It not what yu think.' And then she say, 'Yu only a young woman Gloria and already yu see so much man trouble. Yu going spend yu whole life running from them?' She get up and reach over the table to pour more rum punch into my glass. 'Yu nuh think that maybe there got to be something better than that?'

So I say, 'Something better than being poor and feeling shame?'

'Yu feel shame, Gloria? When yu feel shame? When every man

want to stop what him doing just to look at yu? When they whispering and laughing behind yu back or maybe it worse when it to yu face? Or when they don't even bother whisper, they just say what they want to straight out so everybody can hear and join in the joke and yu too fraid to say nothing back to them? When even the bwoy pickney is chasing after yu down the road repeating all the dirty things him hear from somewhere else?'

I think about Auntie's yard, and the man rubbing himself on the bus, and the crowd that making fun in the shop, and him leaning on every doorpost and saying to me, 'Since when a thing like that matter to a girl like you.' I think about the youths on the road when Henry Wong turn up. And I think about Barrington Maxwell. But I don't say nothing to her.

Sybil sit there a good long while before she say, 'To them every woman is a whore so they can tek what they want from her because she is not a real person. She is a thing. A thing for their comfort and pleasure, their pride or amusement. She there to mek them feel good. People think being a whore got to do with what gwaan in the bedroom but it not. Being a whore is about who is in charge. And who can mek who do exactly what they want the other one to do however menial or shameful. However much it against the person's own self-interest or self-love. Because we just here to work for them, including in the bedroom. That is what they think. Every woman, from baby to old gramma, is only there to serve some purpose a theirs. And that is OK wid dem because one way or another, they reckon they paying hard cash for it anyway.

'It like yu back in slavery. A hundred years ago they free the slave but they nuh free the woman. The woman is still living her life under the control a the man, under his law and regulation and goodwill. And her body is occupied. It is his. It belong to him just like the body a the slave belong to the slave master.

'And when yu suffer that realisation day in day out, year after year, life after life, what it do is shape how every woman see herself. Weak and subservient like she cyan do nothing without him say so, she cyan even think nothing for herself. She completely relying on him to know who she is, and all she can do is carry on just the way him want her to and hope for the best. Just like the slave.'

I wait because she talk so long I not sure she finish. But she lighting another cigarette so I reckon she done. So I say, 'Yu really believe all a that?'

'Me believe it? You better believe it sista because that is the only way yu going mek yuself a life that is your own, where yu not beholden to no man for the roof over yu head or have to be grateful to him for putting a ring pon yu finger. Instead all yu do is provide a service and they pay the bill and yu go about yu business. And nobody got to have nothing to say 'bout how yu look or how much weight yu carrying, or how yu keep house or cook, or mind the pickney. Nobody there to judge or criticise yu. Nobody there to tell yu what to do or imagine what they want to do to yu. They just say it straight out and yu say 'yes' or 'no' and how much it going cost. It simple. Everybody know where they stand. There not nuh guesswork and worrying involved. No tiptoeing. Because there not nobody to persuade and soothe and reassure, and feel fraid 'bout what going happen if they nuh like what yu doing.'

And then Beryl say, 'And no dirty underpants or stinky socks for yu to be soaking and washing week after week.' And they laugh.

'Yu think that better than getting a job that mek enough wages so yu can be yu own woman?'

'You show me that job Gloria and I will be the first in line to tek it. That is if yu think they going give that job to a poor black woman because from where I sit there is only two jobs open to a black woman like you or me. The one I am doing, and the one you just get through doing uptown. Or this third one that yu doing right now working for a pittance in the Chinaman shop.'

And then Beryl say, 'Or carrying di fruit and vegetable on yu head and resting down di basket when yu squat pon yu stool at Coronation Market.'

Mr Ho say Lynette got a cousin that need work and he going have to let me go.

'I sorry Gloria. This nothing to do with you, but my hands tied. I got to give Lynette cousin yu job.'

'Mr Ho I work for yu this long time. Is something I do? Is something mek yu feel yu cyan trust me? I nuh training Lynette good enough?'

'No Gloria.' And then he start wring him hands and some little eyewata run down him face. Me and him standing in the back room straightening up after Lynette long gone.

'Lynette say she pregnant and the baby mine.' I cyan believe my ears. I would never have tek Mr Ho for that sorta man. 'But I never touch her, Gloria. Honest to God. She just mek up story and say she going tell wife unless I give her cousin job and I cyan afford keep three a yu.' That is when I start cry.

'I sorry, Gloria. I truly sorry because yu a good girl. Hard-working and honest.' He tek some Kleenex off the shelf and hand it to me. 'Yu never give me nuh trouble, not a minute's worry. But I got no way to prove the chile not mine and I cyan tek the shame.'

'Yu sure she pregnant?'

'So she say.'

I tek the tissue and wipe my face and then I blow my nose and I say to him, 'I feel bad for yu Mr Ho. It is a wicked situation Lynette got yu in. But if yu give in to her I nuh think it the end a anything. I think it the beginning.'

When I tell Marcia what happen she just say, 'Sybil and Beryl got two room spare,' like it was what she was wishing for.

'We cyan just go move over there.'

'Yu got a better idea?'

I sit on the edge a the little bed but I don't say nothing.

'Come Friday Miss Sissy going want the week rent. Yu know where we going get that from?'

'Mr Ho give me two week pay.'

'And what going happen after that gone? Yu think Miss Sissy going let us stay here on fresh air and a promise while yu look for more work?'

CHAPTER 6

THE MINUTE HENRY Wong hear what happen he jump in a buggy and come to East Kingston. When I reach him at the door he walk straight past me and go inside like he own the place.

'What this you do?'

'What this I do? Who yu think yu is coming in here like yu got any right to ask me any question?'

'I ask you question like papa.'

'What papa? Yu mean you?' I want to tell the man to get out and leave us alone. We can fend for ourselves. But now him sitting down on the sofa wid him hat in him lap. He look so fretful I say to him, 'Yu want a glass a water?'

And then I hear Beryl behind me, 'Or maybe yu like a nice cup a tea. Lipton Yellow Label?' And then she disappear into the kitchen and start rattle some pan even though Henry never say nothing to her.

'Mr Henry we not nothing for yu to be fretting over like this. Yu kind enough to give me a ride on the road and I was grateful. And yu tek us to Miss Sissy and we rest there for a little while, but yu not responsible for us. Yu hardly even know us.'

'I have daughter same as you.' He say it almost like he pleading.

'Yu keep telling me that but I don't know why it mek such a difference to yu. Anyway, I sure yu dawta not nothing like me.'

Henry stand up and start reach in him pocket. And then he pull out a leather wallet ram full a notes.

'Put the money back inna yu pocket man. What yu think this is?'

'I pay. You go back. Miss Sissy take you. I already ask.'

I don't know what is possessing this man. This complete stranger of a man that suddenly decide he going adopt us.

Beryl come in the room wid the teapot and cups. Where she learn to drink tea and milk I don't know. I reckon it musta been some Englishman she busying her time wid. She settle the tray on the table and start pour the tea into the cup. Henry sit down still holding the wallet in him hand, watching her like he witness this sorta thing every day a him life.

Then she say to him, 'Sugar?'

And he say, 'Just one.' After she hand him the cup he just sit there holding it and looking at me. But him cyan think what to say. He just staring.

'Mr Henry, we not your responsibility.' But him nuh say nothing. 'We come from country and we have to mek a life. We not expecting for anybody to ease our way.' He look at me. 'I am not doing anything here but a little housework. Sybil and Beryl be good to us. We got room and board as long as I do the cooking and cleaning. And Marcia get to go the school, which is good, very good Mr Henry.'

'That is very good, about the school. But Gloria, you know . . .' and he lean forward like he want to whisper to me '. . . these women' wid him eyes wandering to Beryl and back '. . . not good girls.' He stop. He serious. 'Miss Sissy say . . .' and then he start shake him head from side to side. I wait, but it seem like Henry cyan even bring himself to finish what he saying. So after some long while I go sit down next to him on the chair and I tek his hand.

'Is OK.' I sorta stroke the back of him hand gentle like. 'Nothing going happen to us. We doing good here. It just like staying wid Miss Sissy, only over here they looking out for us instead a we paying them rent. Everything will work out fine. Nothing for you to be fretting yuself over.' I give him a minute to tek it all in and then I say to him, 'Put yu wallet back in yu pocket. We not needing nothing from yu. We just happy and grateful that yu tek the time to come check us. Yu a good man Henry Wong. I hope yu dawta appreciate yu.'

After Henry gone Beryl start laugh. So I say to her, 'That man help me one day when if it wasn't for him God knows what would a happen to me. And is him that bring me to Miss Sissy, which is how come I end up 'cross the road there. And now I am here wid you. Yu see, is Henry Wong doing all a this. Trust Providence. That man, he going mean something to all a us one day. You mark my words.'

Everything go fine because Sybil and Beryl busy. Not only wid the local but wid the British army boys from Up Park Camp and all dem sailors they bring down here after the British government decide that the Americans could set up bases in British territories of which Jamaica was one. Business was good. And all I had to do was keep the place clean and tidy, and the two a them happy. It was easy. Easier than working in the shop with all dem bwoys standing and staring, and the old women cussing and complaining 'bout how the saltfish bony or the salt beef fatty, and the pickney wid the fast hands into the pocket, and heaving the flour and the rice, and all the time watching Lynette outta the corner a my eye. In truth, this was nothing but joy compare to that. Marcia even going to school every day seeming like she enjoying it.

And then on a Sunday we sit on the veranda and Sybil light a cigarette and Beryl serve food, and Marcia pour drinks, wid the music pumping out from Station ZQI. Because even though the radio set cost so much, Sybil say it nuh matter. We got to have the sounds. So Beryl is dancing and swirling and I got my feet up on a crate with Marcia sitting there painting the nail polish on my toes.

'What yu mean she sick?'

'She sick man. I cyan tell yu nothing more than that.'

'But I come here every Wednesday. Two 'til two-thirty. A drink a rum and I am on my way. Every Wednesday, regular as clockwork.'

'Well the rum I can see to. But Beryl she sick. That is it.'

Then he start walk through the house opening every door and shouting, 'Where she at?' like he going find her laying in her bed and do it to her anyway.

'She down the hospital waiting in line since early morning for whatever medicine they got to give her. That is what I already tell yu.'

'So where di other one? The big brown one?'

'She not here. She gwaan a town.'

'She gwaan town? While me standing here wid a stiff piece a wood inna my pants.'

'Beryl think she was going come back in time.'

'Come back in time?' Him stand and stare at me. And then him start walking again and opening up some more doors.

'So which one a dis room belong to you?'

'My room?'

'Yes. You going have to do it.'

'I am not doing it! Look at me in this old housecoat. I am the live-in domestic. I cook and clean, and wash and iron. I don't have nothing to do wid no men.'

'Well yu look ready to me.'

'Ready! Yu serious?'

'Yah man. Come on we going do it in here.' Him standing holding open the door and pointing wid him finger like for me to go in there.

'That bed nuh got no sheets on.'

'Sheets?' And he stick him head 'round the door to see.

'I just wash and put dem on the line this morning.'

'You nuh worry yuself 'bout no sheets. You worry that it gone quarter pass two and I not even drop my pants yet.' I just stand there and look at him. 'Come nuh, what yu waiting for? Move yuself gal.' And he walk into the room and start tek off him shoes and pants.

Lord God Almighty what am I thinking? Because what is going through my head is that I should just go in there and do it. After all, I been sitting down here in this house all these months watching Sybil and Beryl do it every day, day in day out, and they still good people. They kind and honest. They generous enough to be letting me and Marcia live here for nothing. They not even say a bad word 'bout Miss Sissy who we can hear from right 'cross the street cussing and carrying on alarming 'bout them. All Beryl do is turn up the radio little bit more. I even done trust dem wid my life not to go blabbing all my troubles so I end up in jail. Me really think me better than them? And then I think yu know girl this thing been plaguing yu since Barrington Maxwell. At least if I go do it Beryl can have one day sick without having to tek no aggravation over it. So I walk inside.

When I get in there him laying on him back on the bare bed in him socks and shirt, wid his hands behind his head and his thing stick up in the air ready for me to go sidung pon it. I drop my drawers and go do it. I never even tek off the old blue housecoat wid the little white flowers and edge piping and the cotton so thin from age yu could put yu finger through it. I just hitch up the hem and climb on the bed, and he turn over and get on top a me.

It musta tek a minute or maybe two and he was done. He breathe out real heavy and stop wid his body like a dead weight pressing the air outta me. Hot and clammy and rank from the smell a sweat and what come outta him.

And then he get up and put on him pants and shoes and say, 'Yu going get the rum?'

So I get up and go in the next room and pick up the Wray & Nephew bottle and pour it out. He drink it down in one gulp. And then he reach in him pocket and pull out the money and put it on the table. And just as him walking out the door him turn back and say, 'Tell Beryl I hope she feel better soon and I see her next week.'

It was nearly four o'clock before Beryl come back. She step in the house like she a walking duppy and she head toward her room. When she get there she stop and rest her hand on the doorpost and say to me, 'Him come at two o'clock?'

And I say, 'Yes.'

'So what happen?'

'I do it.'

She turn 'round and look at me with her eyes open wide, and then she say, 'Yu all right?'

'It not so hard as yu think.'

'Only on di soul, darling. Only on di soul.' And then she ease up her body and walk into her room and close the door.

So I shout, 'He leave the money on the table.'

And she shout back, 'You tek it. Yu earn it.'

Beryl was in her bed for near on three weeks with what, we don't know. The medicine she get from the hospital didn't do nothing at all. So I go down to Chinatown and tell the herbalist how she ailing and he mix up some dry dis and dat that I tek home and boil and give her to drink three times a day 'til she get up. And then I carry on do it another week just like he tell me. And after that, Beryl was back. And Sunday become Sunday again.

All the time Beryl sick I was helping out. Just wid regulars. Not no strangers walking in off the street. That way it mean they didn't lose no custom. But even though these men familiar, it was a different thing now. Different from when I used to just say a good morning or afternoon to the British army man, or sailor from the US base, or the almost white wee-dropper that run the dry goods store 'cross town, or the red-skin office manager or bank clerk. And the black men whether they peeling off the notes or digging deep in their pocket for the pennies and ha'pennies that going mek up the change they putting on the table. It was different. But it was also the same because I become what I had always been in their mind. A source of satisfaction that whether they get from me or Beryl didn't matter. To me, it was routine. It was business. It stop me from pretending to myself that I was special. Resisting what been waiting for me ever since Barrington Maxwell. The men, they were all a blur. Except the ones that mek yu laugh. Whether they mean to or not. And the ones that would pass an evening exchanging a few words on their favourite topic. How to put Jamaica right.

In truth, it seem sorta natural. Me a full and proper member a the house. Bringing in money. Not just running after Sybil and Beryl and hoping for the best. I could join in now, and add my tuppence to whatever they talking 'bout.

And even after Beryl get better it seem we all three a us busy as ever. So the liquor was flowing and the music pumping, and the money was rolling in. But then, and I dunno if it to do with how unemployment bad, or mawga wages, or everybody on strike and the war prices so high, but as we go on it seem more and more was asking for favour. Like they want do it today but they nuh want pay 'til next week. We know it not a good state of affairs. But when some a dem start ask us to lend them money that is when we realise how bad the situation get.

Sybil say we cyan carry on like this. She say we got to put down the rates, or get more customers. Better still, she say, 'Get these men some money.' And that is when I think a Henry Wong.

When I go to the wine merchant to see him Henry was eating a bowl a rice and a omelette cook with scallion. And some chicken soup that he was slurping straight from the basin without even bothering wid no spoon. He look up from behind the counter and wave for me to sit down.

'Gloria, you want soup?'

'No thank yu Mr Henry.'

'You call me Henry. That is enough.'

So I say it, 'Henry.' Like I testing it out.

Him tek him face outta the soup and wipe him mouth wid the little white cloth napkin he got tuck in him collar and hang 'round him neck. I don't know how to start so I just say him name again, 'Henry.' And him look curious at me like he know something big is coming. So he put down the bowl and tek the cloth outta him shirt and fold it neat and rest it on the counter. And then he settle himself.

'This is about money.' Henry nuh say nothing. 'Yu have money Henry, that is the thing.'

'You have something ask me, Gloria?'

'It not easy Henry. It delicate.'

'Delicate? Money not delicate. Money is money. You make it, you win it, you lose it, you count it, you spend it, you plan for it, you balance the in and out of it, and then you think how you going make some more. But you never break it. That is the one thing you never do with money. Money not delicate like a flower. It sturdy like the land.'

'Henry, we got a problem over the house that I think yu can help us wid.'

'I always look help you, Gloria, but you know how I feel 'bout business you girls carrying on over there.'

'It not to do wid that Henry. The thing is I was wondering if yu would think about lending us, or me, some money.'

'Lend you money, Gloria?' So I tell him what happen and he listen and then he start eat the omelette and rice again. And drink the soup. And after some long time he say to me, 'I don't want lend you money, Gloria.' My heart sink because Henry Wong is the only person any a us can think of that got the money and half a mind to even consider giving any a it to us. And then he say, 'But what I will do is this.' And he tell me.

When I go back to the house I explain to them how Henry going put up all the money that anybody want to borrow, but is us that going have to do the transacting. That is what him call it because he don't want nobody knowing he got anything to do wid it in case it ruin his reputation as a upstanding businessman. And for our part we going get 30 per cent a the interest. But we got to make sure we secure the loan. That is what him say. So people know they got to settle up and nuh think they can just skip town or pay us nuh mind. Especially wid us being a bunch a women. And right then Beryl just say 'Trevor' and Sybil smile and say yes.

The house we living in own by Pops next door. That is who we paying the rent to each and every month. Pops got a son, Trevor. He a big man, Trevor. Plenty muscle but no work. So that was it and when Beryl go ask him, Trevor give her a big grin and say he would be honoured to help us. Beryl say he even tek off him hat and do a little bow when he say it.

1945

'When the sun first shines its light.'

CHAPTER 7

BUSINESS WAS BOOMING when the war ended. By that time Henry done buy himself a house up on the north coast outside Ocho Rios because that was where he live when he first come to Jamaica, and the four a us save a pile a money that one day we going use to buy the house from Pops next door. Plus, Henry say, I need to learn to talk and act like a lady. So every Saturday morning I was teking the tram to Constant Spring Road where this old English woman with grey hair and wrinkle hands was busy trying her best to mek something respectable outta me, suffering every minute a that hour because me and learning never get on too good. She tek her time wid me though and every week it seem she tell Henry I was meking progress.

I say to Henry, 'Why yu decide to pick me off the street and help me this way?'

'You not need help?'

'Yes I need it. But that nuh different from the dozen other women yu must have pass on the road that day. And don't tell me it was all because I was carrying a Hong Zi grocery bag.'

'I see bag before I see you. And when I see bag I know you sensible girl.' And he laugh. But it not that funny. And it not no answer. But then Henry don't like to give no answer 'bout anything. Like when I ask him why he keep telling me he got a daughter like me he say, 'Fay same age maybe as you. But Fay not like you. Fay not work. Fay spend. Fay not care for little sister. Fay care for Fay. You Gloria, you not take nothing for nothing.' But that still don't explain to me why Henry keep talking 'bout me and Fay in the same breath. So I reckon there is something that he see 'bout how me and Fay is the same. He just not telling me 'bout it.

Then one day some sailor bwoy decide that he not going pay back the money he owe. He overdue three, four weeks now, and nuh matter how much I talk to him it nuh seem like he going put his hand in his pocket for one penny. He don't even seem to care that the interest is adding up all the time he fuming 'bout how we tek advantage a him.

'Not nobody tek advantage a yu. Yu come and yu ask me for the money and I give it to yu. I explain the terms and yu accept them. Nobody beg yu to come tek the money. If yu wasn't such a drinker and gambler yu wouldn't have get yourself into such a state. All me do is help yu because it seem yu cyan help yuself.'

Henry say we should do something. But then another two week pass and still nothing is happening. We nuh see trouble like this before. Usually one visit from Trevor would do the trick. But not with this one. Henry say we need something more than talk so I tell Trevor to tek a friend and go find the sailor in the bar downtown he always drinking in and tek him out back and show him that we not going just sidung and let him play the fool wid us. So that what happen. Trevor just rough him up little bit. But it turn out it mek the sailor so mad he decide to come up the house and give us some worse trouble than we give him.

So two days later he come and find Marcia on her own in the house because since she finish school she got nothing to do. Half the time she cyan even raise herself to go to the interviews I arranging for her. Good clerical positions wid men we already know. But she nuh care. She just lazing about every day and that is how he find her, and beat her. He beat her so bad we have to get a ambulance to tek her to the hospital. I feel so much to blame I didn't know what to do wid myself except stay there and hold her hand while the slime and blood was thickening on her puff-up face. After they finish look at her the doctor say she got a broken arm and two broken rib. And that was on top a all the cuts and bruises she get from where he punch and kick her all over her body. She covered. Her back, arms, legs. Her face such a mess I couldn't even recognise her. And she cyan see nothing because her eyes swell shut.

Henry say the situation bad outta hand. Not that I need him to come tell me that. He say we got to go get some proper help, and that there is a man down Chinatown that do this sorta thing for all the shops and such like down there. That we got to go talk to him to get some protection.

'This not the same as protecting no grocery store from all the thieving and burning that go on down there. This is a different thing entirely. Yu think he going care 'bout us?'

'You got suggestion? You know somebody make sure you safe?' I cyan say nothing because all I can think about is how Marcia laying in the general hospital smash up like a rag doll and fighting to get the breath back into her body.

'You go see.'

'The Chinaman?'

'Yes, Gloria. You go see. He see you he be kind. Take pity. Give good price.'

71

But I know Henry not just worried 'bout the money. He fretful for us as well. So I say OK, I will go. But that not enough for Henry.

'You wear blue dress and head wrap.'

'I am not going down to West Street dress in a get-up like that! Yu mad? Yu think I going get off the bus in King Street and walk down Barry Street dress like that? I wouldn't even mek it the two blocks to Orange Street without some man trying to grab a piece a me and dragging me down into the gutter. Never mind how many women would be cutting their eye at me because they tek one look and decide they know my business. No man. It dangerous.'

Henry so fix on the blue dress he decide to tek a buggy and come wid me. He say the driver going drop me nearly outside the shop and he going wait 'round the corner 'til I finish.

The day we go down there it was hot-hot. And the dress so tight I was boiling up like a live lobster inside a it. I couldn't hardly move without oozing six ounces a water from every pore. But that is what Henry want and that is what I do.

When I get there I just stand up in the doorway and stare at the three a them sitting there wid the beer bottles in their hand. The one Henry send me to see was wearing some shabby old cotton pants and a vest that he should have had the good manners to put a shirt on over. How Henry think this man can do anything to help us I don't know. It seem he cyan even dress himself decent.

They jump up when them see me and brush themself down. I look straight at him and I say, 'Yang Pao?' I know it is him because he a Chinaman and the other two black African.

'What can we do for you miss?' Which is the big muscle one that decide to talk to me. So I look at the Chinaman direct and I say, 'I understand you will sometimes offer a hand of help.'

'What kinda help would that be?'

'Help with a US sailor following an incident with my sista that put her in the hospital all beat up.'

'So what he beat her for?' the muscle man ask.

'Just go see her,' I say to the Chinaman. 'That is all I am asking of you.' And then I look directly at him firm and steady and I say, 'Can you do that?' And he say yes so I give him the piece a paper with the hospital details and tell him that if he want to help Marcia will let him know how to get hold a me. And I turn 'round and walk out.

Henry waiting in the buggy 'round the corner and tek me straight back to East Kingston where I go strip down and tek a shower and put on a fresh, cool housecoat.

Three days later Trevor come running into the house like a bat outta hell all full a excitement and jubilation.

Beryl say to him, 'What fire catch your ass bwoy?'

'The sailor tek a licking. Good and proper man.' Trevor flicking his wrist and clicking his fingers so to make that sound a the lash of leather on skin.

'Yu serious?'

'Yah man. So bad deh have a put him in di naval hospital. The bwoy well and truly mash up.'

A couple days later I go down to West Street and find the Chinaman and say to him that I come to pay for the help he give. He tell me he don't need nothing. The sailor bwoy had it coming. So I put the money back in my purse and I ask him if he would keep a eye on us like he watch over Chinatown. I say it just like Henry tell me. Watch over Chinatown. And this is the first time he actually turn his head and take me in, like even though I go there the week before he got no idea what I look like.

And after some long time he just say, 'What do you have in mind?'

Henry over the moon. He reckon he can relax now and stop worrying 'bout who might tek a fancy in their mind to nuh pay us. Business is secure now as far as Henry is concerned, even though all Yang Pao think he doing is protecting us women and don't know nothing 'bout the money business. Henry say it nuh matter. All we got to do is say we under Yang Pao wing and everything is taken care of. Ain't nobody going ask no questions 'bout that or even entertain any idea 'bout crossing us. That, according to Henry, is the benefit of doing business with a proper businessman.

'No need depend on next door, fool boy Trevor. Now have business on business footing. Just like grocery store and wine merchant.'

When Marcia come home from the hospital she come in the house and go straight to her room and shut the door. She nuh say nothing to nobody. A little later I go tek her some hot chicken noodle soup and when I go in there she is sitting on the edge a the bed wid her feet flat on the floor and her knees together staring at the ground. She never even look up at me when I go in the room.

I rest the tray on top a the dresser and I say to her, 'Marcia yu want me help yu tek off yu clothes so yu can get in the bed?' But she nuh say nothing to me. She just carry on sit there like I not even there. 'Marcia yu need to get some rest. The hospital say. Bed rest.' And I wait, and then I say, 'Yu nuh feel tired from all the waiting to discharge yu and the journey home? Yu nuh think that maybe yu should just ease back and rest 'til yu get yu strength back?' But I am talking to a blank wall.

And then suddenly she just stand up and walk over and pick up the tray with the soup and throw it 'cross the room. Everything go flying through the air like it been propel outta a cannon. That is how hard she throw it. The soup wet up the wall and the bed and the floor. And when I think God, this girl got some feeling inside her I realise she was just getting started.

She throw off the bedspread and sheets and she start tear them up. I think maybe I should grab her and try calm her down. But when I see the vengefulness in her face I realise she would most likely kill me before she let me stop her from doing whatever was in her mind to do.

She tear the sheets and pillowcase into white cotton ribbon. And then she open the wardrobe and tek out every stitch a clothes, one by one, and rip it up. If it got a collar, it was off. Cuffs, lace, edging and trimming, a pocket, everything was gone. I never think a person could tear into fabric like that with their bare hands. Every little weakness in a seam her fingers could find. So by the time both her hands pull out to shoulder width the dress was in two pieces, or three or four depending on how many times she pull and tug, and wrench and claw. And when she come to the end, when nothing else would give way for her, she reach inside and grab the next dress, or blouse, or whatever her hand come to first. And she start with it all over again.

When she done with that, she pull down every picture off the wall and smash it on the floor. Then she swipe her hand across the dresser and every flat surface in that room 'til every little bottle and dish and hairbrush, and nail file and powder puff and lipstick, and hand mirror and perfume and crochet doily was on the floor where she kick and stamp on it and open up the top so she can pour out the liquid or scrape out the powder with her fingers and mash it all together on the hard tile floor under the weight a the old lace-up school shoes that Beryl tek to the hospital for her to come home in. And just when I think she was going to stop, she open up the drawers and start.

I got no idea how long Marcia spend doing all a this. But in all that time, she never say a word. She not even mek a noise. Nothing was coming outta her except the silent tears that was running down her face, that she wipe on the sleeve of her blouse and just carry on.

When she completely wear herself out she lay down on the floor in the middle a the mess and curl up into a ball with her arms wrap 'round her knees. So I lay down behind her and reach round and enclose her in my arms. And I just lay there, holding her rigid body close to me and listening to the sound of the wailing that was finally coming outta her. Wailing that was vigorous and bottom-less. Wailing like a woman because she wasn't a girl no more.

After that we let her rest. Sleep and eat and sit in the yard, silent as she was under the almond tree. And three weeks later when she feel up to it we invite Yang Pao over to the house for a celebration dinner. And even though it Beryl usually cook a meal like this, this time I decide to do it myself. Rice and peas and stew chicken with coleslaw and cho-cho.

It was carnival, with food and rum and music and happiness. We even get up and dance. Just like we do on the veranda on Sunday – a twist and a twizzle, a swivel and a swirl. And another glass a white rum. Yang Pao just sit there and look at us like he never see nothing like it in his life. And why would he? Where would he ever have seen four women so free and easy, one minute twirling 'round in each other's arms and the next minute sitting at the table, Sybil with cigarette in hand, talking 'bout how Bustamante come outta jail after a year and a half detention to set up his own Jamaica Labour Party and go win the election from Manley.

Afterwards when it late into evening he tek his leave and I walk out to the car with him. We stand up in the street under the clear night sky and stars.

He look up and breathe a sigh and then he say, 'Gloria Campbell you are quite some surprise.'

'How so?'

He just stand there. And then he step off the sidewalk and stroll 'round the car and get in it and drive off down the road.

CHAPTER 8

I GOT NO idea how Auntie find out what happen to Marcia or what mek her decide to pick herself up from Back-O-Wall and tek the bus 'cross town to come knock at the door like it was something she do every day. When I see her standing there I almost drop down wid shock. Didn't hardly recognise her anyway because it was the first time I ever see her outside a that yard and that dark little room.

'Yu going invite me in?'

'Yes Auntie. I just surprise to see yu that is all.'

I wrap the string a the Lipton Yellow Label tea bag through the pot handle before I pour in the hot water and tek the tray and cups into the front room. When I hand Auntie the tea she just sit there and stare into the cup like maybe she was expecting to see something swimming there. She never even bother to tek the saucer outta my hand.

'Yu nuh like drink tea?'

'Tea? Where yu get a thing like dat? Yu nuh know tea is di drink a di slave master? Sitting in di shade a di veranda sipping di piss-piss little juicy-juice all day long while di slave burning up in di heat cutting cane or tending di bananas wid barely a drop a water to moisten dem lips. And now yu sit here wid yu little tea pot like yu Lady Gloria in di Great House. Not that this place much like di plantation except I understand a lot a seed get sow here.'

'That was a hundred years ago Auntie.'

'A hundred years, yes. But di white man still sitting on di veranda and di black man still digging in di field and sweating in di factory. It seem like dat is how it is. And dat not even di worse part. The worse part is di black man still looking to di white man to tell him what to do, and tell him how to think, and tell him he all right. Because in his own mind, the black man is still a slave. And in di white man mind, he is still di slave master. So a hundred years later di two a dem still rubbing along fine.'

I reckon Auntie got more going on in her head than the grumbling and cussing I had to listen to every day I spend living in that nasty room a hers. She right 'bout the black man. Sybil right 'bout the black woman. That is our life.

So I say to her, 'Yu want something else to drink?'

Auntie tek up residence in the room off the kitchen. Not all at once, just little little. One night here, two night there, until one day we wake up and realise Auntie been living in the house for weeks. Cooking, cleaning, washing and mending. But most of all what she doing is tending Marcia. Like Marcia was her own sick daughter. So now Auntie a part a everything in the house, even though all the time she muttering and cussing 'bout what kinda shameful house we got her living in and how the Lord going bring down everlasting damnation on our heads and we all going burn in hell for eternity.

I say to her, 'So why yu nuh go back to Back-O-Wall and save yu soul?' But she don't have no answer for me. Every single night though she do the same thing. Soon as nightfall come she tek up some bulla bun and jug a ice sorrel and she tek it in her room and shut the door and nuh show her face again 'til daybreak. This is Auntie's one protest against the evil that is going on in this house. All she say is, 'If yu nuh want eat frog nuh play wid snake.'

The other thing that happen was Yang Pao, because for no good reason he decide to come sit down in the house every day and look at me. The man got nothing to say. All he do is sit and stare. And every once in a while he think a something to pass five minutes and then we go back to the same silence that been going on day in day out for weeks. All I doing is filling him up with Lipton Yellow Label because the last thing I want is him sitting down here all day drinking liquor. I don't even know if he like the tea. All I know is he drinking it down and never say no when I go to top up the cup.

Sometime he leave a hat or a newspaper that mek him have to come back the next day to fetch it. Seem like he never tire. Any time from ten o'clock in the morning 'til ten o'clock at night he can be sitting there with his knees together prim and the teacup in his hand. It get so bad every now and again I have to actually tell him to go so I can go about my business and he get up straight outta the chair and leave without a single word.

So after this go on and on I say to him one day, 'Yu know when I ask yu to watch over us I didn't mean for yu to be sitting down here every day looking at me. I already broadcast the news that we under yu wing so everything is fine.'

He just rest the cup in the saucer and put the saucer on the table and stand up and say, 'That is good.' And then he turn 'round and walk out. After he gone I stay put, staring at the empty chair almost like he was still sitting there with no conversation passing between us. I just sit there with nothing in my head about what I should be doing next. Like I was in a dream until Sybil come to say we got customers waiting.

I never see nothing a him for a few days and then one afternoon I come home to find him in the back yard fixing the fence. So I go lean up on the back door and say to him, 'We can get people to do that yu know.'

And he turn 'round and put down the hammer and say to me, 'Why pay good money when it just as easy for me to do it?'

Yang Pao standing there in his vest just like the first time I see him in the shop. He not scrawny exactly, but there hardly anything on him. What there is, though, is firm. He sturdy. He solid.

'I never tek yu for a man to be doing handiwork.'

He smile. 'To tell yu the truth, Gloria, I not that experienced with it.'

He got a nice smile. It gentle. It innocent. If I didn't know no better I could think he was a overgrown schoolboy doing errands for a few shillings not the grown man that is running protection and gambling, and liquor and cigarettes and US Navy surplus all over town.

'Yu want something to drink?'

'Yu mean tea?'

I laugh, even though I try not to. It creep out before I get a chance to fix my face.

'I mean water.'

'Water?' And then he pull a kerchief outta his pants pocket and mop his brow. Meaningful like.

I get up and walk inside and pour out two long glasses a sorrel from the jug that Auntie keep in the fridge. When I hand him the glass he smile and put it to his lips and drink half a it down straight just like that. I rest my drink on the concrete step and gather up my skirt between my legs and sit down. The sorrel cold and sweet with a bite a ginger that catch yu long after yu swallow.

'The two yu run with, a where yu meet them?'

'Hampton and Finley?'

'Same so.'

'Hampton was the pushcart boy that carry our bags from the wharf to Matthews Lane when we first get here from China.'

'So when that?'

'Seven years back. 1938. Right in the middle of all the riots 'bout unemployment and such. Nice eh?' And he smile again. He squat down on his haunches and cross his arms over his knees like a true Chinaman or a boy scout squaring up to the camp fire.

'Yu know 'bout Zhang?'

'I hear a him. Godfather a Chinatown since 1912. That is what they say.'

'They say "uncle", Gloria. That is what they say. Uncle.' And he look at me serious so I know I say something outta turn. I nuh say nothing else. I just shut up and let him carry on.

'Zhang and my father was comrades since they young boys. They fight for Dr Sun Yat-sen until they declare the Republic in 1912. But then Sun Yat-sen hand over power to the warlord Yuan Shikai and Zhang lose faith. So when my father marry my mother and go back to farming Zhang come here to Jamaica where the Chinese shopkeepers invite him to come help them with the people burning and looting their shops and such.'

He tek another drink a sorrel. 'After my father get killed by the British, Zhang send for us and that is how me and Mama and my brother Xiuquan end up here.'

'So how old yu was when yu come?'

'Fourteen. And I meet Hampton and he introduce me to Finley who his cousin and that is it. That is us.'

'So where yu brother now?'

'Gone to America 1943 to go farm and support the war effort.'

I look at him over the top a the glass while I taste the sorrel and I think he not a bad-looking man this near scrawny Chinaman. He got nice straight hair and his nose small and sorta cute. His lips thin. But the thing about him is how smooth his skin is. His shoulders and arms not got one single blemish on them.

'So now you the boss a Chinatown.'

'Uncle, Gloria. Uncle. Yu uncle is somebody that not yu papa but who watch over yu just the same. Like you his own and he got your welfare and interests at heart. That is what a uncle is. Family.'

Right then Beryl step outta the house and say Hampton at the front door asking for him. He put on the blue short-sleeve shirt he have hang up in the tree and walk towards me. I stand up so he can pass and just as he get to the door I say, 'Yu going leave all these tools and things there just like that?'

He turn and look at me and then start back to go tidy up.

'Is all right,' I say to him. 'Leave it. I will see to them.'

He smile. And then he was gone.

When I look at the fence I see it no better than before he start his handiwork. If anything, it in a worse condition. So for sure now we going have to go get somebody to come fix it.

Next time I see him he got the cupboard door prop up on the side and busy with a screwdriver on the hinge.

'Yu not got nothing better to do than this?'

'The thing was falling off, Gloria.'

I just stand there. And what I realise is Yang Pao would sooner be mending the cupboard door than tek the hint I been giving him not to be coming here all hours. Who would have thought it? The uncle a Chinatown, Mr Inscrutable himself, on his knees on the kitchen floor looking up at me through those dark brown eyes.

'The last time when yu fix the fence I had to go get someone to sort it out yu know that?'

He put down the screwdriver and stand up straight. He brush down his pants.

'I just trying to help.' But he look hurt. Dejected.

'I know, but yu not cut out for this kinda helping.'

He smile like as to say thank you. And just as we standing there a big water jug fall down outta the open cupboard and smash on the hard tile floor and the glass catch my ankle. And there was blood.

I feel the sting and bend down to see what happen but just as I doing it he rush over and brush my hand away.

'It cut bad, Gloria.' He grab a towel and wrap it 'round my foot. And then he pick me up in his arms and put me in the car and drive to the hospital like he was Flash Gordon on his way to save the world.

They clean it up and give me three stitches and say it not going scar too bad. When he leave me back at the house I know what I wanted was for him to hold me. Actually put his arms 'round me. Not like how the others grip the bedstead or steady themselves with their palms flat on the mattress. But he didn't do it. He just sit me down in the chair and fetch a little table and put a cushion on it for me to rest my leg. He even pick up my foot and lay it down soft and gentle. But apart from that he never touch me.

He just step back and say, 'Plenty people here to look after yu.'

And I say, 'Yes.'

After that he visiting me so much and fussing and fretting everyone think it a joke. They even laughing out loud now every time they see him coming.

'What yu see in him anyway?'

'I don't see nothing in him Marcia. I cyan get rid a the man.'

Sybil say, 'Why yu think he nuh just pay the money and do his business? Yu think maybe he waiting to get it for free?'

'Yu think that is what he after?'

Sybil throw her head back and laugh. She laugh so much she nearly fall down.

'What he after? What you think he after?'

I cyan answer her because I don't know what Yang Pao want. I cyan figure him. He tough on the outside. He run his little posse a three and it seem he do good wid it. Seem like him and Hampton and Finley know what they doing. They got Chinatown clamp down tight. People show respect when yu say his name even though Hampton nothing more than a hunk a muscle wid a baby face and Finley tall and wiry and silent, wid a look like he thinking something he happier not to say.

But inside, what Yang Pao like? What really going on in that head? He want something that is for sure. I just not convince it what Sybil think it is. Well, not that alone anyway. Yang Pao want something, he just cyan bring himself to ask for it. Maybe he don't even know himself what it is. I can feel it though. I see it in his body, how he hold it so tight and keep his distance from me. I hear it in his voice because as it turn out Yang Pao got a beautiful singing voice that boom out 'Roses of Picardy' all over the yard as he hammering and sawing things he should be leaving alone. It smooth and even. It sensitive like a act of kindness that touch yu deep inside.

And what I realise is that when I tell Marcia I couldn't get rid a him it wasn't the truth. Not the whole truth anyway. Sure enough the man spending too much time in the house, but then again I feel comfortable in his company. Or maybe comforted or secure or just plain relaxed. Maybe I even feel happy. And that is a first for me to feel that peaceful with a man.

So one day I say to him, 'Yu remember that first time yu come here after Marcia come back from the hospital?' He just sit there and nod. But it not a nod. Not like how most people head go down. With Yang Pao his head go up like he jut out his chin but only little bit.

'When we standing by the car yu say to me that I was a surprise but yu never answer my question when I ask yu what yu mean.' I look at him but not a word is coming back to me. 'Yu not going say nothing?'

'I don't know what to say, Gloria.' He pause like he thinking deep and hard. 'I suppose I had in my mind a idea 'bout what a woman in your line a business would be like. But when I come here that night yu wasn't nothing like what I expect.'

'So what yu expect?'

'Yu know . . . forward and, I dunno . . . common.' He hold his breath a while and then he say, 'But yu not like that. Yu nothing like that. Yu talk serious 'bout what going on in the country and yu mek joke and eat and jig just like ordinary people.'

'Ordinary people?'

'I don't mean it like that. I mean yu live like yu free. Not like yu burdened down with yu situation. You are yu own woman. All four a yu. Yu smart and yu got more going on in yu head than what yu do here behind closed doors. There not nothing forward or common 'bout any a yu. Yu refined. Yu good company, Gloria.'

I think to myself you are the surprise Yang Pao, with yu eagerness to help and the caring yu show the time my leg get cut and the sweet singing 'bout the rose in yu heart that don't die with the summertime, and the fact that in all these months yu never once suggest that yu want anything from me. Not even a hint come from yu. And what that mek you is a man like no man I ever know before.

So when I tell Sybil I cyan figure yu I suppose that is it. Because I also had in my mind what a man in your line a business would be like but yu not that at all. You are a contradiction Yang Pao. That is what you are. And the day that truly come home to me was the day I find yu doing yu exercise out back when yu thought the house was lock up and it was only you here alone with the fence. And even though yu embarrassed and tell me tai chi is a martial art, I could see from the way yu was moving your arms and turning your body that what yu was doing wasn't making no war. It was making peace. And how I know was from the gentle beauty of your hands and the deep stillness of the energy in yu. That is what I saw from the kitchen window and later leaning up against the back door. Not Yang Pao Chinatown hoodlum but a different man entirely.

I just say to him, 'So yu think I good company?'

And he smile that smile and nod that nod and say, 'Yah man.'

CHAPTER 9

THEN ALL OF a sudden he stop come. And when it turn Friday is Hampton who show up to pick up the money. I hand him the envelope and he tek it but he don't say nothing. I think maybe I going ask him what happen to his boss, but I don't. I just bite my tongue. The next week Finley show up and so it go on.

The thing is, I miss him. I miss him sitting there. I miss watching him drink the tea and search his brain for some small thing he can say 'bout what the new government doing, or how prices high. I miss the newspaper resting on the chair knowing that he going come back. I miss the singing in the yard. I miss calling the carpenter and plumber to come fix things every time he do his handiwork. I miss the way he smile like he half happy and half fraid. I miss that nod.

So after I get used to nuh seeing him, one Friday night he show up. Just like that. He stand up in the room, like he not even sure if he here or in this world at all. The music is playing, the liquor is flowing, the place is buzzing. But him, he is all alone. And I realise I feel sorry for him and there is nothing else I would rather do than put my arms 'round him and tek him into the warmth and safety of a place where he can rest. Where he can find some peace. But maybe it not just sorry I feel. Maybe I feel something else. Like maybe with my arms 'round him I could rest and I could stop and I could find some peace.

When I go over and hand him the envelope he reach out and tek it even though it seem like it a struggle for him to put out his hand and pull it back again. I look at him willing him to say something to me, but he don't say nothing. He just stand there like he made a cement.

After that I never see him for weeks 'til one Friday morning I step outta Times Store and walk into him standing up in King Street. He turn his head and see me but I not sure if he going say hello. So I say, 'Long time no see.' But he don't say nothing. 'I reckon yu business must be keeping yu from sitting down anywhere, or maybe yu just decide yu cyan tek no more Lipton Yellow Label.'

'It not that, Gloria.'

'It not the tea?'

He turn 'round and look at me and then he stare off into the street again. I think to myself what yu going to do with this man because sooner or later something got to happen. So I say to him, 'You keep thinking all the time about what I am. But maybe you should concentrate on who I am, the sort of person I am, and maybe that way you might get to know how you feel. I see the way you look at me. And how you stand far from me in case you might touch me by accident. And how when you have to come close to me you hold your breath like you think something bad about to happen. Well maybe you just need to let yourself breathe.'

He just stand there like a statue gazing out into the street. He cyan even bring himself to look at me. So I say, 'Next Monday and

Tuesday the rest of the girls are taking themselves up to the north coast to Ocho Rios. They reckon we not so busy then and they can spare the time to have a break. But I am not going with them. I am just going to close up the house so I can get some time to myself. So Monday night I will be there in the house on my own. And what I am saying to you is you can come over for the night if you want to.'

And still he cyan even turn his head. So I say, 'You don't seem to think that maybe I have some feelings as well.' I stop. 'But I have to tell you that this is a one-time offer. If you decide not to come then it will be strictly business between you and me from that point on because we can't carry on like this.' And then I step out into the street and walk off into the buzz and hum a cars and buses and pushcarts and crowd, and the heat shimmering off the road.

And as I weave my way through the throng I can feel how upright I am. I feel good. I feel strong. For the first time in my life I feel like I tek control a something. For the first time I wasn't the one that someone else was doing something to. I wasn't the one that was waiting to see, or feeling nervous or fraid 'bout what going happen next. I just say what I wanted to. Plain and simple. And really, it was the first time that I think all them dreary Saturday mornings with the English woman was doing any good, because right then I talk different to him. Not just in the way that I put to him what I had to say, but in how it feel. It feel like a force that was inside a me had finally come out.

Sybil say she think I lose my mind.

'What yu want to tek up with a scrawny little Chinaman like that for? It not enough for yu that he been sitting down here all this long time drinking every drop a tea we got in the place? Yu should be happy to see the back a him now it seem he find something better to do.'

Beryl just laugh. She packing her bag to go stay up Henry Wong's house in Ocho Rios and she cyan get enough entertainment outta the idea a Yang Pao spending the night.

'The whole night? What the two a yu going do all night?'

Auntie, she don't say nothing. She just happy she going catch some breeze on the north coast. Marcia is the only one that seem like she concerned.

'Yu sure yu going be all right? Yu want me to stay?'

'No Marcia, what would I want yu to stay for? I invite him over because yu all going to Ocho Rios.'

She look at me like she cyan figure out what going on.

'What is it yu see in him?' I not got no answer for her because I cyan explain that Yang Pao not what everybody think he is. I not got the words to describe his tai chi hands and the pleasure I see in his eyes when he look at me.

When he turn up I realise I knew he would come. He stand in the doorway all showered and scrubbed, with the smell of the Old Spice coming off him and a smile on his face like somebody who was expecting something but they didn't know what it was.

He come inside and I tek him into the living room and he sit down on the sofa sorta prim.

'Nice room. I never sit in here before.'

'Yu want a drink?'

'What, a real drink?'

So I nod my head.

'Maybe a Red Stripe.'

I go fetch the bottle outta the fridge. When I come back I pour the beer into a glass and remember how the first time I see him he was sitting there with the beer bottle in his hand. He tek the glass from me and sip. And then with his other hand he wipe the sweat from his brow and pass his fingers through his hair.

And right then, it suddenly dawn on me. Yang Pao never do this before. He busy wheeling and dealing and putting the fear a God into whoever he want to, strutting like a lord all over town, but he never been with a woman.

So it was me that had to tek off his clothes. And me that had to stroke his face and rub his arms and shoulders and chest, and gently squeeze the muscle that was under my fingertips. It was me that had to caress his lips. It was me that had to take him.

Afterwards he lay there on his back still and silent. And then he turn over and rest himself on my breast with his head buried in my neck. I reach out and wrap both my arms 'round him and hold him close.

I think about every other time I see him. How he so self-contained and in charge, like he a island. And I realise that Yang Pao never let himself feel anything. He just do the next thing, and the next, and the next. That is his refuge, his hiding place. Right up until now because that is when I hear the soft snivelling and feel his body forcing itself to hold back the tears that was welling up inside a him. But he couldn't do it. And in the end he decide to let himself go. I just keep my arms tight 'round him and let him do what he needed to. And when he start to slow down I reach out to the side table and grab a Kleenex and give it to him. And he blow and wipe his nose.

He raise himself up and look at me.

'Is all right,' I say to him. And I stroke his head of beautiful soft hair.

'Yu know why I suddenly stop coming to the house?'

'Why?'

'Because I didn't know what to do with how I was feeling for yu. It nuh seem like the way a man should be feeling 'bout a woman in this kinda situation. But no matter how much I try stop think about yu I couldn't do it. It was even interfering with my work. And then that time I come here few Fridays back and nuh say nothing to yu, it was because I was trying to harden my heart against yu. That is why I just stand there and tek the money from yu like that. But it didn't work. So when I bump into yu outside Times Store last week it was a blessing to me because I didn't know how I was going to face yu after what I done.'

'Yu didn't do nothing Pao. Yu just had some feelings. It happen to everybody. It was new to yu that was all.' And I stroke his smooth, smooth back. 'Yu not as alone in this world as yu think.'

He smile. But it was a different smile. This smile didn't have no question in it.

When Sybil come back from Ocho Rios she say to me if I know what I am doing.

'How yu mean?'

'Like maybe yu forget what this is?' She pause and then she say, 'This is a business, Gloria. It not no courtship. And there not nobody in this house giving it away for free.'

I hear what she saying so the next time I see him I tell him that we have to put things on a business basis.

'Yu mean yu want me to pay?'

I don't say nothing at first because what my head tell me and what my heart feel is two completely different things.

'Pao, I am what I am.'

He look at me quizzical and then he say, 'If that is what yu want.' But even then there was sadness in his eyes.

After that he was coming regular, Tuesday, Thursday and Friday afternoon and then Friday evening when he come to pick up the protection money. That was his business. My business was awkward, like a shadow that fall across us everytime he turn his back and put the money on the table, and me waiting 'til he was long gone before I pick it up. It injure us even though I know it was the right thing. I didn't want nobody getting any fancy ideas 'bout what was going on. Not Sybil and Beryl because all the money we mek go into the same pot. Not him. And especially not me.

CHAPTER 10

'THE CHINAMAN.'

'What Chinaman Auntie? Yu mean Yang Pao?'

'Yu think I nuh know him di way him coming here all these months? No, I mean di other one. Di one yu work for in di grocery store.'

'Yu mean Mr Ho?'

'Me nuh know what him call. Me just know him turn up here two, three hours back looking fi yu, saying him need to ask yu something.'

The next day I go down to Barry Street to see what Mr Ho want. But when he see me come through the shop door he rush over and push me back out into the street like he worried somebody going see me. And then he whisper, 'I come see you. When?'

So I say, 'Tomorrow, three o'clock.'

'Good, good,' and he hurry back inside.

'Lynette never have baby. I give cousin job but the baby thing just a lie. Then they in shop with things going missing off shelf and out back and money take from drawer. So in end I fire them. But they come back. They come back every day. They just open door and walk in and start serve customers like they still work for me. Even after I stop pay them wages. No matter, because they taking what they want from shop anyway to fill their bellies and feed their whole family. And the money, they just tek it.'

Mr Ho sweating and curling up his hat in his hand. And all the time he sitting there so far on the edge of the chair I think his backside going slide off and slap on the hard tile floor.

'They do all this little little because they not trying bankrupt me. They want me going on year after year so they can keep on and on. Take more and more. And they know if they do it too bad shop going shut down and they won't get nothing at all and they nuh want that.'

'Yu nuh go to the police Mr Ho?'

'It Chinatown! Who go police?'

Mr Ho fretting like some cornered mouse just before the cat pounce on it.

'What mek yu come see me Mr Ho?' He nuh say nothing. He just look at the floor.

'The thing is, Gloria, it get worse. It one thing me going year after year with everything just trickling away. But now Lynette and cousin want me give them shop. Sign it over to them just like that.'

'What yu talking 'bout? What mek them think yu would do a thing like that?'

'Well, Gloria, they got some man, and these man they following wife and daughters every time they go to store, to school, the Chinese Athletic Club; when they visit family, the herbalist, the temple. Everywhere. Any time I not with them. They doing this for weeks and now they start say dirty, nasty things and open up girly magazine to show picture and say this what going happen to you. Wife and daughters very frighten. And Lynette say this going on 'til I give her shop. That is what she say. And she say if anything happen to family it my fault for being so stubborn.'

I cyan believe what Mr Ho telling me. I suspect all along that Lynette was a thief but this is something else. It so wicked yu cyan even begin to imagine that somebody could think of a thing like that.

'But what yu going do Mr Ho if yu nuh want go to the police?'

'Even if I could go, what I going tell police? That I got two women working in shop for no wages? And how I going explain what going on with these man?'

'How yu think I can help yu?' Mr Ho sit there quiet like he turning over in his mind what he want to say to me.

And then he say, 'I think Uncle can help.'

'Yu mean Yang Pao?'

'You know him, Gloria. You can ask him for me.'

'Why yu nuh ask him yourself?' Mr Ho wring his hands some more and start swallow hard and lick his lips like his mouth all of a sudden dry up.

'I not pay protection.'

'Yu nuh pay it?'

'Times is hard, Gloria. I not got the extra money what with everything going on with Lynette and cousin taking away every little scrap profit. I just not see my way to do it. So I say to him that I nuh want to pay it.'

'And what he say to yu?'

'He say if you nuh pay insurance you can't make no claim if anything happen. And him and the other two just turn and walk out. That was maybe two year back, and I never see nothing of him since.'

'Yu know if yu pay him in the first place none a this would a happen.'

'Yes, that was mistake. But I think if you ask him for me maybe he take some pity.'

The man got a calamity. That is for sure and I feel sorry for him. But more than that, I worried for his wife and daughters. No woman should have to go through a thing like that. So I say to him, 'I will ask him. I cyan mek yu no promise 'bout what he going to say, but I will talk to him and try mek him see how much yu need him help.'

Mr Ho shoot outta the chair and start bowing and bending 'til he almost on his knees holding on to the hem of my skirt and whispering like he praying to me, 'Thank you, Gloria. Thank you.'

CHAPTER 11

'NO. HO MEK up his mind long time back. It done. It over. Let him go find somebody else to fix his problem.'

'Who he going find?'

'I dunno. All I know is it not nothing to do with me.'

I can feel my shoulders sagging. Right out there in the street under the shade of the big Bombay mango tree in the front of the house.

'Pao, he got nobody else to turn to.'

He let out one a them hefty puff-out-yu-cheek breath he like to.

'What I should do it for, Gloria? Ho say he going pay?'

'I already tell yu, Lynette robbing the man blind. What he going pay yu wid? If he could a do it he would a pay yu years back. Now he got this situation and is only you can help him.'

He think on it and then he reach in his pocket for the car key and start walk off.

'I don't like it, Gloria. I don't want people thinking they can mek a fool outta me and then come bawling to you when they want.' He open the car door and rest his hand on top of it. 'This not the way yu do business, getting some woman mix up in the middle a it.'

And then he get in the car and slam the door and drive off. I stand in the sun on the sidewalk and watch the tail of the blue and white Chevy disappear 'round the corner and then I go back inside and pour myself a drink. I got no idea if he going do anything but I reckon I do my best. I do what I tell Mr Ho, so at least I keep my word.

Next day I go down to the wine merchant to talk to Henry 'bout money because it seem like maybe we got a chance to expand the business. But when I get there he gone to Ocho Rios and not coming back for another week. So the bwoy tell me anyway. And right as I turn 'round to leave a woman step through the door and the bwoy say, 'Good afternoon, Miss Fay.'

It stop me in my track. I look at her and I think so here you are. I never imagine I would ever meet yu. Never mind run into yu just like that outta the blue. I transfix. She tall like her papa and she slim. She not curvy like me. She got on a beautiful frock with some pretty little yellow flowers in the pattern and it hang so yu know that it musta come off the sewing machine of one of the most expensive dressmakers in town. Even the fabric itself tell yu how much that dress cost. It was elegant, that is what it was. Simple and stylish. It was class. And her standing there with her light skin that she shading under her regal wide-brim hat. I couldn't understand how Henry could possibly look at her and think of me. I was nothing like Fay Wong.

'Come sit yuself down, Miss Fay.' And the bwoy pull out a stool and dust it off with a rag for her. 'Let me fetch yu something cool to drink and then yu can tell me what yu want.'

She sit down and the bwoy rush out the back. When he come back he carrying a jug of lemonade with the ice cubes rattling in it. I dawdle. I picking up this bottle and that like I cyan mek up my mind what it is I am after.

She reach in her purse for a piece a paper and unfold it. And then she pass it to him. 'I made a list, Alvin.'

What is her voice like? It is like something smooth. Something even and rounded, softened at the edges. Almost like the wrinkle-hand English woman on a Saturday morning, excepting it definitely Jamaican. It got the tone and rhythm of a island born.

Alvin study the list and then he say, 'Yes, Miss Fay, this all fine.' He wait a minute before he raise his eyes to her. 'Mr Henry say this going be some big-big birthday party for Miss Daphne. He say yu inviting half a Kingston. Yu sista going love it.'

But Fay not even listening to him because all she say is, 'You think my choice of champagne worthy of the occasion?'

And he just say, 'Yes. Perfect choice, Miss Fay.'

She drink two sip of the lemonade that Alvin pour for her and then she stand up. She pick up her purse off the counter and turn to him and say, 'So everything is fine for next Saturday then?'

'Yes, all is good. I will get these things together for yu and deliver dem up to Lady Musgrave Road middle a di week so to mek sure all is in good time. Everything will be perfect, Miss Fay, trust me.'

She nod her head at him and start walk toward the door. Alvin rush round quick to mek sure he get there before her so he can open it and stand back for her to pass. Just as she stepping out she turn her head and look at me like it is the first time she notice me there. She look me up and down and then she smile. But it not the sorta smile that leave yu feeling good. It the sorta smile where yu could almost hear her thinking to herself, 'You poor thing.' It leave a sour taste in yu mouth and a sinking feeling in yu heart.

★   ★   ★

Almost two week later Henry come by the house to find out what I want because Alvin tell him I was down the shop. He walk in the house and go straight to the liquor and pour himself a drink.

I never see Henry tek no drink before so I say, 'You all right?'

And he say yes just before he down the rum in one gulp and slap the empty glass on the table so hard I think the thing would a break.

'Yu sure yu all right?'

Henry straighten himself up.

'Yu party go OK?' He seem like he got no idea what I am talking about, and I think to myself if yu don't know then I sure don't need to be telling you.

'You mean Daphne birthday?' So I nod. 'If one thing make Fay happy is throw party.' I wait because I can see Henry got plenty more to say.

'At least when she doing that she not arguing with her mother.'

'I see her in the shop the other day. She beautiful, Henry. Gorgeous.'

He nuh say nothing at first, and then he turn to me with a face so tender I never see before. 'You also beautiful, Gloria.' It shock me because Henry not the sorta man to say something like that to a woman. Henry talk business, that is what Henry do. Or Henry talk like papa. But this thing, this is new. And then almost like he embarrass himself he pick up the glass and walk 'cross the room and start pour himself another drink.

'What happen to yu? Yu fight wid somebody?'

'You nuh need hear all this, Gloria. A man in a house of women is a very difficult thing. Women not argue like men. Women fuss and find fault. Then they want you say who right and who wrong.

So you in middle with one pull you this way and other one pull you that way. And all that happen is you tear in half.' He stop like he think he already say too much. And then he say, 'What business you want talk?'

So I tell him. Sybil got a friend that she think maybe interested in lending money as well. She nuh tell her nothing too much but she sound her out and say it seem promising.

'Too much people know make problem.'

'What she got to know? All she do is make a introduction here and there. Collect her share and that is that. She don't need to know nothing more than that.' Henry thinking on it so I say, 'Excepting if I increase the business then I want increase my share as well. Make you and me real partners. Fifty-fifty.'

'Fifty-fifty, Gloria? How you come to that?'

'Henry yu not doing nothing apart from putting in the money and turning a good profit. Yu don't have to deal wid these people. Yu don't have to worry 'bout collecting. Yu don't have to try mek Trevor understand what yu want him to do. Yu don't have to keep check on who yu can trust. Yu don't even have to keep count. I doing everything for us. You give me money, I give yu more back. Yu nuh think that is worth half?'

'Where you learn think and talk like that? That is Gloria Campbell business woman talking. But is it wise business woman? Or is it just business woman with ideas too big for self?'

'Yu think I am over-reaching?'

'I think you smart, Gloria. Mean what you say. But can you do it without causing too much waves? Not draw so much attention wrong people start take interest?'

'I can do it Henry. And the more money I make, the more money you going make.'

He stare at me long and hard and then he say, 'Fifty per cent mean you the one make sure this thing not turn out bad.'

'I understand that.'

I tell them what Henry got to say and everybody happy. Sybil say we got to set up a meeting with the two a them and she going come.

'What two?'

'Is two a dem over deh.'

'Yu tell me is one friend.'

'One friend. But is two a dem over deh.'

So all right. She know them. Beryl say she nuh care, she got better things to do. But Marcia say she going come and I have to tell her we cyan all be traipsing over there like we a mob. Is only the two a them, so two a us is plenty. Marcia not teking no for an answer. She say she my sista and she want to play her full part.

'This not no game Marcia. Nobody playing nothing. Me and Sybil can go see to this. It is a piece a business that is all.'

But Marcia talk-talk while Sybil roll her eyes and light a cigarette and Beryl tek herself off to go do something she think more interesting than sidung here listening to Marcia explain why she think it so important that she go. So in the end I cyan tek it no more and I say gwaan, come.

We go meet these two women over the house in Passmore Town. It simple and tidy with a dirt yard out front that somebody just get through sweeping because yu can still see the lines the hard broom leave behind. We sit down on the veranda on some hard plastic pretend wicker chair that got a back shape like a fan, and they bring out some cold oversweet sorrel.

Sybil introduce everybody and tell them that we going put up the money and manage it so all they have to do is act like a go-between in sending the people direct to us. That they not going have to handle no actual money as such. We going do all a that. All they doing is putting one person in touch wid another person. Simple as that. And we see to everything else.

Sybil friend sitting there plump and satisfied. 'So what we get for our trouble?'

'Ten per cent a the interest.'

'Ten per cent!' The two a them say it together at the same time. Surprise and vex. And then the little skinny one say, 'That is it?'

So I say, 'Yu not hardly doing nothing. How hard is it to say to a man, or woman come to that, I know somebody that can help yu? And then put one and two together. That is easy. Yu could do that in yu sleep.'

'But you meking 90 per cent.'

'We putting up the money. We taking the risk that maybe they skip town and nuh pay us back. We got to worry 'bout how the pounds, shillings and pence flowing this way and that. All you got to do is say, "Yes sir, help is on the way." People feel relief when they hear that. They count you as a blessing. I am not a blessing to them. I am a woe. That is how you and me are different. And that is why you get 10 per cent and I get 90 per cent. Anyway, it is my money.'

She scratch her cheek with some long fingernail that the red varnish chipping on. The other one kiss her teeth and I look at Sybil so as to say, 'What kinda friend yu call this?'

But even though they thinking on it and they surely want to, they cyan come up with any good reason why I should give them more. So I wait, and in the end I put them outta their misery.

'OK, all right, I give yu twelve and a half.'

And they say yes. They feel they strike a bargain. They win the negotiations. And that is fine with me because before I go over there I had it in my mind that maybe I would have to give them fifteen, so everybody happy.

Sybil friend say we must have a drink to seal the deal and I say OK, so she go out back and come with a bottle and five glasses. She pour out the rum and we mek a toast.

'To success in our new business.' That is what she say and we clink the glasses and taste the nasty cheap thing that scorch yu mouth and burn yu throat on the way down. I reckon I cyan drink no more a this so I just hold the glass and swish the liquid round for as long as it seem decent and then I tell them we got to go. We shaking hands. It done. It over.

And then Marcia for no good reason just say, 'You mind yu do this right now because the man don't want no trouble.' I cyan believe she do that. What she go open her mouth like that for?

So right away Fingernail say, 'What man?' And I can feel the whole thing spinning outta control. My mind not working fast enough to come up with no answer and I fraid Marcia going tek it on herself to tell them what she mean.

But thank God Sybil got her wits about her. 'The man we got to chase down the bad debt.' And the two a them seem to tek that even though I not convince Fingernail fully swallow it.

After we leave I say to Marcia, 'What yu go say a thing like that for? Yu nuh know Henry Wong don't want no association with this?' But she don't say nothing to me. She just carry on walk down the road to the tram stop and we ride the journey in silence.

Marcia never been the same since the business with the sailor. One minute she high as a kite and the next minute she land like a lead balloon to ground. And then for no reason, she up again. She start tek customers as well after the sailor thing, even though I beg her not to do it. But she not listening. All she doing is getting ready for the next man that she got running in and outta the house fast and furious. It don't even seem like it a business to her. More like it a punishment she giving to herself. I talk to her but it nuh do no good. She just sit there and listen and afterwards she get up and walk off. Nobody know what to do with her, although some evenings I hear her in the room with Auntie making some muffled sound. Maybe she crying. I don't know. She not showing none a this to me. All I see is the big smiling face one day, and the empty dead one the next. It mek me think that maybe she blame me for what happen to her. But Marcia a grown woman now, and in truth coming to this house was her idea. But maybe. Maybe if I done mek Mama do something 'bout Barrington Maxwell then none a this would have happen. But that wasn't what I choose to do. And even now I think to myself how I never send word to Mama. How many letters I start write and never finish, 'til in the end I stop even trying to put pen to paper, because I couldn't face telling her what happen to us. What I bring her favourite daughter, Marcia, to. The bottom a anybody's idea of a decent life.

Pao go beat up the men prowling Mr Ho wife and daughters. Well, he send Hampton to go do it. Trevor say Lynette musta give up the men when Pao go talk to her at the shop because otherwise he don't know how he would a find out who they was. Anyway, Hampton tek somebody wid him and the whole thing get outta hand. It turn into some big brawl right out in the open in North Parade and in the middle a it the police show up, because it was more like a riot with all sorta passing strangers deciding to go pitch in and exchange a few blows for themselves. It was a small wonder nobody get arrested, so Trevor say anyway, although some had to tek to hospital.

Next thing I know the police was knocking at the door asking questions 'bout how I connected to Mr Ho and what I know 'bout Lynette and what go on down the shop. I say I didn't know nothing. I used to work in the shop years back that is all. But I don't reckon the constable believe a word I am telling him because all the time he standing there his eyes roaming 'round the veranda and looking me up and down like he convince some kinda crime being committed only he dunno what it is.

And then he start mek like he want to step inside so I say to him, 'Is there something else we can help yu with constable?' And he just say no and put his hat back on his head and walk out the yard. When he get to the gate he stop and turn 'round and stare at me. And then he lower the latch and tek a last long look at the house like there is something in his mind he just can't put his finger on it.

CHAPTER 12

A WEEK LATER the police come back, only this time is two a them and they not asking no questions 'bout Mr Ho. What they interested in is how I know Yang Pao.

'Yang Pao?'

'The Chinaman wid the shop in West Street. Yu know him?'

I know if I tell a lie it going come back to haunt me. So I say, 'I hear a him.'

'Yu hear a him? Yu nuh know him?'

'Well, he sort of a friend of a friend.' And as soon as I say it I know it was a big mistake, because there was no way I was going to mention Henry Wong's name.

'A friend of a friend?'

The first constable tek a deep breath. And then the other one say, 'Miss, this man is up to all sorta mischief. Yu don't want to be getting yuself into nuh hot water over him.' And they look at me like they expecting some kinda confession.

'I don't understand what this is all about.'

'Yu hear 'bout the brawl in North Parade last week? And a constable come ask yu 'bout it few days back?'

'Yes, and I already tell him everything I know.'

'Well we think maybe yu know more than yu telling.'

No matter how much I try to hide the panic I was feeling I know for sure I musta look as guilty as sin. Written all over me for the constables to see, plain as day.

'Well he not a friend exactly.'

They sigh. Both together like they rehearse it so many times before. And then the first one reach into his pocket and fetch out a piece of paper and hand it to me. It the address of the police station in North Street.

'Yu going have to come down the station because we not getting nowhere standing on this veranda. We not going ask yu to come wid us right now but tomorrow, 'bout two o'clock, mek sure yu there. Tell the officer at the desk yu name and we will come talk to yu.' And then he have another thought and say, 'Tonight yu can have a real good think to yuself 'bout what yu want to say to us.'

Sybil say the police just fishing. 'Is not even you they interested in.'

But that is no consolation because I know for sure the more questions they ask me the bigger the hole I digging for myself.

'Don't bother go down there then.'

'I cyan do that! Yu want them put out a warrant for my arrest?'

'Warrant? Yu think yu that important? Cho, they must have a dozen men just like Yang Pao they busy chasing down right now and most a them doing worse things than him.'

'I not worried 'bout what the police going find out about Yang Pao. A worried 'bout what they going find out about us, and me, and Henry. I would hate anything to happen to Henry on account a all a this.'

★   ★   ★

'Yu got a middle name there, Gloria Campbell?'

The constable sitting across the table from me writing in his little notebook. The table and the chairs made of metal. They cold and hard. And when he come in the room and tek the chair that was propping open the door he drag it 'cross the floor so it mek a din of screeching and scratching. And then he position it left a centre a the table and sidung. And tek out the notebook from the breast pocket a his shirt and rest it on the table and start write.

'My middle name is Antoinette.'

'Antoinette!' And he smirk. 'So where yu get a name like that, Gloria Antoinette?'

'My mother name me it after a story she hear 'bout a French planter and the slave girl he tek for his wife.'

'So after that Antoinette not nuh slave no more.'

'So the story go.'

The walls a the room paint yellow. Not a bright yellow, rich and lively, but a pale wash-out sorta colour that barely cover the white a the concrete that was under it. All the woodwork and things grey. The metal furniture grey as well. And the tile floor. Grey. What kinda colour scheme is that for a police station? I reckon a police station should be blue and white. I don't know why. Maybe the yellow mek people forget where they is. Maybe it mek them talk more than they should for their own good. Whereas blue and white would remind yu to keep yu mouth shut. This yellow is like a school room where yu talk-talk because yu eager to please the teacher with how smart yu is and how hard yu work. Yu want her to know yu conscientious. And then I remember yellow was the colour of my school room but back then, me pleasing the teacher never happen too often. Mostly I just sit there and feel anxious and fraid that maybe she ask me something, because I knew I would have no idea what to say to her. So I would just open my mouth and see what come out. And even though I was talking I never really know what I was saying because all I could hear was the sound of my own heart beating. And then the whole room laughing.

The window high on the wall and it got a black wrought-iron grid over it, so as to stop me from escaping. That is what I reckon. But it so little and covered over it mek the room dark even though it mid-afternoon and there is bright Jamaican sunshine out there. Maybe that is why they paint the room yellow. And the corridor outside and the main room yu come into off the street as well. And because they not got much window, they have to switch on the electric light even in the middle a the day.

'So Gloria, where yu live?' And I tell him. 'So that would be Franklyn Town?' I dunno why he saying this. It was only yesterday he was standing there on the veranda wid his friend. And just as I think that, the other constable open the door and walk in.

'Miss Campbell, can I fetch you something to drink? A little ice water maybe?'

And I say, 'Yes, thank yu.'

He open the door and stick his head into the corridor and shout 'Water' and then he bring the fold-up metal chair he carrying and sit down next to his friend. They nuh say nothing but soon after that a policewoman come in the door with a glass a water and her own chair and sidung next to me. They got me well and truly surrounded now with nowhere to go.

And then the first one start up again. 'So, Miss Gloria Antoinette Campbell of Franklyn Town, what would you say would be your occupation as such?'

'My occupation?'

'That is correct. Your occupation.'

So I say, 'I am a housekeeper.'

'Housekeeper?' And he laugh.

'Yes, before that I was in service with a family uptown but now I am a housekeeper.'

'At this address here?' And he use the end a his pencil to point to the place on the page.

'Yes, that is correct.'

He just roll his eyes.

The second one lean forward with his elbows on the table and say, 'To tell yu the truth, Miss Campbell, we know what yu do. And we know what gwaan in that house in Franklyn Town.' And then he stop and glance at the policewoman sit next to me before he carry on. 'We know all about that. We not interested in yu little girly business. What we want to talk about is Yang Pao.'

'I don't know nothing 'bout him.'

'Nothing?'

'He come to the house once in a while. That is all. A lot a people come to the house.'

'Sure enough.' And he laugh. And then he tek a finger and fiddle with something in his teeth. 'The thing is, we hear it more than that.'

I don't say nothing.

'We always know more than you people credit us for. Yu nuh think yu already in enough trouble? I could stick yu behind bars right now for what yu and yu girlfriends doing over there. But why waste the cell when yu could be sitting here telling me all about yu boyfriend?' I sit there feeling all their eyes resting on me.

And then the other one say, 'Yu born in Kingston, Miss Gloria Antoinette Campbell?' My heart miss a beat I so fraid where all a this is going.

'No. Westmoreland.'

'Westmoreland. What part a Westmoreland would that be?'

'Near Petersfield.'

'Near Petersfield. So yu come from country.'

He wait a minute and then say, 'When yu come from country?'

I drink down the water and ask the policewoman if I can have another glass and she get up and step out into the corridor.

'1938.'

'1938. A good year for rioting that.' And he sit. Still, like he thinking something important. 'What mek yu come to Kingston in 1938, Miss Gloria Antoinette Campbell?'

My mouth parch but there is not a drop a water leave in the little plastic glass on the table.

'I think maybe me and my sista could mek a better life in town.'

'Yu have a sista? Right here in town? Live wid yu in the house there?'

'Yes sir.'

'Now that is a thing. A sista.'

They not got nothing to say except asking me the same questions round and round in circles 'bout what I know a Yang Pao and what he up to. And since I nuh telling them nothing, in the end they let me go.

When I step outside the sunlight almost blind me. Sybil and Marcia waiting for me. They sitting on a wooden bench in the shade 'cross the street.

'What tek yu so long?'

'I have to answer their questions Marcia. It tek as long as it tek.'
And the two a them stand up and we start walk.

Sybil say to me, 'Yu all right?'

And I say, 'Yes. I didn't tell them nothing, but I got a feeling
inside my belly that this thing not done with yet.'

CHAPTER 13

I DIDN'T SAY nothing to Pao 'bout the constable or the police station. There wasn't no need for him to get himself any more involve. I just carry on and he carry on coming to the house three times a week like always and life go on.

Time pass and since I never hear no more from the police I reckon I could let myself believe that they finish with their enquiries or maybe decide to leave me out of it. I try to believe that anyway. And in some small way it work. My mind didn't have to think on it every second a every day, even though it was always there. Something in a shadow that I could reach for unwillingly, or maybe sometimes on purpose to make myself feel afraid or just to remind me that I had no reason to feel content never mind happy about anything.

Every week Henry come tell me how Fay arguing with her mother. 'The two do nothing but cuss all day and all night. That is what they do.'

'What they cuss about?' Asking him like I am interested, which I am not.

'Anything and everything. Anything and everything.'

'So like give me an example.'

'Cicely say to Fay, "You going out again?" And Fay say, "That is none of your business. I am a grown woman and I go where I please." Then Cicely say, "You go where you please but you not going there with any money you earn. When you start pay your own way that is when you can talk about what a grown woman you are." And Fay say, "What like you mean how you pay your own way?" And that is how it go until one of them walk out room or Fay jump in car and leave it in dust behind her.'

'So is money they always arguing 'bout?'

'Money, where Fay go, what she do, who she see, what she say. Anything and everything.' He pause. 'You know one time she argue with her mother and leave the house and not come back for six months. Six months, Gloria! And when she come in she just carry on like nothing happen.'

'So where is go?'

'Stay with friend. That is all she tell me.'

I wait a minute and then I say, 'Life up the house must be miserable Henry.' He look at me like that is the most ridiculous thing I could a said to him. It so obvious.

All this go on and on, every week a report of another argument between Fay and Cicely, until in the end I realise Henry not got a soul he can talk to. He reduce to me, a woman with barely any schooling that nobody can find no use for apart from laying on her back.

Then one day I inside and I hear a booming voice on a bullhorn so I step on to the veranda and see the car with the loudspeaker strap to the roof and I listen to the message, up and down the street, over and over. It go on for a week with the same thing: 'Come Friday night, corner a Jackson Road and Giltress Street, and hear the leaders of the People's National Party share wid yu how they going serve the whole country and mek life better for all the masses a working men and women.'

Sybil hear the message as well and say we should go over there and see what gwaan. I say to her, 'What mek yu think they have any interest in the likes a us?'

'Well yu not going know unless yu go find out.'

So come Friday night me and Sybil stroll over to Jackson Road. What we find when we get there is music and dancing and a big high platform with banners and lights that the speakers going stand on so we can all see them when they tell us what they got to say. The crowd was like nothing I ever see before. It was a multitude, happy and jigging and calling each other comrade. Like I go to a carnival in the middle a the street. And when the speakers step up, the people go wild, cheering and clapping and whistling. It was pure jubilation. A man come to the microphone and say, 'Comrades, hush yuself nuh,' so everybody simmer down.

Then he say, 'I give you the Member of Parliament for East Kingston and Port Royal, the Brown Bomber, Florizel Augustus Glasspole,' and the commotion start up again, hooting and hollering and making so much merriment the man couldn't even talk. All he could do was stand there with the banners flapping behind him and his arms waving in the air trying to calm them so he could start his speech.

And what all the speakers got to say is how the PNP going get education for all, and how important this is because most people in the country can't read or write. That full and proper self-government is going to be our future, which is better than talking 'bout a little more bread and a little more butter like what Mr Bustamante and the Jamaica Labour Party always going on about. And just so, the crowd start up shouting, 'Sweep them out! Sweep them out!' with a whole heap of the comrades raising the broom they bring with them to show just how they going sweep out the JLP.

And when Norman Washington Manley walk up to the microphone I swear people must a heard the uproar from as far away as Savanna-la-Mar or Port Antonio, or any damn place on this island, there was so much excitement. He stand there in a long-sleeve blue shirt, his arms at his side and a half-smile on his face. And when he finally open his mouth yu know right away this man know how to use the English language. My Saturday morning wrinkle hand was not a patch on him. But it wasn't just the way he talk it, it was how he was in himself. He take you in. He capture you. He mesmerise you. This was a educated man. So you know for sure, a educated person would join the PNP. And when he finish talk, the crowd start sing. I don't know how many hundreds a people singing these songs they all know the words to. But they was singing like it was a Sunday morning service and a true act a worship.

After that, Sybil join the local PNP group and she start go down the local kindergarten school one afternoon a week to sit with the little ones and help them with their reading and writing.

'Yu want come wid me?'

'Sybil, I not hardly got no schooling. And even that was shameful wid me meking a laughing stock a myself every time I open my mouth.'

'Yu know enough to sit with a five-year old.'

I think on it and then I say, 'You gwaan. I got no intention a going down there to mek a fool a myself.'

1950

'Of the rarest Chinese jade.'

CHAPTER 14

HENRY SAY YANG Pao been visiting the house up Lady Musgrave Road.

'Yu mean your house?' And he nod. 'What he doing up there?'

'Visit with Fay, or more like, Cicely.'

'What yu mean?'

Henry wait. I can tell he not happy 'bout what he got to say. So even before I hear it I know I not going like whatever it is he feel so strong I got to listen to.

'He visiting with Fay.'

'Yu say that already.' But Henry don't want to say no more.

'Yu mean visiting? Like in *visiting*?'

And he just say 'Yes.'

'How long this been going on?'

'A time, I know that.'

I not going say nothing to Pao. I want him to tell me of his own accord because it seem to me that it should be him that bring up the subject a Fay Wong, not me. But weeks come and weeks go and the months pass by but still there is not a single word from him about Fay. Not a whisper. Not a slip. It as if the woman don't even exist.

So I turn cool. I not tek no initiative with him. I just let him do what he do. Then one day we laying in the bed and outta the blue he say to me, 'Did I do something, Gloria? Something wrong, all them years back?'

'How yu mean?'

'Something to vex yu?'

'Vex me?'

'Why yu mek me start paying yu?' He pause and then he say, 'Or was it because I was weak, yu know, crying like I did?'

I look at him leaning up there on his elbow staring down at me with his hand resting on my naked stomach.

'It wasn't nothing to do with that.'

'So what was it to do with?'

'I tell yu at the time. It was to do with business.'

And even though I could see his mind working on something, he didn't say nothing else. He just get up and dress himself and reach in his pocket for the money he put on the table.

When he reach the door he turn to me and say, 'That was well over four years ago and yu telling me that nothing changed in all that time?'

He stand there waiting for an answer that I didn't have. And then he turn 'round and walk out.

Henry say Pao done ask Miss Cicely if he can marry Fay.

'Marry Fay!' I so shocked it mek Henry worried, like maybe he think he shouldn't a tell me.

So I say, 'Thank yu Henry.' But still he anxious and waiting for some other reaction from me. Me, I only feel disbelief that Pao could go and do a thing like that.

'Where he know her from anyway?'

'Chinese Athletic Club.'

I let the news sit with me for a moment and then I say, 'I cyan understand what your daughter would see in a man like Yang Pao.'

'Is Cicely. Fay not hardly talk to him. That is what maids say anyway.'

I start to mek myself breathe as slow and even as I can because now there is a growing pain in my chest. Tight like I cyan catch no air at all.

'So yu going let her marry him?'

'It not up to me, Gloria. Is Cicely decide.'

'Not Fay?' And he just shrug his shoulders like the conversation already gone beyond anything he can talk about with any certainty.

So that was it. Miss Cicely say yes and the deal was done. A couple days later when Pao come over the house I blurt it out.

'Is it true what I hear 'bout you marrying Fay Wong?' I just say it because I couldn't tek the shame of standing there while he mek his announcement like it was the news a the year. And he admit it like a schoolboy that the teacher catch cheating in an examination with a look on his face like, 'Give me the punishment and let it be over.'

'I can't marry you, Gloria, you know that.'

'I didn't expect you to marry me.'

'So what you expect?'

'I didn't expect you to go marry somebody else.' And I think to myself, 'Especially somebody like Fay Wong,' but I nuh say it. I don't want to be saying nothing 'bout Fay. I didn't even want to be hearing her name mention to me ever again, never mind have it pass over my own lips. All he got to say is he got to give his children a name. And I think yu could have give any child we have a name.

I turn away from him and I start cry. I didn't want to do it. I even mek a promise to myself not to. But it just well up inside a me and it come out no matter how much I try to breathe and swallow it down. When he rest his hand on my shoulder I just shrug it off and tell him to get out because I couldn't stand to even look at him.

Sybil and Beryl, Marcia and Auntie, none a them surprise.

'There is only one reason why this thing upset yu so much.' Sybil drag on her cigarette.

'And what would that be?'

'That yu forget yu a whore.' And then she say, 'Who going marry a whore when they can marry Fay Wong?'

That night I lay in my bed and I weep. I sob like I never know sobbing before even though I know Sybil right. What man in his right mind would do that, marry a whore? Fay rich, she beautiful, she educated, she light-skin. What I got to offer when yu comparing me with a woman like Fay Wong?

But in truth I didn't know what I was crying for. It not like I think I wanted to be married to him, or married to anybody come to that. Because what would I do being somebody's wife? No, it wasn't that. And in the end through all the tears and commotion that I was muffling into the pillow I realise what it was. It was jealousy. Jealousy that even though I was his first I wouldn't be his only woman no more. Maybe I wouldn't even be his woman at all. That was what hurt because I remember how much I miss him that time he stop coming to the house. And it ache me to know that somebody else was going see the funny way he smile and hear the way he laugh from deep down in his belly, even sitting bolt upright in the bed sometimes when something amuse him bad. And how he talk. And that nod. And the singing, sweet and low late at night or early in the morning. And that smooth, smooth skin. But it was more than that because that feeling a jealousy go way back. Back to the time I find Barrington with Marcia and discover that I wasn't the only one.

A few days later Pao come back and I know what he want because he still nuh understand how it is that I could ask him about Fay before he tell me. But I not about to bring Henry into it, so when I see the car pull up at the kerb I quickly run and shut the door. That way, he got to knock. I tek my time to go open it, and when I get there I just look him up and down and then reach for the handle and close the door in his face. I didn't even say a word to him. I just leave him standing there and a few minutes later I watch the car disappear down the road.

The next time he come I let him walk in and sit down in the front room. And then I go out. I pick up my purse from the kitchen and walk out the back door and tek myself into town. Not to do nothing in particular, just to walk and call into Times Store for a coffee and browse the counters at Issa's. I didn't even buy nothing. I just feel the quality of a piece a cloth, and admire a vase, and try on a pair a shoes in the Bata shop. And then I go see Mr Ho and check how he doing now that the Lynette thing pass him by. He good. Business fine. And that please me.

When I get back to the house Marcia tell me that Pao sit down there for a good hour. Just waiting like he got nothing better to do. And when she tell him I gone to town he so surprised he didn't know what to do with himself. He just carry on sitting there like maybe he would stay never mind me having no intention a seeing him that day.

The Friday night he show up. He stand in the doorway and just look at me. I see him, but I had no idea what was in his eyes. Whether it was rage or repentance, or sadness or jealousy at me teking a drink and exchanging a few words and a joke with some a the customers.

When I go 'cross the room to hand him the envelope he step outside on to the veranda so I have to follow him. I am standing there with the money still in my hand when he start to complain 'bout how I treat him this week, so I have to tell him how much him marrying Fay Wong hurt me and how it put me in my place as his three-time-a-week whore.

'Gloria, it not like that. It not like that at all.' And then he give me some long speech about a beautiful tiger running wild that a man admire and love and how caging the tiger would kill it spirit because it wouldn't be strong and independent no more, it would just be laying there in the cage waiting for this man to feed and clean and entertain it, and tend it when it sick. And that would be vexing because instead of running free and full of life, the tiger would be lazy. And the man wouldn't get no pleasure from this tiger no more because it would be dead and he would be the one that kill it.

So I say to him, 'That is all about you. You ever think that maybe the tiger, as well as wanting to be free, also sometimes want some security and some rest so maybe it don't have to fret every day 'bout where the next meal coming from or how it going defend itself against everything out there that want to hunt it down. That maybe the tiger want to be able to look forward to some support and company, especially when it getting older and it not so independent, or strong, or beautiful. That maybe the tiger just want some day to find some peace?'

All he say to me is how I don't need no cage to have all that. I just stand there on the veranda listening to him and the sound of the crickets on the evening lawn, and wondering who I think I am to be punishing him the way I did or talking 'bout peace or company. I fret so much 'bout what I mean to him when it was me that close the door between us. It was me that turn myself into his three-time-a-week whore. Me that tell him, 'I am what I am.' Me that had no answer for him when he ask me 'bout what had changed over all these years together. It was me. Because being a whore is what I am in my own head never mind what Yang Pao think.

The wedding happen at Holy Trinity Cathedral on a bright Saturday morning with half a Kingston inside dress up like it a royal coronation, and the other half a the town outside to witness the grandness and splendour. It was a rich do. And even though I didn't want to, Sybil and the rest a them talk me into going.

'Yu nuh want to go see it for real?'

No I didn't. It was already real enough for me. All that tek me there in the end was wanting to see what he look like all suited and respectable on his wedding day. And what Fay would look like. And see the two of them step together outta the front door of the cathedral into the noonday sun. So I go and I see him in the white suit and her in the dress that flowing so much behind it tek two women to run along fixing and fussing every move she mek.

I think, what kinda marriage this going to be? Fay wouldn't even tek his arm as they walking down the path. They get in the car and I see him gaze out the window up at the white cathedral dome. And then the car move off and I wish I had decide to go do something else rather than stand out there in the street looking at Henry as he watch the car disappear down the road.

CHAPTER 15

THEY GO UP to the north coast for the honeymoon and spend a week in a hotel in Ocho Rios that Henry tell me is a most beautiful and peaceful place with it own sandy beach and luscious gardens. It call the Jamaica Inn and Henry say it the place that the American movie stars stay when they up there. Why Henry think I need to listen to all a this I don't know. It seem like he don't trust himself to decide what he going tell me and what he not so he just give me everything and hope for the best. Me, I don't want to hear none a it, and I want to hear it all. Maybe it better to know rather than not even if it pain you. Maybe the pain comforting. At least that way yu know you still feeling something, which is better than feeling nothing at all.

I nuh see Yang Pao for a good month after the wedding. And then one day he just show up at the house. He come in the room with a face on him like he want to smile but he nuh dare do it 'til he see what kinda mood I am in. I wait for him to say something. But his lips cyan move. Then he bring his hand from behind his back and he got a narrow oblong parcel that he open out in his palm to show me.

'I got this for yu.' It wrap in some pretty green tissue paper.

'What is it?'

'Open it and see, nuh.' And then he do a smile even though it sorta nervous. I cyan even bother reach out my hand to tek it from him. So he push his arm towards me and motion like gwaan tek it.

'What yu bring this here for?'

'Gloria, please. I want to give yu something. Something nice. What is wrong with that? It not like I ever give yu anything before.'

'And yu think this is the time to do it? After yu go marry Fay Wong?'

He just look at the floor like I tek all the wind outta his sail, and his hand drop a little as his shoulder fall.

'I didn't mean to hurt yu, Gloria. Yu must know that. It just . . .'

But I don't want him to start give me no explanation, so I just say, 'What you do is your business. I got no claim on yu. Yu a free man Yang Pao to do exactly what you please.'

He quiet a minute and then he say, 'I bring this for yu and I want yu to have it. Cyan yu just tek it and maybe see what it is?' So I reach out and lift it outta his hand. It heavy. When I tek off the wrapping I see it a box from Lee Jewellery store. And inside it is the most beautiful gleaming gold necklace with a line of jade stones along the whole length. It look like something that should be hanging 'round the neck a Queen Cleopatra. It that gorgeous.

'I cyan tek this from yu Pao.'

He nuh say nothing, and then he say, 'Gloria, who can say what might have happen with us? We start out the way we did and now we here. Yes, I go marry Fay but that not the whole story. Yu know that.' He tek a little pause and then he say, 'I love yu, Gloria.' And after a while he turn 'round and walk out.

After he gone I put the necklace on top a the dresser in my bedroom. Still in the box. Just like that.

Two nights later when we busy in the front room with customers Beryl step through the door and the only thing that catch my eye is the jade necklace hanging 'round her neck. Everything in me freeze. I think even my heart stop beating. I cyan believe she go do that. Especially knowing like she do that I not even wear the thing myself yet. And if I say anything to her 'bout it I know what her defence is going to be. She just going say, 'Everything in this house get borrow by everybody all the time. What yu so huffy 'bout?' And what can I say to that? It true. So I decide to let it go. I know she go put it back tomorrow and that will be that.

But when the next day come, that vision a Beryl in the doorway still edged on my mind. And that feeling a outrage still wedged in my heart. So late morning when she finally raise herself and sitting on the veranda with her second cup a coffee I step outside and I say to her, 'The necklace yu wearing last night, I would prefer it if yu nuh do that again. Yu know where it come from and I don't want to see nobody wearing it. Not right now anyway.' She look up at me from where she sitting with her feet rest on the little wicker stool.

'Everything belong to everybody. Yu know that. That necklace not no different from the blouse yu borrow from Sybil last week or the shoes a mine Marcia like to wear so much.' And then she turn 'round and carry on drink the coffee because for Beryl, it is over.

'Yang Pao give me that necklace after he go marry Fay Wong. That mek it a bit different from a blouse or a pair a old shoes.'

She spin 'round with her body rigid and her face vex like I never see before. 'Yu remember when yu first come to this house, what did yu bring wid yu that was so precious yu couldn't share? And what did we share wid you?'

I got no answer for her so I just stand there. But a part a me cyan believe what she say to me. I stare at the side of her head as she carry on sip from the cup like nothing happen.

Afterwards I think maybe I mek a mistake saying anything to her about it. After all, she right and I knew beforehand what her attitude was going to be. And since she go put the necklace back in my room anyway, what else was there to say? Except there was still something in me that I was carrying 'round the house in the silent way I was dragging my feet and letting a door slam heavy once in a while and picking on every small thing that gwaan 'til eventually Sybil say to me, 'Something eating yu?'

'It nothing.'

'Don't tell me it nothing. The whole house can see it something.'

'It nothing Sybil, honestly. Not anything you can fix. I just have to sort myself out that is all.' But she not swallowing it.

'Yu think this house survive as long as it do wid people who nuh say what they got on their mind?' She stop a while and then she say, 'Beryl tell me 'bout yu talk wid her over the necklace.'

I lean my back against the sink and look at her.

'What yu expect me to say?'

'I don't expect nothing. Beryl tell me what yu say to her and now I just asking yu what else yu still harbouring 'bout it because everybody can see yu not done wid this yet.'

'It was just because Yang Pao give it to me and before I know what Beryl got it 'round her neck.'

'And so yu feel what?' Sybil lean against the wall and light a cigarette.

I tek a minute and then I say, 'I feel like she rob me. Rob me of the time that I needed to mek up my mind what the necklace mean to me.'

'Mean to yu? It was a morsel to throw to yu after the wedding. And the only reason he do it is because even though he married he still want to come here every week getting what he always get.' She walk over to me and ash the cigarette in the sink. 'No man is worth it Gloria.' And then she wet the butt under the pipe and walk off.

Next thing Marcia is asking me 'bout it and I have to tell her it got nothing to do with anybody but me and Beryl.

'Sybil vex over it yu know.'

'Everybody vex over it Marcia. You just stay outta it yu understand me?'

Two days later Beryl go 'round the house and pick up everything that she reckon belong to her. She go in Marcia room and tek back some lipstick and a skirt and the shoes she mention to me before. And she go into my room and gather up all the things she ever give me over the years for a Christmas or birthday present. So I decide I go talk to her 'bout it. When I find her she sitting in the kitchen with Marcia drinking and joking and laughing. But no sooner than I step through the door they stop.

I say to Beryl, 'Yu go tek back everything yu ever give me?'

'What is yours is yours, so what is mine is mine.' And they laugh. And just like when I was in school it mek me feel young and foolish, and shameful.

'Beryl, Yang Pao give me that necklace after he go marry another woman. Yu nuh think that mek it different from all the other things that we all bring in this house?'

135

'Yu think it cost so much money?' And they laugh some more.

So I gather myself together and I say, 'Of course it cost. Yu only have to feel the weight a it to know that. But it not the money. It the fact that he give me something. Have any a these men that come here week in week out ever give you anything?' And as soon as I say it I know I should a keep my mouth shut.

But Marcia jump in. 'It just a necklace. We going fall out over a string a jade from a stupid little Chiney?'

'Don't call him that. If it wasn't for him we would still be living in dread that what happen to yu could happen to any one a us at any time.'

'What happen to me wasn't anything to do wid the business. It was to do wid you and Henry and the money.'

'And you not making enough outta that yuself?'

'I never say that. I just say you and Henry go get Yang Pao to protect yu own interests that is all.' And she turn 'round in the chair sitting there with her back to me.

Then Beryl say, 'So he come and protect us and mek himself your personal man. Your personal man, Gloria, like yu special when all we got is the same good-for-nothing oafs that come here week after week counting out the change on the table. And now he give yu a serious piece a jewellery. Well bully for him. But he still a Chiney. At least we know this one got legs.'

'Legs?'

And then her face turn real nasty before she say, 'Yu nuh know what deh say? The Chiney not got no legs because every time yu see dem deh standing behind di shop counter.'

I tek a deep breath and I say, 'Come on Marcia let us go tek a walk and let everybody calm themself down.'

But she never move a inch. She just sit there and say, 'Gloria, I was sitting in this kitchen before yu come in here and turn everything sour.'

So I turn 'round to go because I cyan believe that even my own sista is going turn on me over this. But before I get a chance to leave she say, 'Yu always right Gloria, eh? Always the one that can see the fault in what everybody else is doing. Like how yu say Mama nuh treat yu good like she treat me. Joking 'bout it but still complaining. And how Lynette dim-witted and Miss Sissy scratching her head over the food she cooking. And even when Auntie show some kindness yu was too high and mighty to sleep in the bed wid her or go tek a shower in the yard.'

I listen to all a this still standing there with my back to her, choking on the tears because to have Marcia turn on me like this was one thing, but to have her do it in front a Beryl was like teking her hand and ripping out my heart.

Then Beryl say, 'So I tek the necklace, so what? Yu think I too trashy to be wearing yu 24-carat-gold? Yu think that because he give it to yu it mek yu better than me? Well yu just a whore Gloria Campbell, just like the rest a us. Even despite all yu airs and graces, and Saturday morning English lesson, and fancy clothes yu buying wid Henry Wong's money, which come to think of it, only mek yu a different sorta whore to him as well. Yu expensive jade necklace? All that mek yu is a high-class whore. Not for one but two Chiney.'

Marcia laugh. Right out loud like she couldn't give one damn how it hurt me. I feel like I want to grab her up and slap her 'til her face black and blue, even though my heart is breaking that she would want to wound me like this.

Next thing Sybil step through the door and say, 'The three a yu so busy cussing in here yu cyan hear someone knocking at the door?'

So I go out there because the way my stomach heaving I think it good to walk away from the air in that room before I throw up on the floor. And still Beryl is shouting to me, 'Chiney stick together, Gloria. It time you learn to do the same.'

My heart beating so hard and legs so weak I didn't even know if I going mek it to the door. When I get there I find a tall, broad man that flash me a smile a white teeth against his dark skin.

'Sorry. Yu been knocking long?'

'A little while. Actually I was starting to wonder if it was a convenient time and maybe I should come back tomorrow.'

I got nothing in my head to say to him, so I just stand there. And then he reach out his hand and pass me a little piece of card that say: 'Sgt Clifton Brown, North Street Police Station'.

CHAPTER 16

IT TURN OUT Sergeant Brown didn't want nothing that day except to tell me that he recently arrive in Kingston and station at North Street in case there is anything I need. I didn't ask him nothing 'bout it because entering into conversation with him was the last thing I wanted to do at that moment, so I just leave it, and he turn and go out the yard and shut the gate behind him.

What kinda curious thing was that? It unsettle me but then I reckon he a sergeant so maybe he come to tek charge of the two constables that was asking so much questions 'bout Mr Ho and Pao and the ruckus in North Parade. But after all this time?

And just as I was trying to put the whole thing outta my mind Pao come tell me that some big police officer been sent from Montego Bay to fight corruption in the downtown area, which he, Pao, think is some kinda joke. He say they get the Chinatown Merchants Association to invite the sergeant to come talk to them so as to meet this man face to face. But when it happen it seem the sergeant not what he appear to be. So I ask him what the sergeant called and he say, 'Clifton Brown.'

'Yu mean that sergeant down North Street police station?'

'Yu know him?'

I hesitate but then I say, 'So what nuh right 'bout this man?'

'That is for me to know.' He smile. 'I tell yu something for nothing though, I going get that man come do a thing or two for me.'

'What would mek a man like Clifton Brown want to run wid you?'

'Because, Gloria, everybody got secrets.'

I fretting so much 'bout what going on in the house, and how Marcia turn on me over the necklace, and what Pao doing with Sergeant Brown and what the sergeant want with me anyway that I cyan settle to anything. So I ask Henry if he want to spend a couple days with me in Ocho Rios and he say yes.

Henry's house in a little cove with a soft white sandy beach all of its own. It small, but it breezy with a veranda facing out to sea. It is a place to rest. A place to ease back and let the worries of Kingston fall off your shoulders.

We get up there early evening just as the sun was setting with its orange glow sinking into the distant water. The caretaker, Abraham, already been to the market so everything is here that we need. I cook up some corned beef and cabbage with rice because I know Henry like it so much, and we eat out on the veranda under the clear night sky.

'What bother you, Gloria? Something heavy you wrestle with?'

I look at him. He old, Henry. Old enough to be my father. He ordinary. Just a regular, taller than average Chinese man. Not the sorta man that would turn anybody's head. But there is something about Henry. Something solid and reliable. Yu feel calm in his company. Yu feel safe. Yu feel yu can trust him, and that whatever yu say or do is going to be all right with him. He not going judge or punish you. He not going laugh or criticise. And that is because Henry Wong is content with himself. He know who he is and what he has accomplished, and he don't need to be proving anything or making a show of anybody else. And that is what make this ordinary man so handsome. He got the kindness to listen to yu without making yu feel like a fool.

'A lot going on in the house.'

'And the wedding?'

'Well that was something else Henry.'

He look at me. 'Gloria, you smart. You good business woman. You caring and beautiful. You everything a woman would want to be. Not your fault that sometimes other people not see it.' Henry got brown eyes and long lashes for a man. And he got majestic grey hair that just touch gentle on his collar.

It quiet between us for a while and then I say, 'Tell me 'bout Fay.'

'Fay?' He take another drink of the ice water and then pile some rice on his fork. He chew and swallow.

'When Fay born, her head, blonde hair. Imagine that, Chinese-African baby with fair skin and blonde hair. Nobody believe it. And it stay just so until she almost five years old. Long curls. That is what she had. It make all the maids and everybody fuss her like she princess. She love it. She like Shirley Temple on the *Good Ship Lollipop* every single day. The only person that take exception was Cicely. What Cicely think was that Fay spoil from the day she born. That was how it start. And nothing change since then. All that different now is Fay big enough to argue back. She stop being little child that Cicely chastise morning, noon and night. Because as Fay grow she understand more and more how

Cicely feel, and she let out her own anger over how her mother treat her bad.'

He pick up some corned beef and cabbage, and then he rest down the fork. 'Cicely beat her, and lock her in room with piano. Sometimes she even leave house with child lock in there.'

I don't know what he expecting from me so I just sit there with my attention full on him because I can feel that there is a lot Henry want to say and I don't want to be getting in his way.

'Fay go inside self. That was what she do, because under the anger was pain. Deep, deep hurt inside. And that is what you do, Gloria. You inside self.'

He tek me by surprise because I wasn't expecting him to suddenly start talking 'bout me like that.

'Is that what yu see the day you pick me off the road?'

'That day? No. What I see that day was you have mind of your own. You your own person. That not easy thing for woman to be. Most women just do what somebody else want them to do, whether it their mother or father or husband. There always somebody else they paying better attention to than themselves. Women not trust themselves. You notice that? But not you, Gloria. And not Fay. Cicely, she think she do, but she spend too much time calling on the good Lord to convince me that it true. You, Gloria, not calling on nobody help you.' Henry finish his food and sit back in the chair.

'What make yu think I not calling on nobody?'

He look at me quizzical. And then he rest his elbow on the arm of the chair with his thumb on his cheek and his hand spread out across his forehead. And I see how his long, thin fingers end in neat-neat cuticles and perfect filed fingernails. Henry Wong got a beautician giving him elegant hands. Hands that are graceful and full of tenderness.

'Who you calling on then?'

'I didn't say I was calling on anybody. I just don't know what make yu so sure I am not.'

He reach out his other hand and pick up the glass of water and sip it. 'Your loneliness.' And then he look at me straight in the eye and say, 'You strong woman, Gloria, who I think been made that way by the many, many woes you have from early age. That is what I believe. And that strength come out in how you do things now. You are in charge. You not letting nobody take liberty with you. You happy talk straight and conduct business way you want to. On your terms. You tough. But inside, you lonely. And I think if there was somebody you calling on, then that emptiness inside of you not be there.'

And just as we sitting there Abraham come to the door to ask if there is anything else we need this evening. So Henry get up and step inside with him and say it all right, he can go home and we will see to everything.

When he come back, Henry is carrying a bottle of Appleton Special. He pour out two glasses of rum and set the bottle down on the table, and then he sit back in the chair.

'Fay got that loneliness inside too. Oh yes, she hard on outside, because that the only way she see to survive her mother. But inside, she just like you. She crying out for somebody to reach in and see who she is. Well, that is one part anyway. The other part is that if anybody try reach in, she more likely bite off their hand than welcome it. So with her it is always come-come, go-go.'

I ask myself is it true? Not 'bout Fay, I don't know nothing about her. But is it true about me? I take a drink and turn my head to sea. And I know Henry is right. There is a wall inside of me. A high concrete wall that I am stuck behind. A wall that I am always trying to climb to the top of and reach over. But I can never make it. All I do is stand back here and listen to the people on the other side who sound like they belong together. They included in something.

'And what about you, Henry?'

'Me?'

'You. Are you inside yuself as well?'

He think on it and then he say, 'I am Chinese man living in fancy house uptown Lady Musgrave Road where I don't know anybody and nobody know me, where I come and go like a ghost. But that what Cicely want. Just like she want import all the furniture from England and surround herself with servants and fine living, and serve Earl Grey tea every afternoon.' And then he stop and drink some rum.

'You not got no say in any of that?'

He swirl the liquid 'round in the glass a while and then he say, 'I am like one of those women I talking about earlier. Just doing what Cicely want me to do.' He take another sip from the glass. 'Me and Cicely start out as convenience. She need husband and I need wife. Good African wife to make me part of community so I not pose threat to anybody who maybe think I criticising them by not joining in. I just set self up in shop. I trying to make way. Marry Cicely good for business.'

We both reach for the next taste of rum. 'Why did she need a husband?'

'She expecting baby.'

'But it not yours, Henry?'

'No. Not mine. It a difficult situation for her. So we get married and all the problems solved.' Henry get up and pour some more rum into the almost empty glasses.

I say to him, 'Yu should be careful with that. I don't know how well yu can hold yu liquor.' And he laugh and swallow down some more.

'I sleep in separate room on old-fashion wood and canvas cot. Not in oak-frame bed that Cicely got all over house. I keep clothes in same camphor-wood chest I bring from China all those years back. That how it always been except for when Cicely want next child. First Fay, then Daphne, and after long time when nobody except her think she can do it, she get Kenneth. Daphne, she one of those waiting for her mother tell her what to do. Kenneth, unruly and heading for trouble, but he still just child. Fay only one got strength stand up to Cicely. Me, my head been bowed to her since the beginning of time.' And he take another drink.

'This don't seem like you Henry. To me yu are a strong man who come to this country and made his fortune with a dedication that most people would envy.' He just laugh. Not a big throw-yu-head-back laugh, but one that start low and disappear into his chest.

'You see, you can fool all the people all the time.' And he raise the glass to his lips again.

'I live in exile, Gloria, but I not have courage enough to leave and go Chinatown. I lazy. Lazy coward who never lift finger, or voice, to help Fay when her mother cuss and cuss, and beat and punish her. Never once. But I can pick you off the road and show you some kindness because I not have to cross Cicely to do it.'

We sit there in silence and finish the rum in the glasses. And then he say to me that the mosquitoes biting and we should tidy up and go inside. So we clear the table and stand up in the kitchen while I scrape and rinse through the dishes and Henry watch.

Afterwards I make some coffee and Henry say he going put on some music. What he choose is a Mario Lanza record, which surprise me because I never take Henry to be the sorta man to like that kinda thing.

We sit on the settee next to each other while I pour the coffee from the pot. And as we settle back I say, 'What is it, the hold Miss Cicely got over you?'

He stare down into the cup. 'She the only person I ever fully give myself to. I wouldn't know what to do without her, even though most times I think she be happy to do without me.'

Henry's spirit dipping down. So to raise it up I say, 'What happen to Miss Cicely's first born?'

'Stanley? He grow up wild and when war come he go to England and join Royal Air Force.' And then after a while he say, 'I think he happy to say goodbye to his mother and Jamaica and everything that remind him of who he was.'

'Who he was?'

'Who his father was.' And as soon as he say it, it make me think of all the questions I ask my own mother about who my father was and never get no answer.

'Who was that?'

'Stanley Johnson. The man young Stanley believe was his grandfather. And it true. Stanley was his grandfather. But when young Stanley turn fifteen Cicely decide tell him truth. I don't know why. I sure she had own good reasons. Maybe it was to make the boy feel sorry for her for the disgrace her father bring upon her. But that is not what happen. Young Stanley blame her for shame instead. And after that he barely had two words say to her. And as soon as he could, he leave Jamaica and she never hear a word from him since that day.'

I sit there and watch Henry as he close his eyes and lean back in the chair. And then I reach over and take his hand remembering the first time I do it that day in Franklyn Town. But this time it wasn't to reassure him. This time it was something else. I caress it. Stroking with one finger the back and the palm. Slowly and gently. And then I start work my way over and across each and every finger, up the outside and down the inside, from the thumb to the little one on the end. Back and forth, top and bottom, while Mario Lanza was singing 'Be My Love' and 'The Loveliest Night of the Year' and the music was vibrating through me like it was playing deep inside my body.

Henry just sit there and let me do it without saying a single word or even opening his eyes. And after some long time, when the record finish, he get up and say we should go to bed.

I go in the bathroom and when I come out I step into the bedroom I always sleep in up there in the house. It the second bedroom. And then I hear Henry come out the bathroom and go into the other room and close the door. I wait to see what going happen next but all I hear is the click as he turn off the bedside lamp. How long I was laying there in that bed I don't know, with the rum spinning my head and my mind turning over every question about what I should do. And no matter how much I try to fall asleep there was something constantly pulling me back, urging me to just get up and take the short walk to Henry's room. So after I toss and turn and toss some more, I finally decide to get outta the bed. I wrap a shawl 'round my shoulders and slide my feet into the slippers to cross the cold tile floor.

When I open the door I can sense that he is laying there wide awake. Even in the pitch dark I can feel it. But he don't say nothing to me. So I just walk over and throw the shawl on the chair and get into the bed next to him. And in that silence all I could hear was his breathing, deep and even like he was concentrating on calming himself. He didn't move. Not one inch. So I just lay there and after a time I fall asleep.

Next morning when I wake up I can hear Henry in the kitchen talking to Dolores, Abraham's wife, who do cooking and cleaning for him. I tiptoe back to my room and pull on some clothes and as I go into the kitchen I see Henry is showered and dressed and sitting at the table eating some saltfish and callaloo.

'Yu sleep well Miss Gloria?'

'Yes, thank you Dolores. And how are you today?'

'Cyan complain Miss. The good Lord is providing well for me. That is the truth.'

Henry's head is down like he don't want to raise his eyes to me.

After breakfast he decide to show me the banana plantation he live on when he first come to Jamaica. So we drive out there and even though it still working, it seem a little run down. But it nuh matter. Henry get one of the workers to lend him a horse and cart and we ride the narrow path through the trees with the hands of fruit hanging full and low. When we get to the top of a big hill he stop and point down to the Great House with its eight white columns out front and the lattice windows and red tile roof. And gardens that lay out prim and proper like some grand English mansion you see in the school books.

'When I come here I was young boy. Mr Johnson, Cicely's father, plantation foreman who bring me from docks in Kingston to do cooking and clearing-up for all the African labourers because he think it better for time and money if all of them eat together instead each family fend for self. I cook and clear, fetch and carry, and help with laundry when Great House overburden. That is how I earn my way as the only Chinaman on this plantation. I live here ten years and in all that time I never see white Englishman that own this place, or any member of his family. Never once. That was how it was. All I had every day was cooking and washing, and smell of burning and horseshit, and self for company. And when I finally leave I realise that only people I know was Mr Johnson and Cicely. Imagine that, after all that time. I use money I save and gold mother give me when I leave China to buy shop in Ocho Rios. And that is how it all start.'

And then he raise his hand and point. 'That is White River Gorge down there. And from up here, you can see Cuba on a clear day.'

Afterwards we call by Dunn's River Falls but Henry not putting on no bathing suit. He just stood at the bottom while I climb the six hundred feet over the rocks and through the water to the top of the falls. And then he sit in the shade while I take a dip in the clear blue sea.

That night when we turn in I just go straight to his room. I feel I owe it to him, he been so good to me. But it is more than that. Henry Wong in his own quiet, gentle way is a wonderful man. Yu feel secure with him. Yu feel like he is genuinely interested. Yu feel like yu spirit can rest with Henry. And for him, I feel there is something he wants with me as well, because even though he hold himself so still the night before he didn't tell me to go. He let me stay there curled up against his back, the whole night through. So I go to his room and get in the bed.

I was laying there when he come through the door from the bathroom. He didn't say nothing. He just walk 'round the bed and get in the other side. He lay down and turn to me. So I wait a minute and then I kiss him. And even though he had a little hesitation, he kiss me back. Soft and gentle. I ease back and start unbutton the shirt of these blue cotton pyjamas he wearing. But when I reach halfway he raise his hand and rest it on mine.

We stop like that a time and then he say, 'I can't, Gloria.' He think some more. 'This is special what we have. After all these years I finally find someone who seem happy to be with me.' He stop. Then he say, 'I can talk to you, Gloria. I whole person when I with you. Not just fraction of Henry Wong. That is joyous to me. This other thing, that would change it. And me, I would feel like old man who don't know right way to respect friendship. It would be shameful.'

I was like a statue, laying there on my side with my hands on the button. I never thought a man would ever refuse me. All my life it was always them wanting me whether it was out of lust or greed, or just because they was paying. That was what I was used to. That was what I come to accept. This I never expected.

I ease my hand from under his and I button up his pyjama shirt and pat him on the chest. Light and playful. And I say, 'Turn over.' And with his back to me I wrap my arm 'round his waist. And what I feel, in truth, was relief that I didn't go do something else to make my life more complicated than it already was. So I was grateful to Henry for that. And wrap up together we fall asleep.

Henry didn't want to do it. But I make him tek me to the Jamaica Inn. I just wanted a glimpse of this hotel that Pao take Fay for the honeymoon. Maybe I was punishing myself. That is what Henry think. But something in me had to see this place.

After I get dress I fetch out the jade necklace that I bring with me and hang it 'round my neck. I look in the mirror and it gleaming.

When Henry see me he say, 'So that is necklace?'

'What yu mean?'

'I catch everything on wind, Gloria. In house. With Sybil and Beryl.' And then he say, 'Fay know about necklace as well.' And he lower his head and nod.

'How she know?'

'Assistant in jewellery store think Pao buy for her and ask her how she like. So she find out he buy it. How she know it for you? That is a mystery. But her mouth busy at Lady Musgrave Road telling everyone who want to listen 'bout woman Pao have in East Kingston.'

The Jamaica Inn is everything I imagine and more. The white sandy cove, the banana and coconut trees, the blushing jacaranda and bougainvillea, the shrimp plant and red ginger filling up the flower beds, the blue-blue sea stretching out as far as the eyes can see. It gorgeous. Honeymoon, that is what this place is made for.

Henry say, 'Pao tell me Marilyn Monroe and Henry Miller come here for their honeymoon as well.'

'Who is Henry Miller?'

'Her husband?'

'The photograph standing on the piano in there say Arthur Miller.'

'Arthur Miller? Pao say it was Henry. I remember because it my name. Henry.'

'The bottom of the photograph say Arthur.'

'Arthur?'

'Arthur.'

It quiet between us for a while and then he say, 'Last night. What happen. And the night before that. We never need mention. Not even between you and me. A mistake. Too much rum and night air.'

We sit on the terrace while Henry order up some rum punch, which come on a little silver tray carried by a waiter in a white jacket. It was class, even though the waiter look sideways at me when he put the glasses on the table. And then he look at Henry and I could see in his eyes what he thought was between us. Me, a black woman, with a old Chinese man in a place like this. Who wouldn't want to make something out of that?

When the waiter gone Henry say, 'Too much shame inside your head, Gloria. Too much disapproval and doubt. Waiter not think nothing at all. He just serve drinks.'

What I know for sure is that Fay wouldn't have bothered herself. She would have just sit here in the necklace and smile, and admire the view while she drink her punch. And as for whether it was Arthur or Henry, she wouldn't have give a damn.

CHAPTER 17

WHEN I GET back I decide it time to stop. I not going tek no more customers. Sybil say it up to me what I want to do.

'What yu think I should say to Beryl and Marcia?'

'What yu want to say?'

I think on it. 'That everybody got to do what she think is right for her. We got choices now. Not like how it was before.'

'Before Henry's money yu mean?'

I nod. 'Yu think they going see it as me disapproving of them?'

'Gloria, every woman makes her choices. Should I feel criticised by what you do?'

So I tell them and they wounded but they don't say nothing. And then Sybil just stand up and say, 'When I start out in this business it was my liberation. Freedom from the shackles of bowing down to some man. So let us not go put chains on each other now.'

A couple days afterwards Sybil say she want me come do something with her.

'Me?'

'This not no job for Beryl.'

I got the next question on the tip a my tongue but I can see she not fixing to tek no more queries. She just waiting for a simple yes or no.

When we get there it a butcher shop in Cross Roads. Sybil walk through the place and give the man a nod like she know him and then she go behind the counter and tek some back steps up to a landing with a toilet yu can smell soon as yu pass it and little further down the corridor she open the door and I see him laying there in the bed wid his big feet sticking out the end. Dry and cracking. And black, like the rest a him. A full-size African wid giant hands that pulling up the sheet under his neck.

'Junior tell me yu sick bad.'

'Yes, bad-bad. It good to see yu, girl.' And he smile, showing off teeth that shiny and even, not coarse like his voice.

'Never yu mind good to see me. What is it yu want?'

'Wait yu hurry nuh. Yu cyan tek two minutes to exchange a how yu do?'

'I can see how yu do Isaac. I don't need no two minutes to do that.'

Sybil walk 'cross the room and pick up a shirt and pair a pants off the chair. She do it with her two fingers pinch together like she would prefer not to be touching them at all. And then she drop them on the floor, and dust off the chair before she sit down.

'So who dis?' And he motion his head towards me.

'That is no concern a yours. She wid me. That is all yu need to know.'

'Yu mean yu cyan even come see me without yu bring protection? After all these years, Sybil? And me in dis condition? What yu think I going do to yu?'

'Isaac, I didn't come here to have no chinwag wid yu. The boy tell me yu sick and want see me so here I am.'

'So where Beryl? She nuh want see me? She nuh care how I almost at death's door?'

Sybil sigh hefty and then she reach in her purse and pull out a cigarette and light it.

'Yu got a ashtray in here?'

He raise up his arm and point to the little table in the corner. So she get up and go over there and search under the newspaper and 'round the plates a leftover food and empty beer bottles and some odd socks and receipts and a can a Campbell's chicken soup and a couple pencils and a bottle opener and two spoons and some loose change until she find it, so full up that she couldn't even pick it up without spilling ash and a few dead butts. All this time I am still standing in the doorway.

'Yu nuh worry 'bout causing a fire?'

'What fire? Anyway, is only me and few pigs and cows in here and dem dead already.'

She tek the ashtray and sit back in the chair. I say to her, 'Yu want maybe I go wait downstairs?'

'You stay right there. This not going tek long.' And then she turn to Isaac and say, 'So what yu want?'

'I bad sick well over three weeks now. Just lying here sweating in dis bed. So the man downstairs not paying me no wages and I falling behind wid the rent and not got nothing to pay for the medicine I need.'

'Yu go to the hospital?'

'I cyan go to no hospital! I can barely raise myself to go tek a piss. I cyan do nothing, girl. Not even fix no food. All I got is the little soup and leftover him downstairs bring me when him feel like it. I wasting away here, girl.'

'So how yu know what medicine yu need?'

'I know. Believe me. I know.'

Sybil look 'round the room with her nose turn up and that is right because the place stink not just from the stench a raw meat that wafting up from down below but the heavy air a sweat and dirty clothes.

'Yu not got nobody to come see to yu, Isaac?' She wait but he don't say nothing. He just look at her like she should know better than to be asking him a thing like that. 'I not going tek yu in, Isaac. That is the last thing I would do.'

'It not that. But if yu could find yu way to leave me some money him downstairs know a woman can come by daily to help me out. That is all I need, girl. That is all.'

I hear the pleading in his voice and I see the determination in her face and I can tell these two got history, and it hurtful and ugly.

'So how much money yu want?'

'Whatever yu can spare, girl. But I need it regular 'til I can get back on my feet.'

She laugh, good and loud. ''Til yu get back on yu feet! Yu joking? Knowing you, Isaac, yu will be laying here playing dead 'til hell freeze over. No man. I am not the fool yu tek me for. I never was.'

'Sybil, yu cyan see the pitiful condition I am in?'

She tek a long look at him while she crush out the cigarette in the ashtray. And then she get up and walk over to the table and put it down in the mess where she find it.

'What say I should even help yu anyway given everything yu do to me?'

'Ah Sybil, girl, that was such a long time back. Yu nuh think enough water already pass under that bridge?'

She reach into her purse and pull out some bills and put them on the table. Still standing there with her back to him.

'That is it, Isaac. I not going give yu another shilling. Yu going have to reach out to somebody else after this. I sure there is plenty other women yu got to lean on.' Then she turn to him and say, 'The money on the table just the same way yu show me all them years back.'

She close her purse and come over to me and rest her hand on my shoulder to turn me 'round and we walk back down the stairs.

'Yu not worried 'bout the poor condition he in?'

'Isaac? Not a damn thing wrong wid him. I seen it all before, Gloria. He will be back on his feet ruining women again in no time. Believe me.'

Then she say for us to go get something to drink. So we jump on the Constant Spring bus to Half Way Tree and mek our way to York Pharmacy.

We walk up the stairs to the soda fountain and sitting there in the booth she say, 'Yu wondering what all that about?'

'I only wondering if yu want to tell me. Otherwise that is between you and Isaac . . . and Beryl.'

She twirl the ice cream 'round on top of the cream soda.

'Isaac used to run Trench Town. Back in his day. He used to supply things, yu know, that people need. Yu want a cook pot, a frock, a hat, a pair of shoes. Even food. Isaac could get it for yu. So everybody owe him. Not just money, but favours, if yu get what I mean. So one way or another yu pay. Not always immediately, but sooner or later. Sooner or later yu pay, one way or another. That is how it was. And people so poor they couldn't do nothing else but deal with Isaac.' She stop mess with the soda and light a cigarette. 'Then one day my mother owe him so much money he tell her he wanted me.'

'To have sex wid yu?'

'No. He wanted her to give me to him.'

'Give yu to him? Like you his property?'

She nod her head. 'So that is what she do. She give me to Isaac. I was thirteen years old, cooking and cleaning and washing his clothes while he go about his business or just lay on the nasty couch he had or sit outside in the yard drinking a beer and smoking a cigarette or maybe some weed. And when he feel like it, or couldn't track down any a the grown women he was running, I do the other thing as well.'

She spin 'round and stare at the three schoolgirls making a ruckus settling themselves in the booth behind her. When she turn back I see her eyes wet. Just little bit. Not like she crying as such. Just moist. She tek her finger and wipe them dry and then she say, 'That is how it gwaan 'til one day he decide to bring back some man wid him from the bar. Well it wasn't just one a dem, it was two. And all three a dem drunk as lords.'

I reach out and rest my hand on hers as her fingers drumming on the table, and she gazing off into the distance wid the tears slowly rolling down her cheeks.

'And afterwards they put the money on the table and I become one a Isaac's regulars. And then one day he turn up wid Beryl.' She tek the paper napkin and wipe her eyes. 'But Beryl younger than me, and she timid. So he beat her. He beat on her for anything. Anything at all, but mostly because he feel bad in himself. And when he drunk, he beat her worse. So right from the beginning I was trying to look out for her the best I could because funny thing was, he never lay a finger on me that way.

Maybe he never expect me to grow up so sturdy. I think he was fraid of me. God knows why. All I know is he used to say, "Don't look at me that way, girl," and then he would go beat Beryl. It mek me feel bad. Guilty. Because when I look at him all I was thinking was yu can do anything to me yu want but yu never going own me like yu think yu do. That was the only thing in my mind that keep me going.'

I want to say to her, 'Sybil, yu sure yu want to be telling me all a this?' but I don't say it. I just sit there with my heart breaking over what she been through, and Beryl too. And feeling bad that I mek such a fuss over the necklace and realising that everybody got a story to tell 'bout how life been cruel to them. Everybody got their pain and mine wasn't no worse than anybody else. It wasn't even special. It was ordinary. The ordinary life of a woman who happen to be born black and poor.

'How yu get away from him Sybil?'

'One day, I don't know what come over me but I just tell Beryl to come and we walk out. We just tek off.' And she laugh. 'That is how easy it was. Because he never even bother to lock the door or nothing. So yu see, being Isaac's prisoner was all in our own minds. Four long years I stay with Isaac when at any time I could have just leave.' She smile. 'Funny that.'

'And he never come after yu?'

'Yes, he come and he find us too, in the little room we rent from a old woman over Jones Town. And all he do is stand up in the doorway and laugh. Yu know what he say to us? He say, "There's plenty more where you come from." That was all. And then he turn 'round and walk off still laughing to himself.'

She not crying no more, Sybil. She released. And just so, she start drink the soda. Then she say, 'The whole thing tek me and Beryl different. That is why I couldn't tek her over there with me today. But I didn't want to go there on my own. Yu understand that?'

I just nod my head and pat her hand.

'Beryl hate Isaac for what he do to her. Vengeful hating. Me? I see him for what he is. A sorry excuse for a man. And as for what he do to me. That was a education.'

When we on the bus going back to Franklyn Town I say to her, 'Why yu bother go up Cross Roads and give him the money?'

'For Junior. I do it for Junior.'

'A who that anyway?'

'Junior? That is a very good question. Yu know, I never see nothing a Isaac for years and then one day, just sudden like that, he show up at the house wid this baby in his arms saying the mother leave it on the doorstep a the butchers and he dunno what to do wid it.'

'Is his baby?'

'So he say. But the mother? God knows. And knowing Isaac it could have been any of a dozen women he busy sexing at the time. So what? Who that baby ever hurt, eh? And sure as eggs is eggs Isaac wasn't no fit father. So I tek it to the orphanage the Sisters got in South Camp Road and leave it there. That was maybe three years back.'

'And yu go visit him?'

'That boy not got a single soul in this world that give one damn about him. Two hours a my time once a week that is all he got.'

'Yu never think maybe yu keep him yuself?'

'Me? What would I do wid a baby, the life I got? Crying and messing up the place and taking everybody's time and worry. And anyway, what would I want with the seed a Isaac under my roof?' She pause and then she say, 'Beryl would have kill me. Can yu imagine?' And she laugh. She laugh so much she nearly fall down the steps a the bus as we getting off.

Walking down the road I say to her, 'Yu ever see yu mother again?'

'One time. When I go over her house in Trench Town she just look at me like she didn't even recognise me. So I say, "Is me, Mama. Sybil." And she just carry on stirring the pea soup like she didn't have nothing to say to me. So I leave and I never go back again.'

When we reach the house I go find Beryl in the kitchen and I say to her, 'I sorry 'bout the commotion I cause over the necklace.'

She sour at first. But then her face melt. 'I should a pay more mind to where yu get it from.'

She sitting 'cross the table from me. And with me standing there it seem like a big, broad wooden barrier was between us. Not that me and Beryl do hugging. That is not how we are. But still, it feel like something else was needed. So I say, 'I had no right to tek out my hurt on you.'

'I would have hurt just the same way, darling. What stop me from seeing that was my own selfishness knowing that no man would ever gift me a thing like that.'

When I turn 'round I see Marcia leaning on the doorpost.

'Yu going apologise to me as well?'

But before I could say anything Beryl butt in. 'Enough is enough.'

CHAPTER 18

SIX MONTHS LATER I shocked when the doctor tell me I am pregnant even though I already know it in myself. It just startling to get it confirm like that. I dunno how I going tell Pao. What his reaction going be. And then I think, actually, it no matter. Is my baby. If he want something to do with it then fine. If not, that is fine as well. It not like I depending on him for anything. I am a woman of independent means. I can do just about anything I please whatever Yang Pao got to say 'bout it.

Harder than telling him was telling everybody in the house. Things been better these last few months never mind Marcia blowing hot and cold with me as the mood tek her. Even Auntie stop professing 'bout wickedness and damnation. She not even complaining no more 'bout the rudeness of the bus driver or the high price of rice. She is going about her business like her lips been stitch together down the hospital and the only time she open her mouth is to tell somebody she going to town or she want clothes put out for the next-day laundry.

When I tell them 'bout the baby they just sit there in the kitchen. Then Marcia say, 'Yu tell him yet?'

And I say no.

'It a accident or yu plan it?' I stand there expecting that maybe Sybil and Beryl would say something but they don't.

So I say, 'It no matter whether it plan or accident. It here.'

'So yu going keep it?' I look at Sybil and I remember how she tell me she couldn't have no baby crying and messing up the place. And I think how I going miss sitting on the veranda on a Sunday and dancing and laughing 'bout the clumsy oaf that come in here and how she talk 'bout every woman being a whore, and how the government not doing nothing to help the real poor in this country or change the colour bar so that maybe a black woman could have some ambition or even hope.

'Yes, I going keep it.'

The three a them just sit there with Auntie watching from the corner making like she busy-busy with her mending but who yu know for sure is keeping quiet pace with every single word.

'So what going happen?'

'I don't know yet Marcia. We have to figure it out.'

Few days later Pao come give me a jade ring. It match the necklace, which, after I come back from Ocho Rios, I put back in the box and stick in my wardrobe. But the ring I put straight on my finger. I don't know why. And I admire it with my arm stretch out because it so elegant and fit perfect. I was going ask him what he bring me this for, but I decide against it as there was something more important to tell him.

So I say, 'I have something to tell you.'

And he say, 'What?' So I tell him 'bout the baby. He shocked. Rigid he was, like maybe I just get through telling him something impossible and he cyan believe it.

And then he start asking all sorta questions 'bout how long I know and what I going do with it.

'Yu mean get rid of it?'

'No. I mean what you want to do? You want to keep it or what?'

'What you want to do?'

'It not got nothing to do with me, Gloria. Is not my baby, is yours.'

'Yu nuh know it take two people to make a baby?'

'Yu saying it mine? How yu so sure?' I nuh feel like explaining nothing to him 'bout how long it is since I last tek a customer. So I just say all right is my baby and I will go about my own business.

But then he want to change his mind. 'If you say the baby mine, then it mine.' And then he start talking 'bout how I going have to move house and let him tek care a me, and stop teking customers because this is not no business for a pregnant woman.

So I just laugh and say to him, 'Some men come on strong with a pregnant woman.'

But he nuh like it. 'Not on top of my son.'

'Who say it going be a boy? Maybe it be a girl. Maybe she become the first woman prime minister of Jamaica.'

Pao not that often right 'bout anything to do with me, but this time he know something without even knowing it. I got to move outta the house. Not because he want me to but because I couldn't see myself forcing everybody to live in a situation that Sybil already tell me she wouldn't choose for herself.

When I go tell them Marcia get up and flounce out the kitchen.

'Yu sure yu doing the right thing?' But I don't say nothing back to Sybil so she say, 'Is Yang Pao idea? Him want yu to do it?'

'Yu nuh think it better?'

'What is better is for a baby to have people 'round it. People to look after it and mek sure it OK.' She surprise me. I never expected Beryl to have anything to say 'bout what the baby need.

'I just reckon everybody will be happier without a baby crying and carrying on all hours a the day and night, and diapers hanging all over the place.'

'So who going look after it? You?'

And then I hear this voice come from behind me that I didn't even know was there.

'I will. That is if yu want me to come wid yu?'

So I turn 'round and say to her, 'Thank yu Auntie.'

And Sybil say, 'Yu shouldn't tek it upon yuself to decide what going mek other people happy.'

I didn't say nothing to her. I was still grateful for how she ease my way with Beryl and Marcia when I wanted to get outta the business. And anyway, I reckon she must remember what she said to me 'bout Junior.

Afterwards when I catch her alone I say, 'What about the baby messing up the place and teking everybody's time?'

'Yu doing the right thing, Gloria. This not no place to be bringing up a child. I going miss yu that is all.'

'Yu don't have to miss me. Wherever I go will only be up the road little bit.' I pause and then I say, 'Anyway, I probably be back over here every other day. Yu think I not going miss you too?'

Fay pregnant as well. Pao sheepish when he tell me but I still glad he come and do it and not leave me to get the news from Henry. I cyan believe he get the two of us pregnant at the same time.

His idea is for me to get a house up in Barbican. It all new up there. It safe. I don't know if that is for me, especially after he tek it on himself to go pick it out. So I going here and there all over Kingston, and for her own reason Marcia decide to come help me look. I grateful for the company and even though we nuh say too much at least we together. It like we sisters again and maybe that is as much healing as we can manage right now.

But despite everything the house we find in Barbican perfect. Three bedrooms, two bathrooms, tidy little yard out back with some grass and fruit trees and a shady veranda.

I decide to write to Mama. It time. But what I going say after all these years? So I think I keep it short in case maybe she nuh want hear nothing from me. I just say me and Marcia all right, and that I got a new house and a baby on the way. That was all. I reckon if she interested she going write back and if I nuh hear nothing then I will know how she feel.

I have the baby in the public hospital downtown because Pao want me to go in the private one up Hope Road even though Fay laying up there making out like this is the most trying thing anybody ever been asked to do. He say he going pay, which is what he said about the house, and I told him no, I got enough money I save over the years. Quizzical he was, like as to say how come yu have so much money, but he didn't say nothing and I didn't offer no explanation. Me and Henry business got nothing to do with him.

When it finally happen it wasn't what I expected. I didn't even know it was a girl 'til they put her in my arms and I lift up the blanket to see. I stare into her face trying to make out this little human being that I think should be familiar to me after this long time the two of us been wrapped together. But it wasn't so because what I saw wasn't any person I had ever seen before. Not even in a dream. And even though she African through and through with skin as dark as mine and a head of curly black hair, she was also Chinese with the little telltale in the eyes and lips thinner than you would expect. She was beautiful. A small bundle of individual who was going to get an education and have all the choices I didn't have. A woman who was going to be free to make of this life what she will.

Sybil and Beryl come to the hospital with Marcia and Auntie. And they love the baby and fuss her.

'What we going call her?'

And I say, 'Esther.'

'What, after Mama?' I just smile. And Marcia smile back, a genuine warm-hearted smile, which is the first time she do that since I can't remember when.

Marcia got the baby rocking in her arms whispering to her, 'Baby Esther, this is your Aunt Marcia, remember that.'

When we get back to the house Marcia tell me that Mama and Babs coming to town to see me. 'They hear the baby come and they going tek the bus from Savanna-la-Mar tomorrow.'

I can't tek in what she saying to me.

So she say, 'I send them a telegram.'

I wait a minute and then I say, 'I write her a letter yu know, but she never write back to me.'

'That was because yu never say nothing to her and she didn't know what she should be saying to you.'

'Yu know 'bout it?'

'She tell me in a letter I get little while back.'

'Yu been writing to her? Since when?'

Over the top a the baby in her arms she say, 'Since I run from Miss Vilma and yu send me back and I didn't have nobody to tell how I feel so I start write to her.'

'And she write back?' Marcia just nod her head.

'She never ask yu nothing 'bout how come I nuh write to her?'

'I tell her yu busy and that yu say for me to keep her up to date.'

'Yu tell her everything that gwaan?'

'No, but she not no fool, Gloria. That is one thing she is not.'

When Mama come I realise that it was fourteen years since I see her. And in truth she almost look like a stranger to me. So much had happened in that time. I wasn't a child no more. I was a woman living a life completely different from the one she knew or the one I expected.

She come in the house and hug and kiss Marcia but she didn't know what to do with me. She just stood there across the room with the little gifts in her hand and never take one step towards me. All she do was reach out her arm until Auntie come and take the things from her and she turn and throw herself 'round Auntie in a genuine act of gladness at the sight of her.

When they finish I just say, 'Thank yu for coming Mama.'

And she say, 'Yu all right? Di baby all right?'

And I say, 'Yes.'

And that was it. The moment was gone because the next thing I know she was sitting down with the coffee cup in her hand and Beryl was serving cake.

Auntie proud-proud. She 'Esther this and Esther that'. Every little thing Esther do she want show and tell. Plus with Marcia, Sybil and Beryl it some gathering of women that is for sure.

Late evening Mama come out on the veranda when I out there taking in some night air. She sidung there in the dark with me and for some long time she nuh say nothing.

So I say to her, 'Yu all right?'

She breathe three slow deep breath and then she say, 'I not going ask yu no question 'bout what gwaan here all these years. I reckon if yu wanted me to know the two a yu would a tell me by now. It enough for me to see that yu alive and well and got yuself a good home. I not even going ask yu 'bout the baby papa. That is your business. I would be the last one to talk 'bout who is anybody papa.' She stop.

So I ask her, 'Yu want me to fetch yu something cool to drink?'

'No, I want yu to just sit there a minute and listen to me.' She pause. Then she say, 'Yu a mother now, Gloria, to a beautiful baby girl that yu pleasure me by calling Esther. So I thank yu for that. It is a honour. Truly.' She wait a little before she carry on. 'Being a mother is a very important thing. Yu know that? It is a very special bond yu have wid that little one. She is your life now.'

'What all this about Mama?'

'Bear wid me.' I wait.

'Yu know how yu always use to joke 'bout Marcia being my favourite daughter? Well, she not my favourite, but she was my first born.'

I turn full 'round and face her in the half-light coming from the street lamp.

'I raise yu like my own, but yu not.'

My mind was swirling. 'Yu mean after all these years yu going tell me that somebody else my real mama?'

'Gloria, I didn't born yu but yu as much mine as if I did.'

'So who born me?'

She move her head like she motioning inside the house. But I cyan see what she doing in the dim light, so I get up and walk over to her.

'What yu just do wid yu head?'

And she just say, almost in a whisper, 'It Auntie.'

The whole a me freeze to the spot. And then I just say to her, 'I don't believe yu.'

'I wouldn't mek up a thing like that, Gloria. Why would I do that? I telling yu now because I think it time. Yu have little Esther now and I think yu will understand why it important that yu know. Is Auntie that the real grandmother, not me. She deserve to have that blessing, especially now the two a yu in the house together wid the baby. Yu cyan understand that?'

I stare at her firm and hard like maybe if I look with enough conviction I would be able to see the truth.

'Why she nuh keep me?'

'That is for you and Auntie. She got to be the one to explain everything to yu.' She wait and then she say, 'She had her reasons I can tell yu that.'

'So the day yu tell me my papa die, who was that?'

'That was yu papa for real, Gloria. But yu have to talk to Auntie 'bout that.'

When I go back inside I didn't say nothing to nobody. I just look at Auntie with the baby in her arms and she look back at me like nothing different, so I wonder if she know 'bout what Mama tell me on the veranda. And then she shift her eyes off me and start talk to Beryl and I think to myself that one day I will be ready to ask her all the questions that only now is coming into my head. But that day is not now. That day I got to prepare for.

★   ★   ★

170

A week later after everybody go back to country Pao turn up. He bring some peanut brittle but since Esther only two weeks old I think maybe it for me so I just say thank yu and I rest it on the table.

He stand there like a loose end and then he say, 'I glad to see yu get yuself some help anyway.'

'What yu talking 'bout?'

'The old woman there.' And he motion his head toward the kitchen.

'Yu mean Auntie?'

'That what yu call her? Well whatever, good yu have some help.' And after a while he say, 'Especially with the baby and all.'

Then he walk over to the cot and peer into it with his hands hold firm behind his back.

'Baby girl, eh?'

'Yes.'

He stand there a minute looking at her and then he sit down.

'Yu want pick her up?'

He think on it and then he say, 'No, it OK. She sleeping sound.' After that he think some more and say, 'I don't know nothing 'bout babies, Gloria. It best you be the one to do wid it.'

'Yu don't have to know nothing. Yu just sit there and I will rest her in your arms.'

So he reposition himself fixed and steady in the chair and hold out his arms. I pick up the baby and place her head in the crook of his elbow and he sit there as still as a statue with that same concentration I see before on his tai chi face. And then he start to cry. Just a slow little trickle that was running down his cheek.

'So this is our baby eh, Gloria? You and me. I never dreamed in my life I could make anything so beautiful.'

Then he tek his little finger and put it near her lips and she open her mouth and draw it in and suck. He sit there looking down at her almost like his heart wasn't even beating except I could see that it was. It was. Beating, and full of a joy he never could have imagined.

'Did yu ever think a this, Gloria? All them years back?'

'No.'

'Me neither.'

And it was then, with him sitting there holding Esther in his arms and crying, that I see the love that was in him and feel the contentment that was in me and realise that regardless of what happen before me and him had created one perfect moment.

The next week I feel bad when Henry tell me that Fay have a baby boy but the labour hard. I was ashamed of the meanness of my thoughts towards her laying up there in the private hospital. Because the way Henry tell it she had blood pressure so bad they start think she going get epileptic. And she was pushing but the baby breech and wasn't coming and finally when he mek it, the child blue from head to toe. And how the doctor think the two of them was going die. And how they have to call another doctor to come sew her up because she tear so bad. It made me feel guilty that Esther come so easy. And for the first time I actually feel sorry for her, Fay.

When Pao come by he say he call the baby boy Xiuquan after Zhang Xiuquan.

So I say, 'That is good to honour Zhang like that. He been like a true father to yu.'

'Zhang been everything to me. Ever since I was a boy. I owe him.'

'I know that.'

'If it wasn't for Zhang I wouldn't be nobody.'

So I just say it again, 'I know that.' And I think to myself that baby, being a boy and name after Zhang, and from his legal married wife, always going mean more to him than little Esther, sleeping so sound in her cot.

CHAPTER 19

TWO YEARS SINCE Esther born and Pao still come over the house. But not so regular. It a different thing now because since Esther come I reckon it time for him to stop paying. That was my way to make it more like family.

'Stop paying? Yu sure that is what yu want?'

'Yes, I sure.'

He think a little while and then he say, 'That mek things different between us.'

And with his back to me and the money in his hand, he reach into his pocket for the roll he always carry and fold the bills back on to the wad. Then he turn to face me and say, 'Yu still going tek other customers?'

'Pao, I not been doing that for a very long time. That was how come I know for sure Esther was your baby.'

He want to smile but he stop himself. And then he turn 'round and walk out and just as he reach the door he say, 'It wouldn't a matter yu know. She your baby and that is good enough for me.'

But even so, he can't hardly bring himself to pay Esther no mind. He don't even seem to notice how she growing into a bright

174

and cheerful little girl. And how she happy to see him every time he set foot in the house. Rushing up to him with her arms outstretched like she expecting something. And how, if yu tek away her black skin, is him she resemble not me, with the little nose and pout 'round her mouth. All he can manage is to say a good morning or afternoon to her. That is all.

Me, he happy to talk to 'bout how excited he is because the newly crown Queen Elizabeth coming to Jamaica for two days on her way to Australia and he done get a invitation to some big reception at Kings House for Fay's mama and her little sister to go meet her. Why he think I should care about any of this I don't know. Especially since I tell him right after he go marry Fay that I didn't want to hear nothing about her.

I intrigued by the high society he moving in though, so I say to him, 'Where yu get the invitation?'

And he say, 'Clifton Brown.'

'Yu mean the police sergeant?'

'What is it wid you and this policeman?'

'What yu mean?'

'What I mean? Every time I mention the man it like yu jumping on hot coals. Yu nuh know that?'

I think on it and then I say, 'I just don't understand how come you and him so tight.'

'What did I say to you? I say I would get that man to do a thing or two for me. That is what I say and that is what I do. And all that hullabaloo over Ho and the mix-up in North Parade and everything else. Gone. Every little misunderstanding taken care of. That is Clifton Brown doing his job fighting corruption downtown. Handy and reliable, that is Clifton. Plus, he know how to keep his mouth shut. So that mek him just about the most perfect policeman yu could have the good fortune to come across.' And then he start strutting 'round the room like he vex with the conversation. 'Anyway, what is it to you?'

I don't feel like I want to say nothing to him so I just let the silence rest between us.

Then he say, 'How Esther doing?'

'She fine.'

'Good.' And just so, he turn 'round and leave.

Esther is fine all right with Auntie doing everything for her. She need feeding, changing, putting down to rest, soothing, entertaining, Auntie is here. And in between seeing to the baby she is cooking and shopping and cleaning and doing everything that need doing.

I say to her, 'Auntie, yu want us get some help? Yu don't have to be taking on to yuself every scrap a everything that need doing yu know.'

'Yu cyan just leave me to do what meking me happy?'

So I let it pass. I know that she not just doing this for Esther. She doing it to make up for all the years she wasn't my mother. All the years she feel she owe me. And I grateful. Because without Auntie it would be just me here trying to be a mother, trying to understand how to make Esther feel like she belong just like how Mama never do for me. But even though Auntie so attentive day to day, I would hate for Esther to think I nuh love her. God forbid that she should grow up like me, feeling alone and deserted. So every night when I say goodnight to her and wish her a peaceful sleep I bend over and stroke her hair and whisper 'I love you' and hope she will remember that sound in her ear for as long as she lives. And know that I love her. Love her with such a determination that I will never give up. Not like what Auntie do to me.

*　　*　　*

Next time Marcia come over the house she sitting on the veranda leaning down playing with the baby crawling 'round her feet. So I tek some cool lemonade out there and I settle down in a chair across the way from her.

'It good of yu to keep coming here to see Esther. She enjoy the time she have wid yu and it mean a lot to me as well.'

She look up at me. 'She my only niece. What else would I do?'

'I just saying it good of yu that is all.'

She ease back in the chair and tek a sip a lemonade. 'Things not the same over the house since yu gone.'

'No?'

'No. It different wid three. Especially since, well, Sybil and Beryl go a long way back together and even though they ask me if I want to join in wid them when they buy the house from Pops I didn't feel like it was what I wanted.' She wait a minute. 'Wid you and Auntie there it was more like family. Now it more like, well, what it is.'

'Yu nuh happy there Marcia?'

She think on it and then she say, 'I am as happy there as I reckon I going be anywhere. I don't think me and happiness going mek likely companions.'

I can see the sadness deep inside of her. It not loneliness like me. It more empty than that. Like a void. Like there is nothing there beyond the body that everyone can see.

'Yu want come live here?'

She laugh. 'Here? Where I going sleep? In the backroom wid Auntie squash up in the bed? Or maybe under the table in there.'

I get up and move my chair closer to her. 'I never mean for yu life to turn out this way. When we come to town it was because I didn't know what else to do.'

She reach down and fiddle with a couple a the little wooden shapes Esther busy fitting into the slots. The red square in here, the green triangle in there, the yellow circle in this one. And while she still bending down she say, 'There wasn't nothing else to do. I didn't blame you for nothing to do wid that.'

'So what yu blame me for?'

She look up. 'I never say I blame yu for anything. What happen is what happen. Moving in with Sybil and Beryl, the sailor, and everything. It happen. It done. No use crying over that.'

I sit there a long while watching her make funny faces trying to amuse the child. Then Esther smile and hold up her arms to Marcia and say, 'Up.' So Marcia lift her on to her lap and start bouncing her up and down while Esther throwing her head back and laughing.

And then she turn to me and say, 'I don't know what to say except I sorry how I treat yu over the necklace.' She wait and then she say, 'I was angry wid yu. Angry that yu a better person than the rest a us. Because no matter what happen there always seem to be some goodness inside yu that mek you right. No matter how shocking things get.'

'I am not good Marcia.'

'No? But yu still all right, Gloria. Yu still know who yu are. Me, I got no idea. Every day I just tek the next customer and once in a while I come over here and look at you and Esther and Auntie living like yu normal and for a few hours I forget. But that is all, because then I go back to Franklyn Town and it all start over again.'

Marcia turn to Esther and start playing with her fingers like incy wincy spider but even though Esther usually like it, right now she not interested. She want to come to me so I get up and go take her. And right then Auntie step out and say maybe Esther need to go get her afternoon nap, so she take her from me and go back inside.

'Yu got Esther. Yu a mother. Yu even got Pao for what that is worth, and yu have a home. Yu life change. I don't know what it would tek for my life to change.'

'One day it will Marcia. Who knows, maybe yu go back to school and learn something to get yuself a good job. Or maybe yu meet somebody.'

'Really? Doing what I do?' She drink some lemonade and I drink some too.

We quiet. Then I say, 'I am so sorry, Marcia. Sorry for everything. Sorry for the mess I get yu in when I beat Barrington and bring yu here to Kingston and Franklyn Town. All of it. It was my doing.'

'It was my doing as well. The two a us did what we had to. Anyway, that is all in the past. I am a grown woman now. Have been for a very long time. So the situation I am in is my responsibility. Nobody else but me.'

'I am here too. Your sister. Remember that.'

I see the tears welling up inside her, but nothing come and we fall quiet again.

Then she say, 'That policeman, the one that come knocking on the door the day we arguing over the necklace. He come back.'

'For me?'

'No, that part funny because it seem he already know yu move.'

'So what he want?'

'Him nuh say. He just come and sit down and stare at me like there is something he think I got to give him.'

'He come from Montego Bay yu know.'

'How yu know that?'

'Pao. The two a them tight-tight.'

'For real?'

Marcia quiet a minute and then she say, 'Yu know that bwoy Milton that Pao got working for him? He been hanging 'round the house every week when Hampton come to collect the money. He just stand there in the doorway while Hampton drinking so much rum he can hardly walk straight. It a wonder he nuh fall down flat on his little baby face.'

'Yu think maybe Milton know something?'

'They all a them know everything. That is how they are. But Finley and Hampton wouldn't never tell yu nothing. Only Milton young enough and innocent enough to maybe let something slip.'

A few weeks later Marcia tell me that when Pao tek Milton on it was for the sole purpose a following Clifton Brown.

'So what he see?'

'He didn't see nothing because in no time at all the sergeant grab him in a alley and had him bent over a barrel with his pants down threatening the worse and telling him he wanted to see his boss. And Milton so fraid he never tell Yang Pao for two whole months, meanwhile Clifton was going about his business free and easy.'

'So what happen?'

'Clifton go meet with Yang Pao at the Blue Lagoon bar and they mek some deal, and next thing Clifton in the fold doing what Pao want him to do and taking his cut.' Marcia pause. 'Milton say Clifton Brown all right though. He a good man. Trustworthy. Reliable. He say everything going fine with Clifton.'

'How come Milton tell yu all a this?' She just ease back in the chair with a satisfied smile on her face.

I telephone Mr Chen in the grocery store I used to work at back home in country.

'Gloria, such a long time since me nuh hear from yu, though yu mother keeping me abreast. How yu going girl?'

'I am fine and well Mr Chen. Thank yu. I have a little dawta now I name Esther after Mama.'

'That is good, Gloria. Very good.'

And then I ask him if he remember back all those years after Barrington Maxwell get killed and the name of the policeman that come from Montego Bay, because everybody was talking 'bout waiting for the man to come.

'Ah Gloria, that was when yu leave us so sudden. They enquire after you yu know. Even tek yu mother to the police station but nobody would say a word about what happen to yu and yu sista even though they know yu tek the bus to Kingston. So in the end they just forget about it.'

'Yu cyan remember the name a the policeman?'

'No, not the sergeant but I can find out for yu if yu want. I remember the young constable that come wid him though because it was that little whippersnapper Clifton Brown who spend all his time worrying my chickens in the yard chasing dem dis way and dat just for fun. And every day I would talk to his mother but it wouldn't do the damnedest bit a good.'

'Mr Chen, yu saying Clifton Brown was a bwoy near to where yu live?'

'Right next door, Gloria. Right next door. Live there 'til his mother die and then later he go join the police in Mo Bay. You most likely nuh remember him because he a fair bit older than you.'

Then after that, Marcia tell me that Beryl go get Hampton so drunk he got no idea what he saying, and tell her that Clifton Brown a battyman. That he and Pao catch Clifton in a alley one night wid some bwoy and that is how come Pao hire Milton to follow him and then go mek the deal so Clifton got to do what Yang Pao say. But, according to Hampton, none a them care 'bout the battyman thing because he a good man Clifton, and it reassuring to have him on their side.

And then she say, 'Beryl say to tell yu that she do that for yu to make up for what happen over the necklace.'

After Marcia finish visit with Esther and leave I telephone Beryl and thank her. And she just say, 'It nothing.'

'It not nothing Beryl. I know that.'

'That good a yu. But yu nuh owe me nothing. It was the least I could do after all what happen.'

I can see Clifton Brown got a situation and how that would wind him up with Pao, but that still don't explain what he want with me. So I find the piece a card he give me that day on the front step in Franklyn Town and I ring the police station. They say he not there and I must leave a message but I don't feel like I want to do that.

It was almost a week a me ringing every other day before I actually get hold of Clifton. When he pick up the telephone he say, 'So you are my mystery woman?'

'What mystery woman would that be?'

'The one that cyan stop ringing the station and getting all these constables into a sweat 'bout what I been up to that have some woman so eager to talk to me. And so private she won't even leave her name nor no message.' I don't say nothing. Then he say, 'I think I must be talking to a Miss Gloria Campbell. Miss Gloria Antoinette Campbell if I am not mistaken.'

And still I don't say nothing, so he say, 'It time we talk. There is a place over Windward Road call Club Havana. It busy-busy at night but early evening not too bad. The food is good as well. How about we catch a bite together? This evening? Six-thirty suit yu?'

And I just say OK and hang up the telephone.

I tek a Checker Cab over there and the place dark and empty except for a barman and one waitress and the Cuban Son playing low in the background. Clifton Brown sitting on a bar stool with a highball glass in his hand full of mint and liquor that later on, when he ask me if I want one, he tell me is a mojito. But I don't want no cocktail not even if, as he say, it a Cuban special.

We go tek a table booth in the corner and I order some Appleton on ice.

'So now, Gloria, what mek yu decide to come find me after this long time?'

'Clifton, I know yu thick with Yang Pao. That is your business. But what is it yu want wid me?'

'Well now, what do you think that could be?'

'If I know I wouldn't be sitting here asking yu.'

The waitress put down the Appleton and look at us. And then she kiss her teeth before she turn 'round and walk off.

'All the waitress in here so facety?'

'Only because she suspect you a business woman working in her bar. Yu know what I mean?'

And I think, yes. After all these years it still the same. One look and they already know all there is to know about me.

'Yu going tell me what yu want or just have me sit here and play yu guessing game?'

'I was in the police station in Montego Bay when a request come through from Kingston for any information we had regarding two young women who skip Petersfield in 1938, maybe in suspicious circumstances. And what we had from the time was an unsolved murder and two missing girls. And when I follow up wid the constables that mek the request, it seem like maybe these two girls had turn up in Kingston. And I thought it curious. Yu see where I am going wid this, Gloria?'

I sip the drink and inspect him over the rim of the glass.

'And wasn't you the little constable they send wid the sergeant from Mo Bay when he come to investigate?'

'I was.'

'So yu going arrest me?'

'Now that is a very good question. What do yu think I should be arresting yu for? What crime you committed, eh Gloria? And was that before yu leave Petersfield or after yu get to Kingston? How should I take my pick?'

'Did yu invite me all the way over here so yu can toy wid me? Or is there something concrete yu got on your mind?'

Clifton taste his mojito and stir it up some more spinning the mint round and round.

'This is the thing, Gloria, evidence. Suspicion I have. Evidence I don't. So what can a man do?'

'What can a man do who is in your position?'

'My position?' And then he think and say, 'Oh yu mean with Yang Pao. Well, Gloria, you need not worry yuself about that. That little arrangement not stopping me from carrying out my other important duties in the Jamaican Constabulary. And chief among those is to bring murders to justice.'

My heart tek a leap and I think I musta physically sit back in the chair from the grin a satisfaction he give me.

'Tell me Clifton, why you and me sitting in a dark nightclub off Windward Road having this conversation when rightly we should be in North Street in one a them little yellow room wid the grey tiles on the floor? Why is that?'

It wipe the smile off his face.

'Gloria, yu smart. I give yu that.' He sit there nodding his head and turning round the drink in the glass. 'This I will tell yu. I don't want to tek yu to the police station to ask yu nuh questions about Barrington Maxwell. But I need to know for sure that there not nobody else I should be looking for. Yu understand what I am saying to yu?'

'I not going sit here and write out no confession for yu sergeant.'

He raise his eyebrows. 'Yu think I should be looking for somebody else in connection wid this or not?'

'That is up to you. But it almost seem like yu don't want to catch the culprit. So why would yu be wasting more a yu time on it?'

'Because this not about catching. It about knowing. Knowing who not to catch.'

'Who not to catch?' I pause and then I say, 'They tell me yu a good man, Clifton Brown. I hope they right.'

CHAPTER 20

NINETEEN FIFTY-FIVE WAS the three-hundredth anniversary of the coming of Penn and Venables. That is what the whole island was celebrating. When the English come and run out the Spanish and claim Jamaica for themself. Beryl and Marcia excited and say we must join in the jubilation and go see the touring Bandwagon show. Sybil, she not interested. She vex. She say we shouldn't be wasting our time making merriment over the British coming here and turning us into a piece of their empire.

'If yu want to go have yuself a good time then celebrate the fact that the People's National Party win the election and Mr Manley become chief minister. Go enjoy clapping and cheering that. And then go put yu back into something that matter because right now there is work to be done to mek Jamaica a better place for everyone.'

This is how Sybil gwaan morning, noon and night. Marcia say she boring the hind legs off everybody in the house. Even Trevor keeping himself quiet next door because he can't take Sybil and her politics in his ear. All he do is come in and give her the money he collecting from the loans and then he is gone with his cut in his pocket.

And when she not in the house telling everybody how things is, she at the PNP meetings in East Kingston where they busy talking 'bout how the English-speaking Caribbean islands going form a single-state federation and get independence from Britain.

Next thing, Henry come tell me that Fay pregnant again. I think it sad that is him have to bring the news but after all it under my instruction that Pao nuh mention Fay to me so I guess that is on me. She have a baby girl they call Mui, but Henry say Fay not happy. She suppose to be living down Matthews Lane with Pao and his mama and Zhang but in truth she spend most her time back up Lady Musgrave Road arguing with Miss Cicely and driving Henry outta the house to Chinatown where he playing mahjong all hours of the day and night. He say the situation real bad up there.

'Now priest come to house all time Fay there. Talk talk, that is all he do. Cicely, she play piano and call down all sort fire and hell and brimstone over what she think bad relation with priest.'

'Yu mean Fay and the priest?'

'I not know what they do. I only know what Cicely think, which, when it come to Fay, is always bad.'

I wait and wait to see what Pao going say to me 'bout the girl child, but him nuh say nothing. It almost like she don't exist. But then it don't seem like there is a lot he got to say 'bout anything except telling me what I already know 'bout how he and Henry Wong in business together running liquor and groceries to the hotels that springing up on the north coast due to the money Jamaica making since they discover the bauxite and all the Americans that want to come down here to catch the sun and rest in the breeze.

And then one day he tell me that he got a doctor if me and the girls or Esther need anything.

'What, yu own personal physician?'

'Yes, Gloria. That is what I am telling yu.'

'So where yu get him from?'

'You don't worry yourself 'bout that. All you got to know is that yu nuh need to be waiting on line at no hospital or paying no more doctor bills. George Morrison going take care a everything.'

When Dr Morrison turn up at Franklyn Town he a big ginger-hair white man with almost see-through skin that burn red from the sun and podgy hands, who tek offence when Beryl call him English and say he is Scottish from Edinburgh. Like that mean anything to us. But he all right, Morrison, even if he like the taste of Appleton a little bit too much for the good teetotal Presbyterian he supposed to be.

The thing about Morrison, though, is cards. So before we know what he is asking me what I think about him running a card club.

'Card club! Yu serious?'

He just sit there and smile like he is talking about the most ordinary thing in the world. Like maybe he just invite me to dinner.

'We cyan have no card club running in the house, doctor. I am sorry.' And then I think on it and I say, 'Unless yu telling me that it Yang Pao the one behind this.'

'No, this would just be a private matter.'

'Well you going to have to take yu private matter somewhere else.'

He tek a sip a rum and gaze out 'cross the street at Miss Sissy rocking there in the chair with the pipe in her mouth. We sit there quiet for a spell until he say, 'I have been thinking about it and it seems that Trevor would be amenable to host the club at his house.'

'Yu mean Trevor next door? And his papa happy for him to be doing this under his roof?'

'So it seems.'

'That is good. You and Trevor go run your card club over there then and leave us outta it.'

'The thing is, Gloria, we need a banker.'

'A banker! Yu can't play cards with yu own money?'

Dr Morrison draw breath before he explain to me in this deep, calm, Scottish voice how regulars would play blackjack against the house and how in time he will organise big-money poker games that players pay a stake to join. And how he going get white men he know from his doctoring and British army soldiers from Up Park Camp and such. So no matter what happen the bank always win.

I listen to him with the same patience he talk to me and then I say, 'You a big-time gambler, doctor? Yu sure yu know what yu doing?'

He just smile like a little bwoy yu catch stealing candy from the store.

'I know about this, Gloria. You can trust me.'

So after I talk to Sybil and she tell me it true 'bout Trevor's eagerness to be doing something more than running 'round town collecting money I say OK. And before we can turn 'round twice men is coming in and outta the house next door and Trevor is serving drinks and the doctor is dealing cards, and we are making money and everybody is happy. Even Pops, who manage to get himself a cut for the convenience of them using his house.

★ ★ ★

When I tell Henry 'bout the card club he just say no.

'It not your business to be saying yes or no. This is our money we using to do this. It got nothing to do wid you. I just telling yu for information that is all.'

'Too much, Gloria. Too much activity. Too much attention.' He strut 'round the room a little to show me how he vex, and then he walk out.

Two minutes later he come back. He stand up in the doorway. 'This English doctor.'

'Scottish.'

He sigh. And then he say, 'This white doctor. He young like you or old like me?'

I cyan believe Henry actually fussing himself over a thing like this.

'It not nothing for you to be worrying yourself about. This is a piece a business. That is all it is. This not cutting across anything to do wid you and me.'

He stand there looking a me for a good while. And then he turn 'round and walk out.

It turn out Dr Morrison got a wife, Margaret, who busy running a house for young mothers downtown. He say it was Margaret that make them come to Jamaica after she see an advertisement in her church newspaper 'bout how good Christian men and women can do charitable work helping us poor and unfortunate people in underdeveloped countries. So she pack up and come here and decide to give her attention to girls who get pregnant and got nobody to care for them.

'I mean very young girls, Gloria. Ten, eleven years old. And she is always in need of help. Jamaican women who can set a good example. Role models if you like.' I just laugh. Laugh out loud at the very thought of it.

'I don't think yu wife will be wanting no help from a woman like me.'

'What kind of woman is that, Gloria? Do you mean kind and caring? Someone who is always looking out for others, her younger sister, her friends, her daughter? Someone who is fair and compassionate in her dealings with people? Someone who understands the black Jamaican woman's experience? Someone who is a constant reminder that goodness can be found in sometimes unexpected places? Is that the kind of woman you mean?'

'Yu not listening to me George. I am a whore. Yu forget that?'

'That was an unfortunate twist of fate. History, Gloria. Something you were driven to as a result of the very same circumstances many of these young girls find themselves in. It is not who you are. And no, I am not listening to you. That is what you think of yourself. Much better than that, I have observed you and from what I see you are exactly the kind of woman to help these girls understand what has happened to them and, importantly, help them to make a better future than one might foresee given their current dire situation.'

'I think it should be Sybil yu asking 'bout this, not me.'

'Sybil is a lovely woman. She cares deeply about her politics. Quite admirable. I take my hat off to her. But you, Gloria, you care about people. That is the difference.'

I don't bother say nothing to him 'bout how Sybil going regular to the school helping the little ones to read, nor the two hours she spend every week at the orphanage with Junior because even after Isaac get better he still wasn't paying the boy no mind and she is the only family he got. Excepting his mama, whoever she might be. No, that is her business.

So I go over there and as I step through the door Margaret Morrison greet me like some long-lost friend from her Bible group. She hugging and thanking me like I already do something wonderful by just showing up.

'George told me you would come.'

'He did?'

'Yes. He said he would ask you but that he knew you would.'

And then she tek me by the elbow and march me through the house into the little back yard where the girls sitting under the mango tree with their needlework. She clap her hands twice so everyone stop what they doing and give their attention.

'Girls, this is Gloria.' And then she say the next thing with such jubilation in her voice I thought maybe she think I was the saviour God Almighty send himself. 'She has come to help!' And they all cheered. They actually rest their work in their laps and put their hands together and applaud. And all I could do was stand there and realise there was no turning back. Because the gratitude on these girls' faces let me know for sure that this wasn't no one-off visit.

What I discover about Margaret is that even though she a holier-than-thou Presbyterian Scottish woman, she also got a good heart. She mean well. And actually, she really care for the young girls in the house. So I go there and I sit and listen and talk, hoping that maybe me giving that time might change something for these girls. Maybe make their lives different. Not that they won't be poor or young no more, but maybe they start think different about themselves, what they worth and what they can do and what they should have a right to expect.

Then one day I turn up and the police was there. They just bring back Hyacinth after she been missing for three whole weeks. Margaret say they find her downtown in the backroom of some bar.

'How they find her?'

'It seems some anonymous man reported they had a girl back there.' And she look at me meaningful like I should know what was going on.

'She all right?'

'She is dirty and distressed. She is in the shower right now but perhaps when she comes out and has had something to eat you could have a word with her.'

'Me?'

'You, Gloria.' So I nod my head although God knows what I am going to say to her. And then Margaret rest her hand on my shoulder and say, 'It will be fine. Hyacinth respects you and your experience.'

She thirteen years old this girl and she already have the baby we send to the orphanage. And by rights she shouldn't even be here no more except she got nowhere to go and Margaret will never put a child out like that. We sitting together under the mango tree when I say to her, 'Yu all right now Hyacinth?' And she nod her head. But she keep it bowed with her hands clasp together in her lap. 'When yu run off from here, where yu reckon yu was going?'

She shrug her shoulders.

'Did yu have somewhere to go?'

'No Miss Gloria.'

'So what yu doing?'

'I cyan stay here no more Miss. The baby gone. I pass my time.'

I breathe and then I say, 'Yu not got no family Hyacinth? No uncle or auntie?'

She shrug.

The thing is, Hyacinth not alone. Every one of these girls got a story that would make yu weep. And in every case there is a man, father, grandfather, uncle, brother, mother's manfriend, neighbour, shopkeeper, even school teacher that busy doing things to these girls that any decent human being would know is a act of wickedness and shame. And because they so young these men reckon the child not going get pregnant or maybe they don't care. With Hyacinth it was her brother. So she run off and find her way to Margaret and say she never going back.

'Yu don't need to be doing that yu know. Nobody trying to put yu outta here. Sister Margaret going find yu somewhere. Yu just have to bear wid her.'

She look at me. 'Who going want me? I ugly and foolish. I good for nothing. I cyan even boil the pot right or mek a even stitch.'

Sure enough Hyacinth got a harelip and she have a lot to learn. But she not ugly as such and she not stupid.

'Sister Margaret know plenty people that would be happy to take in a girl that is honest and hard-working and kind to others. A girl just like you.'

She don't say nothing for a while and then she say, 'Yu mean as a domestic?'

'It not like that. They care for yu. Put a roof over yu head. Yu part a the family. And just like in any family yu help. Yu contribute.' I pause and then I say, 'A good Christian family, Hyacinth. Yu been here long enough to see other girls go to good homes. Someone will want yu.'

'Nobody ever wanted me. Not even my own mother.'

I think about Auntie and then I say, 'The road can be hard sometimes, but it is a journey yu on. A journey that have its twists and turns. But believe me Hyacinth when I tell yu, the road has an end. A happy end if yu can stop yuself from thinking that there is only one way for you. Yu not good for nothing. Yu good for everything and yu don't need to be doing nothing in nuh back-room or anywhere else to bring yuself more heartache. Somebody else started you on that road but now what yu have to do is make that journey yu own. And I know because I been down that same road myself. And just like me yu will meet people who help yu and right now that is Sister Margaret. So just trust her and give it time. And meanwhile, know that we want you. We want yu enough to send the police to find yu and bring yu home.'

And she just get up and throw herself into my arms and cry.

When I get back to the house I find Auntie in a mood. She bang-ing and crashing the pans in the kitchen just like she used to in that dark little room at Back-O-Wall. So I go in there and lean on the doorpost and say to her, 'Something happen?'

'Something happen? What yu think happen?'

'I don't know, Auntie. That is why I am asking you.'

She never even bother to look at me. She just carry on washing and rinsing the same dishes over and over. Then she say, 'He been here yu know.'

'Who?'

'Who yu think? Yang Pao.'

'So what he want?'

'What he want? Yu asking me? All I know is he come here talk-ing to me like I am some maid. The hired domestic. That is what. Asking me fi ice water and meking himself familiar with Esther. At least when yu here he focus himself on you.'

'What yu mean familiar?'

'Come ask how she doing and how she a get along wid me. If I treat her good. Di man too faass and facety.'

'He her father, Auntie. What yu expect?'

'Expect? Me?' She dry her hands on the cloth. 'Who he think I am?'

'Who yu want him to think yu are?'

She really vex now, standing there with the pan in her hand like what she want to do more than anything is throw it at me. So I calm myself and I say to her, 'Mama tell me yu know. When Esther born and she come from country. She tell me.'

'What she tell yu?'

'That yu my real mama.'

'She tell yu that?'

'Uh-huh.'

'What else she tell yu?'

'Nothing. She say it between you and me.'

And just when I think she going say something meaningful to me she tek off her apron and throw it down on the counter and walk off. So I follow her into her bedroom where she sitting in the armchair making like she doing her mending.

'Yu nuh think maybe it time we talk?'

'Talk? When we going do that? Everyday yu busy-busy go-a Franklyn Town 'bout yu business or downtown wiping the runny nose a dem pickney mother. Like deh not got enough people waiting on dem hand and foot and telling dem it OK. Who yu think was there to help me? I will tell yu. Nobody. That was who. Just me, you and nobody.'

'Auntie, I know it musta been hard.'

'Hard? Hard? You got no idea what hard is. All yu do is run 'round town while I am here tending to little Esther all day long.

And if that not enough, yu know what she say to me today? She say, "You are not my mommy." That is what she say when I was telling her to behave herself.'

And then I see the tear in her eye that she quickly wipe away and act like nothing happen.

'I bring yu from country because I reckon I could mek yu a life away from all di misery back there. But yu got no idea what it like for a woman to be trying to mek a living wid a pickney strap to her back. No idea. And living in dat yard in Back-O-Wall when what I was used to was di open sky wid orange and mango trees, and di breadfruit and ackee and pear yu could reach for to mek something to fill yu belly. Wid not a soul to talk to, and di men a prowl 'round because yu young and already got a chile so deh think yu must be easy.'

I sit on the edge of the bed.

'Auntie, I sorry what happen today.'

'So I tek yu to Esther and I leave yu. She was my best friend from when we young. Di only person in dis world I could turn to. And I write her every week so she could tell me how yu gwaan even though my reading and writing not so good. Every week I put down a few words to mek sure she write back and tell me something.'

She stop a while and then she say, 'It wasn't hard fi yu because yu didn't know nothing 'bout it. It was hard fi me. That is who it was hard fah.'

I reckon there not much point trying to talk to her while she this way so I get up and go over like as to give her a hug but she don't want it. And then I hear Esther crying.

'Yu see now, di baby wake up and I only put her down just before yu come in.' And just as she resting the blouse and needle on the table I say, 'I will get her.'

But it not me that Esther want. It Auntie. And even though I got her in my arms trying to hush her tears she reaching over my shoulder for 'Gang-gang'. Next thing I know Auntie standing behind me with the baby pillow from Esther's cot.

'Yu nuh think she too old for that?'

'It the only thing that comfort her, Gloria.'

Esther tek the pillow and press it to her chest. Then she grab the corner in her fist and stick her thumb in her mouth while she rub her nose with the pointed end of the pillowcase. And just so, she stop crying. Still hanging there in my arms lighter than yu would expect for a healthy four-year-old.

When I talk to Sybil 'bout it she say I should have more trust in myself.

'A child always love their mother. Yu nuh know that? No matter how bad that mother gwaan. Even the day I go back to Trench Town to see my own mother it was because I still love her. After everything. And when I turn 'round and walk off it wasn't because I didn't love no more. It was because I thought she didn't love me. Auntie not cutting 'cross nothing. So yu nuh need worry yuself 'bout how Esther feel. What yu need to do is understand that she is your child and you are her mother. And nothing in this world is going to change that. That bond not like a brittle piece a stick that going to break in your hand. And as for the other thing that I know playing on your mind, being a whore don't mek yu a bad mother. Being a bad mother is what mek yu a bad mother. So have faith, Gloria Campbell. Whatever failings yu think yu have because of the wounds of your past. It nuh matter. Yu a righteous woman. So smile at the present and know that your love is good enough for the child.'

Esther tek the pillowcase with her the day she start

kindergarten, even though she mek a commotion to tek the whole pillow and we have to explain to her that she too big for that. So she mek do with just the case.

Me and Auntie stand there at the door of Holy Childhood and wave goodbye to her like we didn't expect to ever see her again. Like she was going to be lost to us for ever. It remind me of the day I leave Marcia in service at that house in Cross Roads. And then I wonder how Auntie musta feel the day she leave me with Mama and if I knew, little as I was, that this was my real mother walking away from me.

But little Esther wasn't lost to us because four hours later she was running 'cross the schoolroom with her arms outstretched. And it was me she run to. Like she didn't expect to see me. Me who sweep her up in my arms. Me she want to tell 'bout all her new adventures. And after I put her down she take my hand on one side and Auntie's on the other and walk to the street to catch the cab.

1960

'From the land where palm trees grow.'

CHAPTER 21

SYBIL TRANSFIX WITH Cuba. All we hear from her is how the fighting going on over there, and how Castro come outta prison and go to Mexico and come back with a boat full a soldiers to go really start the revolution in earnest.

I say to her, 'Yu nuh think all this talk 'bout Cuba a waste a time?'

'Waste a time? They showing us the way. That is what they are doing.'

'The way to what? It not like we got a dictator slaughtering innocent people in the street and need another Paul Bogle to come set things right. The sufferers not suffering so much as to go tek up armed struggle.'

But Sybil not paying me no mind. All she can say is how everything going to be different over there.

So when Castro finally tek over she was rejoicing like there was no tomorrow. She even throw a party over the house in Franklyn Town and invite a whole heapa people I never see before. Some of them were part of the Party faithful that was for sure. But the others God knows, because I couldn't begin to imagine where she know them from. She never tell nobody what she was celebrating though. Probably if she did, some a them wouldn't have come because the Party already divided with this one accusing the other one of being a communist and arguing over who is rank and who is file. So it was just a case of come eat my food and drink my liquor and dance to my music. Still, it no matter. Sybil knew what was in her heart, and she had her party and everybody had themselves a damn good time.

Me, I could see her point because Esther growing and it as clear as day that, whatever the government got to say, Jamaica not changing fast enough to give her a chance to have the dreams and ambitions that is the right of every woman.

Six months later Sybil tell me the East Kingston PNP setting up a women's group and she want me to join. But going to some school room to argue about what the Party doing or what it ought to do, even with a group of women, wasn't for me.

Still, it seem the group do good because a little while after that she say she running a big, open meeting and want me to come.

'What would mek me want to do a thing like that?'

'Because yu care, Gloria. Yu care 'bout the girls down Margaret Morrison's place and yu care 'bout what kinda future Esther going to have. And I think yu care enough to want to help mek something different.'

So I go to East Kingston. When I get there the school room got the seating arrange in a big circle. It look like they expecting a good few. The wooden chairs for little children so yu have to squat down to fix yuself in it, but it fine. They got coffee and ice water so I tek some and wait while people settling themselves and a hefty woman in a bright floral frock is going 'round welcoming everybody and saying how excited she is to see so many turning out.

Next thing I see is Sybil. She waltz into the room in a flurry with two other women trailing after her. She really in charge the serious way she calling the meeting to order and inviting everybody to sit down and give her their attention. When she notice me in the crowd, her eyes light up. It like she genuinely pleased to see me. Maybe because she wasn't sure whether or not I would come. So now she is striding 'cross the room with her arms hold out like she preparing for a big embrace. And when she get to me, she do it, she hug me. A big, warm, full arms-round-yu-body hug like she never do before in all the long years we know each other.

She ease back and look at me and then she say, 'It good to see yu mek the journey.' She carry on stare at me with her hands steadying my shoulders and then she let me go and turn 'round and walk off.

The meeting all about how the PNP working to improve education and the quality of life for children and families especially the poorest in Jamaica so they can have different economic choices, and understand their history and identity and destiny.

It remind me of all those hours I spend sitting at that kitchen table in Franklyn Town listening to her spout forth with the cigarette smoke wafting 'round her head. Excepting this time she not got a audience of four, it more like a audience of forty. And the speech she giving not just coming from her and the sense she mek of what she see. It coming from the Party and I know that because I never hear Sybil use no words like economic choice before. This was a whole new thing. And what give it away completely was when she start talk 'bout destiny because that is what Mr Manley was always talking 'bout. It put me in mind of all those girls over

Margaret Morrison's place and I know Sybil right. You have to learn to read and write and get yourself a education.

Sybil pause and tek a drink of water and then she say, 'What I want you to understand is the invaluable contribution that women have to make. That is because women have the patience and love to sit down with somebody, be it a child or a grown woman or man, and give them the attention and confidence they need to learn to do something like read.

'But this is not all one-way traffic. Women also have a need to develop our skills and increase our confidence and our pride. Because every woman deserves to have dignity and choices. Opportunity and equality. That is how to create a Jamaica that will truly progress and prosper.'

The whole room erupt in so much clapping and cheering, I never hear nothing like it in my life. Not indoors anyway. It so loud and raucous I start think maybe it 140 women in that room.

'Next year starting on 1 January is the Year of Literacy in Cuba when the government has committed itself to education. They are going to build schools, train teachers and recruit volunteers to teach reading and writing to everybody, especially those in rural areas. So what I am asking is who among us is prepared to go to Cuba to help with this great undertaking? Who would give up a week or two of her life, or whatever time you can spare, to help our comrades in Cuba and learn how we ourselves can build a better future?' She pause, then she say, 'Yu don't have to tell me now, just wait at the end and I will get yu name before yu go.'

At the end of the meeting she come straight up to me and say, 'So yu going come? To Cuba?'

'I cyan go to Cuba, Sybil.' I pause. 'Not that I don't think what yu doing good and worthy. It just that . . . all a this don't mean the same to me as it do you. All the talk and the organising too much for me. Besides, I couldn't leave Esther like that. And anyway, I don't speak no Spanish so what kinda help I going to be?'

'It not just the teaching they need help wid. It building the school and cooking some food and tending the babies and little ones while the mothers and fathers trying to learn something. It helping to do anything that need doing. So nuh worry yuself 'bout nuh Spanish. If yu want to go they will welcome yu with open arms, believe me.'

But it wasn't Sybil who change my mind. It was Pao. Because two weeks later he turn up and start tell Esther that she need to behave herself and curb the way she talking to me because she too fresh.

'What yu doing coming in here talking to the child like that? Yu think after all these years yu can suddenly come act like a father?'

'Gloria, the girl outta order. Her mouth is running off at the slightest thing yu say to her. Yu nuh think it rude?'

'What I think is what I think. It not got nothing to do wid you.' And then I notice Esther still sitting there after what she say to me, which in truth was rude. Because lately Esther very fast with her anger close to the surface. Ever since she leave kindergarten and start at this new primary school she fresh and she screaming and ready to argue over any little thing. And no matter how much I talk to her it don't seem to mek no difference. One minute she nice, the next minute she nasty. And after that she apologising but it don't seem to stop her from doing the very same thing the next day. Auntie say the child need a strap taking to her. That is the Jamaican way. But I not about to start that. Esther already got enough burden without me adding to it.

So I just say to her, 'Go sort yuself out in yu bedroom. There not no need for you to be standing here listening to this.'

She look at me and then she look at him but she nuh move. So Auntie sweep into the living room and take her by the hand outta the way.

I step out on to the veranda and he follow me.

'This is my house, Pao. I not going let just anybody come in here and think they can start dishing out the discipline. Yu voice been missing since Esther born. Yu cyan come now and start like this.'

'Am I just anybody, Gloria?'

'I don't mean it like that. All I am saying is yu overstep a mark.'

'But the old woman in there, she can tell Esther anything she want.'

'The old woman in there is her grandmother not nuh maid like yu think she is.'

'Her grandmother? Yu mean the woman that bring yu up in country not yu mother?'

But I don't feel like explaining anything to him. I wouldn't know where to begin even if I wanted to.

'She her grandmother. So that is her position.'

He look at me with such a sadness I never see in him before. Excepting the day all them years back when I tell him I wanted him to pay. Then he say, 'So what is my position, Gloria?'

'Yu got to earn that, Pao. That don't come by right.'

'So how I going do that?'

'Yu start by doing what Auntie already do. Put in eight years a love and attention into the child's life.'

He walk off down the steps and get into the car and drive off. And I know for sure, by the way he never even look back, that

I wasn't going see him again 'til I pick up the telephone and tell him it all right for him to come over.

When I go back inside Auntie in the kitchen boiling water and meking tea.

'Tea, Auntie?'

'I reckon that is what yu need.'

After she put the Lipton's in the pot and fix the cups and saucers she turn to me and say, 'Yu need a break, Gloria. Yu know, a rest from all a dis aggravation.' She wait while she pouring the tea and then she say, 'Why yu nuh go to Cuba wid Sybil like she want?'

'I cyan just tek off to Cuba like that.'

'What stopping yu? Yu business over Franklyn Town? That will tek care a itself. And Esther. She will be fine. I am here like I always am.'

Then I remember Esther still in her room so I go in there and she sitting on the bed in her pyjamas. I rest myself next to her and put my arm 'round her shoulder.

'How yu doing baby?'

'All right.'

'Yu father love yu. Yu know that? He just don't know how to show it.' I pause and then I say, 'He was trying to get involved. That is all he was doing. He didn't mean no harm by it.'

She turn and put her arms full 'round me and then she whisper into my ear, 'I love you Mommy and I'm sorry for being rude to you.'

A week later when I go talk to her 'bout maybe me going to Cuba she say, 'Gang-gang already told me.' And I think, whoever told yu to call her that because I can't remember. Or maybe it was you who decide the first time yu wanted to call her something. Because the only time yu ever see the woman everybody think is yu grand-mother yu were one week old.

'She did? So what yu think?'

'We will be all right. I understand what you are doing, but you will telephone me, won't you, Mommy?'

'Of course I will. Yu think I not going miss you too?'

CHAPTER 22

WHEN WE GET off the boat in Santiago de Cuba it hot-hot. There not even a little drop a breeze coming off the sea. And with the mountains right behind yu, there not no relief from that direction neither. Rodolfo and Matilde meet us because we going stay with them. Their English good so we can feel at home. Rodolfo light-skinned, but he tanned. A Spaniard with short, tight, curly hair. Matilde, she homely, like her favourite outfit would be an apron, wrapped 'round her as she cooking and serving the food she fond of to the people she love.

The house just outside the city because Rodolfo and Matilde are farmers. In truth, it not that unlike a Jamaican house with a little veranda out front and some blue iron gate, and inside a room yu walk through to the kitchen. And then out back a real nice big sitting area shady under the trees. This is where it seem they live because inside the house dark and it not really got no furniture. It barely got any windows and the bedrooms little more than a couple alcoves off the walk-through living room hid behind some curtains they must pull across at night. So I reckon we going boil up in there, which don't seem that encouraging if you actually want to get some sleep. Matilde say me and Sybil going share the room next to the one the children in and she and Rodolfo going sleep out back. The bathroom outside. It primitive but it got everything yu need.

After we tour the house we settle down to eat. Yellow rice with red beans and fried plantain. It not nuh Jamaican rice and peas but it tasty, and even though there not no meat it welcoming after the long journey. Sybil seem like she make herself at home already. Especially since it turn out she know more Spanish than she let on learning it like she was these last months. Me, I sit there under the tree and give myself a talking to because these people good enough to let me stay with them and all I am doing in my head is comparing and complaining. That is truly ungracious when what I should be is grateful and have the generosity in my heart towards them just the same way they have been hospitable to me.

Afterwards my eyes wander 'round for where the telephone at but I cyan see nothing. So I whisper to Sybil, 'They got a phone?'

And she shake her head. 'It next door.' So I just raise my eyebrows and then she say something in Spanish to Matilde who get up out the chair fast and say, 'Yes, I understand. Of course.'

Matilde walk me out the house and 'cross the street, and down the road a ways through an iron gate, up the path on to a veranda and into a door while she calling out, 'Celia, Celia.' When this woman come out she explain to her and Celia smile at me. She dry her hands on her apron and then she tek me by the hand and lead me to the telephone like it was the holy grail. That revered it was. She even dust it off with her cloth before she point at it as if to say, 'There you are.' So I smile and say, 'Thank you.'

But then I am fumbling because I never mek a phone call from abroad before. Matilde come up behind me and tek the receiver out my hand and dial all the code and then she hand me the phone and say, 'You can call now.'

When I get through Auntie say everything is all right. Esther have a good day at school and eat her dinner and almost ready for bed.

'Hello Mommy.'

'Hello baby. Gang-gang say all is well and yu doing fine.'

'Yes. I miss you.'

'I miss you too but I can't talk long because I don't want to be running up these people's phone bill. Yu understand? I just wanted to let yu know we arrive safe and everything is fine. And check that you OK as well.'

'Yes, we are all right.'

'Good. I will ring again when I find a public phone OK?'

'OK.'

'I love you.'

'I love you too, Mommy.'

I tell Matilde that I want to pay Celia for the phone call but both of them say no. Celia even tek the money I am offering and hold my hand while she push it back into my purse and close the catch. And then she give it a little pat and say something which Matilde tell me she say: 'That is a small gift from us in respect for your large gift to Cuba.'

When morning come I so relieved to get outta the bed I was in the shower at sunup. And even after the water run over me I don't think I was any more wet than lying there with the thin sheets sticking to me like plastic on a damp surface. When Sybil finally get up she look refreshed. I couldn't believe it. How she managed to sleep and rest in that heat.

While we eating breakfast Matilde say, 'The Cuban Literacy Campaign is the world's most ambitious and organised literacy campaign. This is the year of education that will bring equality between the classes and urban and rural citizens, and create a national identity of unity, sense of history, courage, intelligence and combat. It is a movement of the people. A movement for solidarity.'

Matilde sound like she reading straight from Fidel Castro's manifesto, which I suppose she is. But when she show us the grey uniform and blanket and hammock and textbooks the volunteers have to take to the rural areas I can tell it not just talk. She proud. She really believe in what they doing because the way she holding up these books is like she think they have the answer to their prayers. And what these books are called are *We Shall Read* and *We Shall Conquer*.

And then Rodolfo say, 'Education and revolution are the same thing.' His English not so good as Matilde's so he don't say so much.

We drive up the mountain in a little old army jeep that mek yu feel every lump and bump on the road. It jerk yu outta the seat so much yu have to hold on tight in case yu head hit the roof or when yu land back yu break yu backside, or give it a damn good bruise anyway. And the more up the hillside we go the slower yu moving because the road is running out until eventually all yu got is a hard-packed red dirt track with a heap a rocks and boulders that yu have to steer your way 'round.

When we get there, the school not finish build. It look like maybe it used to be some kinda storage shed but never mind, it a school now and it full a women that have come from all over this mountain so they can learn to read. The children running 'round except the ones that too young to even crawl, and the game they all playing is just the one thing. This one is Fidel, this one is Che or Raúl or Camilo Cienfuegos. Even the girls in it, they Haydée Santamaría or Melba Hernández. And every stick under their arm is shooting at the soldiers of the cruel and unjust tyrant Fulgencio Batista. And every shout and scream is the same, *Patria o muerte!* Homeland or death! Because for them it is as real as anything else they know living right here in the Sierra Maestra mountains.

Matilde say Sybil going sit in the class with the women but I going help her with the children. So we gather them 'round and she and Joaquina, who is a real schoolteacher, set to. Me, I just ease up and when a child losing interest I go sit down next to him or her and try get them to pay the lesson some attention.

Later on another woman come ask me to help with the food so I do that. More rice and beans. And after that I lean up by a stand-pipe and wash the pots and plates as they get pile up next to me and I pass them on to the woman that drying and stacking. She called Aida and she look as African as me.

When she see me staring at her she say, 'Santiago was the first city in Cuba to get African slaves.'

I so surprised I just say to her, 'Yu speak English.'

'My people come from Jamaica little time back.'

We carry on with the dishes and then she say, 'Plenty French here as well after the slave uprising in Haiti. So Santiago different from other towns in Cuba. More mix.' She stop. 'But there is one thing that all of Cuba shares.' And then she straighten herself up like she about to salute the national flag. 'The island will sink into the sea before the Cuban people let ourselves be slaves to anyone. That is Señor Fidel Castro.' And she tek the cloth and start drying the dishes again.

At the end of the day I go back to another sleepless night even though I so tired, not from the work but from the bumpy road and the airless heat. Next day, same thing. But this time it don't seem so hard. Maybe I getting used to it. Or maybe I starting to see the good all of this is doing because even though I cyan hardly talk to anybody I can look. And what I see is pride. They have overcome. And if education and revolution are the same thing as Rodolfo say, then the pencil in these children's hand is like the stick under their arm.

When we get back from the mountain I tek a shower and put on a fresh housecoat to cool down and relax. Matilde say me and Sybil must come out front on the veranda where we can see the sun set. And just as we sitting there I notice Rodolfo standing at the gate talking to a man. A man with beautiful hair. Hair that dark and full, but short and cultured. Hair that bouncy and soft. And when he turn 'round his eyes catch me and they are laughing and gentle. The kindest eyes I have ever seen.

I say to Matilde, 'Who is that?'

'Rodolfo's cousin.' And she stop, so I just carry on look at her 'til she say, 'Ernesto Sánchez.'

And just as I turn my head I see him look at me and say something to Rodolfo, and I catch a hint of the Spanish faint on the breeze. So I say to Sybil, 'What did he say?'

'He said, "Who is that?"'

I sit there thinking that maybe when he finish talking he will tek a stroll up the path, but he don't. He just shake Rodolfo hand and wave, the smallest little now-yu-see-me, now-yu-don't wave of the hand, and then he turn and walk off.

'He fought you know, Ernesto, alongside Fidel and Che up in the mountains. Both he and Rodolfo.'

Next morning Rodolfo tell us that Ernesto coming to dinner that evening. And from that moment on what a state my mind is in. All through the lesson, and the pots and plates, and the sticks that are shooting bullets, and the cries for 'Homeland', and the bumping down the mountain road, all I can think about is that hair and those eyes.

When I reach the house I go straight in the shower and come out and put on something nice, not that I got anything really presentable with me, but I have a blue skirt and a white blouse with some frill down the front and I reckon that will do. I fix up my face with the little something I bring, and even as I am putting on the lipstick I am wondering what the hell it is I think I am doing. How can I be acting this way over a man I don't even know? Me, a woman with a child and the history I got.

It so obvious the way I going on Sybil say to me, 'Yu sure yu know what yu doing?'

'What it look like?'

'You know what it look like. It look like what it is.' And she narrow her eyes at me. 'Just think before yu leap that is all I am saying.'

When Ernesto show up he is wearing green army trousers and shirt with the sleeves rolled up to the elbow, and black army boots. Completely different from how he was the day before in the pants and sport shirt. But even so, what is still the same is the hair so soft and the eyes that sparkle.

I am awkward and clumsy and don't know what has come over me. I am like a schoolgirl who dunno what to do with herself. Not that there is much for me to do or say. Matilde busy-busy doing everything and insisting that we sit there at the table and 'make conversation', but what conversation am I making when I can't understand a word of Spanish? Every now and again Sybil join in or Ernesto give some translation, like, 'Fidel says, "When men carry the same ideals in their hearts, nothing can keep them isolated".' Or, 'Che Guevara say, "We should defend the right of all peoples to achieve their liberty".'

This is all they talk about. The revolution. And when Matilde lean in my ear to whisper, she say the only English Ernesto know is to quote Fidel and Che. That is all he knows to do.

But that is not all Ernesto is doing. He is also looking. He is looking and he is smiling. And when it come time to clear the table he jump up quick and say to Matilde that me and him going do it. So we clear and wash the dishes standing side by side at the sink while he taking care to make sure he nuh touch me. Not even by accident.

When we finish he say, 'It is a beautiful country, Cuba.' But I don't say nothing to him. So he say, 'You will have some time before you go to see a little of it.'

'I will?'

'Yes, I already asked Rodolfo.' He pause and then he say, 'And your friend too. Of course.'

So I think quoting Fidel and Che not the only English you know after all.

That night when I go to bed my mind is churning. Half a me so eager to be with him it frighten me. The other half telling me I am a stupid old woman. Ernesto got to be ten years younger than me if not more. What would a man like that want with a woman like me? And even if his interest not just to show me this country he love so much, what is the point of all of this when I going back to Jamaica in two weeks?

Sybil don't say nothing 'bout it. Maybe she reckon she already say her piece. What she do instead is lay in the darkness every night and tell me how things would be different in Jamaica if we had unity like the Cubans. And I say, 'And hope. The same hope that carry these people 'cross this mountain every day to sit hour after hour trying to read and write and learn.'

Halfway through the week Ernesto come early one morning. He exchange few words with Rodolfo and then put us in his little army jeep and drive to Cementerio Santa Ifigenia to see where José Martí buried. Ernesto say José Martí is the Apostle of Cuban Independence and he always quoting from him. He love José Martí for what he say about oppression and justice. And for his poetry as well. Poems about love and liberty and compassion. Like he say Martí write:

> I have a white rose to tend
> I give it to the true friend
> And to the cruel one
> For him, too, I have a white rose.

Ernesto say every Cuban is a revolutionary and a poet. And every ten minutes there is something else from Martí or Fidel or Che that he got to tell us. That is Ernesto. Sybil just sit there in the back a the jeep or walk slowly behind. But she nuh say nothing. I guess she reckon she know what going on and it got nothing to do with her.

We drive into Santiago where Ernesto say is home to the two most important landmarks of the revolution, Moncada garrison and La Granjita Siboney. He park the jeep because he want to walk us to the cathedral. So we wander down and down past some streets that got the house right on the narrow cobble road with no yard or nothing. Just a concrete step at the door and a little balcony upstairs to hang out your washing. That is it. Spanish. Spanish like the adventurers and merchants and conquerors that been flocking to this island since Christopher Columbus, sauntering free and easy along to the sound of that same song that is coming at you from every direction because that is the only tune anybody want to play. 'Guantanamera'. So it nuh surprise me when Ernesto tell me the words a the song based on poems by José Martí. That would figure.

When we finally get down to Parque Céspedes the cathedral is beautiful with the columns out front and the two towers with the dome roof and the statue of the angel in the middle. I ask Ernesto if we going to go inside but he say no, it too cold and dark. Instead, we going sit on the balcony of the Hotel Casa Granda and admire the cathedral from over there. We climb the steps and reach the balcony where we overlooking the park with the men sitting under the shady trees playing dominoes and slapping the tiles on the table just the same way they do it in Jamaica. Hard and loud. And what else I can hear is the man and his guitar playing 'Guantanamera', singing like he doing it for a sweetheart that sitting right there in front of him.

Ernesto order three mojitos. He say we got to try it because it a national drink of Cuba. So I say, 'Jamaica the one that mek rum. Yu nuh know that?'

And he say, 'Cuba make rum. Cuban rum is the best rum in the world. Just like Cuban coffee.'

So I laugh, 'No man, Jamaican coffee is the best coffee in the world. There is no arguing over that.'

'You come taste my coffee and you decide which you think better.'

It turn out Ernesto is the supervisor at some big coffee plantation in the hills above Santiago. And it also turn out the mojito good. It sweet and refreshing and it got a good kick.

We sit up there on the balcony drinking down a second mojito and me remembering the time in Club Havana that Clifton Brown offer me one and I order some Appleton instead. When we ready to go I ask Ernesto if there is any public telephone I can use to call Jamaica. And he say yes and walk us 'round the corner to the general telephone company.

Esther tell me all about what she been doing at school and how she and Auntie been baking cakes and playing cards and reading books together. She sound happy. Auntie in good spirits too. I relieved. But a little part of me also envious. Envious of the time they sharing together, and how is seem like they nuh miss me. When I finishing the call I say to Esther, 'I love yu.' And she say, 'I love you too Mommy but I have to go now. Talk to you soon.'

Next day we back up the mountain. And I really start notice the little ones and think how all of this is going to change their lives. Not just because they learning to read and write but because their mothers learning too, which going give them different opportunities and so the children going have different experiences and different choices. And I start to wonder how Esther's life would have been different if I had made some different choices. Like the choices I made over Barrington and going to Kingston, and moving in with Sybil and Beryl, and Henry, and Pao, and Morrison and the card club. With each turn putting myself further and further out of reach of the kind of life a normal person supposed to have. Further and further into a place of no return.

Then I think 'bout Marcia and how her life been shaped by the choices I made. And me, my life, how that would have been if Auntie had kept me with her in Kingston. But none of that I will ever know. Yet what is for certain is that the lives of these people, young and old, up in these mountains going to be something it would never have been without Fidel Castro and his revolution. A revolution that is in the soul of each and every one of them every time they quoting from him or shouting *Patria o muerte!*

Ernesto come at the weekend to take us to the Gran Piedra from where he say you can see Jamaica on a clear day. Me and Sybil get in the jeep and he drive. Everywhere you go yu see billboards that in Jamaica would say 'Milo' or 'Craven A' or 'Tide', but here they say '¡*Viva el Socialismo Cubano!*' and '*Unidad, firmeza y victoria*' and '*Las banderas de la revolución y el socialismo no se entregan sin combatir*'.

All along the way to the Gran Piedra there are monuments by the roadside to fallen heroes of the revolution with their names and occupations carved on boulders. And every single one a these Ernesto is eager to point out and tell us about.

1,234 metres. That is how high this thing is. And to get to it you have to climb 454 steps.

I say, 'No man, yu joking. I not going up a thing like that, I would be dead before I reach.'

But he say, 'We can do it. We just take our time.'

So the progress slow and then halfway up it start to rain. It come down so fast and heavy that in no time at all the water was running like a river down the steps.

'There is a boulder up ahead. We can shelter.' So we follow him and even though it just tek a little while by the time we get there we are soaked, our clothes sticking to us like paste.

And standing there so close to him under the overhanging rock I notice the muscle 'cross his chest and arms. Not bulky like Pao's man Hampton, just firm and strong and sort of deliberate. His arms look like they have intention. I just stand there, letting the rain fall with half of me hoping it soon stop, and the other half wishing it never stop, ever.

But even though I tugging inside the rain stop anyway and Ernesto say we can make it to the top. Up there, the sun is shining bright as any Jamaican day. Brighter than sometimes after an afternoon rain because the light got a sheen to it. Like it reflecting off a giant crystal somewhere in the sky. The view, if you nuh care too much 'bout the buzzards circling you, truly take your breath away. But Jamaica on a clear day? Maybe not. More likely the lights on a clear night. And still, I nuh care. Me, I can see Jamaica.

On the way back down the hill I ask Ernesto to tek me to a public phone, which he do. But even though I let the thing ring and ring, and I hang up and ring back, there is no answer. I can't imagine what Auntie and Esther doing that they nuh pick up the telephone.

When we get back Sybil fretting, sitting there on the little bed in the stifling alcove we sleeping in. So I say to her, 'Just say it.'

She look at me with her hand resting over her mouth, and then she drop it and say, 'Yu sure yu know what yu doing?'

'Yu ask me that already.'

'But I don't hear no answer. What I see though is you going headlong into something. I not even sure yu know what it is.' She pause and then she say, 'Do yu know what it is?'

I think on it. 'I never met no man like this before, Sybil. You ever? You ever meet somebody like this? Somebody that mek yu heart leap just to look at him or him look at you. Where it feel like electricity just to have him stand next to yu or rest his hand on the gearstick so close to yu knee. And all the time yu have to concentrate real hard not to let yourself reach out and touch him. Touch any part a him. Just so yu can feel the warmth of his skin under yu fingers. Yu ever feel like that about anybody?'

'Gloria, yu head running away wid yu.'

'It not my head Sybil.'

'Well whatever it is, it need to slow down. We in this country for one more week and that is it. And if yu remember we come here to do something and it not this.'

I know she right. So I just get into the bed and turn off the light that not worth the effort anyway because the thing must be a ten-watt bulb it so dim.

When we laying there in the still, airless dark I say to her, 'Yu ever think yu would want to get yuself a man?'

She laugh. 'Yu nuh think I had enough men?'

'No. Yu know. A man.'

'Yu mean like Pao?'

'No not like that. Or maybe. I don't know. Someone regular. A regular man and a regular life.'

She nuh say nothing, but I can hear her mind working on it. Then she say, 'I don't think I ever wanted to have a regular man. To me, that is too much compromise. And as for a regular life, who got that Gloria, eh?'

We lay there in the quiet a time and then I say, 'Or a woman?'

'A woman! Yu joking? In Jamaica?'

'I know. But did yu ever think about it? After all, you and Beryl been together all this long while?'

She quiet at first and then she say, 'Yu need to go to sleep. We got another long day tomorrow.'

CHAPTER 23

I GOT NO idea when Ernesto going show up next, so when we get back from the mountain, even though I feel reluctant to be taking people for granted, I ask Matilde if I can walk down aways to ask Celia to use the telephone. And straight away she jump up and tek me by the hand and walk me outta the door.

Out on the street I see the horse-drawn bus going into town with the wooden cart it pulling and the long bench seats full in the back. The thing so packed there was even people standing up between the benches, sorta bent over because the roof not high enough for them to stand up straight. And because nobody know when the bus coming, which not that often anyway, there is people waiting on the road waving down any vehicle that passing to hitch a ride with them. Matilde say there not much gasoline and it expensive so everyone got to help their neighbour.

When I get through to Auntie she say they not there when I ring because she and Esther go on Saturday to the pictures at Harbour View and Prospect Beach on Sunday.

'Yu mean the drive-in at Harbour View?'

'What other pictures yu know out there?'

'But how yu get there?'

'Clifton come tek us.'

'Clifton Brown the policeman?'

'Same one. He come looking fi yu but yu not here so he tek me and Esther out for a trip.'

'And who tek yu to the beach on Sunday?'

'Clifton.'

'Yu happy for the two a yu to just tek off with some strange man just like that?'

'He not strange to me, Gloria. Anyway, he a policeman.'

When I talk to Esther she OK. She having a good time. She happy. And then she say, 'Uncle Clifton was nice at the weekend, Mommy.'

'He not yu uncle, Esther. He a policeman.'

All week we up the mountain and then back at the house dog tired for dinner and a restless sleep. And then two days before we going back to Jamaica Ernesto show up and say he come to tek us to his plantation because we not tasted his coffee yet. Sybil say she not coming. She and Matilde got business to do.

'You have to decide whatever it is yu decide. Just remember what I say to yu.'

We didn't get a hundred yards down the road before some woman wave down the jeep and Ernesto stop. After they exchange a few words he get out and ease up the seat so she get in the back. When we set off again he say to me, 'She works at the botanical garden and needs a ride.' So he drive, while the two a them chat and I gaze at the road and another billboard that say '¡*Ya vencimos, y seguiremos venciendo!*' with the people walking under it going about their business, strolling the street and catching the bus like any day in downtown Kingston. Almost like they unaware, or maybe overaccustomed to what going on over their head.

When we reach the garden she thank him and say she will get the university professor-turn-gardener to show us 'round because I am a visitor and she think it would be nice for me. And sure enough the professor come out in a creased floral shirt and dirty pants and some rubber slippers on his feet that make outta a old truck tyre just like they do back in country. And what he show us, marching up and down and through this garden, is the butterfly flower that smell like honey, and the orchid that smell like chocolate, and the toothpaste mint anthurium, and elephant ear cactus, and bird of paradise, and Japanese bamboo and the majestic Royal Palm that you see so tall and proud all over Cuba, and everything else on this used-to-be coffee plantation. All the time Ernesto standing so close to me I can hardly breathe. Leaning over my shoulder to smell a plant or touching a leaf with his hand brushing lightly against mine. And even though I was trying to smell the honey and the chocolate and the mint all I can smell is Ernesto, fresh, like he just step outta the shower.

And then it start to rain. Fast and heavy just like it do the last time we out together.

We run back to the shack, slipping and sliding over the mud, and we wait there while the rain hammering down and a heavy mist is settling as far as the eye can see. When it ease, Ernesto say we should try mek it to the plantation because the road will be turning to mud. So I say to him 'bout paying for the garden tour and he say, 'That is a gift from Cuba.'

The further we go up the mountain the less and less like you travelling on any kinda actual road as such. In the end all yu got is a sticky red track that the jeep wheels spinning in. But I don't care. The mountain might be falling down in a landslide for all I know.

Because my mind only got one thing on it. Being alone with Ernesto. For the first time. And feeling the ease and the tension that go with that.

Ernesto house originally build by a French Haitian planter with brick and clay roof tiles. It little and cosy with one of everything. One kitchen, one bathroom, one living room and right next to that one bedroom with French doors just like the ones in the living room opening on to that same one terrace sitting up high over the coffee hills. He say we should tek off our wet clothes and I think he right. He give me a dry shirt to put on, which long and decent, and he tek my things to go hang out in what used to be, in the old days, a storage room for the coffee beans under the house. He say that was OK back then because the house didn't have no kitchen and so the beans wasn't anywhere near anything that smell. Ernesto put in the kitchen and bathroom himself when he come to live here five years back because nowadays all the drying and storing of the coffee beans happen away from here over the ridge.

I stand in the doorway and watch him fix some rice and beans and pork, which surprise me, the meat, but it welcome. He handy in the kitchen that is for sure. Washing the rice, stirring in the beans. He look comfortable at the stove, which is another surprise because I never see no Jamaican man busying himself like this before. Cooking the jerk pork over an open fire, sure. But turning down the heat under the rice, no.

After we eat, we sit there in the living room listening to the rain fall slow and steady.

'You have a husband in Jamaica?'

'A husband?'

'Who you have to telephone?'

228

I laugh. 'No, no husband. I have a daughter though. Nine years old this year.'

'Your daughter she is called?'

'Esther, after my mother.' But then I think no that not true but I don't bother explain nothing to him.

'It is good of you to give your time to help us. Cuba is grateful.'

'Is it only Cuba that is grateful?'

He think for a while and then he say, 'I am not grateful.' And he think some more. 'I am overwhelmed.' He stop and then he say, 'Or perhaps that is not the right word.' And he get up and walk inside.

Later when he come back he carrying a tray and say we should step on to the terrace since it stop raining. He pour out the coffee into two tiny cups and then he say, 'Just a small taste of Cuban cane.' And offer me the spoon and sugar pot. So I just take half a teaspoon and stir it in. And in truth, the coffee is good. It rich and smooth. It heavy on your tongue with a flavour almost nutty. It is truly lovely coffee. He just look at me sideways and smile, as we sitting there, the two of us on his terrace after the rain.

He sip slow and gentle from the cup and after some good while he say, 'So is Jamaican coffee still the best coffee in the world?'

And I say, 'Yu coffee come a good equal. That is all I am willing to say.' And he throw his head back and laugh.

Ernesto say the road too bad to mek it back to town so we going have to spend the night. And in truth, that was the words my ears wanted to hear all evening. Next thing he go inside and come out with a cigar and sit down and light it.

Then he turn to me and say, 'This is a celebration.'

'What you celebrating?'

'The same thing I celebrate every day. The revolution.' And then he wave the cigar in the air and say, 'Would you like one?'

And I say no because really I just happy to sit here beside him with the smell of the Cuban tobacco wafting over and seeing the smoke disappear on the breeze.

When I get into the bed the rain is coming down again and it is thundering and lightning. He come to the door and say to me, 'You OK?'

'I can't sleep.'

So he leave the makeshift bed he got in the living room and get in next to me. When I turn my back to him, he say, 'I will stroke you to sleep.' And just as soon as he say it I feel his hand creeping under the shirt, caressing my back in long gentle lines and small tight circles. And then wider curves and wavy motions until every inch of my skin was being touched, all at the same time, by his one single finger. In all of my life, and after all the men I been with, I never feel anything like this before. Not even with Pao as gentle and caring as he is. Because what I feel now is a presence, a connection between two people who are both fully awake and fully aware of being here together. Present instead of absent. Engaged instead of detached. A bonding not just of the body, but of the mind, even the spirit.

And as I am laying there thinking this, I feel him reach round and start stroke my stomach with a hand that is moving so light and slow it is sending waves through me like I am riding the surf. And I am wondering how much further I am going to let this man go. And what it means that I am laying here letting this happen. And why I don't just open my mouth and say, 'No.' But what I realise is, it not Ernesto that begin all of this. It was me. Because it didn't just start now with his hand on my back. It started from the moment I ask Matilde, 'Who is that?' and the dressing-up I do that evening, and the way I let him smile at me over the dinner, and how I wash the dishes with a welcoming body standing next to him at the sink, and the stirrings I had standing under the rock in the rain, and talking to him on the terrace like I did so open and familiar, and telling him I couldn't sleep, and letting him get into the bed with me. That was all me starting something, even if I never admit it to myself before now. And then I think about Pao. What loyalty do I owe him? Because even though he go marry someone else, that was a very long time ago and me and him still regular, and he still the father of my child.

But even as my mind is spinning on all of this, my body is moving in unison with the ebb and flow of this electricity that Ernesto is making with his fingertips touching alive every nerve in me.

When he move his hand to my breasts I realise there is nothing I can do. I am powerless. If I do not keep my mouth shut I will say yes, not no. So I lay there while I feel his hand moving down my stomach and round and round, until it stop between my legs, stroking my thighs and tracing the creases so dangerously close to the place where I am now aching for his hand to come to rest.

So I reach back to find where he is behind me. And just as I do it he pull his hips away, out of range, and say, 'No. This is for you.'

And right then I just turn 'round and I kiss him. With a full and open mouth like I never done before with anyone in my whole life. And he kiss me back with a tongue that was entwined with mine and a mouth that was giving and taking and guessing my every wish, even the ones I never knew I had. And just when I thought I was lost to every sight and sound of thunder and lightning and everything else in this living world, he slide down my body and put his head between my legs. And a soaring excitement and pleasure come over me from right down there in the depths rising up over my head.

He stop and say, 'You like this?' And then right after he put his head down again and start his mouth and tongue moving.

No man ever do this before. This was for me. It had nothing to do with money or him satisfying himself. Nobody was pretending anything. It was real and true and genuine. And I was real and I was true and I was genuine.

I didn't say nothing to him even though I could hear some moaning and long, deep gasping that I think was coming to me through the darkness. Except I knew it wasn't. It was coming out of me. Escaping. From a place I had never been to before.

Afterwards, he ease himself up the bed and with my back turned to him and our fingers entwined high above our heads over the pillow, he wrap his other arm 'round my waist and we fall asleep.

The half-light of dawn wake me up coming through the calico curtains. But I not ready for this to be over so I just take my hand and pull his arm further, tighter into me. And I close my eyes again.

When I finally wake up, the bed next to me is empty. The French doors is open so I can see clear 'cross the terrace with its little cobblestone wall to the hills beyond. The curtain pull back and wafting on the breeze, brushing the polished mahogany floor.

And then Ernesto is coming through the door, wearing nothing more than some loose cotton pants and bare feet, and carrying a tray with tostada and café con leche made, he says, 'With the best coffee in the world.' And I laugh.

He rest the tray on the foot a the bed and sit himself on the edge. Then he take off the pants and drop them on the floor, and slide himself between the white cotton sheets. He turn to me and say, 'How you doing?'

And I say, 'I am doing good. Thank you.'

We eat and drink, sitting up in the bed, breaking the tostada into pieces and dipping it into the coffee. Just quietly, taking in the view. Then he rest the tray on the floor. And while he doing it, I reach for the hem and pull the shirt off over my head. When he take me in his arms it seem like that is what his arms always intended to do.

I am encircled. Skin to skin. And then I am filled with peace and calm, and tenderness and joy, and anticipation. All at the same time. Purposeful but gentle, like the morning mist rising over the mountains on a bright, sunny Cuban day.

CHAPTER 24

WHEN I COME back and ask Auntie what Clifton Brown want she just shrug her shoulders and walk off.

And then I get a letter from Ernesto that I didn't even know if I wanted to open. Because after everything, we shower and sit on his terrace and eat the fruit plate and omelette while I listen to him talk more about the right to insurrection in the face of tyranny, and how we must work every day to make our successes greater and our failures fewer.

And then finally he say to me, 'You could stay. Stay here in Cuba.'

'I have a child Ernesto. I can't do that.'

'Then you get her, bring her back.' And he turn 'round and wave his hand towards the house. 'There is plenty space. I build two, three more rooms if you like. It is easy.'

When I look at him everything in my heart want to say, 'Yes, yes.' Like when yu struggling with something and can't make it work and then somebody come along and just say 'forget it' you don't have to bother doing that no more. It is relief. That is what you feel. You breathe out and your shoulders fall even though yu know the answer come too easy.

'What I realise this last two weeks is how much there is to do in Jamaica. How far we still have to go. And how important it is for everyone to make a contribution. Can you understand that?'

'Jamaicans are not revolutionaries.'

'Maybe not like you, but it doesn't mean we can't try to do something to bring some fairness and mek life better for people.'

'No. But Che says the true revolutionary is guided by great feelings of love. Is there great love of the people in Jamaica, Gloria? Is there love of the cause?'

And even after that, after he swerve the jeep coming down the mountain so he don't run over the fat ten-foot snake that the rain wash outta the undergrowth into the middle of the road, after we pass another billboard that say '*Los principios no se negocian*', he stand up with me at Rodolfo and Matilde's gate and say, 'There is still time to change your mind.'

I say, 'Ernesto, I am not what you think.'

'I know. Rodolfo told me.' He pause and then he say, 'And it is all right.'

My blood just boil. It heat up and bubble over. And everything that I was feeling about him and turning over in my mind and wondering what future we could make together come to a dead stop in that one moment. And in a voice full with rage and scorn I say to him, 'Who are you to decide whether it is all right or not?'

'I mean all right with me. Everybody deserves a second chance.' I don't say nothing, so he say, 'I know it is what you do, not who you are.'

'You have no idea who I am. Yu spend a few days with me that is all. Whoever yu think I am is something you made up. You imagined me, Ernesto.'

And just as I start to walk off he say, 'We even have programmes for women like you.'

So I turn 'round and I say to him, 'Yes, since yu make prostitution illegal and decide yu have to re-educate us.' And I turn 'round and go inside the house and shut the door and never even look back.

The thing that hurt wasn't so much the thought that all the time we were together he was thinking I was a whore. Even though what attract me to him was the look in his eyes that didn't have that question, 'How much?' What really hurt was that after all these years and after so long of not seeing no customers, I still think of myself as a whore. So Ernesto was wrong. Being a whore wasn't what I did. It was who I am, and that realisation I couldn't run from. Not even if I run to Cuba and into the arms of the revolution and Ernesto Sánchez.

When I open the letter it says: *Nothing is perfect, Gloria. You have to work at it. But you have to work at it with a forgiving heart. And I don't know if you can forgive me when there is still so much you have not yet forgiven yourself for.* I think the man presumptuous, even though I know what he say is true.

Then he tell me how the suffering in Cuba getting worse with the US not buying their sugar and refusing to sell them the oil and agricultural machinery they need. And then he write a poem.

> For you there was anger.
> For me there is anguish.
> And a longing so strong
> as to take the green from the hills
> and the aroma from the coffee
> and the light from the early morning
> in which I saw, and held, and touched you.

It made the tears roll down my cheek. Not the sort of crying where your chest heave and your nose run. Just a quiet, slow line of moisture that yu can wipe away with a single finger and rub against your thumb almost like it was a memory of something past. But under it, under the tears, the anger was still there because I let Ernesto reach me and then he let me down. Or maybe I was angry with myself for wanting him and then afterwards not knowing what to do with him.

And when Pao turn up I didn't know what to do with him either. I just let him stand there on the veranda 'til he say, 'So where yu been anyway?'

'Since when I got to explain myself to you?'

He stare at me long and hard and then he step past me and go inside. That evening when we go to bed we both knew something was different because halfway through I just stopped and rolled over with my back to him. So he reach his arm over me and rest his lips against my cheek. I thought he would say something but he didn't. He just lay there pulling me closer into him and breathing like he choking back his worry.

Auntie say Esther too sullen for a child. A child should be happy and laughing and talk-talk 'bout her school day and such like. But instead, she say, Esther just come in the house and go in the bedroom and lock the door. And when she come out to eat her dinner she not got no more than two words to say to anybody. Auntie say, 'Yu see di hole, someting a-go drop in-a-it.'

'Yu think I nuh notice it myself?'

'I don't know what yu notice. Question is, what yu going do 'bout it?' And she pick up the breakfast dishes and flounce into the kitchen.

So that afternoon when Esther come back from school I go knock on the bedroom door and stick my head inside.

'How yu doing baby?'

She look up at me from where she sitting on the bed reading a *Archie* comic book. She don't say nothing to me so I step into the room and walk over to the bed and sit down next to her.

'Everything all right at school?' She shrug her shoulders. 'Something bothering yu? Yu got something on your mind?'

'No.'

'No? So how come yu so quiet and not got nothing to say to nobody?'

She turn to me. 'Is there something you want to say to me?'

It take me aback. And then I see how she pile up in a corner all the presents I ever give her for birthday and Christmas that I say come from Pao. Some of them look like she never even bother open the box.

So I jut out my chin at them and say, 'What happen to all a that?'

'What do you mean?'

'The presents from your father.'

'My father?'

I put my arm 'round her shoulder and I say, 'Come on now Esther, yu know he is your father and he love yu.' But she just shrug off my arm and ease herself away from me.

'Esther, he love yu.' I can see she trying hard to stop the tears from falling. Using that same swallowing motion I did the night Pao tell me he was going to marry Fay Wong.

I ease myself up close to her. 'Why don't yu just tell me what it is?'

'Because it isn't going to change anything.'

'So what yu want to change?'

She sit there and let me put my arm 'round her and then she lean into me little bit.

'How come he never wants to see me? Don't you want to see somebody if you love them?'

'He come to see yu.'

'No. He comes to see you.' She pause and then she say, 'You know he never came over all the time you were in Cuba? Not once. It was Uncle Clifton who made sure we were all right. Don't you think he should have come?'

'He didn't know Esther. I didn't tell him about Cuba.' And I want to say to her again that Clifton not her uncle but I decide to leave it.

She sit there completely still, staring at me, and then she say, 'Why doesn't he ever talk to me, Mommy? Ask me about school or take me for a drive, or do anything with me? Why doesn't he ever do anything more than come in the house and talk to you?'

'That is how he is Esther. It nuh mean he don't love yu.'

But that not doing anything to calm the questions in her head. And since I not got nothing sensible to say to her she just decide to get up and walk out the room, and a little while later I see her through the window standing in the yard swinging a hula hoop 'round her waist.

Auntie say the other children keep asking Esther who her papa is, and what he do for a living, and what they do together on a weekend, and why he never come up the school to see any of the activities that go on up there.

So I say to Pao that maybe he could make a point to have some kinda conversation direct with Esther. And he try, but he can't make it last longer than two sentences.

'She a child. What yu expect me to say to her?'

'Say whatever yu say to Xiuquan or Mui. What yu say to them?'

He think long and hard and then he say, 'I don't know. I don't think I say anything to them.' And then he think some more and say, 'They come and they go and mama see to them. And they play some stupid little games wid Hampton. And on the weekend they come wid me while I pick up the money 'round Chinatown and such. But talk to them? All I say is put on yu shoes, get in the car, mind what yu doing when yu outta doors, smile at the people when they smile to yu, say thank yu when people give yu something. That is all.' And then he pause before he say, 'Cho, Gloria, children not there for yu to be talking to.'

I let a few weeks pass and then I say to him that maybe he could go show his face up the school so that everyone can see the child got a father, and he say he going do it. But every time I tell him 'bout some event going on up there he say he busy. Week come and week go, and still he never make no move. In the end I just give up because it don't seem like any fruit is going to come from my labouring with him over this.

Next thing I get a message from the school that they want to see me. When I get up there Sister Emmanuel tell me that Esther been telling lies 'bout who her father is and what he do. 'She is telling everyone that her father works at a hotel in Miami and is seldom here on the island. However, she seems extremely vague on details, for example, the name of the hotel or the precise nature of his responsibilities there.' And then she look at me over the top of the skinny little glasses she got perch on the end of her straight white nose.

'Let me ask you Sister. How many children Esther's age know so much details of what their father do? Is that common to you?'

'I am not here to debate the issue with you, Mrs Campbell. Or should I say Miss.' And then she straighten the few pages on the desk in front of her and sit herself upright and prim.

'Is there something else on your mind Sister apart from what Esther say about how her father earn his living?'

'As I have already said, I am not here to debate the issue. This is a liberal-minded school. It is 1961 after all. But we have our reputation to think of and well, suffice it to say, there is a problem.'

'A problem?'

She sigh and then she say, 'Perhaps you could have a word with the child.' And then she stand up and smooth down her white-white habit and tidy the ebony rosary beads hanging 'round her waist.

But when I talk to Esther she got nothing to say. She just shrug her shoulders like she don't know what all the fuss is about. And when I ask her why she telling these lies she just say, 'What do you expect me to say?'

'Say he is a shopkeeper. He Chinese. They will understand that.'

A little while later I got to go up the school again because they say Esther giving too much backchat to the teachers. I sit in that deadly office sweating and leaning over to catch some relief from the electric fan the Sister got standing on the edge of her desk, but nothing is making me feel any better. All I can do is remember how I used to hear the other children laughing at me in that yellow schoolroom, and feel the dryness in my mouth, and listen to my own heart pounding like it is me that Sister Emmanuel is reprimanding for the trouble I have caused. And maybe that is just what is happening because what she got to say to me?

'I suggest you take a firmer hand.' And then she gently close the Bible she have open on her desk like as to say we finish. Conversation over.

But nothing was over because three weeks later I was back in her office again. Only this time Esther been fighting with her classmates, scratching and kicking and screaming, and rolling 'round in the schoolyard dirt.

'Do you know what they were fighting about Sister?'

'That is of little relevance, Miss Campbell. The point is, such behaviour cannot be tolerated. Not in a reputable school such as this. Not with our responsibilities to parents. Respectable people with expectations about the sort of children with whom their child associates. Not with a child who is so obviously delinquent.'

'She is nine years old Sister. Are you telling me that all the adults in this school cannot control a nine-year-old child?'

'Our responsibility is to educate children, Miss Campbell, not control the excesses of their insolence or wanton acts of violence against each other, or property for that matter.'

'She damaged property?'

Sister exasperated. 'No, Miss Campbell. I simply mentioned it as an ancillary.' She take off her glasses and give them a wipe with a little pink cloth. And then she put them back on her skinny nose.

I sit there feeling like my whole body burning up from the inside. And what I want to do more than anything else is reach over and slap the stupid little glasses off her face. All that is stopping me is the picture in my head of a Cuban mountain school and my worry about what will happen to Esther if she don't get a good education.

So I calm myself and I say, 'What can we do to help the situation Sister?'

'Do? Surely I have already made myself clear. The situation cannot be tolerated.'

'So you throwing her out the school?'

'That is not how we would put it. But that is the only solution we can see.'

'That is the Christian answer all you educated people come up with?'

Her whole body stiffen and her eyes flash with a sudden anger that come over her.

'To be frank, Miss Campbell, certain matters have come to my attention. Firstly, Esther's father is not a hotel manager in Miami, nor is he a shopkeeper come to that. We know about him and his escapades.'

'Escapades?'

'Further, there is the question of your, let us say, occupation.' And she open her eyes wide. 'You asked about help and since it is my opinion that Esther's difficulties originate in the home I would suggest that you concentrate your attention in that direction.'

I open my mouth to speak but she just ignore me and carry on. 'Guidance can be found in the teachings of the Good Book and the Grace of the Lord.'

So at least we get to the bottom of it and since no amount of arguing was going to change anything I just stand up and take my purse and walk to the door. When I get there I turn 'round and say to her, 'So maybe yu not so Christian and liberal-minded as yu think if all yu want to do is punish a child for the sins of her father and mother.'

When I tell Pao he angry, which is the first time he ever show any concern over what happening with Esther.

243

'She cyan treat the child like that. It outta order. Yu want me go over there and talk to her?'

'I don't think talking going do any good.' And then I quickly say, 'I don't want yu doing nothing else either.'

'Cho, Gloria. What yu tek me for? I just trying to help that is all.'

And then he strut off into the kitchen. When he come back he swigging from a Red Stripe and toying with the bottle cap in his other hand.

'If she don't want the money there is plenty other places that will be happy to tek it.' Which is true but Esther still struggling with something that she going take with her wherever she go.

All Esther got to say is she don't care. She don't like the school anyway. Even when I ask her what she fighting over she just say it nuh matter.

'Esther, baby, something is troubling you. Yu don't want to talk 'bout it?'

But all she do is shrug her shoulders and carry on reading the comic book that resting in her lap.

So it was Sybil who say to me, 'What about the priest Henry tell yu 'bout?'

'The priest! Yu serious?'

She just sit there on the veranda looking at Miss Sissy 'cross the road and then she turn her head back to me.

'So what, yu think because Henry bring me over there he be the one to point me in that direction as well?'

'Yu got a better idea?'

'Henry don't know the priest. All he do is see him knocking at his door and hear the commotion going on between Fay and Miss Cicely over it. Yu think that is a recommendation? Anyway, I tek enough Catholics already.'

'What is more important to you, the shame yu feel with Sister Emmanuel or the chance that maybe this man could give Esther the help she need?'

'Since when you start falling on the side of God?'

'It is a suggestion, Gloria. That is all.' And then she peer at me sideways and say, 'Ernesto is here.'

I can't believe my ears so I just look at her but I don't say nothing.

'He come to find yu and was staying in a boarding house downtown but I tell him to come here. No point him spending his money like that.'

'Here? In this house? Yu not worried that maybe Pao come here and find him?'

'Pao don't come here no more, Gloria. Not since you leave.'

And just as she say it Ernesto step on to the veranda with a coffee cup in his hand and a smile of confidence that he had no right to feel. When Sybil see him she get up and walk inside.

'What yu doing here Ernesto?'

He jut out his chin towards me. 'You, Gloria.'

'Yu shouldn't have come.'

'No?'

'No.'

But what I realise is even though I still angry all I want to do is reach out and touch that hair and stroke that face and put my lips to his.

'Yu should know when to leave something alone.'

'I cannot leave this alone.'

I didn't say another word. I just take my purse and walk down the veranda steps, out the yard and into the quiet afternoon.

Three hours later I had Sybil on the telephone asking me what I am going to do about Ernesto. So I tell her I wasn't the one to invite him and she say she didn't invite him either.

'Well, I am not the one that got him sleeping over there in the house.'

She wait and then she say, 'He didn't come here for me, Gloria. He come for you.'

'I don't know what to do with him Sybil.'

'So what?'

'So he just going have to stay there 'til I figure out what to do.'

When I ask Henry 'bout the priest he tell me that he called Father Michael Kealey and he downtown at Bishop's Lodge. I think to hell with Fay. The man is a priest. It is his job to keep people's confidences. So I forget about Sister Emmanuel and I telephone the Lodge because I can't think where else to turn.

Father Kealey is a handsome man with a gentle face and grey hair at his temples. And a dimple in his chin. He mixed, maybe African and Indian. I don't know and I not about to ask him.

'Miss Campbell.' And he put out his hand to shake.

'Thank you for seeing me Father.'

'It is my pleasure. What can I do for you?'

I explain to him all about Esther and I ask him to excuse me as well because I am not a Catholic but brought up Baptist even though I can't say I been to any church in recent days, or years.

And he just smile and say, 'What would you like me to do?'

'I was wondering if yu would consider seeing Esther. Having a talk with her about all these troubles she having at school.'

He sit there nodding his head with his hands clasp together

across his chest. 'I don't really know how you think I might be able to help.'

'I don't know either Father. But Esther not talking to anybody.'

He think on it and then he say, 'Who did you say the child's father is?'

A dumbness suddenly come over me. I never expected him to ask me that. Not right now, just like that. There no point in lying so I just say it: 'Yang Pao.'

'Yang Pao?'

I don't know whether the expression on his face is horror or just ordinary surprise. So I sit there and wait.

And after a while he take out his little book and say, 'Why don't you bring Esther over next week. Monday, about 3 p.m. Will that be agreeable?'

'Yes Father. Thank you.'

Father Kealey sit with Esther for well over an hour while I was waiting outside in the garden lush and peaceful, and full of poinsettia and bird of paradise and little wild banana plants.

Afterwards, when we travelling home she suddenly say to me, 'I miss you when you go to Cuba you know?'

'Yu did? I thought you and Gang-gang had a real pleasing time together.' And then I say, 'And Uncle Clifton too.'

She sit quiet for a while and then she say, 'I saw the letter that came from Cuba.'

'The letter?'

'Yes. And I heard you on the telephone talking to Aunt Sybil.'

'That isn't nothing for you to be worrying about, Esther.'

She turn herself 'round and look straight at me. 'Are you going to leave me, Mommy? Because if you do I will have no father and no mother either.'

My heart leap out to her because it pain me to hear that this is what she think. So I put my arm 'round her shoulder and pull her to me and I say, 'I not going to leave you Esther. I never going leave you. You and me, we going to be together for ever and ever. Long after you get yourself a husband and have your own children and even after that, I will be loving the grandbaby and looking out for all three of you, or maybe four or five. Every little one that come along. That is how it going to be. Nothing on this earth could take me away from you.'

CHAPTER 25

BUT WAS IT Esther that was keeping me from Ernesto or was it because I was still angry with him, because the day I come home and find him sitting on the veranda anger was all I felt.

I tell Esther to go inside the house and then I say to him, 'What yu doing here?'

'I have been waiting days, Gloria, and nothing from you.'

'I didn't tell yu to come here. In fact, I already tell yu that yu shouldn't have.'

I rest myself in the chair across from him.

'And what we have means nothing to you?'

'What we have is a night and morning at your house and some trips to the mountain.'

He stand up and brush himself down and then he say, 'We cannot talk like this. I will be at Sybil's if you want to see me.'

And then he step off the veranda into the early evening street with his soft hair blowing on a gentle breeze.

When I go inside I take one look at Esther's guilty face and say to her, 'Yu should be in your room seeing to your business not listening to people's conversations.'

'Did he write the letter?'

'It doesn't matter, Esther. It don't concern you. What you need to be doing is getting yuself ready for the new school the Father sort out for yu.'

'I don't want to see any more nuns.'

'What you want? I will tell you what you want, and that is to make sure yu get yuself an education. Yu see those children in Cuba they marching over that mountain every day just so they can sit in a shack and understand how one word follow the next. They not bad-mouthing the teacher or fighting with their friends. They receiving their learning like it a gift not a chore like how you want to gwaan. Father Kealey had to make special arrangements for them to tek yu at the Convent of Mercy and what you should be is grateful. Not standing there telling me what you want. Yu understand me?'

The next day I go over to Franklyn Town even though I knew that all I had to do was sit on it and wait for him to be gone. But I don't. I kid myself into thinking that something had to be done, which most likely was just an excuse for me to go see him.

When I get there he is standing in the back yard painting that same fence Pao labour over all them years back. I pour some sorrel from the fridge and take it to him and then I ease away and gather my skirt and sit down on the concrete step.

'Yu not got nothing better to do than this?'

'This is for daytime.'

'Daytime?'

'Evenings I go with Sybil to her Party group to exchange ideas with the comrades.'

I smile and then I say, 'We got enough trouble here, Ernesto. We don't need you to come stirring everybody up.'

He put down the paintbrush. 'People are already stirred up. And what they seek is an end to their poor conditions. Perhaps my experience is of help.'

'Jamaica not the place for no armed uprising Ernesto.'

'What did you say to me? You said inequality is unjust and must be overcome.'

When I talk to Sybil 'bout how she change her attitude to him, she say Ernesto is inspiring. That people can't get enough of how he listen and think about things, and reflect back to them their own thoughts and experiences woven together with stories of Cuba and the wisdom of Fidel and Che. She say the referendum coming up over whether Jamaica should stay in the West Indies Federation and Ernesto helping them to get people interested and involved.

So how it end up was with the three of us, me, Sybil and Ernesto, going all over Kingston talking to every woman and man that would listen, about how Jamaica would do better as part of a regional federation as opposed to going it alone like Mr Bustamante say. Ernesto stand and sit and smile. And shake the hand of every man that come near him and kiss every woman on both cheeks and every now and again he say something like, 'A better life is not like an apple that falls from the tree when it is ripe. You have to make it happen.'

And just like this the days turn into weeks because the fighting and mayhem that go on after the US try to invade Cuba at Playa Girón meant that Ernesto couldn't make it home. So he stay and we carry on. And what I felt was pride. Proud of Sybil for the energy and commitment she put into caring all of these years. Proud of every Jamaican who take the time to listen and talk and think. Proud of Ernesto for having faith in us as a nation even though we weren't going to take up arms and storm the British at Up Park Camp. Proud to be standing next to him in the street, or watching him deliver a speech to a local Party group, or grabbing a patty with him at Monty's, or a soda at the pharmacy. Because wherever Ernesto go the sun was shining on him. Day or night. And I didn't even have to fret that Pao would see me. Or Henry for that matter. After all, what was I doing? Political work for a better Jamaica.

What I discover was that I had something to offer. Not only the personal experience that I share with Margaret Morrison's girls but also the thinking that I could do. I was uneducated but I wasn't stupid after all. I could actually think. And I could talk about what was best for Jamaica. Think and talk with complete strangers. And even though I couldn't quote Norman Manley or Che Guevara the way Sybil and Ernesto do, the struggle was still real and important to me. And I could add my voice to it. Not just sit on the veranda and hope for the best. I could contribute to our future.

But the night I decide to stay at Franklyn Town was the mistake that maybe half of me had been planning all along.

We come back to the house after a rally where Ernesto stand on the platform and tell the crowd in that cricket ground packed to the hilt that we have to learn to overcome our oppression. Capitalism made us weak. But with hard work, unity and sacrifice we can do it. Victory is ahead. They love it. They clap and cheer so much he could hardly finish what he was saying 'bout how we have to be firm in our faith and go forward with our eyes on the future and our feet on the ground.

The whole place erupt when he was done, bringing their hands together high above their heads and making so much noise they must have hear it all the way to Montego Bay. Whistling and hollering with so much excitement and appreciation it could have been Che Guevara himself standing there with the gentle smile in his eyes and the breeze fluttering the bunting behind him.

And it was in the spirit of that jubilation that I step up to him and throw my arms 'round him and held him to me. And he held me. And we stood there like we were alone again on his terrace overlooking the coffee hills. So alone I couldn't even hear the crowd no more or remember where I was. Not 'til Sybil tap me on the shoulder and I turn 'round and see the blanket of outstretched arms waiting to carry him off 'round the park.

When we finally come back to the house our feelings were running high. And a couple rums later it seem like the only thing to do was stay. I telephone Auntie so she wouldn't fret and I go with Ernesto to the room he sleeping in that used to be mine.

And the excitement I felt even before he touch me was filled with a yearning and longing I never imagine existed, never mind was possible for me to feel. He lay there looking down at me for some long time and then he take a finger and slowly encircle my lips. Round and round until all I wanted to do was take it into my mouth and suck. And just doing that one single thing set my whole body soaring as I taste him and watch him watching me. And then he kissed me with a mouth so firm, yet so gentle, while my arms closed fully 'round him.

The next morning when I wake up I realise I sleep with Ernesto naked. And that all night long all I wanted was to feel the warmth of his back or the firmness of his arm 'round me. Even his feet I wanted to feel resting gently on mine. And whereas with Pao I always put on a nightdress, and he pull on his shorts, with Ernesto it would have seemed like a retreat. A withdrawal from what we had shared.

I lay there in the early light of dawn thinking about him and me. And Esther and Auntie, and Marcia. And Pao. And Margaret's girls. And how Sybil so eager for every minute that Ernesto is with us talking about the marvels of Cuba and the revolution. And the great achievements of the women's federation with their daycare centres and education and work programmes. She cannot get enough of it even though it not all glorious because there is also plenty people wanting to shout down Ernesto and tell him to go back to Cuba because they don't want no communism here in Jamaica. One time it get so bad even I had to stick in my oar and say to them, 'Yu forget what all a this about? It nuh matter whether yu call it communism, or socialism, or democracy or anything else. The point is we want a better life. Fairness, equality, opportunity. That is what we want. Education, good health, a respectable job, a decent home. So we all on the same side. Remember that. Because at the end a this is people. Ordinary people wid ordinary lives. Not Party members who got nothing better to do than sit down here arguing and bickering with one another.' And they simmer down. But it is still there. The quarrel.

So even though I agree with Sybil that what happening in Cuba is truly marvellous, there is a part of me that is still holding back. Not from the good I think we doing right here right now, but from where this kind of pressuring people's opinion and party-line debating might tek me. And the expectation that Ernesto might have about what this time together mean.

Because in truth there was no future for me and Ernesto. After all, what did I ever hear from him apart from another quotation from Che or Fidel? We hardly knew each other. Except for what go on in the bed, and even though it like nothing else on this earth, it wasn't enough to build a life on. Not when you leaving behind everything and everyone you know, and uprooting your child for a foreign land. Because that is what Ernesto have in mind. He wouldn't give a second thought to him coming to Jamaica. So I get up and leave.

When I get back to Barbican Auntie was vex. Stirring Esther's porridge and crashing and banging every pot and pan she could find to boil an egg and butter some bread.

I don't say nothing to her, I just go take a shower and go to my bed. Later when I get up the house was empty. Esther gone to school and Auntie about her business. But before I could even turn 'round twice Ernesto was at the door asking me why I run off from him.

'I didn't run off from you.'

'So what happened?'

I look at him standing there on the veranda in his khaki pants and white shirt but I didn't say nothing.

'I am leaving tomorrow. Sybil's friends have found a way for me to return home via Moscow.'

'I know.'

'Will you come to Cuba? Not now but some time. Come and be with me.'

'Ernesto.'

'What do I have to do to make you say yes?'

I want to step across and hold him and stroke his head and calm his worried brow but I don't do it. I just stand there.

'I shouldn't have stayed with you last night. It was selfish. I let my feelings rule my head.'

'You regret it?'

'No Ernesto.'

'So come.'

'I can't. I belong here. Just like you belong in Cuba. But the gift you have given me, the truly wonderful gift, is me realising that I do have something to give and I want to do it. All those nights at the Party meetings and neighbourhood gather-ins, listening to you and hearing my own voice with ideas I am sharing with others, that was my awakening. My revolution. And now I have to carry on and build like yu said.'

He stand there a long time not saying anything, just getting more and more sad, with the realisation of what I am saying.

'I love you, Gloria.'

And right then all I want to say is 'I love you too' but I don't do it. I just hold myself still and hope the ache in me will pass.

'You will always be special to me Ernesto. Always in my heart and on my mind.'

'And I will always love you.' And he turn 'round and walk away. And I wept.

When Esther come back from school she wasn't talking to me. She wouldn't even look in my direction. So I just say to her, 'Cat got yu tongue?'

'You stayed with him last night?'

'What I do isn't your or anybody else's business.' Which I realise afterwards was sort of curt, covering over the guilt I felt.

She wait and then she say, 'I am not sure my father would agree.'

The next day I can't decide whether or not to go to the airport. And with all my dithering I leave it too late so by the time I get there he had already gone through the departure gate. I see Sybil waiting by the glass window and I walk over to her. And as we standing there looking out on to the empty runway she reach out and put her arm 'round my shoulder.

A month later I get a letter from him.

I have been trying to forget. It seems the only thing for me to do to keep my sanity. So I tend to the coffee, and I eat and drink and go about my daily business, and once in a while, for a minute or an hour, I am free. But each evening when I sit alone on the terrace with my coffee and cigar, and I go to my empty bed all I do is remember.

    Your back is on my mind
    with the little mole in the middle that I stroked and kissed.
    Your lips are on my mind
    As I slowly encircle them with my finger
    Your eyes are on my mind
    with their yearning and longing and laughter.

I hope that you are well, and Esther too. I send you the best of all things.

As always. Ernesto.

CHAPTER 26

SO THE REFERENDUM happen and Mr Bustamante get his way. Jamaica withdraw from the West Indies Federation. After that Mr Manley say the only way forward was for us to get self-government, so he and Busta go to England where Queen Elizabeth say we can have our independence from the mother country and they set the date for 6 August 1962.

The celebrations include eight days of rejoicing all over the island and a right stately visit from Her Royal Highness Princess Margaret and her husband the Earl of Snowdon. And to top it all they say we going have a big to-do in the new National Stadium the night when they take down the British flag and haul up the yellow, black and green that was for us and our future. Yellow for our natural riches, black for the struggle and green for hope.

But when the time come hope was the last thing I was feeling because instead of Norman Manley being the first prime minister of an independent Jamaica it was Busta and somehow I couldn't see him managing to do what Jamaica needed because no matter how much the elected government felt itself committed to a cause it didn't have the power to get the people to organise. And no amount of instructing or cajoling was going to make it so. Not like how the Cubans want to do everything for Fidel. There wasn't going to be no national literacy campaign that was for sure. No mass volunteering. There wasn't enough unity for that. We could sing and eat and dance. But was there enough love of the people? Enough love of the cause? I didn't think so.

So we nuh bother take ourselves to no street parade or the National Stadium to sing the new national anthem and watch the firework display. We just sit there in Franklyn Town, me and Sybil and Beryl and Auntie and Marcia, and watch Esther get entertained by the nonsense songs Trevor was busy making up and singing to us like he think some record producer going seriously take him on. Not that there wasn't music pouring outta every young man on this island because there certainly was that. Every one of them thinking that Prince Buster or Leslie Kong was going produce their record for the sound systems they got blasting out at the lawns. But Trevor, I didn't think so. For one thing, he only had the one song even though he switch 'round some of the words every time he say 'Here is another one', but it was still the same song. And whereas everybody else was singing 'bout independence and forward march and freedom sound, all Trevor had on his mind was how everybody and everything in this world let him down. The other thing, he only had the one tune. And when you hear that same tune over and over, even if it got different words, your mind switch off. So there was only Esther listening to him. Not that it matter to Trevor because all day long he was coming and going from the house with that twangy little guitar of his telling us 'Here is another one' like he just make it up in the hour or so since we last see him.

In between we do what we always do. Sit on the veranda with the radio playing and shaking the drink to cool it 'round the ice; and listening to Sybil talk 'bout how things need to get better for the working man, and more, working woman; and looking at Miss Sissy 'cross the road with her thin grey balding head sitting in her rocking chair rolling backward and forward smoking her pipe and when the thing not in her mouth watching her lips moving so you could almost hear the tut-tutting that was coming from her.

And while I was sitting there I realise that, even though I was happy that the white man and his queen wasn't ruling over their slave nation no more, the only thing I could think about was what Ernesto say to me about liberation not being achieved through the mere act of proclaiming independence but when economic domination of a people is brought to an end.

A week later Pao come over to Barbican. It a long time since I see him and longer since I get a chance to talk to him because all he say to me is, 'Yu and Sybil finish running 'round town getting everybody to go to Cuba?'

So I tell him it not what we doing and he say, 'Well, whatever it is it suit yu. It put a liveliness in yu. Yu sure yu not up to something I don't know about?'

'Like what? What yu think I got time for?'

He laugh. That same laugh that been making me smile all these years. Like a mischievous schoolboy with his head lowered and a big grin on his face. It was open-hearted and undefended. A look I couldn't imagine him showing to anybody else but me.

After that all he was doing was fretting over how some British army captain get a little Chinese girl called Merleen Chin pregnant. And she only twelve years old. And how her grandfather looking to him to fix it and he don't know how to work it out without old man Chin losing face which is the worse thing that can happen to a Chinese.

'Why this so important to yu?'

'Important! Yu serious? Chin is the head a the Chinatown Committee. If I cyan fix this I cyan fix anything.'

Truth was Dr Morrison already tell me all about it. Late one night in Franklyn Town after the card club finish and he come next door for one last drink and some peppermints before he go home. Told me all about how Pao going let him and Margaret adopt Merleen's baby because Margaret can't have none herself. And what I thought was how good that was of Pao to give the baby and the Morrisons a chance. And to give Merleen the chance to finish her schooling and have a life without a baby dragging on her heels. Not like those girls over Margaret's home or Auntie running away to Kingston with me wrapped in a shawl.

The captain wasn't no news to me. I already hear all about him from Fingernail over Passmore Town because a while back he was asking her if she have any young-young girls. And she tell him, 'Go 'way man, what yu think this is?' That is what she say anyway. But her telling me, that whole conversation, was just a bit of tittle-tattle so she could build herself up to asking me if they could increase their percentage on the money we lending.

So I say to her, 'No man. A deal is a deal. Nothing change since we shake hands and drink down the rum together.'

And she scratch her head with that same nasty fingernail that I swear the nail varnish must be so cheap it chipping off before it even dry, because every time you see her it look just the same.

'Yu not even going tek a minute to think 'bout it, Gloria?'

'There not nothing to think about. If yu want more money, mek more business.' And even as I say it I knew she wasn't going take no for an answer. And the sideways glance Sybil give me, the one I catch outta the corner of my eye, tell me the same thing. But more. That maybe I was too hasty turning Fingernail down like that. Maybe I should have sweeten it a little bit more. Maybe I was storing up trouble for down the road.

But that was then, and right now what I wanted to talk to Pao about was how we going make sure Esther get herself a good education, because there was no way I wanted her to end up like me. Or like him come to that. Jamaica didn't have no tolerance for the likes of us no more. Those days had gone. And just like I said to the Party faithful, the future had to have equality and opportunity in it. For women as well as men. And education was the key to that.

'The child only ten years old. What yu fret yuself about?'

'Ten years old, that is exactly when yu have to be fretting. Next year she not a baby any more. She got to go to high school and where yu think she going go?'

Pao think I want Esther to go to Immaculate Conception where he worried the nuns going want to know who her papa is and he don't want Fay finding out because according to him she don't know nothing about him having a child with me.

'You think Fay dunno? What daydream yu living in if yu think Fay don't know?'

But he just stand there in the kitchen like he forget about the school troubles Esther already have. Or maybe it don't matter. And even though I keep mentioning it to him it not doing no good.

Then he disappear. No hide nor hair of him did I see. When he finally turn up he say St Andrew and Alpha Academy two good schools. And yes, he would think that because they both got plenty black girls. Not like the great Immaculate that so white. And even thinking that way not worrying him because Pao consider himself enlightened. He run with his little gang of black boys and that is good enough for him. But inside I know he really fixing on how dark Esther's skin is. So I decide to tell him some home truth 'bout how independence didn't change anything in Jamaica. That it wasn't no Chinese revolution like he always telling me Zhang talking 'bout. The peasants didn't get no liberation. And it wasn't no Cuba either.

'The same thing that was going on before is the same thing that is going on now. The British take all the profit from the plantations, and they still taking it. And now the Americans and the rest of them going take the big profit from the bauxite and all the hotels and factories they busy throwing up all over the place, and Jamaica going to be left exactly where we always been.

'Jamaica look good on the surface, but unless yu make sure your daughter get a good education she going end up with the same choices I had, the same two choices that is waiting for her because she is a woman and because of the colour of her skin. And I don't see her wanting to be no domestic, not any more than I did.'

He silent like he can't believe I am talking this way to him. The funny thing about St Andrew and Alpha was that it was the same two schools Father Michael mention to me. So right away I knew where Pao been to get his advice. And when I tell him it the same priest that Fay running to with her woes all he do is vex some more over how I know 'bout Father Michael, 'til in the end I say to him, 'You give up the right to say anything to me 'bout what

I do or what I know when you decide to go marry Fay Wong.' And that shut him up. It surprise me though, because I never take Pao for the sorta man to go talking to a priest.

Esther say she don't want to go to any more convent school so I put her name down at St Andrew High School for Girls and she take the entrance examination and pass it. We go get the uniform and such, which she excited about because she know St Andrew is a good school. The little white blouse fit perfect but we have to get the pinafore altered. When it done I say to her that she should put it on and go show to her father the next time he come.

She do it. She go in the living room and twizzle 'round in front of him two times and then she just walk out without saying a single word to him. I feel sorry for her that she got no idea how to be with him even though I keep encouraging her to tell him something or maybe ask him a question. And to be fair to her, she been trying her best but it not getting her nowhere because Pao can't make it beyond, 'Hello, how yu doing?'

When Pao gone I say to her, 'Yu don't want to say nothing to yu father?'

'Like what?'

'Like maybe thank him for paying the school fees, or ask him if he think the uniform pretty.'

'What would I have to thank him for? You could have paid the fees yourself. We didn't need anything from him.'

She right and the only reason I let him do it was because I wanted him to feel like he was taking some responsibility. But the way she say it and then ease her weight back on her leg it was like she steadying herself to have some big fight with me.

'Esther he is still your father.'

And then she really set herself and say, 'I heard him. In the kitchen the day you were fighting about Immaculate.'

'That was just a misunderstanding Esther.'

'What, that the nuns might misunderstand that he is my father? Or his wife might misunderstand that I am his daughter? I was standing behind the dining-room door. I heard every single word. And I heard you too, telling him about how I am going to end up with the same two choices you had and not wanting to be a domestic.' She pause and then she say, 'What was the other choice?'

'The other choice?'

'Apart from being a domestic.'

It was like being plunged into water so deep and so cold your whole body go into shock. You freeze and you can't breathe.

'It don't matter. It not important.'

'It is what they said isn't it?'

'Who?'

'The girls at school.'

'That is what yu fighting about?'

Her face was pure anger. Rage, right down to its core.

'Esther . . .'

'Don't Esther me.'

'It was a long time ago. Long before you were born. It all behind us now.'

'Is it?'

'Esther, I love you. Your father love you. Isn't that enough?'

She think on it and then she say, 'It would be better if I didn't have any father at all. If maybe he was dead, or you never knew who he was in the first place.'

'Don't talk like that girl. Yu know yu don't mean it.'

'I do mean it. I already told Father Michael. And I also told him about the letter and him from Cuba.'

'Yu tell him that!' I can hear how my voice raising so I calm myself and I say, 'Yu got to have roots Esther. Otherwise yu can never make sense of your life.'

'I've got roots. I have you and Gang-gang, and Aunt Marcia and Aunt Sybil. That is enough for me. I don't need a father, especially one that can't even bring himself to say, "Yes, that is my daughter right there."' And then she walk off into her bedroom and shut the door.

Two minutes later she open it again and say to me, 'Will you come with me to Father Michael some time?'

'I thought your chats with him was private. Between you and him. That is what he tell me.'

'Not if I ask you to come.'

So I say yes and she close the door.

Later on when Esther fast asleep and me and Auntie catching some night air on the veranda I turn to her and I say, 'Tell me 'bout Antoinette.'

'What Antoinette?'

'Yu know, Gloria Antoinette Campbell.'

She stare straight into my eyes like she searching for something, like she probing deep into my soul. And then she turn her head away to the street and the dark.

'Antoinette was a slave. When she come to di plantation she was just a girl and di slave master tek one look at her and give her that name straight off. And after that she never have no other name. Not even di one she come wid from Africa because she was Antoinette and she never wanted to be nothing else. So di story go. And right away he tek her into di big house and bed her and she become his in every way possible. Everybody think he just going keep her like dis 'til di next young slave girl come along to turn his head. But then he surprise everybody when he go marry her and Antoinette was so happy she was singing and dancing all over di place. And then after that he tek her to Haiti because he was a Frenchman and that was where he come from. And Antoinette wasn't no slave no more. She was a lady and she leave all a that behind her.'

'And when she go to Haiti did she go live on another plantation? Another plantation with African slaves?'

'That was where di story end, Gloria. With happiness that Antoinette not no slave no more.'

'But it not happy is it? Because when she go to Haiti Antoinette would have live on another plantation where she wouldn't be nobody. She wouldn't be slave and she wouldn't be mistress. She wouldn't belong anywhere at all. She would be a lonely island.'

I think on it little bit more and then I say, 'You think the story end happy but it didn't. It end sad because Antoinette wouldn't have nowhere to settle her heart. Yu cyan be happy for not being a slave while slavery still going on and yu people still in chains. Yu have to get rid a slavery before yu can be happy.'

Auntie take a long time before she speak and then she say, 'I tell yu this di first time I come to Franklyn Town and yu try give me tea to drink. Slavery not only di chains that bind yu hands and feet, it di chains that bind yu mind. So yu can still be a slave even after all di slaves in di land been set free. I tek what yu saying 'bout Antoinette. I think yu have a point. But this not just some old story 'bout a slave girl. Slavery done and gone a long time back. But you Gloria, yu still a slave. A slave that still not forgive herself for letting them catch you. Like it was your fault, maybe for being so stupid or slow, or maybe careless or irresponsible.

'At least Antoinette was free in her head. She tek di name and she mek it her salvation no matter whether she fit in or she a island like yu say on that plantation in Haiti. You got di name but yu still not free in yu head. Yu still got di chains a slavery wrap 'round yu soul. The chains a all di generations that come before yu and everything that happen to yu since yu born. And even though yu stop yu dirty business this long time back, yu still a slave to it in yu head.

'The good Lord say we have to repent for di sins we commit and forgive dem that sin against us. But we have to forgive ourself as well for di sins that get commit against us. Nobody ever mention that part, but that, Gloria, is di hardest part. When yu do that, that is when yu will set yuself free. And you, like Antoinette, won't be no slave no more.'

I sit there looking at her a good long while remembering Ernesto's letter 'bout having a forgiving heart and then I say, 'What about you, Auntie? What about the sins that commit against you?'

'That is another story. A very long story for a different time.'

I go with Esther to see Father Michael and what she want is for me to see how he talk to her. Or listen more like because in truth the Father not saying that much. He just sit there with his hands folded in his lap, and every now and again he ask her a question or repeat back what she just say to him. But it not no question like I would say, 'How yu doing baby?' He giving her clues. And the other thing I notice is he talk to her like she smart and got a head on her shoulders. Like she can think for herself. And that is right because Esther older than her years.

So she tell him 'bout the conversation me and her have 'bout the school uniform and such and he say, 'How did you feel after that? Did you feel listened to?'

'No, because I never got to say anything I really wanted to.' He just sit there and nod. And then she say, 'About how it feels with him not loving me.'

'And the things the girls said about your mother?'

'Yes.' And then she take a sideways glance at me and say, 'I felt ashamed. And I was angry that they knew and I didn't.'

He take a hand and stroke his face, round the cheeks and lips and jaw. 'How, I wonder, would a mother tell a child, especially one of your tender age, a thing like that?' But the way he say it make it clear he didn't expect an answer. He was just ruminating on it.

And what I realise is my conversation with her always full of excuses for Pao. Defending him and chastising her. And even though I might be thinking all sorts of things 'bout what a rough time she having and how he could do better, I never say it. All I say is, 'He is your father and he love you.'

Father Michael is calm. His voice is even and gentle. He not forcing her to accept anything. She can say whatever she want and he will listen to it. And the way he talk to her is open. Not like he telling her but more like he thinking about things himself. Mulling it over in his mind. So after that, I realise it was me. Me who had to change. Because all Esther was doing was following my cantankerous ways.

On the way home I say to her, 'I didn't mean what I said to Pao about the two choices. I was just trying to provoke him.'

'I know.'

'And the other thing, about the past . . .'

'Was a long time ago.' And then she say, 'And the Cuban? Is he in the past as well?'

And I just say, 'Yes.'

CHAPTER 27

'WHAT SHE CALLED?'

'Loretta.'

'Loretta?'

'Loretta.'

'How long she and you . . . yu know?'

'Since independence week.' And then Marcia stop. And I just look at her because I can't believe what she is telling me.

'Yu already meet her.'

'I did?'

'Remember the meeting you and Sybil organise independence week 'bout how women going contribute to building Jamaica's future? And the play they put on? Well, the woman that come from Miami to help write it, that was her. Loretta.'

I take a deep breath and hope to God that Auntie stay out the house long enough so I can talk sensible to Marcia without no interference from her. I think the supermarket trip must take her at least two hours so I reckon we still got time.

'So what yu asking me?'

Marcia take a sip of the sweet sorrel and let her eyes pass over the bougainvillea that busting purple all over the fence.

'I asking yu what yu think.'

'What I think? This is Jamaica, Marcia!' I pause and then I say, 'This woman mean that much to yu that yu willing to tek all the nastiness people going throw at yu never mind the brick through yu window or the fire they going set over that house in Franklyn Town?'

She ease forward on the chair and rest her elbows on her knees. And then she clasp her hands together before she start talking.

'When I first meet her I think she smart. She smart, Gloria, yu know that. The way she talk 'bout women and power and such yu know this woman read a lot a books and she thinking and turning ideas over in her mind all the time. Everybody wanted to talk to her and listen to what she got to say. We all like bees 'round a honey pot. And it not only because she bringing new thoughts to people's experience, it because she got energy. And she funny, Gloria, she really funny. I cyan remember the last time I laugh so much. Sybil say Loretta's energy and humour is magnetic.'

'So Sybil know all about this?'

She just nod her head. 'And afterwards I ask yu if we could tek her up to Ochie for a few days in Henry's house and yu say yes. And that is when it start.'

'With Sybil and Beryl in the house!'

'Gloria, yu got to share rooms. You know that. So Sybil and Beryl share, and me and Loretta.'

I lean over to her and I say, 'Keep yu voice down. I don't want all a this news carrying on the breeze to the whole street.'

So she sit back in the chair and reach for the glass. After she finish drink she rest it back on the little round formica table next to her.

'It not like anything I ever experience in my whole life before. It was different and lovely. So lovely yu cannot imagine. Kissing a woman, Gloria, it is lovely.'

'Don't talk to me 'bout kissing no woman. This is Jamaica, Marcia.'

'Being with a woman is like being together in a gentle flowing river. It is soft and soothing and calm. And everything is like it moving in unison. So yu can't even tell any more where you end and she begin. And it is all giving. There not nobody taking nothing from the other one. Both of yu is giving and receiving in the same measure. It equal. It honest.'

She stop, and I think thank God because I don't know if I want to hear any more. It horrifying me. But then I think who am I to be horrified about anything that anybody does? Me, of all people.

'Marcia, Jamaica not got no patience for this sorta thing.' But she don't say nothing, so I say, 'What Sybil and Beryl say 'bout it?'

'Sybil think Loretta wonderful. She love Loretta for everything she got to say 'bout women and men, and power and resistance. Beryl, she just glad to see me happy.'

'Yu happy Marcia?'

She lift up her head and turn to me. And then I see a curious look in her eye. It almost like pain, but it not pain. It confusion.

'Yu nuh happy then?'

'I am happy, Gloria. Happier than I ever imagine I could be. I just don't know if I ought to be.'

'What yu mean?'

'Like if it right for someone to feel so happy over a perversion. I mean, Gloria, it not really natural is it?'

'Yu think what yu been doing with them men all these years is natural? Did it feel natural to yu?'

She think on it and then she say, 'It feel like what a woman supposed to do. Yu know, do it with a man. That is God's way.' She stop and then she start again. 'I did have a real man yu know. Eugene.'

'So who that?'

'Just a man I meet. But he didn't know nothing 'bout the other business.'

'And what happen?'

'He vex me and I couldn't get over it. So after that I was angry wid him all the time over every little thing and it wear us both down.' She wait. 'And then there was Milton.'

'Yu do it with Milton?'

She smile. A big broad smile. 'I tell yu before how he was hanging 'round the place every Friday night watching and waiting while Hampton collect the money. I could see it in his whole body what he wanted, so yes. And it was nice, yu know. He sweet and young and eager to please. Milton was like a little treasure 'til Hampton tell him he had to get himself a proper woman.'

And just then I see Auntie stepping outta the taxi cab and the driver rushing to the trunk to offload the Hong Zi grocery store bags. She come back sooner than I expected. He carry the groceries to the veranda and Auntie reach in her purse for his tip and he was gone.

'Esther not back from school yet?'

'No Auntie, she got her choir practice.'

'Well, I going unpack these things. You two want some coffee or something?' And she disappear into the house.

Well, I think, maybe it not such a revelation. Maybe I should even have seen something like this coming. Some serious way that

Marcia was going take one step beyond, because she been hurting her whole womanhood. But another woman?

I lean over and whisper, 'So this is why yu been going to Miami? Not just the shopping like yu tell me?'

'Yes, and Loretta come down every month as well. And we got the telephone every night.'

'Every night! So it serious then this nine months since independence?'

'I think so. The thing is, Gloria, she coming down for the cele-bration next weekend and I want yu to meet her. Meet her properly.'

We sit there quiet for a spell and then I say, 'This Loretta, she been with a woman before?'

'She never been wid a man, Gloria. She never even seen a grown man naked.'

So come Saturday I go over to East Kingston to the church hall I organise for the evening. The place full-full. It was a joy to see all these women crowded into the room drinking rum punch and eating curry goat and rice, and talking with so much excitement and expectation. It was a relief as well after all the weeks we spend at Party meetings, church groups and school gates. Even the emer-gency room at the hospital. Wearing out shoe leather telling women to come enjoy some fun and entertainment 'bout the life of women in Jamaica.

Then Marcia walk 'cross the room to me with this woman by her side. She is tall and slim and black and beautiful. I remember her, looking like she should be running in the Commonwealth Games not sitting down with a pen in her hand writing no plays.

'This is Loretta.'

I reach out my arm and shake her hand while I notice what a sparkle her eyes got to them.

'So nice to meet you.' That is what she say in her Miami-American voice, which is fine, except me, I got no voice. I got no idea what to say to this woman. So I just stand there thinking to myself so this is what a homosexual woman look like. And then I realise how foolish that is because I got no idea how many of them are standing right here in this room with me. Because when yu look, yu can't tell nothing. After all, who would see Marcia and think a thing like that?

Sybil come over to where we standing and I say to her, 'Good turnout gal.' And she laugh. Then she say to Loretta she need her and the two of them walk off with Sybil glancing at me over her shoulder like, 'So now yu know.'

Ten minutes later we all sitting down in front of the stage. And what happen next was the most incredible display of Jamaican womanhood with women singing songs and acting little skits and reciting their poems. They so clever with the words and so brave to be standing up there performing in front of all these people. Not trained actresses, but the ordinary, everyday women we meet on the street and at church and outside the school gate. And the fun they poke at how women and men gwaan with each other was unbelievable. It cut right through all the manoeuvring we do this way and that, all the blustering and ranting and piggishness you get from men, and the conniving that women do to get what we want. I laugh so much I thought my belly would bust. Even the two nuns standing at the side was laughing. Though every now and again they put their hand over their mouth like maybe they nervous 'bout enjoying themselves too much.

But it was seriousness as well. Because all the joking aside there was a message. A message about how we need to take charge of ourselves and our lives, and stop playing all the same damn-fool games we doing since the beginning of time, and give up acting like we too weak and too stupid to do anything worth doing. That we have to behave like the intelligent and courageous people we are. And always have been.

Then almost like my eyes deceiving me, I see Marcia standing there in the spotlight saying she got a poem to share. I turn and look at Beryl sitting next to me but she just give me a quick glance before putting her attention back on the stage like she knew it was going to happen. And after all the clapping and cheering, because this audience very enthusiastic to listen to any woman who got the nerve to get up there and say more than two words, Marcia begin.

'Di man dem come, di man dem go.
Deh mek their vibration and tek their jubilation
off of my inhalation
and then deh swallow di intoxication.
Dem nuh fret 'bout what deh do
because di money on di table is fah yu
and since it yu dat choose
who going talk about abuse?
But who in her right mind would favour this
if she could have di kinda bliss
deh say every woman can get if she find di right man?
That is di illusion dem sell to yu
to secure di fusion of your labour in di kitchen and wash-house and bed.
Because when all is said
and done, that is just another set a chains

not fah your hands and feet but fah your heart and head.

So it nuh matter if there not no opportunities or education or work

Why yu fuss so much 'bout being a wage clerk.

Yu already got all yu need to serve and satisfy and feed.

So just keep cooking and scrubbing and open yu knees

and he will do what he want nice or nasty as he please.

And di money on di table?

That is to appease for di lack a di ring on yu finger

and di risk yu tek every time yu open di door.'

They clapping and hooting and pounding their feet on the floor. That is how much they love Marcia's poem. Next thing Loretta come up on the stage and hug her and take Marcia's hand and hold it up in the air, which make the crowd go wild with their appreciation and admiration, with some of them whistling and shouting out 'Go sista' and 'Yah man'.

I stunned. I look at Marcia standing there and I think well, listening to you talk 'bout Loretta made me worry that it was she that have you hypnotised, but hearing that poem change my mind completely. Hearing that poem make me realise that you, Marcia, have been on this journey for a very long time. Because that poem, that poem, was pure Sybil.

When all the gaiety done and we go back to Franklyn Town I say to Marcia, 'So when yu start write poem?'

She sit there sheepish like I catch her out with some long-time secret. She nuh say nothing at first and then she say, 'I know it not nearly good enough but I think I got a message to send, yu know? Because what they say is, the personal is the political.'

Then Loretta say, 'She works very hard, Gloria. Reading, going to speeches and rallies when she is in Miami. And the poem she shared tonight is better than she thinks. It's a great poem.' And she smile and take Marcia's hand in hers. 'The work of a truly promising poet.' She pause and then she say, 'Your sister is gorgeous, and kind, and really talented.'

And then she lift up Marcia's hand and kiss it.

Sybil come out with the drinks so I motion my head towards the two of them sitting there side by side and I say to her, 'So what yu mek a all this?'

She rest the tray on the table and smile. 'Jamaica got a bad attitude over this homosexual thing. That is for sure. But you ever ask yuself where it come from? And know that it start way back in the nineteenth century with some law that the British mek. So I say to myself, yes, that was slavery. That was how they enforce their complete domination over us. Including telling us who we can love and who we can tek to our bed. Because that is the most private part of a person's life yu can control. That law was to keep us in our place. Because if men doing it with men, and women doing it with women, it not meking no babies to increase the stock. Yu ever think of it like that?'

'Yu nuh think it because a God and the Bible?'

'Whose God and whose Bible? The white man. And it was the white man mek the law and threaten the punishment and frighten the living daylights outta everyone. And that trepidation come down generation after generation 'til it get fully integrated into the society. Into the culture. Maybe the negativity even a camouflage now for our shame of that history.' She stop and pour out the rum into the glasses. 'Or maybe it just fashion or most likely fear. Because how many ordinary Jamaicans yu think really feel so strong 'bout this thing? Really and truly. Compared to how many, if they wasn't fraid 'bout God's damnation or the trouble they might bring their way, would say, "We free from the chains of slavery. Let every woman and man choose to love whoever they want".'

She light a cigarette and sit down. Then she say, 'We independent now. The national anthem say teach us true respect for all; and justice, truth be ours for ever. That is what everybody so happy busting their lungs singing about. Out of Many, One People nuh? It time we put our money where our mouth is.'

Sybil always talk 'bout everything like it cut and dry. For me it not so straightforward. Because what I see is Marcia making a rod for her own back. And I can't understand why. I can't understand how being with a woman could be so lovely and so important that you willing to take all the nastiness and bigotry and misery that you suffer as a result. Why choose that? And yet when I look at her and the two a them sitting there together, I see a glow in her that I never see before. A contentment like she settled in herself and not struggling no more to put on a face that going keep her demons at bay. She at peace. And I think about how I felt sitting on that terrace with Ernesto drinking the coffee and watching him smoke the cigar and I wonder why I or anybody else would want to rob her of that? But what I know for sure is they can't live like that in Jamaica. So sooner or later Marcia will be packing her bag and getting on that plane to Miami for good. And that part, losing her, that was the part that was really grieving me.

The next day I go have lunch with them over Franklyn Town. Beryl serving macaroni cheese with salad, which I think not that special given Loretta only here for a couple more days. But Marcia say Loretta love macaroni cheese so I guess that is all right.

'It been hard, Gloria. Matching up how I feel about Loretta

with my confusion, yu know, that feeling inside a me telling me that I wasn't no homosexual. Because I had an idea about myself and that wasn't it.'

Just then Sybil step into the dining room with Beryl behind her carrying the plates and things to fix the table. And after that Loretta follow with the glasses and rum punch and fresh sorrel. Marcia give Loretta a smile. And then the two a them sorta nod to each other. A special recognition that was quiet and private even though the room full a people.

The breeze coming through the open window is nice because outside it really hot. Inside it cool, not just from the fresh air, but from the stillness of what passing between everyone. Then Loretta say, 'I don't know if it's appropriate to ask you, Gloria, what you think?'

I can see all of them got the same question on their tongue. Even if they leave it to Loretta to ask.

'Yu two grown women. Yu big enough to choose what yu want to do.' They all just sit there waiting for whatever else is on my mind.

Then Sybil say, 'Well, it been an education for me. Simone de Beauvoir, Betty Friedan and a voice inside a me saying what we need now is to understand how the struggles of women different if you also poor, or black, or homosexual. And that it just as important as anything the white woman got to face.'

Marcia lean into Loretta and the two a them touch hands.

'If yu want the honest truth, I don't understand it. Or maybe I only understand part a it. The part about wanting to be with someone likeminded. About things between you being equal and honest. The sharing. I live long enough in this life to understand that. But the other part, about wanting to be with a woman . . .

like that, I got no idea about that. So I wonder if Marcia sure what she doing. And worry in case she go fix herself into something only to find out later on that it not what she want.'

'Yu could say that 'bout anybody yu wid.'

'This not just anybody though is it Marcia?'

Then Loretta say, 'You are right, Gloria. And I do keep asking Marcia if she's sure and reminding us that we should take things slowly.'

Marcia smile and squeeze Loretta's hand and say, 'I never been more sure of anything in my life.'

Later on when Marcia walk me out to the taxi she say, 'It is lovely being with Loretta.' She pause. 'I feel joy when I am with her. Not just happiness, Gloria. Joy. Just to listen to her talk, or look at her 'cross the table or watch her sleep. I love her, Gloria. And she really love me, even though she see me at my worst as well as my best. She love me. With a passion and patience and devotion I never imagined anyone ever could or would want to.'

CHAPTER 28

TWO MONTHS LATER I discover I was right 'bout Fingernail when Trevor come tell me that she asking him so much question 'bout what gwaan over the house in Franklyn Town and who was coming there.

'She ask me who the man.'

'What man?'

'The man Marcia talking 'bout when she say to Fingernail long time back that the man don't want no trouble.'

It shock me because I thought we were long past that by now. 'So what yu say to her?'

'I didn't say nothing to her. I just tell her I got no idea what she talking 'bout. And then she start ask me what other man coming to the house and I just laugh and say to her the place is a whore house how many men yu think going there? I never say nothing to her, Gloria. Nothing, not even after she tell me she could get me a appointment wid a record producer she acquainted with.'

I didn't mention any of this to Henry. Things good between us even though I was worried we would change after what happen in Ocho Rios. But Henry not like that. To him, business was

283

business and since that time we back to normal. Excepting maybe something did change because he stop talking 'bout me being like a daughter to him. Now we was more like friends. Somewhere beyond friends just short of lovers. Like after the affair finish but yu still care deeply about each other. That is how it was. And the Ochie thing never get mentioned.

Next thing I know Abraham was on the telephone telling me that some man been up the house in Ocho Rios asking questions 'bout Henry, but just like Trevor he didn't say nothing. He just pick up the phone to me because, he say, he didn't want to be alarming Mr Henry with any of this news.

How Fingernail and her mystery man make the connection between me and Henry and the house I couldn't figure out. All I knew was I didn't want anything bad to happen to Henry, especially if it had something to do with me. After I think on it for a few days I realise that Clifton Brown was the only person I could turn to, so I ring the police station and ask him to come meet me.

I take a taxi to the airport and he pick me up in his car and drive over to Port Royal where we go get a drink in Morgan's Harbour. We sit there in the shade gazing out at the blue Caribbean with the tourists going up and down on their waterskis churning a white foam and cutting through the peace and quiet with their motorboat engine.

'What I have to tell yu mean me putting all of my trust in you.'

'All your trust, Gloria? All of it?'

'This not about no murder, Sergeant Brown. It about something completely different.'

He stare into the glass a while and then he turn to me. And just in that split second with him looking at me I remember him going over to the house while I was in Cuba and I decide not to do it.

Not to tell him 'bout Henry and Fingernail and all the situation that unfolding.

'So what it about then?'

I sit there quiet and then I say, 'Nothing. It not about anything.'

He raise his eyebrows at me. 'Yu bring me all the way over here to tell me it nothing?' He pause. 'So it not going surprise yu when I tell yu I don't believe yu.'

'Well maybe I just change my mind about bothering yu with it. Yu busy policeman. I don't want to be taking yu time.'

'Yu taking my time right now. So why yu nuh just tell me?'

My mind in a muddle. 'Clifton, I change my mind.'

He narrow his eyes. 'So be it. So be it, Gloria.'

We finish our drinks and drive back to the airport where I catch a Checker Cab to Franklyn Town.

Sybil think that Fingernail just fishing with Trevor.

'And anyway, who say the man up Ochie got anything to do with her? The two things could be completely disconnected for all you know.'

She right. I just running ahead of myself. So I decide to forget it and hope that I don't hear nothing more. After all, moneylending not actually illegal, even if we not official as such. Even the prime minister, Mr Bustamante, was in the moneylending business at one time with his little office there in Duke Street. But people still frown on it. So if it get out poor Henry's name going get drag through the mud, not just for the money but for who he in business with, a no-good East Kingston brothel keeper.

And that thought made me realise I couldn't leave the situation alone. So I decide to tell Henry what going on and he say, 'Some man go North Street when I not in shop. Ask Alvin all about me.'

'What Alvin say to him?'

'He say, I businessman. Own supermarket and wine merchant and live Lady Musgrave Road with wife and children.'

'Yu got any idea what that all about?'

Henry don't know, but he say nothing else happen since then and it was a good three weeks back.

When Marcia telephone to tell me she think somebody watching the house over Franklyn Town that is when I knew the situation bad outta hand and I had no choice but to go back to Clifton.

'Oh, so now yu want to tell me.'

'What can yu do Clifton?'

He look out to sea just the same way he do the last time we sitting there in the shade at Morgan's Harbour. And then after some long while he say, 'I already do it, Gloria.' And he smile.

'Yu already do what?'

'I already know all about yu mystery man and who hire him and what she want. Everything, Gloria, everything, believe me.'

Clifton pleased with himself. Smug. It wouldn't have surprise me if he pull a big, fat cigar outta his pocket and stick it in his mouth, except Clifton don't smoke.

'So yu going tell me?'

'That depends.'

'On what?'

'On whether or not I change my mind.' And then he laugh. A great guffaw of a laugh. Clifton well satisfied with himself that is for sure.

We sit there a while longer and then he say, 'The man, the one watching the house and asking so much questions, he a ex-police-man renting himself out to go spy on people and report their business. He get hired by a woman over Passmore Town. I think she a friend a yours.'

'Fingernail?'

Clifton laugh so much he nearly fall off the chair. 'Fingernail! That is what yu call her?' And he laugh some more.

'Yu ever see her? Yu ever see that nail?'

'No, man.'

'So?'

'So OK, Fingernail hire him to go find out anything he can about you and what gwaan over Franklyn Town. And simple enough he wondering who this house belong to that everybody so busy taking their vacation in Ocho Rios. And that take him straight to Henry Wong. The man we talking 'bout not so bright so that musta been some easy-easy trail to follow.' He stop. And then he say, 'But I tell yu something for nothing. This thing not done yet.'

'What yu mean?'

'Wait nuh sista. I going tell yu. Just wait yu hurry.'

'I am not yu sista, man.' And then I have to bite my tongue because I can feel I am getting ready to give this man a piece of my mind, and in the circumstances I know that not such a good idea.

The waiter put down the two rum punches and take up the empty glasses and walk off.

'Yu friend, what she want is money. She go up Lady Musgrave Road and tell Cicely Wong that her husband got a woman in Ocho Rios and if she pay she can have all the details she want. But Miss Cicely not interested. She just tell her she can do whatever she want with her information because she not going give her a penny.'

'How yu know all a this?'

'Fingernail tek her detective with her for comfort and one thing about a private dick is that if yu pay him enough he will tell yu anything and everything yu want to know. That is why it always better to put yu trust in the police.' And he smile.

He sip his punch. And then he look out to sea with the breeze blowing in his face and say, 'I know yu don't want nothing happening to Henry Wong to disturb your cosy weekends in Ocho Rios. You and him sipping Appleton on the veranda and doing whatever the two a yu do up there. I know yu don't want that.' And then he turn to me and raise his eyebrows.

CHAPTER 29

HENRY MISERABLE. EVERY day he get up early hours before Fay get outta bed and take himself to Barry Street for his breakfast and then he go sit in the shop all day 'til it time to go back to Barry Street for his dinner and play mah-jong 'til all hours of night to make sure Cicely gone to her bed by the time he get back. And when he not down there losing his money he is sitting here in the house telling me how Fay leave Pao and come back to Lady Musgrave Road and arguing with Cicely morning, noon and night.

'Even sometime when Fay come back from nightclub early morning, Cicely get out bed so two them can argue 'bout hours Fay keeping and how it not seemly for a married woman, and 'bout priest that she busy chasing to Bishop's Lodge and he chasing her up the house. And I know because some time back I had to get out own bed tell him go home when he come knocking at door in middle of night. All this arguing. They even argue over fact that maybe they nuh argue for two hours. That is how bad it is, Gloria. Too much for a man to take. Too much.'

I sit there and I listen to it, not because I am interested in what Fay and Cicely cussing about but because I want to hear the reason why Fay leave Pao. But Henry don't know. Every time I see him I think maybe this time he find out and going tell me, but no. All he say is that it involve some boss in West Kingston. That is it. Except it seem like whatever happen in West Kingston mean that Pao now got Kenneth Wong working for him.

'Yu mean your boy Kenneth?'

'Yes, Gloria. My boy who should be in school learning lessons instead of running on street do errands Pao. So he have money now, buy records and fancy clothes. And school he forget about even though I still pay fees. Kenneth always been wild. I tell you that before. But now he rude and talk back to everybody in house, including his mother! Can you believe?'

'So what you doing 'bout it?'

'Me? Children not to do with me, Gloria. That for Cicely. That is how it always been.'

Henry not mention nothing to me 'bout Fingernail's private detective so I reckon that die a death even though Clifton still convinced she not done yet.

Next thing I get a knock at the door one day and when I go open it Judge Finley is standing there taking a rest from the noonday sun. I so surprised I can hardly believe my eyes. I didn't even know he had the address to come find me.

'I hope I not intruding, Miss Gloria, but I have a favour to ask yu.'

When we settled with the coffee on the veranda I say to him, 'I don't have no envelope a money for yu Finley.' And I laugh.

He a humble man, Finley, so he bow his head a little.

'I know that is the only way you and me meet each other before. But this is a completely different matter I want to ask yu 'bout.'

And what he want is for me to talk to Pao 'bout Kenneth Wong.

'Kenneth is a young and foolish bwoy. I tell Yang Pao that a long time back, long before all this mess. We had a tangle wid some bad people and, well, I don't need to go into details wid yu. The thing is Kenneth working wid us now and Miss Gloria, I can tell yu it a bad situation that can only get worse.'

'Finley, yu work for Pao. Why yu nuh just talk to him 'bout it?'

'I have tried, believe me, but he not listening to a single word I am saying. Even Hampton say to him that Miss Fay not going like it, her little brother involve wid us and all. But Yang Pao don't care. You must know what he get like when his mind fixed on something.'

I think to myself yes, I know, and then I say to him, 'What mek yu think the situation so bad apart from how Fay maybe feel 'bout it?'

'The bwoy is wild, Miss Gloria. He got no discipline. He outta control. He will do anything wid anybody or against anybody at any time. He got no sense, and no understanding a business or respect for anybody or anything. He lie and he cheat and he disloyal. All Kenneth Wong interested in is money and swaggering 'round the place like he a big shot now he running wid us. So trouble is following him everywhere. It get so bad nobody want to go do nothing wid him. Not even run a little errand 'round the corner because it so dangerous.' He pause and then he say, 'I worried people going start tek a hike. Yu know, if the Kenneth thing nuh get sorted out. Or worse that somebody get hurt.'

I look at him bending down his tall wiry frame to sip the coffee. Like he don't know he can raise his arm to bring the cup to his lips.

'I don't see how I can help yu.'

'Talk to him. That is all I am asking.' And then he say, 'Things going OK for us right now but this Kenneth thing, it need put a stop to before it completely get outta hand.'

I got no idea what good they think me talking to Pao going do. But anyway, I say to him that I will try and he grateful. I reckon they must be desperate if they coming to me.

Just before he leave I say to him, 'Tell me something Finley, how yu get the nickname Judge?'

He pull his big lips together tight like maybe he don't want to say, but then he relax and smile.

'Yang Pao give it to me when we was just boys, the first time I meet him and Hampton ask him what he think I look like. Hampton is my cousin, is him introduce me to Yang Pao. Anyway, he think 'bout it and he say I look like I could judge a good horse. And it mek Hampton laugh so much he nearly bust his sides. So that is how it come about, Horse Judge, yu know.'

I can see where Pao get it from because Finley got a face like a horse sure enough.

I smile and I say to him, 'So what yu name?'

'Neville.'

'All right Neville Finley, I will see what I can do.'

Pao not interested. 'That is my business. Finley got no right coming to yu over a thing like that. It got nothing to do wid you.'

'Yu cyan see he must be seriously fretting over this to be coming all the way up here to talk to me 'bout it?'

He stop his fuming. 'Kenneth not that bad. He unruly that is true. But he young. He will learn. All he need to do is simmer down.'

'You, Finley and Hampton been running together since yu fourteen years old. Yu nuh think yu should stop a minute and listen to them?' He thinking on it. 'Yu know, Pao, trouble is brewing. The ink barely dry on the election paper and already there is so much rumbling over unemployment and the poor state a the economy. People running short on patience and hope, especially in West Kingston, which is where I hear yu have some run-in.'

'Where the hell yu hear 'bout that?'

'It nuh matter where I hear it. The thing is t-r-o-u-b-l-e is b-r-e-w-i-n-g. That is what I am saying to yu. Yu nuh know that for yuself?'

He vex. 'Of course I know it. Yu think I been living in a cave? But that is West Kingston, it not Chinatown.'

'There is going to be open warfare in the street. Yu know how easy it is to buy a gun nowadays?'

'Don't talk to me 'bout no gun. That is how all this nonsense start.'

'What yu mean?'

He look at me like he wish he never say what he did. And then he think hard on it and take a deep breath.

'I had a man call Samuels and a while back I discover he was selling guns in Chinatown for a boss in West Kingston called DeFreitas. So anyway, I go deal with that situation and DeFreitas agree to stay outta Chinatown if I give him Samuels so I do it. And next thing I know, Samuels turn up dead. They shoot him in the back a the head and burn his body in a alley.'

'And Kenneth?'

'After Samuels gone I needed somebody to take care of his chores.'

'Even though Finley and Hampton warn yu against it?'

'Yu see, now yu back to that same thing.' He shrug his shoulders and start to walk off.

So I say, 'And Fay?'

He turn 'round. 'What you know about that?'

'I know she leave yu and go back to Lady Musgrave Road.'

He take two deep breath and do one of his big puff-out-yu-cheek sighs. 'She leave me after she hear 'bout Samuels. She even try tek the children with her but I stop that.'

'Yu see, the trouble already start. Yu cyan see how all a this is coming together into one almighty calamity for yu? Turf war, murder, yu wife leaving yu and all this business over Kenneth. It all pointing in the same direction. Yu nuh see that?'

He look at me a good while. 'Yu have any tea?'

When we settled with the Lipton's on the veranda he say in a calm, gentle voice, 'I know how much trouble going on over West Kingston. The thing with DeFreitas was because I didn't want it spreading into Chinatown.'

I sigh and pat his hand as we sitting in the chairs next to each other. 'Che Guevara said that we shouldn't be afraid of violence. It is the midwife of new societies.'

'He said that? Well I guess he would the amount of fighting them Cubans been doing since the first Spaniard set foot in Havana or wherever it was.'

'They doing good yu know, since Castro tek over. With literacy, employment, medical care. They turning the place 'round.'

'Yu think that is the way we should be going? Communist?'

'Maybe not communist as such. But socialist. Socialist enough for every man, woman and child to have a chance.'

'Yu mean like Sun Yat-sen? Liberty, equality and fraternity?'

'As long as fraternity include everybody. Black, white . . .' and then I look at him and say, 'Chinese, Indian, Scottish, Irish, Lebanese, Jew. Everybody, no matter where they come from or the colour or shade of their skin. Out of many, one people.' And then I think on it and I say, 'Even if they homosexual.'

'Homosexual!'

'Yu got a problem wid that?'

He think and then he say, 'No. Actually, I know a homosexual myself and he is a good man. As loyal a friend as anybody could want.'

And then he reach in his pocket and pull out a cigar and stick it in his mouth and light it.

'Since when yu start doing that?'

'This?' And he take the cigar and twizzle it 'round in his hand to admire it.

'This I start do after I settle the business with DeFreitas. I was celebrating.'

'Well I don't want yu celebrating with it here.'

'This here is a real good Havana cigar, Gloria. I would have thought yu would like the smell a that.'

'When the Cubans celebrating with a cigar they celebrating the revolution not some backwater power struggle.'

'Yu take everything too serious, Gloria.'

'Serious? Yu nuh think it serious that people prepared to kill and maim each other over a little more bread and a little more butter? At least the Cubans fighting for liberation. What we doing not going bring down no government. It not even going put a dent in the injustice that going on here.' Then I say, 'The Cubans, they are revolutionaries. We are discontents. And that is a different thing entirely.'

He sit there a while but he don't say nothing. And then he suddenly turn to me and say, 'Esther, she doing all right at St Andrew? She leave all that bad school business behind her?'

I nod my head. 'Yes, she doing fine. Everything turning 'round for her.'

'That is good. Very good.'

And then after a little while he say, 'I will talk to Kenneth.'

We carry on sitting there sipping the tea and looking out on the lawn and the people strolling by on the distant street. And then he take a big puff on the cigar and my nose catch the smoke coming to me on the evening breeze and I remember the green coffee hills, and the morning clouds rising in the bright Cuban sky.

'I don't care what yu celebrating, I don't want yu smoking any cigar in this house. I cyan tek the smell.'

Next time I see Henry he tell me Kenneth still working for Pao.

'Kenneth no respect for anybody or anything. You know he even smoking ganja in the house. Plain as day like it not illegal and he not care.'

So I decide to go see Father Michael. The idea just come to me one afternoon when I was downtown because I think maybe he was the only person that going talk some sense into Pao. But the Father not much help. Even though he give me a warm welcome and ask me 'bout how Esther doing at St Andrew, it seem like he got something else on his mind. All he could say to me before he usher me out the door was he would try to raise the issue with him but that he was powerless to intervene in Pao's business activities. That is how he put it. Somehow I expected more from him than that especially after he been so

296

kind giving his time to Esther and talking with me 'bout her schooling and such.

I walk up the road to find a taxi and as I turn the corner who should I bump into but Fay Wong. She practically walk straight into me. When she see me she stop.

'My, my, Gloria Campbell.'

I so surprised she recognise me I dunno what to say to her.

'You know me?'

'I know you now, but I have known of you for a very long time.' And then she look at me like she was two foot higher staring down her nose at me. She a little taller in truth, but it wasn't by that much. She wearing a beautiful yellow linen dress trimmed in white at the neck and sleeves, and white shoes with little heels, and she clutching a gorgeous white patent leather purse. She make me feel like a shambles in the floral cotton I was wearing even though it was a good frock and not cheap neither.

We stand there silent for a while and then she say, 'I have often wondered what it would be like to meet you face to face. Have you ever wondered that?'

I think on it and then I say, 'We met already. One time long ago, in your father's wine store when you were organising your sister's birthday party.'

'Really?' Then she bite her lip little bit before she say, 'Are you still enjoying the jade necklace?'

It shock me that she so haughty to mention it like that. But I don't see no point in continuing down this track with her. 'You and me been sharing a life for a very long time whether or not we like it. So maybe it is providence that we should meet like this because now we don't have to wonder.'

She take one last look at me and then walk off down the street. And I think to myself now I understand why the Father was in such a hurry to see the back of me.

A few days later for reasons I couldn't understand Pao decide it time for me to meet his children.

'After all these years? What I going meet them for?'

'Because it time, Gloria. Fay gone. We making a real home and family at Matthews Lane now. We not got nobody coming and going disrupting the place like she can't make up her mind where she live. We settled. It good time the children meet you. Xiuquan twelve years old and Mui eight now. It time.'

'So how yu going explain to them who I am?'

'It nuh matter. We can just meet by accident.'

'Accident! Yu serious?'

'It will be all right. You just step outta Times Store this Saturday 'bout two o'clock and we will be there.'

I can't think of anything so ridiculous. 'What is the point a me meeting them? What purpose it going serve? Tell me that.'

'Purpose? For you to know them and them to know you. What more purpose yu want than that?'

So come Saturday afternoon I step outta Times Store and the three of them standing up in the street with Pao acting like he not waiting for me.

'Hello, Gloria. It such a surprise to see you.'

And I say, 'Yes, quite a surprise.' It was comical. He introduce me to the children, first Mui and then Xiuquan. When I look at them I think how fair their skin is. Not dark like Esther. Mui's hair straight. Not even the slightest kink does it have. Neat in two little plaits falling down her back. She bright-eyed with a certain confidence. She will fit fine into Immaculate. Xiuquan got more colour and a wave in his hair. Like he Spanish or Cuban, which make me smile. But he sullen. Sad inside like his mama.

Mui put out her hand to shake. Him, he don't want to know. And when I call him Xiuquan he say that not his name. His name Karl, which is what Pao tell me Fay always call him.

Pao march us into the store like he supervising a military manoeuvre and we go upstairs to the soda fountain where he order up ice cream for the children and I take some coffee and he a glass of ice water. And as soon as we sit down at the little table in the corner I knew it was a mistake because now I am sitting here explaining to these children that I am an old friend of their father knowing full well that Xiuquan don't believe a word of what I am saying.

Then Mui start ask me if I have any children and I tell her 'bout Esther, which set her chatting 'bout everything under the sun while Xiuquan just sit there silent with his back half turned to me. And then she start talk 'bout Father Michael who it seem she worship, and if Esther know the Father. Well Esther and him not anybody's business, especially not Mui or Pao. So I just say Esther not a Catholic, which she can't believe like it unimaginable to her there could be anyone on this earth not Catholic.

'Papa, do you know that Esther is not a Catholic?'

But before Pao can give her an answer Xiuquan just turn 'round and say, 'Yes, he does.' And then he get up from the table and walk off and that was the end of our accidental meeting.

All the way back to Barbican I chastise myself for letting Pao talk me into it. What good did I think it would do? With Fay up Lady Musgrave Road bumping into me and the attitude that Xiuquan got.

When I get back to the house I find Clifton waiting for me.

'Yu nuh got nothing better to do than to be sitting down here drinking my liquor?'

'Gloria, Gloria. It is one small drink that is all.'

'What yu doing here anyway? I thought every time yu see me it had to be in a dark corner in Club Havana or over Morgan's Harbour?'

'That is because it done.'

'What yu mean, done?'

'Done. The murder investigation over, finish, kaput.' And he take a sip from the glass.

'Just like that?'

'Just like that. Old and cold. Nobody care no more.'

I feel my heart settle and a thin smile across my lips as I am coming fully up the veranda steps. I rest my purse on a chair and sit down next to him.

'So where yu been? I been waiting for yu to come tell me something 'bout Fingernail.'

He laugh. 'I been in Miami. I just come back.'

'What yu doing in Miami?'

'I got people there.' I don't say nothing even though I know there got to be more to it than that. I just kick off my shoes and reach over and take a taste from his glass.

'Jesus, Clifton, that is neat Appleton. Yu never hear 'bout a drop a water?'

'Gloria, this is how yu say good afternoon to yu bredda?'

I put the glass back on the table. 'Tell me what yu come over here for. And yu not my bredda.'

'Every Jamaican woman is a sista and every Jamaican man is a bredda. Yu nuh know that?'

I raise my eyebrows just the same way he do to me over Morgan's Harbour.

'I don't want nothing, Gloria. I just come to check yu.'

After Clifton gone I say to Auntie, 'How come yu let Clifton Brown come here and settle himself and drink out my liquor?'

She spin 'round and look at me like she affronted.

'A nuh who yu do fah, a who do fi yu.' And then she turn and walk off into the kitchen while I am wondering what it is Auntie know about what Clifton is doing for me.

When I ask Dr Morrison what Clifton doing in Miami he tell me there was an incident. That is what he say.

'An incident at Club Havana involving two boys.'

'Yu mean the one in the newspaper where the two boys get knived to death?'

He nod.

'So what that got to do with Clifton?'

'There was an English girl, let us say, in the back of her car entertaining a waitress . . .'

'Entertaining? A waitress?'

He look at me like as to say, 'Gloria, please.' Then he nod again, slow and deliberate like his patience running out. 'She was *entertaining* the waitress.'

So I wait while he sipping the rum. 'Anyway, Pao came to the rescue. As always. Cleaning up the mess and dispatching the girl back to England and the waitress to Miami. Escorted by Clifton. So there you have it.'

'So who murder the two boys?'

'The English girl. She was here with her father for the independence anniversary celebrations. Out on her own for the night. With the knife under the car seat.'

I can't believe they let her get away with murder just like that.

And then I think who am I to talk. 'And Pao didn't say nothing 'bout it being two women in the car?'

'The waitress was an innocent bystander, Gloria. A young, impulsive girl who had nothing to do with the wreckless mayhem of that evening. And as for the other one, her father is paying Pao for that, just like he paid for John.'

'It the same man? The father of Merleen Chin's baby?'

'Same one. Anyway, being a British army officer, it's doubtful what kind of justice his daughter would have faced. The most likely outcome would have been our waitress in jail because simply being there, in that car with another woman, would have been guilt enough.'

And then almost like he read my mind he say, 'Pao and Clifton are like brothers. This other thing is just su-su to him. That is what you Jamaicans say, isn't it?'

'Gossip?'

'Yes. The malicious sort that serves only to justify small-mindedness and prejudice. And Yang Pao is not like that. He could see that the waitress going to jail for a crime she hadn't committed would be a travesty.'

Why it surprise me I don't know, especially after what Pao say 'bout Clifton being a loyal friend. And in truth all of them stood by Clifton from the beginning. Pao, Hampton, Finley. And in all these years I never hear any of them, not even once, say anything 'bout battyman or chi-chi. They just leave it be and get on with their business. So I reckon if Pao and them can take it in their stride then I got no business feeling any way 'bout Marcia.

In October the flood rain from Hurricane Flora cause all sorta wicked damage across Jamaica. And just the same way we always expect the worse, we nail wooden planks over the windows, and gather together every bit of food that come dry or in a can, and fill everything we could find that could take fresh water, and sit in the dining room at Franklyn Town with the kerosene lamp and Sybil and Beryl and Auntie and Esther listening to the prime minister on the radio wishing us well and then the crackle on the line as it go dead and then the sound of the wind. We do it. Just like we do for every hurricane that ravage this island.

But even though Jamaica drowning under the water, my mind was not on that. My mind was on Cuba and the four days that Flora hang there causing havoc and mayhem. My mind was on the wind that reached 125 miles per hour and the 100 inches of rain that fall over Santiago de Cuba. My mind was on a house perched on a mountaintop and the coffee crop, and Ernesto Sánchez.

1965

'While more deeper is the wound.'

CHAPTER 30

AFTER THAT, THINGS get bad. What with the almighty mess Flora leave behind, and unemployment and poverty getting worse even though the government was telling us we got more money circulating on the island than ever before. And yes I could see it with the fancy houses they building up the mountain in Beverly Hills and the cars on the road that so pricey and elegant. That was for some. For others it was a gunman waiting behind every corner of West Kingston or somebody with a machete wielding through the air to slice any man, woman or child who belong to, or someone think belong to, the other party be it the Labour Party or the PNP.

Martin Luther King even come here with his message 'bout how we had to face the challenges of the hour with creativity and determination but it didn't make no difference. As if him talking to the privileged at the university could change anything. And then after Mr Seaga make his speech 'bout fire for fire and blood for blood, that was it.

That was when Pao come tell me that Kenneth Wong outta control, running with Louis DeFreitas in West Kingston and getting into some serious business.

'Gloria, Kenneth is bad. The bwoy got a gun sticking outta every pocket. Everything Louis tell him to do, he do it. I try talk to him but it nuh do no good. All he say is Louis his friend. Can yu believe that? And even though I tell him that Louis DeFreitas is a punk who would just as soon put him out front to take a bullet as shoot him in the back if it suit him better Kenneth not taking a blind bit a notice of me. I even talk to Henry 'bout it but that not no good either. The thing is, Kenneth setting a bad example because all Xiuquan can see is how a boy little older than him can make fast money and get a reputation.'

I want to tell him 'I told yu so' but I don't do it. No need to be rubbing salt into the wound.

'What mek yu think Xiuquan would have his head turned that way?'

'Turn that way! The boy already get himself arrested two years back for thiefing outta Times Store and I have to sweeten Mutt and Jeff to let it go.'

'Mutt and Jeff?'

'The two constables that arrest him.'

'Thieving not the same as shooting down somebody in the street, Pao.'

'Yu think?'

Pao not the sorta man to get agitated over nothing. Most times I reckon he could do with paying a bit more attention to what going on 'round him so right now it seem the situation really serious.

'And yu know what happen now?'

I don't say nothing because I know he going to tell me.

'Henry Wong drop down with a stroke in the middle of the street.'

I just stand there silent like maybe I been struck deaf and dumb. Pao look at me hard and then he come over close and say, 'You all right?'

'Yu telling me the man is dead?'

'No, Gloria. He have a stroke that is all. Right now he is sitting up in bed in the Chinese Sanatorium begging everybody that visit him to bring rice and peas and chicken with them. What it matter to you anyway?'

I gather myself. 'Nothing. I just don't like you coming in here telling me somebody is dead. It not the sorta news yu announce just like that.'

He look at me and then he say, 'Sorry.' He wait a while just standing there staring at me like there is something else he want to say. And then just before he turn and walk to the door he say, 'Esther, she all right?'

The next day I go up the sanatorium after visiting hours and pay the nurse to let me see Henry. When I go in the room I shocked to see what a pitiful state he is in. A big man like Henry struck down in his prime. Paralysed down one side of his body. Even his face lopsided.

I draw up a chair close to the bed and take his good hand in mine. And I stroke it just like I did that night in Ocho Rios and before too long he open his eyes.

'Gloria.' He say it in a sort of whisper, which I think is all he could manage. So I just smile at him.

And he say it again, 'Gloria', and smile at me with the bit of his face that he could still move.

'No need for yu to say anything. I can do all the talking for both of us.'

He laugh, but it was just a tiny sound that come out his nose like he just breathe out heavy. Then he start move like he want to sit up in the bed so I get up and fix the pillows and help ease him.

'There many kinds of love, Gloria.' And he swallow hard. 'The love of mother or father for child. The love of man for woman. The love of a brother. The love of a friend.'

I say 'Henry' like to stop him because I can see how much he struggling and I don't think he need to be carrying on this way. But even though he have to wait to catch his breath, he gather himself because there is still more he want to say.

'And there is love that fills the heart and soul with joy. Love that is happy just to look up and see you sitting there and hear your voice and see your smile and know you are all right. And that love, Gloria, is all of love. Every kind of love rolled into one.' He stop and breathe. 'Sometimes it takes many years for that kind of love to grow. Other times it happen just like that, in a flash, a look, a conversation, a joke you share, because that connection is all it takes to turn a life on a sixpence.' He stop again. 'The physical thing, a lot of times is empty. All body and no heart. A recreational activity.'

I reach for a Kleenex and wipe away the spit that dribbling from the corner of his mouth.

'That is what people do even though it not take away their loneliness. It add to it. But when there is love, Gloria, the physical part is an expression of that love. And even then, it is only the finger pointing at the moon. It is not the moon itself.' He stop. 'With you, Gloria, the moon is what I have had all these years and the one thing it is so very hard to let go of.' And then he say, 'The bit about the finger and the moon, that not me. That the Buddha.' And he smile his half-face smile.

'Henry.'

He close his eyes and squeeze his shaky hand over mine. And I feel the life draining out of him.

'You, Gloria, is all any man would want or need. A man younger than me that is.' He open his eyes and look at me with a tenderness that make me think Henry want to cry. But he don't do it.

'Another time, another place, Gloria. Different circumstances. Different ideas about who we think we are or what we should want or deserve, or what is decent or honourable or fair. That is what was needed.'

And then he close his eyes and a little while later I realise Henry gone to sleep.

The next time I go visit Henry I go in daytime because the other night was too late for a man in his condition. I reckon I was taking a risk so I just pray that nobody recognise me and go report to Pao that they see me there. When I open the door Henry sitting up in bed eating ackee and saltfish that he say Hampton bring for him earlier.

'Yu looking good.'

'I know that not true, Gloria, but I thank you for saying.'

He put down the empty plate on the side and want me to get a cloth for him to wipe his hands and mouth so I go to the sink and wet up some paper towel and bring back to him. Henry got his businessman face on.

'You remember Alfred Ho? You work for him in shop.'

I nod my head.

'Want you see him.'

'What all this about Henry?'

'You see him. Ho know what to do.' He pause, and then he say, 'And the money that everybody owe that is for you. You carry on business or not. Whatever you want.'

'Henry.'

'And the house in Ocho Rios, that same as always. Abraham still there but it your house now. Nobody know about it. Not Cicely, nobody. Just you and me and your women friends from Franklyn Town. So no need you do anything. Just use it. Make it home we never had.'

'Henry, there is no need for you to be doing this.'

'Not need, Gloria, want.'

I think on it and then I say, 'What yu going to do about the businesses Henry? The supermarkets and such?'

'You want give Yang Pao? That how it is?'

'The two a yu been running supplies to the hotels for a long time.'

'For you, Gloria. For you.'

I think. 'What about Miss Cicely?'

'Cicely? No need worry 'bout her. She well provided for. All you have to do is see Alfred Ho and collect money he have waiting for you.'

'Waiting for me?'

'US dollars, Gloria. That is the thing to have. You go see him and make it soon. I not be here much longer and I want know you have in your hands. Go now. Go on.'

I stand up and lean over and I kiss him. Just light on the lips and then I ease back and look at him. 'That wasn't for the money. That was for what yu say about love the last time I was here.'

He sit there upright in the bed but he didn't say nothing. He just motion his head towards the door like as to say gwaan, be on your way.

CHAPTER 31

I STEP OUTTA the room and start off down the long corridor that open to the elements with the banana trees and yellow hibiscus. And as I turn the corner I walk straight into Fay Wong.

We stop and she look at me, but this time it was different. It not like the 'you poor thing' she do to me that first time in her father's wine shop. Nor was it like the way she look down her nose at me the last time we meet. This was completely different. It had gentleness in it. Maybe it was because her father was dying. But that look mean that it didn't alarm me when she say, 'Would you like to get some coffee?'

We go down to the restaurant that they have there in the sanatorium and it nice. Not what I expected for a hospital at all. The tables even got a white damask cloth on them and flowers in a vase. We collect the coffee cafeteria-style and sit down. She careful, Fay. She position her skirt neat and tidy, and rest her purse on the table, and check where the chair legs going before she ease it up and settle herself to reach for the coffee. And after she pick up the cup she put a paper napkin in the saucer and rest the cup back in it to make sure nothing drip off the bottom and catch her blouse, which is a beautiful cream silk with a ruffle down the front.

And then she just look straight at me and say, 'Do you love him?'

'Pao?' She nod her head.

So I say, 'Do you?'

'Never even liked him, not in the slightest.'

It startle me. The frankness of her.

'So what you marry him for?'

She take a sip of coffee and then dab the corner of her mouth with another paper napkin.

'When I was a child I had very fair skin and blonde hair. Can you imagine that? And everybody in the house was so pleased and proud all the maids wanted to do was brush and comb it, and every night Mama would have them plait rags into it, you know, so the next morning my hair would flow out into magnificent blonde curls.' And she do a little twizzle with her hands to show me what she mean.

'Everywhere I turned, all I could hear was them telling me I was just like Shirley Temple on the *Good Ship Lollipop*. Actually I have never seen that movie and hope never to for as long as I live.'

I can't believe Fay is talking to me like this so I just sit there mesmerised, wondering if I am in the middle of a dream.

'This will probably be the only time that you and I talk like this so I think we should just be open and honest. There is no reason not to be.'

I sit there in amazement, so she carry on.

'Everybody thought that Mama resented it, my hair and the attention, but that is not true. She was the one, after all, instructing the maids to make the curls. She was the one who had me twisting and turning in front of company to show off what a beautiful blonde daughter she had produced. Mama only turned sour after my hair turned to brown when I was five years old.'

'You think it was disappointment?'

'I think it was shame. The shame of a black African woman who thought she had escaped slavery by virtue of her blonde, fair-skinned baby, only to find that the baby wasn't blonde after all.' She take another sip from her cup and do the same routine with the napkin.

'Why you telling me all this Fay?'

'I am explaining to you why I married Pao. The context. Because every decision we make has context.'

So I nod my head and settle down to listen.

'It was after that, that she started to beat me and scream and shout and find fault. Not that I want to paint myself as a victim, but I was a child and she was my mother. I expected her to look after me, to protect me, but she didn't. She let me down in the most unforgivable way. And so as I grew, we argued and argued and continue to do so to this day.

'Mama was brought up Methodist but she converted to Catholicism so when it came time for me to go to school it was a convent school she chose and then later it was Immaculate Conception because as far as she was concerned it was the best secondary school for girls on the island. To me, it was heaven. Heaven to be away from her, so I pestered Papa until he let me become a boarder because it meant I would no longer have to go home to her at the end of each day. But even though it was she who wanted me to be at Immaculate, she was enraged by the fact that I was happy there and decided that the only reason was because I was playing at being white with my new friends. In fact, nothing could have been further from the truth. The white girls didn't mix with me, and neither did the Chinese because I wasn't full Chinese and that mattered a great deal in those days. Still does. And the black girls, few and far between as they were, stayed together. I was in no man's land, but that didn't matter because the most important part for me was I was away from her.'

Right then a woman come by to collect up the empty cups and Fay just catch her eye and ask her if she can have a top-up. The woman look down at Fay sitting in the chair and turn vex like she thinking to herself, 'What yu asking me for? I am not nuh waitress.'

But even though she feel sour she reach over and pick up the cup and saucer and say, 'I see yu tek milk. Yu want me bring yu back some sugar as well?'

Fay just smile and say, 'No, thank you. That's very kind.' And the woman walk off.

'And just to infuriate her I used to pretend I was with the white girls all the time. I used to even force myself into their company so I could show off to Mama.'

'But I thought she was happy for you to pass. That was what she was proud of.'

'Only if she was in control of it.'

The woman bring the fresh coffee and put it on the table, and Fay say thank you in the sweetest, gentlest voice you could imagine. And as the woman walking away I realise she never ask me if I wanted more coffee or anything. She never even look at me.

'Anyway, much later I met a man. He was standing outside the Carib one night as a friend and I came out of the pictures. In fact I'd seen him there several times before, but that night I took one look at him and when he smiled at me I knew he was perfect. Isaac was as big and as black as any man could be. So I just walked up to him and told him to come with me and I put him in a taxi and took him to Lady Musgrave Road.' And then she laugh. 'Can you imagine? Mama was completely beside herself. A black man sitting on her veranda talking to her fair-skinned daughter. The steam was practically coming out of her ears! It was the most gratifying sight I had ever seen.' Fay laugh and laugh at the memory that even after all this time she was still delighting in.

'Mama hates black men. According to her they are all irresponsible and unreliable. Indolent and slipshod, that is what she says. So Isaac was my revenge on her for all the years and all the ways in which she made my life a living hell.

'So I started with Isaac, who was much older than me and worked in a butcher shop.'

Isaac in the butcher shop? I couldn't believe my ears. She mean that man laying in the stinking bed asking Sybil for money? No, this must be a different Isaac. But standing outside the Carib night after night? Smiling at young women?

'I even used to go and spend time in the one room he rented upstairs filled with the stench of raw meat and blood.'

I think to myself, yes, it him. The same one!

'It was sordid and I revelled in every minute of it. And every time I dropped his name into conversation with her or had him sitting on the veranda while she was inside playing the piano and singing about hell and damnation, it was delicious.'

And the history he got with Sybil and Beryl? And the boy, Junior?

'The funny thing was Isaac was actually good company. Not too bright but very humorous and I thought caring. And after a while I really grew to like him and I thought he liked me. So when

Mama told me she wanted me to marry Pao I thought Isaac would have something to say about it. But all he did was sit there with the cigarette in his hand as if it had nothing to do with him. And eventually when I pressed him, all he could say was, "Do whatever yu want."'

And this thing from Isaac, Fay say in real Jamaican just like him, to show me she could do it. And then she smile with her eyebrows raised at the insolence of the man. My head busy figuring the years so I realise she must be talking 'bout a time long before I meet him.

'So you see, I went with Isaac to spite Mama, and I married Pao to spite Isaac.'

I can't think what to say to her so I just say, 'I thought you married Pao to get away from your mama?'

'That is what I told him, but it was only partly the truth. Isaac was the other part.'

'You ever see Isaac again?'

'Years later I passed him in King Street with some young black woman on his arm. I just walked past and you know, he never even turned his head.'

I sit there looking at her this beautiful, rich, educated woman and think what a mess we all are. Every single one of us, no matter how we appear on the outside.

'Did you love him, Isaac?'

'Love? What is that, Gloria? Do you know?'

She waiting for an answer but there is nothing I have to say, so she carry on.

'All of my life I thought that everything could be solved inside my own head. All I had to do was to be smart enough. And I would disappear into this head for hours and days, thinking and thinking and thinking some more. But you know the problem with that? You can only think what you can think.' And she smile. 'You can only see things the way you see them. You can only understand them the way you understand them. So in the end you just go round and round in circles getting even more confused and exhausted. And when I tired I would just stop and decide that everything would be fine. Just to get a rest. Then I would rally myself and carry on with nothing having been resolved. That is what I did running between school and Mama, and then Matthews Lane and Lady Musgrave Road. It was all I could do because escaping from that internal madness takes courage. You have to step outside of your own head. You have to be prepared to let someone else in and believe that it is possible to expose your vulnerabilities and inner torment to them without feeling invaded. You have to give up fear, and have hope. You have to trust. And most people, Gloria, including me, are not that brave. It took a very long time and many hours of anguish for me to see that. It took Michael Kealey.' And then she look at me and say, 'I know you know.'

So I just smile back at her and we sit there in silence for a while. And then I say to her, 'How did you find out about me?'

'The necklace. I knew Pao was going to the house in Franklyn Town, so when I heard about the argument over the necklace I knew it was you.'

'How you know about that?'

'Sissy. She was my nursemaid before she left us to set up her boarding house. That is how my father knows her.' And then she say, 'I know about your daughter as well, at St Andrew. I know.'

I think on it and then I say, 'Fay, what is all of this about?'

She wait before she start to talk. 'I want you to know that I don't hold any malice towards you. I also want to apologise for my mention of the necklace the last time we met. It was spiteful and I am sorry. The past is the past, Gloria. What happened, happened. So be it, but the future is a different matter. I suppose I just wanted you to understand something about me. Know me, not only what is said about me. We have shared such a lot it seems there should be more between us.'

She stop. And then she turn really serious. 'How old are you, Gloria?'

'Forty-three.'

'I have just turned forty and I have spent almost all of that time trying to spite someone, first Mama, then Isaac, then Pao. And I have never ever stopped to think, I mean really think, about who I am or what I want. I have never had any sense of direction about my life. I have just stumbled from one disaster to the next trying to make the best of a bad job. Trying to salvage something from my misery. And now, finally, I want to change my life.'

And just like that she get up from the table and pick up her purse and say, 'Walk with me to the car park and I'll give you a ride back to Barbican.'

I call by the ladies' room on the way so by the time I get there Fay was already sitting in the maroon Mercedes and drove me home without needing any directions from me.

CHAPTER 32

HENRY'S FUNERAL WAS at Holy Trinity Cathedral. The same place that Pao and Fay get married. Father Michael was up there conducting the service even though he the Roman Catholic Bishop of Kingston now, which maybe was fitting given how rich Henry was and how close the Father is to Fay. The cathedral was full and when I squeeze my head 'round the corner I see Pao standing there with Mui on one side and Xiuquan on the other busy crossing himself and reciting all sorta things about confessing to Almighty God and how he had sinned in thought, word and deed. It was a vision of him I never ever thought I would see in my life. Standing there with the frankincense burning and the little bells ringing almost like he was going to cry. That moved he was by the whole thing.

I walk off before the end when the woman was singing Ave Maria because nobody invited me and I didn't think if they see me they would have wanted to make me that welcome. The Father look good though in the purple and white and gold. And he made it a real gracious send-off for Henry, which I was glad for. Especially when he said the part about Henry resting in the sleep of peace. That was nice.

For me, I couldn't hardly believe he was gone. It seemed like he was all of Kingston to me ever since that day he picked me up off the road when I was so in need of some kindness. And that is what he gave me all of these years, kindness, and even though I still had Sybil and Marcia, Henry's passing made me feel like I had lost my best friend. Even Alfred Ho, the way he was with me when I go pick up the money, seem to know what losing Henry mean to me. So who knows what Henry say to him. All Mr Ho say to me was that Henry wanted me to have what he was keeping. And he hand me the shoebox. And I say thank you.

'That not all, Gloria.'

And then he go out back and come with four more boxes.

'Five boxes a money, Mr Ho?'

'Full, Gloria. Full to the brim.' And he smile. 'You need ride to take you home I think. I get car.'

When we turn 'round to leave I see he got a picture a Chiang Kai-shek hanging on the wall.

'Since when you a supporter of Chiang Kai-shek?'

'Oh, times change, Gloria. Not like old days. Back then, man could sell his rice and flour with no hindrance. Nowadays, since half of Chinatown run here to get away from Mao, businessman have to know which way land lie and breeze blow.'

Henry keep his word and before he die he tell Pao he could have all the supermarket, wholesale and wine merchant businesses. But even though he make this gift to Pao, Henry never get a chance to make a will so now Miss Cicely calling him up to Lady Musgrave Road to tell him that she got no intention of granting Henry's wish because she worried 'bout what Kenneth going to inherit. And what she want is for Pao to take Kenneth under his wing to learn the supermarket trade so that in a few years' time Pao can have the wholesale and wine merchant and Kenneth can have the supermarkets.

'And no matter how much I tell her that Kenneth not got no interest in being a shopkeeper she not listening to me. All she got to say is let's give it a try, and how I am the general manager and Kenneth is my apprentice. The woman is mad you hear me, mad. So now me and her fifty-fifty partners and I have to pay Kenneth outta my share. You ever hear of a thing like that?'

I never know Miss Cicely was such a shrewd businesswoman. I was impressed even though I feel sorry for Pao because he thought he had the whole thing sealed and delivered. Still, I reckon he got a taste of his own medicine after all these years he been fixing everybody else's business.

But, just like anybody could have predicted, Kenneth Wong is no shopkeeper. So now Pao coming 'round the house every night telling me how Kenneth lazy and unreliable and only doing it because Miss Cicely threaten to throw him outta the house at Lady Musgrave Road if he don't. According to Pao, the whole thing is a disaster and there is no way out of it because Miss Cicely got him over a barrel and anyway he need her because what with the political situation the gambling and protection not doing so good no more. And even though he still got the Navy and other surplus off the wharf and hotel construction sites it not enough to keep everybody going. And that this thing with Miss Cicely is his only chance to make a future and even get legal, which for the first time in his life is what it seem he want.

So every night I am listening to this tale of woe, on and on. And I sit there on the veranda or living room or stand up in the kitchen and nod my head and say yes and show some sympathy because I really do feel bad for him.

And in between all of this I got Clifton Brown coming 'round when he feel like it drinking my liquor and making himself at home. One time I even come and find him sitting on the veranda with Auntie passing the time of day. And after she gone inside he start congratulating himself on how the Fingernail thing sort itself out without him having to do nothing because 'the trail' go to the grave with Henry Wong. And then he help himself to another drink.

All of this time the situation was getting worse. Political gang warfare, clashes with security forces, strikes and industrial disputes. The government bulldozing shacks and making people homeless. It was bedlam. Even Haile Selassie coming here cause a stampede with so much people and disorder at the airport. And that is how it gwaan until October 1966 when things get so serious in West Kingston the government have to declare a state of emergency.

And in the middle of all of this Kenneth Wong go get himself shot in some gun battle that it take the police five hours to get under control and during which time Kenneth lay there and bleed to death in the street. This is what Judge Finley come tell me, and how Fay telephone Pao in a state yelling at him because she think it was his fault that Kenneth mixed up with all of this. That if it wasn't for Pao, Kenneth would never have been on the street to meet a man like Louis DeFreitas and none of this would have happened. So now they all worried that Fay going leave and go to England.

'What would she go to England for?'

'It seem she got a brother there.'

I know. Henry already tell me. But I don't say nothing.

'It serious, Miss Gloria. Believe me, serious.'

Then I remember what Fay say to me about changing her life and I say to him, 'Yu think she going try tek the children wid her?'

A couple months later when Clifton gone to Miami to see if the waitress all right that is exactly what Fay do. She jump on a BOAC jet to England and she take Mui and Xiuquan with her. And after Pao scream murdering vengeance on every man and woman that help her and say he going to England to get them back, 'til Clifton and Finley talk him out of it, he open a bottle of Appleton and not put down the glass yet.

When Clifton come tell me I already know something had happened. So I just ask him how she do it.

'The two constables that Yang Pao vex after they arrest Xiuquan and have to let him go, the ones he call Mutt and Jeff, they do it.'

'How Fay know about Mutt and Jeff?'

'God knows. The thing is the children gone and that is that. And even though Pao so drunk he don't know what day a the week it is Hampton and his friend go find the constables and give them a hiding anyway. So they pay for it.'

'They hurt bad?'

'No, Gloria. It was just a little slapping. They off work right now but they will be back in that station in no time. And if they know what is good for them they will carry on like nothing happen because they know they had it coming.'

I just wait out the weeks with Finley coming at regular intervals to tell me that Pao not doing no better. All he do is empty the bottle and walk to Barry Street for the next one because nobody in the house prepared to go fetch it for him. Esther, she can see that something going on so she ask me and I tell her.

She stand there in the kitchen and look at me and then she say, 'You think he can get them back?'

'No. That not going to happen now. They gone until such time as they old enough and want to come back themselves.'

And for the first time in her life Esther seem like she have some sympathy for him.

'So am I the only child he has now?'

'The only child he has in Jamaica. The only one that he can see whenever he want to and talk to and pass the time of day with.'

'You think he would want to do that with me now?'

The thing on the tip of my tongue is to say, 'Esther, he loves you. He just don't know how to show it that is all.' But I don't say it.

Instead I say, 'You would like that? After everything that go on all these years?'

'He is my father.'

'Yes, he is.'

She sit down on the stool like she settling in for a talk she been waiting to have for a long time. Then she say, 'How do you know he loves you?'

I think on it and then I say, 'Because his caring is constant. For twenty-one long years. Through thick and thin. He is always there.'

I can see she turning it over in her mind. 'I don't think he is a bad man you know.'

'No?'

'Father Michael says we are all troubled. And every person has to deal with life as they find it. Whatever circumstances they meet. We have to decide at each and every turn what is the right or best thing to do. That we struggle and sometimes we make mistakes.'

'And then what?'

'We try again.'

'We get another chance?'

'Yes, because all of us suffer. If we didn't suffer we wouldn't do the things we do. So we deserve kindness and compassion.'

'Someone said to me once that nothing is perfect, we have to work at it. But we have to work at it with a forgiving heart.'

She get up from the stool and walk over to me and put her arms 'round me. And after she hold me like that for a good long while she ease back and look me in the eye and say, 'You are my forgiving heart.'

So after that I decide one day to take her to Margaret's with me. She old enough now to understand the tragic predicament these girls are in. When she get there she stand in the doorway silent, hanging on to the doorpost like her life depended on it.

So I say, 'Come on Esther, yu can help these girls with their reading, writing and arithmetic.' And I turn to the girls sitting there in the yard and say, 'This is Esther, my daughter. She has come to help.' And just the same way they put their hands together and clap the first time I go there, they do it again, which bring a smile to Esther's lips and unfreeze her.

Hyacinth still here. Almost grown. But even though she is a really good girl Margaret can't find no family for her. So she in the house earning her keep and a little wage and taking Esther under her wing. Showing her what to do and how to do it. And chat, bwoy can they chat. So much so I have to separate them once in a while so they can get their chores done.

Margaret happy because she think Esther got a calling. Me, I am just relieved to see her taking an interest in something other than a magazine 'bout US movie stars. And quite an interest it was too, because Esther was going there every time she get a spare minute, even on her own, to help Margaret and see Hyacinth.

When I ask her what she like so much 'bout the place she say, 'It's giving people a second chance.'

But I know it more than that, because for the first time it seem Esther actually have a friend. So I tell her she can have Hyacinth come over the house if she want to and it put the biggest smile on her face I ever did see.

When Pao finally turn up it was early evening almost two months after the children gone to England. I just open the door and take him in my arms and hold him.

'I wonder how long it was going to be before you come.'

I walk with him inside and start to boil the kettle.

'You not got no Appleton?'

'From what Finley tell me yu already had plenty enough of that. I fixing us some nice Lipton's.' Right then Esther come into the kitchen. She stand there and look at him like she thinking what it is she want to say, like it matter to her to say something soothing. And then she say, 'I'm sorry to hear about what happen.' She take one more look at him and then she step through the back door into the yard.

After I make the tea I settle us down in the living room while he tell me how since the children leave he feel like somebody reach inside his chest and pull out his heart. And how spending time with Father Michael made him feel like he was connected to Fay. And how he really wanted to make a family with her but now she and children gone.

And then he turn towards me and lean into my arms and cry with the full weight of his body against me. Such sobbing I never thought a man could produce. It was that same sound of despair that come out of Marcia after the business with the sailor. That same pain I emptied into my pillow the night he told me about marrying Fay. That was the depth of the sorrow in him, as his body was heaving and the sweat was creeping through his shirt.

And as I was sitting there holding him and listening and letting my heart go out to him I realise that this is what Fay meant in the postcard she mail to me from the airport. A regular tourist post-card, with a picture of the Jamaican flag and Dunn's River Falls and a sunset on Negril beach. And on the back of which she had written, 'Look after him. You were always more of a wife to him than I ever was.'

But I wasn't thinking so much about being a wife. I was think-ing about devotion and how despite all the searching I did in my head and heart about what I really meant to him, for Pao I was never his three-times-a-week whore. I was always more than that, from that very first night. More than a convenience or recreational activity, more than a respite from Matthews Lane. And for me he was always and would always be there. Because with Pao neither of us had anything to forgive ourselves or each other for. We were authentic and that is the most honest thing a person can be.

CHAPTER 33

IN ALL THE years we spend in Kingston, we never go back to Petersfield because after all what was there apart from bad memories and a heap of people asking questions we didn't want to answer. But now Marcia tell me that Mama sick, serious, and the only decent thing to do is to get ourselves on that country bus for the trip back. But Clifton say no, he will drive us.

'What on earth you want to go over there for Clifton? What is there for you that is anything worth having?'

'It almost thirty years since you and me been there, Gloria, and at the time you was leaving and I was coming both over the same reason. And for both of us too it is a home full a pain and sorrow. Yu nuh think it should be something we do together?'

Auntie think it a good idea as well for Clifton to go but she say I should leave Esther with her because she fourteen now and studying hard with her heart set on university so this not the time for me to be taking her outta school to go gallivanting to country.

'Anyway,' she say, 'who knows what gwaan over deh, so feel before yu mount an remember long look cyan buy talk. If people want to keep their secret deh will do it. But nuh fret yuself.

Everything get sorted out in it own time. Time longer than rope.'

So we take the same road, me, Marcia and Clifton in this new black Chevy Impala that he driving with a bench seat of red leather in the front so all three of us can fit in. A car that he say been shaped like a Coke bottle, which I for one can't see but it seem to please him.

We go through Spanish Town and May Pen and 'cross the mountain to Mandeville and drop down into Black River and along the coast to Savanna-la-Mar. And all the time we travelling I can't get over how everything the same. Exactly as it was thirty years back when me and Marcia do this trip on the bus that tip and turn and swirl and almost fall down 'round every corner. The wild bush and little hamlets where the washing lines is hanging between the breadfruit and mango tree, the multicoloured rickety wooden shacks that wouldn't stand a gust of wind never mind a hurricane, the higgler on the roadside with a row of conk shells and three wet fish, the music blasting out of every meagre shop and bar that got electricity. It was all exactly the same, everything apart from the electricity.

So finally we get up to Petersfield and the little town just outside that was our home. The place we were all in such a hurry to leave and would never have come back if it wasn't for the sense of duty that bring us here.

When we arrive at the house it look just like it did the last time I see it. Same wooden house with the apex roof and three steps up on to the boarded veranda with the railing and everything else that need painting and the scaly door that still wedge wide to let some breeze pass through. And the yard with the banana and breadfruit and mango trees. And the dry, dusty, red earth that used to blow everywhere on a windy day.

And inside, it dark and closed in like it always was, with the air hanging heavy even though every window in the place jam open with a piece of stick trying to let some life in.

Babs happy to see us and open her arms wide so she can hug me and Marcia both at the same time. And then she kiss us and examine us, one at a time, to make sure we are truly the sisters that the good Lord has delivered to her safe and sound because, Marcia tell me, Babs got religion bad. Then she say she going make some coffee we can drink on the veranda and we say good as we walk into the bedroom where Mama laying in the old iron bed that me, Marcia and Babs used to share when we young.

When I see her I startled. I can't believe how grey and frail she get even though I reckon she must be a good age by now. But how old? I don't know because that subject was never a topic of conversation Mama ever wanted to have. And as for birthdays, she never had nothing to do with that neither.

She open her eyes when she hear our footsteps and raise her arm over the thin grey sheet as if to say come here, come closer. I draw up a chair next to the bed and Marcia cotch herself at the foot.

'It so good to see yu. I was wondering if yu would find time to mek the journey.'

Her voice so weak it was a miracle we manage to hear at all what she have to say. So just to soothe her, I take her hand in mine and I say, 'Yu should be resting yuself Mama.'

She nod her head, and then she raise her other arm and make for Marcia to come take her hand. So Marcia move 'round the bed and do it, which spread Mama's wings like she was some archangel in her nightgown passing among her flock.

'You girls turn into some fine women, who go to town and

mek a living and come back here in glory. A good living at that. Yes sir. Wearing fine frocks and driving a beautiful automobile that park there outside dis window.'

'That not our car Mama. It belong to our friend that drive us here.'

'Yu friend bring yu?'

'Yes, he from 'round these parts himself. He called Clifton.'

'Yu mean Clifton Brown that little scallywag that used to plague Mr Chen chicken morning, noon and night?'

'Yu know him?'

'Me know him? He was a rascal that is what he was. And if he nuh join di police force he would a been doing business for di other side that is for sure. Tell him to come in here and let me tek a look at him.'

So I shout Clifton and the next minute he was standing there in the doorway.

'Lord God Almighty! Yu di image of yu father.' Mama so shocked I think her hair turn an even whiter shade of grey.

'Come here bwoy. Come here in the light let me see yu.'

Clifton ease up to the bed and I get up so he can sit on the chair right there next to her. Mama take both her hands and clasp his. And then she look at him, deep, like she studying to see if it really him or his father.

'Clifton Brown.' She wait and then she say, 'You a good man Clifton Brown?'

'I try to be Mama. I try to be.'

'Good. Yu need to be. To make up for di sins a yu father.' And then she take her hand and pat his, light and gentle like it a true act of motherly love while she repeat to herself, 'Yu need to be.' And then she just lay there and fall asleep.

When we step out on to the veranda Babs got the coffee she pouring and the extra chairs she bring from the kitchen so we can all sit down.

'The doctor say she not going last that much longer.'

'What wrong wid her?'

Babs just shrug her shoulders. 'He nuh know.'

'He don't know? So how long she been like this?'

'A few months that is all. She go downhill fast that is why we think she going be quick. Before that she was busy-busy 'bout her business but last little while me and Leroy been coming over every day to see what she need doing and fetching for her.'

I sip the weak instant coffee she serve us with.

'The nearest hospital in Montego Bay so we cyan be trekking her 'cross there every other week. And the doctor that come to Savanna-la-Mar, well it not that regular and him up to him neck because is everybody from miles 'round here knocking down his door.'

'It cyan be easy for yu with a husband and four children to care for yuself.'

'Four children, Gloria. Yu know how much hungah that is? And Leroy got three already and another one on the way. It trying but yu manage. What else can yu do?'

Then she say, 'Oh, I got something for yu.' And she get up and go inside. When she come back she pull a little frock outta a brown paper bag and hold it up so we can all see. It blue and white with some frilly little sleeve and a ribbon tie 'round the back.

'Yu think Esther will like it?'

And just before I know Marcia going open her mouth and spoil the moment, I say, 'It lovely Babs. It good of yu to think of her,' which please her and put a smile on her lips while she fold up the dress and put it back in the bag. I get up and take it from her and hug her and say thank you, knowing that the dress far too small for Esther since it probably made for a five-year-old child. But it nuh matter. She think of it and that was more than I do.

Later on Babs's husband show up. A scrawny little farmer with baggy pants and dirty fingernails, and boots that not got no laces in. He say he leave the children with his mother because it was too far to bring them this time of night, which vex Babs because she wanted them to come meet their aunties from Kingston.

'It nuh matter Babs. We see them tomorrow. We here three days so there is plenty of time.'

But she not listening. She too set on chastising Scrawny and telling him over and over, 'I nuh tell yu to bring dem over here? I nuh tell yu that?' And all he do is walk away from her as she following his every step 'round the kitchen like he fraid she going stretch out her arm and box his ear.

When we finish eat and wash up Babs and Scrawny go home taking off down the dirt track in the rusty little truck he come here in. After we sit on the veranda and drink some of the Appleton that Clifton bring with him, I reckon it time to settle Mama and go to bed. Me and Marcia share the little single bed that Mama used to sleep in while Clifton take the same canvas cot of Leroy's that we put up in the kitchen just like in the old days when the door was shut and the kerosene lamp put out for the night.

Next morning Leroy come with his two boys to see how we doing and if we need anything. He a hefty man, tall and broad with hands that you can tell been labouring year after year for nothing at all.

He hug us hard and afterwards I stand back and look at him and say, 'Yu sure yu my little brother? How come yu get so big?'

He laugh and turn to his boys and say, 'I tell yu she would say that.' And they grin and shuffle their barefoot like they happy their daddy right 'bout everything.

Leroy say he going do some jobs for Mama and since he there all day it all right if we want to go do something else like see Mr Chen or whatnot.

'Mr Chen still got the shop in town?'

'Yah man. But di son do most a di work now. Old Mr Chen all he do is sidung there and shout out his orders and spit in di bucket he got by di side.'

So we go into town but Mr Chen can't hardly remember me. His son say he can't see so good no more and anyway he losing his mind. But when he hear Clifton's voice he remember that fine.

'Clifton Brown is that you bwoy?'

Clifton laugh and bend down where Mr Chen sitting and take his hand and shake it firm.

'Yu sound just like yu father.'

Clifton don't say nothing, and Mr Chen don't have no more conversation neither, so after we buy some patties and soda, and pick up some things for the children, we jump back in the car and head up to the church where me and Marcia sit in that same pew and laugh in unison with our own echo 'bout how the pastor used to slap down on the Bible between every single word while we sing out, 'Hallelujah, praise be to God.'

And then Clifton surprise me because what he want to do is go drive up the hill to the shack that Barrington Maxwell used to live in.

'What yu want to go do a thing like that for?'

'Yu don't want to see it, Gloria? Yu never think of it yuself?'

And while I am wondering what Mama meant 'bout him looking like his father and Mr Chen recognising his voice, Marcia say,
'I never think I would ever set foot inside that place again.'

We sit there silent in the car, and then Clifton just start the
engine and head off towards the mountain road. He park up and
we get out and stand there on the tarmac almost like we couldn't
decide whether or not to actually look for the track that lead down
to Barrington's shack. But we do it and when we reach there we
stop. And even though the roof cave in and the windows broke
and the place tumbling down with all sorta weeds growing over it,
you could still see it was the same coalman's hovel where I beat in
Barrington's head, and before that, where my stomach heave at the
smell of him and my head swirl with the heat and my skin shred
under his big, dry, calloused hands.

And then Marcia start to cry with a wailing that burst outta her
like a dam that well up and rupture because nothing could stop the
water from flooding out. She drop to her knees in the dirt, and
with her hands over her face she bawl. Loud and heavy with a pain
that was coming from so deep inside her it cut through me just to
hear the sound of it.

I bend down and put my arm 'round her shoulder and then I
move in front and take her fully in my arms just as the tears started
to roll down my own cheeks and the rocks dig into my own knees
in a way that gave a physical meaning to the feelings I had inside.

When I look up I see Clifton was crying as well. Silent and
slow, but steady and strong. Standing there with his arms wrapped
'round himself like he was trying to bring some comfort to a body
that remembered some unholy truth about Barrington and that
shack. And then suddenly he launch himself at the wall and pound
so hard with his fists and shoulder and feet that the whole rotten

thing fall to the ground taking with it all the crumbling remains of our torment. All except for what was left inside each one of us.

Babs tell us to come by her house so we can meet her children. The place just like Mama's, wooden and cramped and dingy even though she try to brighten it up with some colourful curtains and a nice fresh tablecloth. I give her the things we pick up for the children in Mr Chen's shop, all the time feeling bad that I never thought to bring anything from Kingston because all the time I was getting ready to come the only thing on my mind was Barrington. Not even Mama like it should have been.

Babs act like she grateful and tell the children they must wait 'til later when she going divvy up the gifts between them. And then she settle us down and serve the oxtail stew she cook special. It taste good and take me way back because it was always a favourite of Mama's.

All through the meal she fussing at the children and chastising Scrawny for this and that. And when we done she pour out some more watery coffee and we step into the yard.

'Babs, we going back to Mama's now and spend the evening and tomorrow with her. But I want to thank yu for how gracious yu been to us coming here. And I want to say that if yu need anything . . .'

'Thank yu, Gloria. I can see that you and Marcia do good fi yuself in Kingston. What wid di frocks yu wearing and di house I come see when little Esther born and di car and everything. That is good fi yu. I am glad. But we don't need nothing from yu. The good Lord is providing all we want for. We content. We happy. And each and every day we give thanks to Jesus Christ, King of Kings, Lord of Lords.' And then she turn to me and smile. A thin smile just across her lips like her face was almost cracking itself to do it.

Mama wasn't no brighter that evening or the next day. She just lay there drifting off to sleep and waking up again. Me and Marcia sit there anyway, and when Mama could raise her head and talk she do it and we pass the time with her, fetching a drop of corn-meal porridge or a glass of water when she wanted it. And all the questions I had in my head about who my father was or what she mean when she say what she did to Clifton couldn't have no answer because there was no way I could bring myself to ask her given the condition she was in. All I could do was sit there and chide myself for never having come back before. And puzzle over how it was that such a strong, vital woman could have shrivelled to the size of this miniature person in front of me.

The next day we drive back to Kingston with Marcia sitting next to Clifton talking so excited like she just been released from years of confinement. Me, I watch the country pass by and wonder how anything was ever going to change in Jamaica. How anything could make a difference to this rural poverty, or bring proper medical care or education.

And as for my worries about people asking us questions we didn't want to answer, nobody asked us anything. And as for my questions for Clifton about his father, and what happen at the shack, that would have to wait for another time.

Three days after we get back Marcia telephone to say that she get a telegram from Babs that Mama had passed.

'Yu think we should go back for the nine nights?'

My heart sink. 'I don't know that I want to do it Marcia. What you think?'

Marcia quiet at the other end, so I say, 'If yu want to we can go, but I don't think we can expect Clifton to be driving back over there so soon.'

Still she nuh say nothing.

'Just tell me what yu thinking 'bout it. There not no point in you and me playing cat and mouse over it.'

She wait a minute and then she say, 'I don't want to do it, Gloria. That last visit was enough for me. Nobody going miss us anyway. They been carrying on all these years without us so what it matter?'

'What about Babs and Leroy? Yu nuh think we should go there for them at least?'

But all I get from her was more silence.

'I don't think I can face it, Gloria. When I think 'bout Petersfield all I can think about is Barrington Maxwell and you and me in that shack that day. And then after we go there with Clifton it was over for me. That is the last memory I want to have. The last tears I want to shed over it. And the last time I want to set foot in that town.'

I think on it and then I say, 'We got to go, Marcia. Never mind 'bout nine nights but we have to go to the funeral.'

'We do?'

'It Mama's funeral. It got nothing to do with Barrington. And if we nuh go, it will only turn into another thing we cyan forgive ourselves for.'

So we go and Clifton drive. The service simple. The pastor preach and slap the Bible and we praise the Lord and sing. The little church cram full of people I never see before and just like Marcia say they none of them pay us any mind at all.

Afterwards when we go back to the house I give Scrawny the envelope with some money and the bank book for the account

I open for them. And he just take it and say thank you like he already expecting what was in it.

Leroy more surprised when he reach out his hand. 'So what dis, Gloria?'

'A little help for the way.'

He peer into the envelope and then he look at me. 'We don't need dis yu know. We doing all right. Not no shame in being poor.'

'I never say it was shameful.'

He stand there like he was turning things over in his mind and then he take out the money and put in his pocket and hand me back the bank book.

'That no use in these parts. A post office order every now and again would help ease di pain though.' And then he smile and wrap his arms 'round me.

CHAPTER 34

I LOOK AT Marcia sitting there on the veranda with the red hibiscus in the flower bed behind her and the light breeze brushing the leaves and I think, 'Yes, I knew it would come.'

'So what yu going to do up there?'

'Loretta got me a job in the women's theatre collective she work in. It nothing special, some office work, helping with marketing and promotion, and getting things ready for each production. The thing is, moving up there will give me the space and time to concentrate on my poetry and that is what I really want to do.'

Sybil and Beryl throw a party over the house to say farewell to Marcia. But in truth it wasn't no party. It was just us with food and drink and merriment. Just like how we use to have Sundays on the veranda. With eating and drinking and high spirits. On the outside. On the inside, my heart was breaking.

'It not like I going the other side a the world. Miami only two hours away.' Then she say, 'Yu the only one that not been up there yet.'

'Yu mean Sybil and Beryl been?'

Beryl say, 'Yah man. Shopping in Miami. Loretta got a beautiful apartment as well.'

I can't believe I am the only one. It make me feel left out. Excluded. Like the time when we argue over the necklace and Marcia turn on me. And then I wonder how come she never ask me if I want to go up with her sometime, all the trips she make.

'Would yu come, Gloria? Come to Miami?'

'Yu asking me?'

'Sure I'm asking yu.'

I smile because something inside me soften. Then she say, 'Would yu come stay in the apartment with me and Loretta?' And the way she look at me tell me what it was that stop her from inviting me before. Me sleeping in the place with two women doing what they doing. Because after that first time I meet Loretta and I say what I say about not understanding it, me and Marcia never talk about it again. Not like that. It was just a kind of information conversation. Loretta coming for the weekend. Loretta going back to Miami. Marcia catching the plane on this day or that. That was all there was to it. She never tell me any more than that. And I never ask. Even when she come tell me she was leaving it was just a matter of practicalities. I didn't have it in me to open my mouth and ask anything. Nothing meaningful. So why would she bother inviting me up there not knowing how it is I really feel?

'I would love to come Marcia.'

And she smile. And take Loretta's hand.

When we go to the airport Marcia got more luggage than anybody could imagine. So much stuff they have to pay extra for the baggage.

'A where yu get all a this?'

She sigh. 'This, Gloria, is the benefit I get from what you and Henry's business do for me. And all the wonderful stores in Miami that I been bringing things back from little-little. Now it all got to go one way. All at the same time.' And she laugh.

'One way Marcia?'

She drop her carry-on bag and throw her arms 'round me. And the two of us bust out crying like a pair of babies testing their lungs for the first time. We just stand there hanging on to each other with the tears rolling down our face 'til we hear them making the final call for her flight and she say, 'I have to go.'

And I say yes and let my arms fall to my side.

And then she hug and kiss Sybil and Beryl and she and Loretta turn and walk off through the departure gate.

We wait 'til the plane actually take off, watching it rise into the sky through the big glass window like maybe expecting she wasn't really on it and next thing she would be walking down the gangway back to me. But it wasn't so. No more than it was with Ernesto. She was gone. And I had to dry my tears and carry on.

When we go back to Franklyn Town the three of us just sit there on the veranda with the ice rattling in the glass as it cooling the rum and the radio tuned to the ska and rocksteady and reggae they busy playing.

CHAPTER 35

DOCTOR MORRISON GOING back to Scotland because Margaret think that Jamaica changing too much for her to still feel like she belong here. She say that Jamaicans have to claim Jamaica for themselves and anyway, she want baby John to go to school in Edinburgh where she and the doctor come from.

'Yu want to go George?'

'It is what Margaret wants. And I do understand her wanting John to be educated in Scotland.'

'So what going happen to the girls?'

'We were hoping you would look after them. With Hyacinth's help, of course.'

'Me?'

'Gloria, truthfully, haven't you been doing so anyway? Ever since Margaret got John? Besides we cannot think of anyone better suited. Can you?'

I don't say nothing but I know my face show him the relief I feel that she not going close the place down.

'And the card club?'

He laugh. 'You know, Gloria, that has gone from strength to strength. It seems that no matter how bad things get men are still eager to chance their hand at a quick fix. And afterwards, win or lose, lament the absence of the services of your good selves next door.'

And that is right because everybody stop doing that now. Sybil too busy with all her politicking, Marcia serious over Loretta even before she go to Miami and Beryl, well, she just do whatever Sybil do.

'So yu going close down the cards then?'

'Hell no! Trevor will take care of that.'

'Trevor?'

He laugh again. 'Trevor is a lot more competent than any of us give him credit for. In all honesty, he has been running it for years.'

For Pao, Morrison leaving was his chance to find out where Fay and the children at because he reckon the doctor could go down to England and do some snooping in London where he think they living.

I say to him, 'That is all well and good for you, but what about how Merleen Chin feel 'bout her baby being taken away to Scotland like that?'

'She give up that boy to Morrison because there was no way a child like her could have keep and care for it. That is what happen. So is them that got to sort out what in his best interest now.' And I think maybe, but it don't mean that she not got no feeling 'bout it.

Right then Esther step on to the veranda with Hyacinth and Pao look at them and smile because Hyacinth looking good since I pay the hospital to fix her harelip.

'You girls off to go do something nice?'

'We going to the volleyball tournament you told me about.'

He reach into his pocket and peel off some notes and hand them to her and say, 'Enjoy yuself. Two a yu.'

Esther take the money and kiss him on the cheek before she and Hyacinth go down the steps and disappear into the street.

'Volleyball tournament?'

He vex. 'Cho, Gloria. I just tell the girl about it that is all.' And then he sit down and say, 'So what, a man cyan talk to his own daughter?'

I get a letter from Ernesto. Hand-delivered by a Guantanamo domestic who say she have a friend in Santiago who ask her to bring it. Her friend named Matilde Alonso, which make sense. It been a long time because nothing been going between Cuba and Jamaica since the US blockade that the Jamaican government decide to join in with. Except the domestics that they fly there on US Navy aeroplanes.

The letter is long because Ernesto distraught that Che Guevara get killed in Bolivia. He say he weep for days and weeks, and in between that all he do is read every speech that Che Guevara make in Cuba and New York and Algiers and Uruguay; and every arti-cle he write in the *Verde Olivo* magazine and *Cuba Socialista*; and every interview he give, that is the ones Ernesto can lay his hands on.

But this time, the poem was different.

> Each day the sun rises
> and I see the blue sky and green hills of Cuba.
> Each day the sun sets

and I see the long shadows of the Royal Palms.
And as the time passes,
more and more
I greet each day with a love of homeland
that stills my restless mind.

I put it in the drawer with the others because I didn't know how to get word to him without asking Matilde 'bout her friend and I didn't want to do that. Not start something again that already finish. Even though I feel sad for Ernesto 'bout Che Guevara. I reckon the poem sound like he found some peace and I should leave well alone.

When Norman Manley have his seventy-fifth birthday celebration in the National Arena we cram in there with god knows how many PNP comrades because that place have six thousand seats. And that was some evening. Sybil beyond herself with excitement which turn to fever when the great man retire and his son, Michael, take over. Because just how Norman Manley say the mission of his generation was to win self-government and the mission for this generation is reconstructing the social and economic society and life of Jamaica, so Michael Manley had the words 'democratic socialism' tripping off his tongue every minute of every day. And she love it. So much so that she throw herself heart and soul into supporting him winning the next general election. Sybil was so busy running here and there organising party groups you could hardly see her for dust. And she turn just like Ernesto, only it was Michael Manley not Che Guevara that she got on her lips morning, noon and night.

It important what she doing for the country. I knew that. But for me, it wasn't the politics. It was the people. So when Esther tell me that the Baptist church at Half Way Tree open up an adult education centre and was giving a hand to people with legal and welfare problems that is where I went. To offer some comfort and support and anything else I could do. Because whatever I feel about God, they were trying to do some good. I help with the basic schools and backyard daycare centres as well. But the speeching and organising and rallying, I left to Sybil.

Then one day she come and tell me she want us to stop the moneylending. She say enough was enough and even though me and her been fifty-fifty partners since Henry gone she think it time we just collect what we can from what still owing and call it a day. She say she and Beryl agree.

'Besides, people barely got the wherewithal to pay what with the unemployment situation and such, it seem almost criminal to be sending Trevor to go harass them when they already got so much troubles.'

I tell her I am happy with that because in truth it Sybil that been taking the lion share of the responsibility and since the actual money not no big concern for any of us no more why buck the cart if that is what they want to do?

'Anyway,' she say, 'the time seem right, now that Jamaica changing to dollars.' She pause and then she say, 'There is just one fly in the ointment.' I raise my eyebrows.

'Fingernail.'

I knew it. Something inside of me expected it to be an altercation with Fingernail.

'What is her problem?'

Sybil take another sip of her coffee. 'She say she want us to pay her off for her losses.'

'What losses? What she talking 'bout?'

'She say we owe her 12.5 per cent a the interest on all the money that due whether or not we collect it. That was the agreement. That was the percentage for all the business she put our way.'

'Even on the money we don't manage to collect?'

'So she say.'

I think on it and then I say, 'What you think?'

'We think we should pay her. Just to get a finish to the thing.'

It vex me. Fingernail been nothing but aggravation from the beginning. But the thing that really stick in my craw is how she try make so much trouble for Henry. And how because he die she get away scot free without having to account one iota for the nasty way she go about her business.

And it was that feeling left inside of me over Henry that make me say, 'She can get her percentage on whatever we collect. But the loans that we let go, she don't get nothing on that. It one thing losing that money, but paying her 12.5 per cent of squat? No.'

Sybil worried 'bout the prospect. 'She not going like that yu know.'

I ease back and I say, 'Yu think it all right me saying that even though we partners and I overriding what you and Beryl already agree?'

'It not that, Gloria. It just that she aggrieved and in a way I can understand it. We mek a hell of a lot of money over the years and she only get the crumbs from it.'

'So yu saying we should give her what she want?'

'No, I just saying what I saying. Whatever yu decide is good. All for one and one for all. That is how we always been and I don't see no reason to change that now. I just wonder if it going turn out to be more trouble than it worth.' And then she wait a minute before she say, 'Is this business or personal? Because I know the business woman in yu would have just say, "Yes, the money a small price to pay to be done with her." So yu surprise me.'

I take two deep breath. 'It personal Sybil. Yu think that is bad?'

'Who can say what is good or bad. It is what it is. Just so we know what going on, that is all.'

Afterwards I wonder if I was too hasty giving my answer to Sybil. But then I think, if it come to it, all we got to do is give Fingernail what she want and no harm would have been done excepting for it hurting to see her get her way.

When I talk to Clifton about it he unimpressed.

'Why yu nuh just give the woman the money and save everybody's time and trouble?'

'I don't like the woman, Clifton. I don't like what she try to do to Henry.'

'The man is dead and gone. Yu think it matter to him? It don't matter to nobody now what she do.'

I know Clifton right. After all, nothing ever come of all her investigating. Not even Miss Cicely was interested. But still, I couldn't stomach the idea that she was going to get the better of me.

It stay on my mind 'til Sybil telephone and say that she tell Fingernail our decision but she didn't say nothing.

'What, nothing at all?'

'Not a single word. She just sit there on her veranda looking at me and then she turn her head and stare at the street. And when she finally open her mouth she just start talk about how good it was that Trevor got to make his record.'

'Trevor make a record?'

'Yeah man. It turn out that Fingernail was serious 'bout knowing some record producer and she fix a meeting for Trevor and he do the record. Some song 'bout how the police not got no right to be chasing innocent criminals.'

I laugh. 'Innocent criminals?'

'Something like that. Anyway, it not doing so good in the hit parade but at least he have the satisfaction of knowing he do it and he got the record spinning on the turntable over and over every single day so the whole street can appreciate it. If appreciate is the right word.'

I think on it a minute. 'So what yu think Fingernail going do?'

'Your guess is as good as mine.'

CHAPTER 36

I TELEPHONE CLIFTON to congratulate him on his promotion to police captain.

'It wasn't no easy thing yu know. They put me through my paces. Well and truly.'

'I wouldn't expect anything less. Giving a man a responsible position like that. You got to know he up to the challenge.' And we laugh.

'Anyway,' he say, 'Trevor in the hospital if yu want to go visit him.'

'What happen to him?'

'He get knifed.'

'Yu serious?'

'Straight up. A rumble over some card game. Another inch to the side and they would a slice his liver and mek him bleed out right there on the floor like a stuck pig. That bad it was. Or nearly was anyway.'

'He all right?'

'All right? He sitting up in that bed there showing off his stitches to everybody and harassing every pretty nurse that passing him by. Go take a look at him. I think he would appreciate it.'

When I go over the hospital Trevor just like Clifton say. Boastful and happy, and full of charm for the nurses.

'What happen?'

'Deh just bust in wid gun and knife. One a dem even had a cricket bat. Can yu believe that? And deh just grab up everything on di table and tell everybody to empty him pocket and when I try wrestle wid one a dem he stick me.' And then he smile and say, 'Yu want to see?' And start raising up his pyjama shirt and pull down the pants little to show me.

'It nasty Trevor. And it not no stick. It more like slice.'

'That not nasty.' He examine himself and sorta rub the stitches light with his finger. 'It mannish. Yu nuh think so?' And then he look over and smile at some young nurse passing by about her business.

'How many men yu think so lucky to have a thing like this to show off? And to say, I get knifed in a card game?' And he smile.

'Trevor, this not no joke. The man nearly kill yu!'

'Nearly, Miss Gloria. Nearly.' And then he smile again. A big, broad grin.

'How they find out 'bout the game and how much big money was passing hands over there?'

He cover himself up and pull the sheet to his neck. 'I think that my fault.'

'How so?'

'Since the doctor gone it not so easy, yu know, to get all dem white men. So maybe I talk little bit too much trying to get people interested.'

'Who yu talk to?'

'Too many people, Miss Gloria. Too many.'

I think on it and then I say, 'Yu think maybe Fingernail got anything to do wid it?'

He quiet at first and then he say, 'I think maybe.' He pause a minute. 'She been complaining bad 'bout how you and Miss Sybil stop the lending and rob her over it. She real sour 'bout it. Real sour.' He stop again. 'Sorry I mek such a mess a everything.'

'You didn't mek no mess, Trevor! It was me and you don't need to be apologising for anything. It me that should be saying sorry to you.'

He laugh. 'Well, it done now. Card club over. And since my latest record doing so good in the hit parade it likely time for me to be thinking 'bout other things anyway.'

'Yu not going get the police to do something 'bout it?'

'Di police not got no time for a thing like this. Not wid di nonstop armed combat they contending with. Anyway, all a them was wearing kerchief over their face like it a cowboy movie.'

When me and Sybil go over Passmore Town we find Fingernail and her friend sitting on the veranda in some brand-new frocks and high-heel shoes. They even wearing hats, sitting there in the shade of their own front yard.

'So Sybil, Gloria, long time since we nuh see yu.'

We walk up the veranda steps and sit down in the sticky plastic chair.

'Yu mek yuself some big money then?'

Fingernail stand up and twirl 'round two times, smiling with her hand raise in the air. 'Yu like it?'

We just sit there and look at her. So she rest herself back down.

'Yu bwoy all right in the hospital?'

I feel like I want to get up and slap her spiteful face. And then maybe take the hat off her head and stamp it into the ground.

'Yu lucky this thing didn't turn into no murder.'

'Murder! Cho, people getting shot for just walking down di street in di wrong-colour shirt. Trevor was nothing.' And she motion her hand like to say enough already, I don't want to hear no more 'bout this.

So I get up and say, 'It over then. We done.' And she just shrug her shoulders.

When we reach the street and drop the gate latch we see the other one with her hand half raise like she tempting to wave but she too nervous to actually do it. Next thing I know Sybil lift her arm and sway it little bit in the breeze. Like a farewell and I think all right, she her friend in the first place.

Sitting in the taxi Sybil say to me there is something she want me to come do with her. And what she want is for me to go to some dancehall with her to listen to Junior playing his trombone.

'What, like in a band yu mean?'

'Yes.'

'He must be a grown man now eh, Sybil?'

'Twenty-two years old. Making his living as a musician. Can yu credit it? And I watch him grow all these years just like he was my own. First in the orphanage and then all the way through school, which is where he learn to play the trombone. Yu know Alpha see that boy right from the first day he set foot in that school yard.'

'I always hear tell how good they do with the boys and the music there.'

'Them nuns save that boy's life. That is the truth.'

★   ★   ★

The dancehall in a downtown backstreet behind a wooden door that got a wrought-iron gate to protect it. Inside it packed, and hot-hot. There so many people in there you almost couldn't even move your arm to reach into your purse for change to pay for your drink. And the outfits these women wearing? Outlandish wasn't the word. Like maybe she got on a lime-green catsuit that so tight the zip only pull up halfway. Or a orange brassiere and some leopardskin something that I not sure if it shorts or dress except it not got no front and barely cover her backside. Or maybe she got a long skirt to the ground but she draped from head to toe in all sorta beads and bangles like she a Egyptian belly dancer. And the hair, that was something else because there was every colour under the sun. Blue, purple, pink, green. You name it, it was there on somebody's head, excepting for the ones that go bleach their hair blonde. But the one thing all of these women have in common is that every one of them dress so they could show off everything they got.

And if that wasn't enough, then the dancing was showing off everything they could do. Winding up every inch of their body in a way that put you in mind of just one thing. And what going on with the men on that dancefloor wasn't anybody's business. While the rest of them stand 'round and watch like it was a floorshow for their entertainment. Which maybe it was. To me it was shameful. Me, a woman who been in the business I been in all those years.

All I feel when the records stop and the deejay finish his toasting, which is what Sybil tell me it called, was relief. And I thank God when Junior's band finally turn up with him blowing some real sweet music outta that trombone.

Afterwards when he come say hello he greet Sybil like she was his true mother. Wrapping his arms 'round her and kissing her on the cheek with love and real affection. And then he shake my hand and say, 'I sorry 'bout what I bring yu to.' And he sorta gesture with his head 'round the room. 'I didn't know it would be like . . . like this. It's just, yu know, my first live gig and I wanted Sybil to come see me because up 'til now all I do is play trombone in the studio for somebody's record.' And he smile. 'Sorry.' And then he kiss Sybil on the cheek again.

Junior was courteous. A gentleman, with manners. Dressed in slacks and a breakneck shirt, with soft, sensitive hands that would never see the blood his father's had. Not the way he play that trombone. And eyes that had the telltale hint, especially when he smile, of a little Chinese, right there in his African face. Just like Esther.

1972

'And so my life its way will wend.'

CHAPTER 37

CLIFTON WAS WAITING for me when I get back from my trip with Hyacinth enrolling her into the community college book-keeping course. And what a happy day that was after years of her trying to get all the qualifications for the entrance.

I see the grave look on his face, so I say, 'What happen?'

'It Auntie. She just collapse and Esther ring a ambulance to tek her to Morrison and he call me.'

'Morrison say what wrong with her?'

'He think it a heart problem that mek it beat funny and that is why she fall down unconscious but then she wake up and she OK. But she off her legs if yu get me.'

'Yu mean she cyan walk?'

'Not at the moment. Morrison say maybe not again, or maybe she get up OK but she always going be unsteady. So anyway, he put her in a nursing home up Constant Spring Road but it expensive and he want to talk to yu 'bout that.'

'We lucky he was on hand.'

Clifton laugh. 'Yah man. Good that he only last six months in Scotland before he had to come back home and open a bottle a rum. He say to me that the cold and sober Presbyterian life was killing him. Yu like that?'

We pull into the car park and the place is beautiful. Gorgeous lawns and gardens and paved walkways with arcades of pink English roses over them and flower beds with hibiscus and anthurium and oleander and periwinkle, and a plumbago hedge sitting right under the big tiled veranda where the nurse greet us and say she will take us directly to Auntie.

Auntie's room is clean and bright and airy. It spacious and the decoration gracious. It seem more like a first-class hotel than a place for sick people. So I think Morrison done good no matter what it cost.

I walk over to her and kiss her head as she sitting there in the wheelchair looking out the French window that got the little balcony on the other side. And then I pull up a chair next to her and sit down.

'How yu doing Auntie?'

She reach over and take my hand in hers. 'I doing fine, Gloria. Just fine. Di people here, deh good to me. Nothing fi yu to fret over. Every long lane have a turning.'

So maybe this is what she needed to finally stop her from doing all the chores she always busying herself with and refusing for me to get some help.

We talk some more while I was pushing her in the wheelchair 'round the garden and then just as I was ready to go she say to me, 'Clifton going talk to yu. Di things yu want to know, I not got di strength fi it but I tell him to tell yu because I understand it not fair fi me to go die and tek all a dat wid me.'

'Don't talk like that. Yu alive and well.' I want to ask her what she mean but there don't seem no point. She already tell me Clifton going do it so that will be soon enough.

Esther serve stew peas and rice for dinner. She home for the holidays before she go to university.

'Yu have a good day with yu father at the races?'

'It was fun but I'm afraid I lost a lot of money.'

'His, I hope.' Clifton laugh. And then I smile to myself about how measly that musta sound.

Me and Clifton step on to the veranda while Esther inside seeing to the dishes. He pick up two glasses and a bottle of rum as we walking out so I know this going to be some long conversation.

He settle himself and pour the drinks. 'I have something to tell yu.'

'Is it something I want to hear?'

'Well yu been asking 'bout it for long enough and Auntie think it time.'

'I am all ears Clifton.'

He swallow down a big gulp of rum. 'It just difficult to know where to begin.' He take another drink. 'There was a man, married man, but he couldn't keep it in his pants. Yu know what I mean? Well, maybe he wasn't so different from any other Jamaican man or any man in truth. Anyway, he do what he do and go about his business. And two a the women that he do, they sisters. And one sister, she had a son. And the other sister, she have a daughter. But the second sister young. She just a young girl.'

'Clifton.'

'Yes, yes I getting there. Patience, Gloria.' And he drink some more rum and then he hold up the glass and turn to me. 'Yu think it could do with some water?'

'Water? Since when you start tek water?'

'It going to be a while, Gloria, and I just wonder if maybe we should slow things down wid a drop a water or even maybe some ice.' And just as he say it he get up and walk inside and a few minutes later he come back with the full ice bucket and a water jug. He sit down and start fussing with the glasses, dropping in the ice cubes and pouring water after them.

'Ice and water Clifton?'

He look down at what he doing. 'Well, it won't do no harm.' And he flick the excess water off his fingers and ease back in the chair with the glass in his hand.

'Anyway, even though this man do what he do, he nuh like it when he find out his wife seeing another man herself. And, Gloria, what he do is he kill her.'

My heart leap. God knows why. Maybe it was just the thought of somebody killing somebody. Like murder following me everywhere I go.

'But not just that. He cut her up. Cut her bad. And it was all to do wid her sex, yu know, the cutting. It was cruel and nasty.' He pause.

'Yu going tell me who this man is?'

'It was our father, Gloria.'

'Our father! Who is the our?'

'You and me, Gloria. You and me.'

I convinced my ears deceiving me. 'Yu trying to tell me yu my brother?'

'Yes, Gloria. And the other man. The one the wife was seeing. That was Barrington Maxwell.'

It was like somebody take a wet rag and slap me in the face because suddenly my body was rigid, suspended in its own space and time completely separate from me, and my thoughts, and my feelings. It was just hanging there in this empty void.

'Barrington Maxwell?'

'Yes, and the thing is, Barrington really love this woman. He really love her, Gloria, so he go over to the house and he burn it to the ground even though there was nobody in it because they already haul our father off to jail.'

'And that was where he die back in '38?'

'Yes, he live out the rest of his days in Kingston Penitentiary and he die.' Clifton take a breath and another drink. 'What Barrington say was that this man tek everything from him and he was going to tek everything from this man. But it only me . . .' He pause '. . . and maybe you that know what Barrington mean.'

I feel the blood drain outta me. 'He do it to you as well?' But Clifton didn't give me no answer so I say, 'Yu ever tell anybody?'

'No, not 'til now. You tell anybody?'

'I told Mama but she wasn't interested. She just boil up some herbs and give me to drink and we never mention it again.'

'Yu think maybe she thought Barrington already seen enough trouble she didn't want to mek no more for him?'

'Yu think? I don't know what she thought.'

It quiet between us while the crickets was clicking and the sound of next door's lawn sprinkler was coming to us over the hedge. But my mind was not still. It was busy with memories of Barrington. Barrington and me. And Marcia. And how I never asked her anything 'bout her and Loretta and how maybe that was the emptiness that lay there between us, why all that time she didn't invite me to Miami even though she had Sybil and Beryl staying up there with them.

And then suddenly I just say, 'Yu think that was what mek you the way you are?' And right afterwards I realise we brush over the bit where he tell me he is my brother so I say, 'Yu me bredda, Clifton?'

365

He turn to me and smile. 'Yah man. I been trying to tell yu for a good while.' And then he get up out the chair and come over and ease me to my feet and hug me. A big, warm bear of a hug that a older bredda would give to a younger sista. It felt reassuring. Like I wasn't alone in the world no more. But in truth, that feeling been with me a long time. Like there was a bond between us. An easiness. An acceptance. And him coming to the house and taking out Auntie and Esther when I was in Cuba. And how Auntie treat him. And Esther taking it on herself to call him uncle. It was all there except I couldn't see it. So maybe when he tell me it wasn't a surprise. It was more like him confirming something I already knew.

He ease back and while we standing there in the dark of night he say, 'That is why Auntie send for me.'

I step back and look at him.

'She send message to me in Montego Bay that the police was after yu and I had to come to Kingston to see to it. That is how come I dig up the query from the constables and wangle the transfer to get here.'

I can't say nothing to him so he carry on. 'She know everything, yu know, Auntie.'

'Why she nuh tell me herself?'

'I should know that, Gloria?' He pause. 'That is like asking me why people nuh tell their secrets. Because it their secret I suppose.' He pause again. 'Maybe she was waiting for the right time and she reckon this is it but she not got the strength right now.' And then he sit down and pick up the glass.

'The thing I don't understand, Gloria, is what yu was doing up there.'

'Up where?'

366

'Up Barrington's shack the day you and Marcia beat his head in.'

I could barely breathe so I didn't say nothing even though I knew he was waiting for something to come from me.

Then I say, 'Why yu think he try do it to Marcia?'

'Gloria, how am I going to know that? Maybe he mistake her for you.'

I sit there a while and then I get up and go inside to put on some light on the veranda.

When I come back I say, 'Yu think what Barrington do to yu is what make yu the way yu are?'

Clifton take his hand and rub his face. His forehead and eyes and nose and cheeks and mouth and chin. He do it over and over. And then he sigh. A deep, heavy, slow sigh.

'In a way, but maybe not the way yu expect.'

'What yu mean?'

He stop and breathe. 'He used to wait for me outside the school gate and tell me to come wid him. Not every day just every now and again. And because I never tell a soul what was going on nobody was paying it any mind. But anyway, I would go wid him to the shack. I would go. And he would do what he do. And afterwards, I would walk home. And after a while it didn't seem so bad. Sometimes I even used to stay afterwards and help him with making and stacking the coal. But the thing about it, Gloria, what it was about, was power. The power a grown man has over a child. A child that was brought up to believe that adults were always right and had to be respected and yu had to do what they tell yu.' He stop and empty his glass and take a refill, ice and water included. And then he shake off his hand like he do before so the excess water from the ice fall in droplets on to the tile floor.

367

'And later, when I try do it wid a woman I found out that I could do it physically, but it didn't feel good. And what it was about was the power. It felt like the same power Barrington had over me. Because yu know, Gloria, in this world the power a man got over a woman is backed up by a whole system and culture that say he is more important and more valuable than her, and his needs and wants got to be met before hers, and she got to serve him and sacrifice for him, and do what he say and keep him happy. He got to have the better cut a meat and the last drop a milk while she settle for the scraps and water. What it say is, she don't really matter. And that apply to every man, the nice home-loving family man as much as the scrawniest, laziest, nastiest, imbecile of a man. The system is there for him. And when yu see that for what it is, it is hard, Gloria, to believe that any woman in her right mind would really want to give herself up, give up her body and her heart to something so personal knowing how uneven and unfair that relationship is. Give herself up of her own free will.' He stop and take another sip. 'And when yu a policeman believe me, Gloria, yu see too much of what a man's acceptance of his position can lead to. It is ugly. It is disgraceful. And, Gloria, it all part of the same shameful thing. The meat and the milk, and the beating and rape and murder. Not just from the nasty ones, but from men yu would think was a nice guy as well.'

I sit there in silent disbelief because I never hear a man talk like this before. It never even dawn on me that any man would give a second thought to what is going on or even care about it.

'It took me a long time to come to where I am now. And in the past there was things I did that I regret. Things wid men younger than me. That was a part of my troubled mind and for my conscience. But there is one thing I know, if I was a woman, under these conditions, I wouldn't want to do that wid any man.'

'Yu a rare man, Clifton Brown.'

'No. Most men know the truth a the situation. They just playing ignorant because it suit them. It comfortable. After all, would you want to give up that kinda power?' He wait a minute. 'And even if yu the kinda man to tek issue wid it how yu going do that without bringing down the wrath a the whole world on yu head? And that not just other men we talking 'bout. It women too because some find the arrangement comfortable as well. It like everybody know their place and just carry on dancing that same dance over and over. It agreed. It easy. It familiar. And it comforting to know that yu in step wid everybody else. There is safety in that. That is what they convince themself of anyway. They reckon it better to be unhappy than risk the hatred of everybody 'round yu.'

He smile. 'Cho, I sure I not telling yu nothing yu didn't know already. I reckon every woman know it, in her heart, even if she don't let it play on her mind because after all she got to get on wid life the way she find it.'

We sit there and let the silence rest between us.

'It a dangerous thing yu do though Clifton, in a place like this.'

He nod his head. 'Life is dangerous, Gloria, and me being the way I am is only one part of it. Yu wouldn't believe the kind a nonsense I have to put up wid being a policeman. Honest to God. Especially wid all the trouble and antics that going on out there right now.'

Esther step out on to the veranda to ask us if we want anything and we say no. She say she going to bed for an early night and so she can carry on reading her book. And then she walk back inside.

Clifton pour himself another drink and come 'cross and top

369

up my glass. When he sit back down he say, 'I been chatting all this long while telling yu everything from A to Z but I notice there was two things we ease over that yu never say nothing 'bout.'

'What that?'

'First, what yu think 'bout our father and what he done. And second, what yu was doing up Barrington's shack that day.'

I rest my finger over my lips a while before I drop my hand to the glass and take a drink.

'I don't know Clifton. I don't know what I think. I spend such a long time meking up the worst stories I could imagine about him and what yu tell me just seem like another one of them. It don't seem real. And even though I tell Esther how important it is to know your roots, right now it don't seem to matter except for explaining why it is I turn out so bad.'

'Yu not bad, Gloria! Is that what yu think? Yu didn't do nothing but do Barrington a favour. Yu put the man outta his misery. That is what yu do.'

'Is that yu policeman verdict?'

'What yu think?'

'I don't know what I think. That is what I just say to yu. How I feel? Empty.' And in truth who my father was is something I stop wondering about a long time back because it didn't seem to have any bearing on anything. Not any more.

'And yu not going tell me 'bout the shack that day?'

'That, Clifton, as Auntie say to me, is for another time.'

But what I never say to him was that when I talk about me being bad it had nothing to do with killing Barrington Maxwell.

The next time I visit Auntie I say to her that Clifton and me had our chat and he tell me everything. And she nod her head and just say, 'Good.'

'I know now why yu say all them things to me when we at Back-O-Wall. I understand that yu was just trying to warn me and protect me from the troubles a young woman can find if she go mix up with some man.'

'It not no excuse, Gloria.' And then she take my hand in both of hers and say, 'I know I treat yu bad when yu first come to Kingston and I am sorry. I get myself into a rut wid yu and I didn't know how to get outta it. I only hope dat these past years in Franklyn Town and me coming to be wid you and Esther go some way to mek up fah it.' And then she look me straight in the eye and say, 'Can yu forgive me?'

'There not nothing to forgive Auntie. I know yu was only talking to me from outta yu own sorrow. And anyway, it me that should be thanking you. For sending for Clifton.' And she just squeeze my hand.

I ask her again if she don't want to come home.

'How many times yu going ask me that? And how many times I going tell yu I happy here? Since deh move me to dis nice little apartment I got everything I need. And on di days I good enough to walk wid di stick I do fah myself. And on di days I not so good, there is plenty people here to do fah me. There is company when I want it and quiet when I don't. It perfect, Gloria.'

CHAPTER 38

MICHAEL MANLEY WIN the election and every week after that Pao was over the house telling me what wonders the government performing with their minimum wage and workers' co-operatives.

Sybil ecstatic as well because, for the first time, the government actually making jobs for women.

'The Women's Auxiliary doing everything, Gloria, to support the work we doing. They even setting up special women's centres so that pregnant schoolgirls can have their babies and still finish their education. That is something eh? Mek your work a bit different. And women's groups as well, all over the island to help raise consciousness. Raise consciousness! It lovely.'

Next thing she tell me is the government re-establishing relations with Cuba and she going on an exchange visit with the Cuban Federation of Women. 'Yu want to come?'

'I cyan go to Cuba.'

'Yu nuh want to see how the federation forging ahead?'

'That is good for you Sybil. My contribution is right here.'

'Yu not even interested to see how Ernesto doing?'

'That ship sailed a very long time ago Sybil. You go and when yu come back yu can tell me all about it.'

Sybil go to Cuba and when she come home she say Havana is magnificent. It bold and proud and mobilising women into the workforce and political work and government administration. Even the ice cream is wonderful. And then she say she going there long-term. To help with some big conference the federation organising.

'To Deepen Women's Revolutionary Action. That is what it is called. Can yu believe that?'

I laugh. 'Yu in yu element girl. But what Beryl going do?'

'What Beryl always do?'

'Stick with you.'

'Same thing.'

'What about Manley?'

'It not going to last, Gloria. Jamaica not got the stomach for what needs to be done.'

I wait a minute to see if she was going to say something 'bout Ernesto but she didn't. And I didn't ask. What would I do with news of him anyway?

Two weeks later we go to the airport, me, Esther and Marcia who come back from Miami so she could say goodbye to them. When time come Sybil squeeze me real tight. Long and close.

'Until such times, Gloria Campbell.'

And then she kiss me, Cuban-style, both cheeks, and she turn 'round and the two of them walk through the departure gate together.

We wait 'til they well and truly gone and we walk outside to catch a cab. And as we standing there in line Esther turn to me and say, 'There is someone I want you to meet.'

Me and Marcia just exchange a glance and raise our eyebrows.

'His name is Rajinder.'

'Indian?'

'You have a problem with that?'

'I just asking that is all.'

Then I say to her, 'Yu never want to introduce me to anybody else before?'

'He is the first one, Mommy. I didn't want to . . .' She stop and look at us and then she say, 'I wanted to think about it.'

Rajinder come to dinner. He is as quiet as a mouse and thin as a rake. But he muscular. Athletic, which make sense because of how she meet him. Playing volleyball on the beach. He intelligent too. At the university with Esther studying some managerial something. And he have good table manners. How Esther is with him? Protective.

Pao vex when I tell him 'bout Rajinder. 'Indian, Gloria?'

'What it matter to you?'

He sheepish. Like a little boy that know it wrong but he going say what he got to say anyway. 'Yu know what they say, Gloria.'

'I know what they say. That coolies dirty and smell bad and rob yu at every turn. But you Yang Pao, of all people, coming in here and saying a thing like that?'

'I didn't say nothing.'

'But yu think it and that was bad enough.'

He stand there a minute and then he turn and hump off, which is what he like to do when a conversation take a turn that displease him. But I didn't follow him inside. I just sit there on the veranda for a good long while, taking in the night air and finishing my drink. When I eventually go in the bedroom I don't say nothing to him even though I know he was laying there wide awake. I just wash myself and brush my teeth and put on my nightdress and get in the bed with my back to him.

And then outta the dark he say to me, 'I didn't mean nothing by it yu know.' He pause. 'I am sure Rajinder a good man. After all Esther choose him nuh?'

'Yes, she choose him.'

He quiet for a while and then he say, 'They say all sorta things about the Chinese as well.' And then he pause before he say, 'But you still chose me.'

I turn 'round. And then I open my arms and welcome him into them.

When I get the postcard from Fay I realise that I still not done nothing 'bout Junior. He just turn up on the doorstep one day saying that since Sybil gone to Cuba he think maybe I could help him.

'How you find me Junior?'

'I telephone Sybil and she say for me to come see yu.'

I tell him to come up on to the veranda outta the sun and I ask him if he want some lemonade and he say yes.

Few minutes later I come back with the jug and glasses and rest them on the table. And then I notice that he still standing there. So I tell him it all right he can sit down and he do it. Careful and gentle with his knees together and his feet firmly on the ground. He tell me what he want and I just say, 'Yu waste yu time coming over here Junior. I sorry but I cyan help yu.'

'The thing is, Miss Gloria, I got the chance to join a band that going on tour. To Europe, and London, England. And I thought since I going there I might take the opportunity to see her. That is if she want to see me.'

'Junior, yu not listening to me. I don't know who yu mother is.'

'Yu do, Miss Gloria. Yu know her.'

And right then I know it true. Looking at those Chinese eyes and finally admitting to myself that I have always known since the first time I meet him in that grisly dancehall. And Fay sitting in the restaurant at the sanatorium sipping coffee and telling me 'bout Isaac.

'Maybe yu father should be the one to be helping yu with this Junior.'

'He don't know how to reach her. All he know is that she go to England.'

'So he actually tell yu who she is?'

'Yes. Little while back but it only now that it have any purpose to it. Yu know, because I going to England. So that is why I wondered if yu know where she is.'

I breathe out heavy and pour some more lemonade.

'What mek yu think I might know?'

'Because yu with Yang Pao. And although I can appreciate that you and his wife probably not likely make the best of friends I reckon that maybe he would know where she at.' He pause and then he say, 'And you could find out from him for me.'

All I say is that I would see what I could do. But actually I didn't do nothing even though I had his telephone number burning a hole in my purse. I didn't feel like I could go give him Fay's address just like that. It felt like I should check with her first. And I didn't know where to begin asking her 'bout a thing like that.

★ ★ ★

Fay's postcard got a picture of the Queen and Buckingham Palace and soldiers with big fur hats. It say, 'Congratulations on Esther's graduation.' And then she write that Mui tell her about it, which make sense because I know Mui been exchanging letters with Pao.

I put the card in the old shoebox with the rest of them that I get from her time to time. The same box in which I keep Ernesto's letters. And looking at them like that I realise it a very long time since I hear anything about him. So I start wonder if he all right and spend days turning over in my mind if I should telephone Matilde. And in the end I do it.

We exchange a few pleasantries and then I say to her, 'Do you see Ernesto, is he OK?'

'He is fine, Gloria. He got married. A little while after Che died. Just like that, having ignored so many women Rodolfo and I introduced him to. Suddenly he started to see one of them and the next thing we knew they were getting married. Two children. Two beautiful, bright, cheerful girls. And he started playing golf.'

'Golf!'

Matilde laugh. 'Yes. Dressed in army fatigues just like Che used to.'

And so I decide to write to Fay. For Junior's sake and for Fay's as well. I think it must be hard to lose a child like that and never see him again. So I reckon I owe it to her as a mother that she should know even if she don't want to do anything about it. And maybe there was another reason. To forgive myself for never having written a single word to Ernesto in all of these years.

CHAPTER 39

'WHAT IS WRONG with you that yu cyan leave this alone?'

Clifton turning over in his mind what it is he want to say to me.

'Yu know, Gloria, yu keep that inside a yu all these years and it eating yu up. I know what yu was doing up at Barrington's shack. Yu think I don't? Yu think I am not the one person who know exactly?'

'Clifton.'

'You were a child. Barrington was a grown man.'

'I was fourteen years old when it first happen and I carry on going there for two long years before me and Marcia run here to Kingston. And if we nuh do that, how much longer would I have keep doing it?'

'Yu have to let it go, Gloria.'

I take a deep-deep breath and then I say, 'Yu know, that day, I still don't know if I beat in his head to protect Marcia or if it was outta jealousy. That I should go there and find him doing that with somebody else. And in truth I pick up the stick and start swinging my arm long before I realise who it was he got there under him. It was pure rage Clifton. And it wasn't to do with her, it was to do with me.'

All the time I am saying this, Clifton is sitting there on the veranda leaning forward in the chair with his elbows on his knees and his hand over his mouth like he stopping himself from talking.

'Why did I do that? Keep going back. Yu know why? Because I felt wanted. Somebody wanted my company. Because no matter how much Mama try treat me like I was part of her it never really feel like it. I used to even make joke that Marcia was her favourite daughter. That much did I feel outside of something.' I pause and then I say, 'Excepting when I was with Barrington. I'm not saying it was Mama's fault. She grow me up a Campbell and she was good to me. Always. But there was something that set us apart, which now I know what that was, but back then I didn't. I was lonely, Clifton, and I thought people didn't want to be with me, except Barrington and doing what he wanted me to do was the price I pay, every once in a while, to escape from feeling so deserted.'

'Yu was a child, Gloria. Barrington tek advantage of yu.'

'I went back Clifton. Yu nuh understand that? I went back and back and back. It was me.'

'It was you but it wasn't your fault.'

'It was my fault. My fault for being wanton, and stupid and irresponsible in the first place like the slave that get caught for being too slow and careless.'

'The slave get caught because somebody is chasing them. Somebody that is more powerful and more conniving. They are not to blame for that. And neither are you. And as for going back all you do was act out of your loneliness and confusion.'

I cyan believe that it could be so simple after all these years.

And then he say, 'Did Auntie ever say to yu that people have to forgive themselves for the blame they take on to themselves

379

thinking it their fault the way other people hurt them? That you, Gloria, tek on that blame for what happen with Barrington and been punishing yuself for it all these years. She ever say that to yu?'

'Auntie don't know nothing 'bout what happen with Barrington.'

'But yu know what she say is true nonetheless.'

We fall quiet.

'How can yu forgive yuself for a thing like that Clifton?'

'Because everything can be forgiven. Because what Barrington do to yu he do out of his own pain and suffering. And what you do with Barrington was out of your pain and your suffering. But he do it to yu, Gloria. And you do it with him. That is the difference. He was a adult man and you was a girl child and right there is that power imbalance we talk 'bout before, you and me. I know what it like to be on the weak end of that power equation, Gloria. I know. And what happen wasn't your fault any more than it was mine. It time yu let it go and know that you are a fine and decent person, and yu always have been. Yu just human, Gloria, that is all. Yu are a human being who mek mistakes, and sometimes get confused and has weaknesses and vulnerabilities. And being like that we don't always do things in a way that leave us feeling good. People, Gloria, we suffer. So what that mek you? It mek yu just the same as every other person on God's good earth.' He pause and then he say, 'It seem like yu already forgive Barrington for what he do to yu so maybe it time yu forgive yuself.'

I sit there with the tears slowly rolling down my face. And then Clifton get up and walk over and as he reach me I just stand up and lean myself into his arms and sob. I cry so much I wet up the whole shoulder and collar of his shirt. And in my grief I realise that Clifton right. Not just about Barrington but also about Auntie and

Pao. Because it come to me that I had forgiven them all. So yes, if the patience and generosity and kindness was in me to do that, then it was time I forgive myself as well.

The day we go to Esther's graduation was joyous, with me and Pao sitting side by side in the beautiful university gardens at Mona on a gorgeous July day clapping and cheering and feeling so proud of our daughter, *our* daughter standing up there on the platform holding her certificate rolled up with the little ribbon 'round it. Proving that no matter who your mother is, with her lack of learning, and all the mistakes she make in her life, she, Esther could do it. Be someone respectable in this world. Get an education, and pass their examinations. In economics as well because she say you cannot change anything in Jamaica without understanding how money works.

Afterwards when she come up to us dressed so pretty in her gown and board hat she go straight up to Pao and kiss him on the cheek. And then she do the same thing to me. And as I glance over her shoulder I see Clifton and Marcia walking over to us, with Hyacinth and Father Michael. All of them looking like they wouldn't have missed this day for the world.

And it was family like we never knew before.

ACKNOWLEDGEMENTS

It takes many people for one person to end up with their name on the cover of a book. In this instance it took my editor, Helen Garnons-Williams, the most insightful, diligent, considerate and all-round wonderful human being who never falters in her belief in me and my ability to do better.

Thanks also to Emily Sweet, Sarah-Jane Forder, Erica Jarnes, Elizabeth Woabank, Oliver Holden-Rea, Trâm-Anh Doan and all the good folk at Bloomsbury.

My agent, Susan Yearwood, for her support and encouragement and for being there through thick and thin and all the ups and downs.

And for friendship as enduring as the path itself, Amanda Harrington.

A NOTE ON THE TYPE

The text of this book is set in Bembo. This type was first used in 1495 by the Venetian printer Aldus Manutius for Cardinal Bembo's *De Aetna*, and was cut for Manutius by Francesco Griffo. It was one of the types used by Claude Garamond (1480–1561) as a model for his Romain de L'Université, and so it was the forerunner of what became standard European type for the following two centuries. Its modern form follows the original types and was designed for Monotype in 1929.

ALSO AVAILABLE BY KERRY YOUNG

PAO

Kingston, 1938. Fourteen-year-old Yang Pao steps off the ship from China with his mother and brother. They are to live with Zhang, the 'godfather' of Chinatown, and Pao is destined to take over his protection business and become a powerful man. He sets his sights on marrying well, but when Gloria Campbell, a black prostitute, comes to him for help he is drawn to her beauty and strength. They begin a relationship that continues even after Pao marries Fay Wong, the headstrong daughter of a Chinese merchant.

But as political violence escalates in the 1960s the lines between Pao's socialist ideals and private ambitions become blurred. Jamaica is transforming, the tides of change are rising, and the one-time boss of Chinatown finds himself cast adrift . . .

'With grace, authenticity and humour, Young lets Jamaica's political history shine through the life story of her charming yet fallible hero. Brilliant'
DAILY MAIL

'[*Pao*] confirms Young as a gifted new writer. Her novel is a blindingly good read . . . both for its mesmeric story-telling and the quality of its prose'
OBSERVER

'A pacy but absorbing saga of domestic struggle and gangland manoeuvring set against the violent backdrop of postwar Jamaican politics . . . [A] punchy tale of pungent characters and impassioned entanglements'
INDEPENDENT ON SUNDAY

'Young's heartfelt, sparky and affecting debut novel is a chronicle of multicultural Jamaica . . . The complexity of Jamaican society in *Pao* is fascinating and bewildering'
GUARDIAN

ORDER BY PHONE: +44 (0)1256 302 699; BY EMAIL: DIRECT@MACMILLAN.CO.UK
DELIVERY IS USUALLY 3–5 WORKING DAYS. POSTAGE AND PACKAGING WILL BE CHARGED.
ONLINE: WWW.BLOOMSBURY.COM/BOOKSHOP
FREE POSTAGE AND PACKAGING FOR ORDERS OVER £20.
PRICES AND AVAILABILITY SUBJECT TO CHANGE WITHOUT NOTICE.

WWW.BLOOMSBURY.COM/KERRYYOUNG

B L O O M S B U R Y